Praise for

DRAGONS DEAL

"Another enjoyable addition to the saga of the McCandles family." —*Night Owl Reviews*

DRAGONS LUCK

"Joyous fantasy with continuous action and a creative cast of characters." —*SFRevu*

DRAGONS WILD

"Asprin tackles a new kind of comic fantasy, a little more serious and hard-boiled than previous books. Featuring a likable rake and plenty of action and quirky humor, this series opener belongs in most adult and YA fantasy collections." —*Library Journal*

"Colorful." —*Publishers Weekly*

"Delightful." —*Monsters and Critics*

Praise for Robert Asprin's MYTH series

"Stuffed with rowdy fun."   —*The Philadelphia Inquirer*

"Give yourself the pleasure of working through the series. But not all at once; you'll wear out your funny bone."
—*The Washington Times*

"Hysterically funny."   —*Analog*

"Breezy, pun-filled fantasy in the vein of Piers Anthony's Xanth series . . . a hilarious bit of froth and frolic."
—*Library Journal*

"Asprin's major achievement as a writer—brisk pacing, wit, and a keen satirical eye."   —*Booklist*

"An excellent, lighthearted fantasy series."   —*Epic Illustrated*

"Tension getting to you? Take an Asprin! . . . His humor is broad and grows out of the fantasy world or dimensions in which his characters operate."   —*Fantasy Review*

Robert Asprin's

DRAGONS RUN

JODY LYNN NYE

ACE BOOKS, NEW YORK

THE BERKLEY PUBLISHING GROUP
Published by the Penguin Group
Penguin Group (USA) LLC
375 Hudson Street, New York, New York 10014

USA • Canada • UK • Ireland • Australia • New Zealand • India • South Africa • China

penguin.com

A Penguin Random House Company

ROBERT ASPRIN'S DRAGONS RUN

An Ace Book / published by arrangement with Bill Fawcett & Associates

Ace Books are published by The Berkley Publishing Group.
ACE and the "A" design are trademarks of Penguin Group (USA) LLC.

For information, address: The Berkley Publishing Group,
a division of Penguin Group (USA) LLC,
375 Hudson Street, New York, New York 10014.

ISBN: 978-0-425-25617-6

PUBLISHING HISTORY
Ace trade paperback edition / October 2013
Ace mass-market edition / December 2014

PRINTED IN THE UNITED STATES OF AMERICA

10 9 8 7 6 5 4 3 2 1

Cover art by Eric Fortune.

Dedicated to my wonderful mother-in-law,
Jeanne Fawcett

One

Griffen McCandles only half listened to his uncle Malcolm's unending tirade. He had to concentrate on driving. The eight lanes of US Highway 10 from the airport heading toward New Orleans were completely tied up with morning rush-hour traffic. High winds from gray, cloud-streaked skies were whipping rain onto his windshield. The red Camry was unfamiliar. He had had to borrow it from one of his poker dealers, who lived in Metairie and had the space to park a car. Brenda had freely handed him the keys but neglected to tell him that she ate most of her meals in it. There had been no time to clean it out before Griffen had to go to the airport to pick up Malcolm McCandles, his father's older brother and his guardian since the disappearance of both of Griffen's parents many years before. He and Malcolm had to shove aside piles of burger and sandwich wrappers, heaps of aluminum cans, and waxed paper bags from pralines and beignets so their long legs would fit. The mess displeased the elder McCandles.

On the other hand, almost everything did.

"Even first-class air travel is a miserable experience these days! The food would be low quality for a prison, and expecting a grown man to cut a steak with a plastic knife is ludicrous and demeaning. Not that the so-called safety provisions are making anyone safer! And the seats! I felt as if I had been packed in with the cargo." Malcolm kicked at a milk shake cup. "Couldn't you find anything better to drive? What happened to your car?"

"It was vandalized," Griffen said, not wanting to go into detail. The wreck of his prized auto had been a murder attempt. He had been in it at the time. Malcolm snorted. Like Griffen, he was above average in height, slender but strongly built, with a long face, a masculine jawline, and slightly hooded eyes. Except for age and coloration, the two men looked very much alike, including, at the moment, disgruntled expressions

"That's what you get for living in an uncivilized environment," Malcolm McCandles declared. "If you weren't too lazy to try and make something of yourself, you could be living in New York or Seattle, or Silicon Valley—one of the centers of business. Not an antique backwater."

Griffen bit back a retort, knowing it would just invite debate. New Orleans was a small city but hardly a backwater. It supported a working port and one of the most thriving tourist cultures in the United States. Except for the central city, you could hardly tell it from any other Southern town, with its apartment houses, shopping malls, and sports arenas lining the very highway they were driving along. Besides, he was happy there. He had hardly ever been able to say that before.

He and his younger sister, Valerie, had spent ten years in their uncle Malcolm's care, with him as a vaguely disapproving, generally absent personage. A housekeeper, also distant and gruff, cared for them most of the time. She had been no more motherly than Uncle Malcolm had been fatherly, but it was far better, he had since been informed by those who knew personally, than the foster-care system. One way or another, he had been unprepared for the realities of adulthood.

On the other hand, how did you tell someone that he was a hereditary dragon? As far as Griffen was concerned, the explanation had come far too late, without sufficient details to assuage his curiosity. Much of what he had learned about himself had come from other people and from experimenting with his budding powers. A glance in the mirror showed a mild, Midwestern American twentysomething male with green eyes, medium brown hair, a long jaw, and a straight nose with somewhat prominent nostrils. Who would guess that beneath that handsome if ordinary visage lay Puff the Magic Dragon?

His uncle looked less friendly and more draconian glaring out the window at the traffic.

"Couldn't you take another way into town?" he asked.

"The other way takes about three times as long," Griffen reminded him. Again. He kept his face as smooth as if he were playing poker. He had trained himself not to have tells. It helped at times like this to keep his emotions concealed.

He was trying not to blow up. The weather was as grim as the company. The Thursday after Mardi Gras stood a good chance of having good weather, since spring came early to the Gulf Coast, but Griffen was glad he hadn't bet on it. Rain spattered the windshield and splashed in through holes in the floor of the car. He was going to have to think about giving Brenda a raise so she could afford to replace this beater. And he was unused to being out of bed before noon. His profession as well as his personal inclination made him a night owl.

His profession, which was being neglected due to Val's disappearance, was president, administrator, and chief executive officer of a free-floating gambling organization handed off to him a few months before by another senior dragon named Mose. He wished Mose could have been in the car with him. He was one of the wisest people Griffen knew. He might have figured out how to solve Griffen's problem before Malcolm showed up, maybe even preventing the elder dragon from getting on a plane.

On the other hand, Mose might have had little more insight into where Valerie had gone than he had. Griffen was beginning to realize how little he knew about the way his sister thought. He was kicking himself for not investigating

further how she really felt about her unborn baby's grandmother. She had distrusted Melinda on sight, as he had, but
they had been forced into a truce with her. The moment the
crisis was over, Melinda had showed her true colors. Or had
she? Was the disappearance Val's idea?

Griffen stared out the windshield at the rain, making sure
he didn't miss his turn. The unfamiliar engine juddered. He
hoped they would not break down. Waiting on the edge of
the road for Triple-A to come and tow them would not improve his temper.

The siblings had been in New Orleans for over a year.
What had precipitated the move south was that people had
started trying to kill or kidnap Griffen. With the help of an
old friend—all right, another dragon—named Jerome, they
had fled to the Crescent City, where they lived in relative
safety.

"Relative" being a relative term, of course. In those
months Griffen had had run-ins with werewolves and other
shape-shifters, government agents, a bounty hunter, enemy
dragons, the element of fire, and, not least, as it happened,
the New Orleans Police Department. He had had to concentrate on staying alive while making a living and dealing with
being actual head of the local dragons, of which there were
many more than he could have dreamed existed. Two of them
were his girlfriends.

He didn't look forward to explaining all that to his uncle.

On the other hand, why *should* he explain anything? Malcolm had pretty much washed his hands of him when he
refused to give Griffen a job in his corporation. Griffen was
prepared to get along on his own.

He decided he was just dealing with too many hands, and
he had no idea what cards were in any of them, including
his own.

If only Valerie would call! He glanced down at his cell
phone, stuck upside down into the cup holder so he could
see the screen. No missed messages. The volume was turned
up all the way.

The phone rang, and he grabbed it.

"Hey, bro," Jerome's smooth voice hummed into his ear.

"Where y'at?" Griffen asked. He had been born and raised in Ann Arbor, Michigan, but the local patois appealed to him enough to adopt some of it.

"Nothing fresh. None of my cabbie friends took a fare matching Val's description anywhere at any time, Mardi Gras, Ash Wednesday, or this morning. Your watchers on the apartments reported in about nine. She wasn't there and hasn't been there, but some of her clothes are missing. Not many things, really. Toiletries, toothbrush, hairbrush all still in place. Did she have a passport?"

"No," Griffen said, thankfully. "We've never been out of the country."

"That wouldn't stop Melinda," Malcolm said. Griffen glanced at him, wondering if he had been able to hear Jerome's side of the conversation. "She could arrange for false papers on a moment's notice. Even genuine ones would not be outside her realm of influence."

Griffen nodded. "Did you hear that?" he said into the phone.

"Sure did. Not around here," Jerome assured him. "Anyone making fake paper with your sister's picture on it would prod someone to call someone who knows you."

"Glad to hear it."

"People want to stay on your good side, King of Fafnir. They all hoping for a favor one day."

"I know. I'll catch up with you later," Griffen said. "Thanks for the update. How's the rest going?"

"We've got one table tonight at the Sonesta, nothing you have to worry about," Jerome said. "You can count on me."

"I know, Jer," Griffen said, sincerely. "Thanks."

"No problem, man." The connection went.

"You've been careless, Griffen," Malcolm said. "Your sister should not have been out of sight at any time."

"Her life is her own business," Griffen said, as evenly as he could. "But what do you care? I haven't seen you taking any particular interest in us. It's been over a year since we moved here, and the first time you call is in the middle of the night on Mardi Gras."

To Griffen's surprise, Malcolm McCandles looked almost sheepish, a far cry from the formidable businessman's mien.

"I have been keeping tabs on you, but you had not caused or been in sufficient trouble for me to step in."

"Thanks a lot!"

Malcolm looked at his neatly trimmed nails as if his thoughts were written there. "I did not mean that to sound deprecating. I have been pleased at the application to task that you have shown while you have been here. You're doing well, better than I would ever have expected. If you had worked so assiduously at your education, you might have had a master's degree right now."

"And do what with it?" Griffen countered, glaring through the windshield at a truck's bumper. "I'd probably be a cog in your machine right now, wouldn't I, fed just enough information about my . . . my secret identity . . . to keep me satisfied, but still under your thumb."

"Griffen, no McCandles lives under the thumb of anyone else! As you grew into your abilities, we would have assumed a role more akin to partnership—"

Griffen snorted, twin jets of steam lancing from his nostrils.

Malcolm continued, "You may not believe me, but it's true. Look at what you have accomplished on your own. Without any guidance or backing from me, you've put yourself into a position of authority here. Once you started to gain confidence, I couldn't force you to comply. You would have declared your independence on your own. I would have had to convince you to ally with me."

Something in the way he said that made Griffen's ears perk up, figuratively.

"Is that why you're here?" he asked. "It's not all about Val, is it? You phoned before you knew she was gone."

Malcolm nodded grimly. "I can't argue with your perception. You have always had a gift for spotting nuance. No, I had no idea. Yes, I am here for another purpose. I have been asked to manage a . . . situation."

Griffen allowed one eyebrow to climb up his forehead. "Well, I appreciate the courtesy call before you came into my territory. I'll drop you at your hotel. Let me know if there's something I can do to help, and I will keep you posted on anything I learn about Val."

Malcolm scowled, his handsome face creasing. "It is not like you to jump to conclusions, Griffen. I do not expect to operate alone, especially, as you say, on your territory. I would appreciate your help."

"On your *situation*. What about my sister?"

"I feel responsible for not insisting you safeguard Valerie more closely, especially considering her . . . condition. I offer you my help, not as quid pro quo, but as a concerned relative."

That sounded better than Griffen would have expected, which immediately made him suspicious. "From what you have said, my guess is that whatever you have cooking is difficult."

"Very." Malcolm grimaced again. "I need information from a very powerful person."

"I have a lot of the local politicians as clients, and a few of them as friends," Griffen said, in the spirit of cooperation. "I can probably arrange a friendly meeting with whoever it is, maybe at a private poker game. Not many of them are dragons, but they like some action."

"Again, I have no intention of denigrating your accomplishments or your acquaintances, Griffen, but I doubt very much whether few, if any, of the local humans have ever met the man I need to see."

"Why not?"

"Because he's been dead for almost eighty years."

Two

The whispers bubbled up as if from the very soil of Odd Fellow's Rest Cemetery long before the dilapidated Camry passed it. Reginaud St. Cyr Duvallier sat on the stone bench outside his family's mausoleum with his well-shod feet crossed in front of him on the wispy grass and drew a long, satisfying drag from his cigar. Cuban. He'd had plenty of cases of his favorite smokes put away in dry, cool storage long before the Bay of Pigs debacle. Had enough to last a century and then some. Some of his admirers made sure he had fresh ones these days, too, smuggled in past the Coast Guard disguised as cases of legal rum. He enjoyed the taste of the smoke on his tongue. No other tobacco in the world had the flavor, the sweetness, or the rich aroma of Cuban. It was almost as good as the taste of power. Not quite, but he liked to say so to seem humble. People liked it when you sounded humble.

"He's in town, Mr. Duvallier," a bloodless voice hissed in his ear. "Landed and on his way in a car."

"Glad to hear it, Pierre," Reginaud said, tapping off a half-inch cylinder of thick ash. It joined the dust of ages on the ground by his feet. "I hate to be disappointed. No one wants me to be disappointed, would they?"

"Nossir!" the whispers erupted again. "Never, sir! Not in a million years!"

No, they wouldn't, Reginaud mused. *They wouldn't be caught* dead *disappointing him.* He chuckled at his own little joke, and the whisperers joined in. *The boy, though.* The boy ought to have come and paid his respects. The older one would make certain he did. There was too much for both of them to lose. He might have to send a few little reminders. He hadn't been bothered with the boy before, but his attention was back now. Must be old age catching up with him. He grinned and clenched his cigar in his front teeth. That was another little joke he liked to make to himself.

"Who's keepin' tabs on all those other little matters?" he asked aloud.

"I just heard from my third cousin twice removed in Surrey, England," a chirpy wave of sound informed him. Daphne Ellswood, a niece and always a good friend. Pity about that violent husband of hers, and she still wouldn't say that her murder was his doing. Reginaud was pretty sure that was the reason she was still around, sixty years on. "He said that Mr. Perricone had a lovely funeral. A glass carriage drawn by black horses with plumes on their heads, and thirty-six cars in the procession. And such a touching graveside service. That vicar had a real pretty voice. He sounded sorrowful that Mr. Perricone had gone to his reward when he was still in the fullness of life."

"Well, Mr. Perricone had it coming, I daresay," Reginaud said. "If only he had shown a little humility, he wouldn't have had to have a funeral so young." He put his thumbs behind the suspenders holding up his old-fashioned trousers. The thumbs weren't in such good shape as the suspenders, but he could replace the latter, not the former. His whole body was a study in contradictions—but, then, so was his existence.

Reginaud disliked looking glasses these days. They reminded him that even his formidable intelligence had its blind spots. He'd read the legend of the Lernean Sibyl and thought he had it all worked out when he had the rituals done over him to give him life after death, but even strong magic wasn't proof against Time itself. His skin had turned leathery, even more than it had been when he'd been out in society and spent his leisure time in the sun. Food didn't nourish him in the same way that it did before though he could and did enjoy it. He'd once had a potbelly, but his midsection had hollowed out, so he could see his internal organs outlined under his skin. His eyes frightened people. That, he actually enjoyed. Once in a while, he did look in a mirror to see those pits of fire glaring back at him and grinned at the sinister effect. Before, he had plain old light brown eyes, a color his late wife, Arabella, called muddy water. This was an improvement. It got people to agree with him a lot more readily, as if they were afraid something would come out of those eyes. But it was his brain they really had to fear. He hadn't missed a trick in life and did not mean to now that he didn't have death constantly preying on his mind.

Some nights, alone in the mausoleum, he wondered whether it had all been worthwhile, going through the transformation. He had had a pretty good life, all told, been respected and rich, had a good wife, and sons and daughters who had grown up and made him proud. But why let go if you didn't have to? There were plenty more fields to conquer. He hadn't been president yet, for example. Hadn't even been governor or mayor.

Pity was, those political dreams had had to take a backseat. His slowly deteriorating appearance even made it difficult to go into town during the day. Reginaud preferred the nighttime anyhow, and he had come to enjoy being the power behind the throne instead of the target sitting in it. The best deals were made after midnight, in the back room of a bar with hot jazz playing and men hunched over a table with everything to lose.

Yessir. That did not and would never change. He could make arrangements. He had a long memory and connections going back over a hundred years. Even he found it a little strange to be dealing with the great-grandsons and -daughters of the men he had grown up with, but he could spot a resemblance a mile off. Landrieus, Carters, and Longs looked and acted the same as their ancestors. And they all wanted the same thing: power. They wanted different facets of it, time and custom allowing, but the most precious was information. Reginaud had access to plenty of that. He doled some out in exchange for favors, money, influence, and more information, which he always managed to turn to his advantage. And people were already starting to ask him about the upcoming elections. So much was at stake. He stood to make a regular little fortune on it and incur favors he could one day call in. Always paid to look to the future.

Reginaud kept tabs on everything. He even had a secretary with a modern computer-thing she lugged out to his mausoleum three times a week to update files with him. The computer had gotten smaller over the years, from the size of a suitcase to no bigger than a hardback book, and a damned sight lighter. The groundskeepers, old black men who had cared for the cemetery for decades, paid no mind to her anymore. She was just one of the regular visitors. But today she was bringing someone else with her. The timing was interesting. Two suitors for his goods. That made him feel very pleased with himself.

He heard a car's engine and the crackle of gravel under the tires as it made the sharp turn up near the entrance to the graveyard from Canal Street. Not the little, chug-chugging Ford that Miss Nita Callaway drove. Interesting. The visitor wanted to show up in his own vehicle. Appearance mattered to him. Reginaud took a drag on his cigar and leaned back to wait.

As the long, shiny, black stretch limousine pulled up near the entrance, he clenched the remaining three inches of stogie in his front teeth and applauded. "Gotta give the man points for style. Good as a parade."

A young black man in a captain's cap and with a bow tie at the neck of his immaculately pressed short-sleeved shirt got out of the driver's seat and ran around to open the right-hand door at the back of the extended vehicle. Nita swiveled to get her feet on the ground. Always a lady. The young man took her hand and helped her to stand up.

Her light café-au-lait skin made Northerners call her Creole though that name properly belonged to the descendants of the French and Spanish settlers of Louisiana territory. Miss Callaway wore a little white blouse over a knee-length blue skirt, and a cardigan sweater the same shade. Reginaud smiled. She always took the effort to look nice. He had given her a pretty little pearl pin that she wore on her left lapel high enough that to glance at it wasn't rude. He had plenty of jewelry and other trinkets he could have given her, but she was modest in her wants. Reginaud never pushed her to accept anything that'd make her uncomfortable. It'd be hard to find someone else like her. She was hardworking, honest, and discreet, plus she accepted what he was without comment. Her hair had turned from dark brown to light brown shot with gray over the years, but her face was still unlined. Perhaps she had gone in for a touch of magic herself. He'd gladly pay for it if she wanted it. She was an excellent secretary and a true lady.

The visitor climbed out behind her and brushed himself down, clearly uncomfortable to be standing in a graveyard. He was a white man about fifty years of age, light brown hair graying at the temples. His dark blue suit was nearly as expensive as Reginaud's but didn't fit as well. He must have put on, Reginaud estimated, maybe twenty extra pounds since he had bought it. His belly strained against the ostrich-skin belt that held his pants up. So there was vanity in play. That was another piece of information that Reginaud could use in their negotiations. The man glanced at Reginaud, who crinkled his eyes over a friendly smile, then opened them up and let him have it.

At the sight of his sunken, fiery orbs, Mr. Sandusky almost fainted right there among the tombstones.

Had to give him credit, though. After a tottery step or two and a couple of deep breaths, he visibly steeled himself and approached Reginaud with his hand out. What he wanted, he wanted real bad.

"Mr. Duvallier, a pleasure. I'm Albert Sandusky."

Reginaud grasped the outstretched hand. The younger man's skin was soft, as if he never did any heavy work. He recoiled at the feel of Reginaud's fingers.

"Mr. Sandusky, good to make your acquaintance. Have a seat." Reginaud patted the bench beside him. He waved the stub of his smoke. "Want a cigar?"

Sandusky wavered. He had ruddy, thick lips in a pale face. His Adam's apple bobbed as he gulped. Couldn't hide the nervousness. Reginaud was enjoying having the upper hand.

"Er, not at the moment, sir. I was hoping that you would accept my hospitality and join me for lunch in town. Er," Sandusky eyed him nervously. "You do eat, don't you?"

"Why, I sure do! Love good food. I'd be most pleased to join you."

"Would you . . . do you . . . mind coming in my car?"

Reginaud stood up and fastened the center button of his jacket. "Mighty nice of you. It's been a while since I took a limousine ride, especially one where I was sitting up."

Sandusky gasped. Chuckling, Reginaud clapped him on the back.

"Just joshing you, son. I like a good joke. Don't you?"

"Er, yes. Yes, I do. I mean, a joke."

"That's fine. Where we goin'?"

"The Court of Two Sisters?"

"You askin' me or tellin' me?"

"Er, tellin'—telling."

"That's fine. My favorite restaurant. All aboard, then, huh?"

Mr. Sandusky nodded, and the chauffeur leaped to open the rear door.

Reginaud waited as Nita slid into the seat and scooched over to where her secretarying bag was lying on the floor. He followed, looking approvingly at the sleek leather seats gleaming with the polish of the truly expensive. Not a rental, then, but the property of the man himself. That meant real money and pride in his position. Another useful couple of facts. With regret, he discarded what was left of his stogie.

He never smoked in an interior room where ladies were present, and a closed car counted, especially to Miss Callaway. Nita would never have said a word, but she'd have thought it at him, and she had some mighty loud thoughts that came out of her eyes. Reginaud held on to the door frame and boosted himself into the interior. Smelled nice in there, too.

Nita flipped open the little computer thing and put it on his lap. The list of messages was a long one. Somehow, she arranged it so the important ones were at the top instead of lined up by date.

"The first three are urgent, Mr. Duvallier," Nita said. She didn't point at the messages. That was unladylike. "I'd appreciate it if you'd answer those right away. The first one's been waiting a solid month. Please stop ignoring it. The next eight are . . . requests. The rest are begging letters and solicitations. Nothing of any importance."

Reginaud did a quick scan of the names in the last-named category. He was amused to see names of old rivals and associates sprinkled among the strangers. He rightly enjoyed wielding the DELETE key.

"Hah!" he said, with a cackle, consigning Laszlo Peary to the outer darkness. An uncomfortable shifting on the expensive leather reminded him they weren't alone. He glanced up with a wry smile. "Excuse me, Mr. Sandusky. Just one of those little pleasures. Wish I'd had one of those in the old days. Wiping people out with one push of a finger, no bullets needed. Very satisfying."

For the first time, Sandusky returned the smile. "I quite agree, Mr. Duvallier. May I . . . may I ask you a question?"

"The air's free, son."

"Mr. Duvallier, are you open to our proposition?"

Reginaud settled back against the lush upholstery, the laptop warm on his bony knees. "Don't believe I'll tell you. Not just yet anyhow. Let's get us a drink or two and get to know one another. Meantime, I'd like to enjoy the ride."

Reginaud rested his elbow on the back of the plush seat. He waved away the laptop computer and admired the scenery. New Orleans had changed for the better since his younger days. The automobiles, now, they were so sleek and fast compared with the boxy models he had learned to drive. Sandusky busied himself with the wet bar, serving drinks to his guests. Nita had a very diluted white-wine spritzer. Reginaud admired the rich gold of the cognac in the balloon glass poured for him. Sandusky took a solid belt of bourbon for himself. A black convertible went by, top down in spite of the drizzle. The driver and passengers, both in their twenties, looked carefree and pleased with themselves.

"What do you think, Albert? Can you picture me behind the wheel of a Mercedes E-class? Fine set of wheels."

"Whatever you say, sir," Sandusky said, uneasily. Reginaud drank down the first brandy as if it were water. The fire going down his throat felt good, very good. An excellent year. A quality year. He extended the empty glass for a refill. The visitor stared at him, then hastily poured more. "Should you drink it that fast, sir?"

"Keeps me alive, son," Reginaud said with a grin that was brilliant in his leathery face. "Keeps me alive."

Three

They took a right off Conti, past Bourbon, and onto Royal. The driver swung around the corner and came to a stop in front of the Court of Two Sisters. Reginaud smiled again. Sandusky had done his homework. The door of the limo cracked open into brilliant sunlight, and the young driver extended a hand to him.

"Thanks, son, I can get out." The youth backed away, openly relieved not to have to touch him. Reginaud led the way into the cool, dim hallway toward the service desk. Marina was working the hostess desk that day. He admired the updo of her thick hair and readied a compliment. Behind her, at the far end of the large, high-ceilinged building, customers came and went from the inside buffet lines before taking their laden plates out to tables in the sunlit courtyard. Reginaud could just hear the warm notes of the jazz trio playing.

Sandusky hustled to get in front of him. He exchanged a few quiet words with the young black woman. Marina glanced up and saw Reginaud coming toward her. He offered her a friendly wave. She spoke into a walkie-talkie, and a green-waistcoated waiter hurried up, an older black man with protuberant, bloodshot eyes. Reginaud recalled that his name was Dempster. The old man steered them off to the right, toward one of the private dining rooms, and stood aside as they entered. The table inside had been laid with white cloths for six.

"Are we expecting anybody else?" Reginaud inquired

politely as soon as Dempster had seated them and closed the door behind him.

"Some of my colleagues were going to join us," Sandusky said, uneasily, toying with his water glass. "But they have, er, other obligations."

"Left you carryin' the can, eh, son? All right, then. Let's talk bricks and mortar. Make me understand why you want me."

Sandusky frowned and shot a sideways glance at Nita. She looked demure and incorruptible. As always.

"My people told me they explained it to you," he said

Reginaud leaned back. He took a cigar out of his pocket, considered Nita, then stuck it between his teeth without lighting it.

"Well, I'd appreciate it if you explained it. Pretend I'm as stupid as you think I am."

"I . . . I don't think—"

"Sure you do. Tell me why you're giving this old, dead man this very fine treatment, Albert. I can call you Albert, can't I?"

Sandusky didn't like it, but he took it. "Certainly, sir. Well, you're a resource for . . . I mean, you have . . . You have a way of getting things done, Mr. Duvallier."

Reginaud nodded, hooking his thumbs behind his suspenders.

"That is very true."

Sandusky pressed on. "You know my . . . friends. They have discussed our needs with you before. We just want to make sure that you are on our side."

Reginaud decided to add a little fuel to the fire. "Well, son, you might have heard that there're other bidders in this sale now. I'm not saying that their money's any greener than yours, but you need to be aware of that."

Sandusky looked horrified. "No! We asked for your help first! We'll give you more!"

Reginaud shook his head. "There are other things in this world than money, you know. Our savior Jesus said that the love of money is the root of all evil, and I never let myself get trapped that way."

"What do you want?"

Reginaud leaned back. "Well . . . I like to have my views taken into account, you know."

"Do you want a position? That might be a little difficult, considering your . . ." Sandusky halted, trying to find the right words.

"State of health? Haw haw haw!" Reginaud grinned over his unlit cigar. "I ain't goin' nowhere. I'm a whole lot more likely to see the next century than you are. No, I'd rather have the ear of the next-but-one president. That's where you're ai-min', isn't it, 2008, or is it 2012? This candidate you're backin' is so big and wonderful that the whole country's gonna be on fire for him once they see him in action."

"Well, you know that's true. But we're not there yet."

"Well, I suppose not; that's for the future. But your man won't be positioned to run unless you get him national at-tention right now, in 2003. You can't do that unless the field's clear for him. He's got one big-time rival, one who is likely to attract interest away from him—good kinds of interest. And that's where I come in, isn't that right?"

Sandusky grimaced. Reginaud read his face and nodded.

"Your man don't even know I exist, do he?"

"No, sir. As far as he knows, we're just an ordinary special-interest group. You're kind of our secret weapon."

"As I was for your daddy before you, and your granddad before him."

"Yes, sir. A lot of people are counting on our man not having to face off against her."

"Well, we'll see," Reginaud said. "I don't like hurting little girls, you know."

"She is not an ordinary little girl—I mean, woman!"

"No, she's not. But I have to be fair and hear the other side of the argument. She might be reasonable, you never know. I don't know. She might even be better for the job than your man."

Albert sulked. "We'll withdraw our offer."

"Then I doubt I'll have the time to listen to anything else you have to say in the future," Reginaud said, with genuine regret. "I've got my pride, young man. Pardon me while I finish my drink. Miss Nita and I will get a taxicab back. Thank you for your hospitality. I genuinely appreciate it."

"No, I didn't mean that!" Albert exclaimed, stretching out his hands. His eyes were wide with alarm. "We want you! We *need* you."

"To do what, exactly?"

"Get her out of the way. She's a bloodthirsty beast! Our man's a rising star. She'll just muddy the issues and set us back to square one. Nothing's off the table, up to and including . . . removal."

"I know what you want," Reginaud said. "That's always my last resort, and it's always on the table. Let you know what's what soon's I hear from the other side."

The look on Sandusky's face was a mixture of skepticism and horror.

"The other side? What do you need, a Ouija board?"

"Nope. Telephone's enough."

Sandusky wasn't happy. "All right. We'll do it your way. But I don't think I'm exaggerating when I say the future of the whole country is on your shoulders."

"Do what I can, but you may have an inflated idea of what I'm capable of, son."

His look said he doubted it, but Albert Sandusky didn't say what he was thinking. Instead, he got up and leaned out the door. Dempster was waiting with a rolling tray full of covered dishes. Reginaud tucked a napkin into his collar. He could smell the veal grillades and shrimp étouffée. Talking business always gave him an appetite.

Four

Watching Malcolm try to get anything out of Val's boy-friend, Gris-gris, was like watching the immovable object take on the irresistible force. Griffen stood beside the hospital bed, wondering whether the effort was harming the patient or adding to his will to live. Gris-gris, even two days after what would have been a fatal injury to a lesser man, was impatient to get out of his bed at Charity Hospital. It was futile, and all of them knew it. Griffen could have held him down with one finger in the middle of his chest. Gris-gris was very slim to begin with, but it seemed that he had lost weight in the two days since they had brought him in with a knife wound in his belly. The apples in his cheeks were thrown into greater prominence because of the hollows below, and his skin, almost ebony black, had a gray cast. Privately, Griffen was worried about him, but he couldn't fault the other man's energy.

"What are you doing, asking me where Val's gone to?" Gris-gris demanded. He shook his armful of tubes and elec-tronic cables at Malcolm. "Do I look like I been out and about, whisking my lady off to the ends of the Earth?"

"You were the last person to see her before she went miss-ing," Malcolm pressed. Griffen could see he was getting nowhere, but the elder dragon had to reinvent the wheel. He wouldn't take anyone's word, not even Griffen's.

Gris-gris was adamant. He glared back at the elder McCandles.

"I am not. The man you're looking for, or woman—I ain't no sexist—is the one who took her away. And if I get my hands on that person, you better get there fast if you want to hear his last words." The heart monitor standing on a white pole next to the bed started beeping alarmingly. The nurse came running: a short-legged, stout, African-American woman with an opera singer's bosom, wearing a green uniform dress under a white smock. She slapped the device in the side with her open palm. It stopped bleating.

"You all right, Gris-gris?" she asked.

"I'm fine, Justine," he said.

She put her hands on her hips.

"Hmmph! Then you calm down. I got better things to do than come running every time you get excited. Give me your arm." She took a sphygmomanometer off the wall and wound the cuff around his biceps. She put her stethoscope's earpieces in and applied the disk end to his inner arm. "Hold still!"

Gris-gris turned pleading eyes to Griffen.

"Griffen, you got to get me out of here. I want to help you. I need to find my lady."

"Gris-gris, you need to heal," Griffen said, seriously. "Val would gouge out my eyeballs if I let you go anywhere until it was safe."

The thin man's deep brown eyes flashed. "Safe? Nothin' in this world is safe."

"Okay, I won't argue with you," Griffen said. "If the doctors will let you out, then I'll drive you home."

"Not a chance," Justine said, waving him back. "He's here for a good while yet. Look at that blood pressure! You could run a hydraulic pump off him!"

Gris-gris shot him a wry look, gambler to gambler, as the nurse unfastened the cuff. "You always do check the odds before you make a bet, man," he said. "No. They got no intention of letting me out on the streets. I keep tellin' 'em I'm fine, and they pump me full of more stuff. All it does is make me pee." He glanced out the window.

"We're keeping your circulation running," the nurse said, pushing Gris-gris by the shoulder so he fell back against the pillows. "You lost a lot of blood. You're not going anywhere for a while."

"I got a business to run, ma'am," Gris-gris said, respectfully if impatiently.

"Can you run it if you're dead?"

This sounded like a long-running argument that must have been repeated numerous times over the last two days.

"I can try," Gris-gris said.

"Well, then, you better try astral projection instead because this is your center of operations for now. You want me to get you some Jell-O?"

Gris-gris sputtered. "And you think *I* got a death wish?"

Laughing, the nurse left the room. The dealer shook his head.

"She won't let me out of here until I pass gas, or better. They got me on liquids and IVs. How am I supposed to do that?"

"I don't know," Griffen said. "I've never been stabbed in the stomach."

"You ain't been in town long enough," Gris-gris said.

Gris-gris knew that Griffen's skin couldn't be penetrated by anything but dragon teeth, but he was quick on the uptake. He must have guessed if Griffen made no reference in front of his uncle to the unusual goings-on during Mardi Gras, then he wouldn't, either. Griffen was grateful. Malcolm impatiently brought them back to the subject of their visit.

"Was Melinda here with Valerie after the parade?"

"For a minute. Mrs. Melinda and Val were kind of tight with each other. Val was mad at you, Grifter, that's for certain. I told her it was my idea to keep quiet about gettin' shanked not to spoil the day for her, but you know what she like."

"Yes," Griffen said. "I do. She was angry because she was worried."

"Do you think that Melinda used that anger to spirit her

away with her?" Malcolm asked. "With every moment that passes, the trail grows colder."

"I know that!" Gris-gris leaned back in bed, looking up at the ceiling. It was a sign of how much pain he was in that he didn't maintain his characteristically fierce eye contact with them. "No. That Mrs. Melinda left before Val did. She said . . . she said she had to go check on her daughter. Val sat with me for a while. I was pretty groggy. They dosed me up for the pain. I closed my eyes, and the next time I opened them, she was gone. That's all I know. She didn't leave me a note. I told Nurse Bossyboots out there to wake me up anytime Val came back, but she didn't. Hasn't even called."

"She hasn't called me, either," Griffen said. "And she's not answering her phone."

"That's bad. If she's in trouble, I want to help."

"You will!" Griffen assured him. "But if you die trying, she'll kill me."

Gris-gris's narrow face split in a brilliant white smile. "That just mean she have two guardian angels."

"And what makes you think you're going to heaven?" Griffen countered. Gris-gris laughed.

Malcolm stepped back from the bedside.

"That's enough, Griffen. There are other people I need to speak to."

"I'll be back," Griffen promised Gris-gris. "Anything you need?

"A one-way ticket out of here," the thin man said with a grin. "But you could pick me up a decent burger next time you come. Maybe from Yo Mama's. The food here's nasty."

"I heard that!" Nurse Bossyboots called. "Don't you dare!"

Griffen followed Malcolm out of the ward to the elevator. They emerged into the streaky sunshine forcing its way through iron gray clouds. The air was thick with humidity and the smell of mold. An ambulance, red roof light flashing, screamed past them into the emergency bay. At the door, medical personnel in anonymous green and white poured out to pull a folding gurney from the rear of the square vehicle. Griffen couldn't tell much about the figure lying on it, only that it was limp and unconscious.

Griffen worried that Val could be somewhere in the city, hooked up to life support, unable to let them know where she was. He could not allow himself to believe that he would never see her again. Their parents had disappeared when he was a boy. He and Val only had each other. He was more determined than ever to track her down and bring her home safely.

"So we have to consider that there might be another agency besides Melinda involved in her disappearance." Malcolm scowled. "That complicates matters."

Griffen studied him. "You don't look surprised."

"Griffen," Malcolm began, then paused. "I regret not having given you more time to absorb the truth about your heritage and to be available to answer questions. But it will have been brought home to you one way or another that an infant dragon of nearly pure blood, as Valerie's will be, is an immensely important asset, either as ally—or pawn."

Griffen felt anger rising in him. "You had the chance to tell us to be more careful. You had *years*."

"I thought you had the common sense to monitor your own fertility." Malcolm sighed. "But I am forgetting what it was like to be twenty. It has been a long time."

The way he said it made Griffen curious. He peered sideways at his uncle.

"How old *are* you?"

"Now, what kind of question is that?"

Griffen was a little embarrassed but told the truth.

"Well, I have been reading up on dragons. Some of the old ones are thousands of years old."

"*Reputed* to be thousands of years old," Malcolm corrected him. "The truly ancient are . . . well, we must speak more deeply on the subject another time."

Griffen felt frustrated. He hated having people hold out on him. "I'll remember that. In the meantime, I put in a call to a friend. She might be able to help us find Val, or at least set us going in the right direction."

Malcolm raised his eyebrows.

"Excellent! Did she witness Valerie's departure?"

Griffen hesitated.

"Not exactly."

"Then what is the nature of her information?"

"Well . . . it's hard to explain. I don't know exactly how she does what she does." That explanation was not going down well with Malcolm. Griffen did a mental shrug. "She's a witch."

"Griffen!"

"I have a lot of faith in her, Uncle Malcolm. She has been a good ally lately."

"An *ally*? In what way?"

Griffen glanced at the people streaming in and out of the hospital entrance.

"That's a long story. I don't think I should go into it here."

"Griffen, it's unwise to associate with others. They are . . . beneath us, you know."

"No, they aren't! They just have different talents!"

"Not as powerful as ours. That can engender jealousy and put you in danger. You can't trust them."

Griffen kept his face as blank as if he held four aces. "I do trust her. She knows about me, Uncle Malcolm. There's nothing to hide and no reason for her to be jealous."

"So the damage is already done," Malcolm said. His face set into a stone mask. "I might have to do something about that."

Griffen felt a chill race down his spine.

"No!"

Malcolm turned and headed toward their parking place. "Come on, then. I don't see how much good it will do, though."

Five

Griffen held his temper as he drove, but inwardly, he was fuming. His uncle sat beside him, surveying the city with a haughty air.

"I cannot believe that you revealed our heritage to outsiders," Malcolm said, for approximately the tenth time. "You endanger us all! Do you know how many humans I have told that we are dragons?"

"None," Griffen said. "And minus-two dragons, Val and me. Holly would have figured it out anyhow. She already knew when we met the first time. I ran a convention for, uh, alternative life-forms. Lycanthropes, fairies, vampires, ghosts, all kinds of people. And witches. I was the only dragon. Well, except for Val, but she wasn't really a participant. I was master of ceremonies. The, er, person who asked me to run things said that only a dragon would have the credibility and power to make the event go smoothly." He hoped Malcolm wouldn't ask if it had. "Then Holly and I were both parade royalty during Mardi Gras. Her title wasn't king, but it meant the same thing." Griffen realized he was babbling. He shook his head. It seemed an eon ago that he had ridden on the Fafnir float, throwing doubloons and beads to the screaming crowds. The last forty-eight hours felt like forty-eight years. He wondered if Val was all right. He glanced at his uncle.

Malcolm hadn't heard a word. His lips were pressed together as he stared out the windshield.

"You may have caused a total breach, Griffen. This is serious. I refuse to compound your error."

"Then don't come with me," Griffen said. He wrenched the wheel, and Brenda's car veered right off Rampart Street onto Canal toward his uncle's hotel. A man in a T-shirt hopped backward out of his way. "I've already put my life in her hands more than once. I trust her. You don't have to. I'll meet you back at your hotel and tell you what she says."

Malcolm grumbled. He hung on to the Jesus strap with both hands. "It isn't that I don't trust you to give me a full briefing," he said.

"But you *don't* trust me."

"No. I think you don't know what questions to ask. Besides, she may be a charlatan."

"No," Griffen said positively. "She's not a charlatan. You may not be able to trust the people you work with, but I can."

"Only because no one else has met their price yet, Griffen. Always remember that."

Bah, Griffen thought. But he steered the car back toward the French Quarter.

For a city as laid-back as New Orleans seemed to be, Griffen was surprised how swiftly all traces of Mardi Gras had been swept away in two days flat. He was afraid that some of the evidence of Val's last movements might have been swept away with them, but he was relieved to see the end of the festival. The purple, gold, and green bunting had been removed from all the storefronts. Images of jesters in motley had receded to the windows of knickknack shops and a few advertising posters. Hanks of beads still hung in nearly every open store in Jackson Square, but those were always there for the tourists. He was frankly relieved it was all over. That seemed to be a common feeling among his fellow denizens. The few tourists left seemed at loose ends, but New Orleans was a town for wandering. They'd find plenty to do, at a much easier pace.

He parked the car in the underground garage of the Royal
Sonesta and led his uncle out into the grand public space of
Jackson Square. The clock on the tower of Saint Louis Cathedral struck two. Griffen remembered he had had nothing
to eat since too early in the morning. He had forced down a
sweet roll and a small cup of coffee. One of his favorite restaurants, Chart House, beckoned at the other corner of the
square. The turtle soup there was the best in town, but his
throat choked up when he thought of rich food. He could
always manage to eat beignets. Café du Monde was just across
St. Peter. But business first.

The park inside the wrought-iron fence was unoccupied
except for a few tourists taking photos of the General Jackson
statue and a couple of gardeners in coolie hats. All the action
was in the space between the three streets that bound the
square and the fence. Artists, seated under standing umbrel-
las come rain or shine, had their work on display attached
to the iron bars.

"Poot nea'ly layaff mysel' to death!" a middle-aged black
man, his hands stained with oil pastels as he filled in the
blue sky on a canvas, shouted to his neighbor, an older white
woman in a smock and with a long braid of graying hair
down her back, who was sketching the caricature of a stout
man in a white polo shirt and a baseball cap.

"Well, honey, what ay-else could you DO?" the woman
bellowed back, adding a camera around the neck of her subject with a few deft strokes.

The lilting local patois was just one more kind of music
of the city. Griffen let the soothing sound of their banter and
laughter calm his jangling nerves. New Orleanians often
carried on conversations across streets, down blocks, or from
an upper-story window to a friend standing on the street
below. Northerners seemed so reserved and quiet by com-
parison, though you would be no more likely to break into
those conversations, however public it appeared, unless the
speakers were friends of yours. Privacy here had a more complex definition.

The cathedral watched over the square like a benevolent uncle, neither forbidding nor disapproving what went on at its feet. The chill wind that swirled around it could not touch its magnificence. Griffen hoped that his uncle might be impressed, but if he didn't play poker, he ought to. His face was as stiff as the statue of Andrew Jackson.

The world seemed to pass through the square daily. Two musicians, on accordion and saxophone, belted jazz music between a tent belonging to a local crystal reader and a face painter. The long lines of people waiting for their services tossed coins and bills into the open instrument cases of the musicians. Griffen turned the corner, looking for Holly.

"Repent NOW, or pay for your sins at the hands of Satan and his army of demons!" An amplified voice close behind them made Griffen jump. He looked back at the skinny frame of Reverend Wildfire, a local preacher who stalked tourists with a megaphone. "Repent! The end of the world is upon us! Jesus is coming, and he accepts into heaven only those who acknowledge their failings in this wicked world!"

Griffen wiggled a finger in his ear. Reverend Wildfire passed by, stinking of sweat and stale liquor. Malcolm gave him a chilly frown. The reverend didn't notice. As far as Griffen knew, he was sincere about his ministry though no one really listened to him. Griffen thought of saying as much to Malcolm, but his uncle's expression of disapproval never wavered.

Malcolm looked disdainfully at the human statues standing on upturned buckets at the corner of St. Peter and St. Ann. Griffen felt a pang for the loss of one of his good friends, who had died during the convention the previous Halloween. Malcolm all but snorted at the kids breakdancing for tips on a sheet of cardboard along St. Peter.

Griffen could tell what he was thinking, that all of this looked unbelievably tacky, worn-out, and low-class. Griffen felt a wave of temper hit him. This was his home. He loved the impromptu showmanship, the people who made a living, however marginal, out of their own skills and wits. Did he prefer that they break into houses or sell drugs? He knew plenty of those who lived on the more sinister side of the city, too. Tee-Bo ran a drug business. They had crossed paths. Griffen wasn't inclined to be judgmental or stop him unless their businesses conflicted. They had come to a mutual respect. He spotted one of the drug lord's runners near the entrance to a hotel on Jackson Square.

"Hey, Mr. Griffen!" the runner shouted.

"Hey, Emmet!" Griffen called back.

This brought an actual snort out of Malcolm.

Griffen felt fire swell in his belly, but he tamped it down. He stopped short, making his uncle halt beside him. The elder McCandles looked at him in surprise. "Uncle Malcolm, do you know the official motto of New Orleans?"

Malcolm raised an eyebrow.

"Yes, it's, er, *Laissez les bon temps roulez*. Bad French for *Let the good times roll*."

"That's for tourists. The locals prefer, *Be nice or go home*. I've already figured out you're not going to like a lot of my friends or acquaintances, but you don't have to. They're my connections, not yours. Just treat them with the respect you'd give the rich hotshots you do business with. You came to me. If I have to, I'll figure out where Val went on my own, and you can do what you need to. Then leave."

Malcolm's face went very still. "Point taken."

Griffen found that he was trembling with reaction. "Good."

His uncle cocked his head and regarded him, as if seeing him for the first time. "I'm impressed, Griffen. You have changed. You never had any real concern for anyone but yourself before. Now you not only are pursuing the well-being of your sister, but you are thinking of the dignity of your adopted city. Well done."

"Thanks," Griffen said, not trusting himself to say any more. He had told off his uncle. He had never done that before.

He *had* changed. Before coming to New Orleans, Griffen

had always gotten by on pure charm and his wits. He was becoming responsible. Things went below the surface. People were getting under his skin. He was vulnerable. That made him nervous. What if he failed them? What if they figured out he was still just a grifter with no skills? The thought made him more nervous.

Halfway down the square from St. Ann, he spotted Holly sitting under a beach umbrella propped up in a stand. A plump black man with graying dreadlocks was standing up from a green-draped chair and feeling in his pocket for his wallet. Leaving a bill with her, he walked away smiling. A woman took his place. A circle was drawn on the cobblestones in bright pink chalk around the chairs. Griffen halted them beyond it, out of earshot to give Holly privacy.

Next to her chair, Holly had a homemade sign made of deal board painted a warm brown. On it "Ask Mother Nature" was hand-lettered in a kind of pretty calligraphy done in comfortable colors like greens and golds. Mystical sigils done with glitter paints in bright blue and silver decorated the rest of the sign. Malcolm eyed it skeptically.

"I thought you said she was a witch," he said.

"Witchcraft is a nature religion," Griffen replied.

Holly didn't look like the Halloween caricature of witches, but neither did any of the others Griffen knew. She looked more like an old-time hippie. Her long, dishwater blond hair was tied back in a black-and-gold scarf, and she wore a gold-and-blue shawl over a moss green T-shirt, a long denim skirt, and sandals. Holly held the hand of a silver-haired woman, whose wrinkled face was rapt as she listened to her. Holly stroked the creased palm with her strong fingers and pointed out various lines and mounds. Griffen shifted from foot to foot, but he didn't interrupt. Malcolm looked at his watch impatiently, though he followed Griffen's lead and remained silent. Holly nodded once in his direction to show that she had seen them. Her voice was swallowed up in the ambient noise of the busy square, enough to keep humans from listening in on what might be a very personal reading. Griffen had keen hearing, a facet of his dragon heritage, but he couldn't make out what she was saying. Holly might have put an extra charm on the circle to keep anyone from eavesdropping. He grinned to himself.

When she was finished, the old woman thanked her warmly and fumbled in the expensive clasp bag on her lap. She extracted a ten-dollar bill and offered it to Holly, who pointed to the basket on a little tray table that had a little hand-lettered sign propped in it that said, "Gifts." The old woman gave a shy glance at Griffen and Malcolm, then hurried away. Holly stood up, stretched her legs, and wrapped the shawl closer around her shoulders.

"Cold today," she said. "But the sun's nice. How you doing, Griffen?"

"Pretty good," he said. "How about you?"

"I'm good," she said. She picked up the basket. "Good day. A bunch of tourists hanging on, taking advantage of the city's emptying out. They still had a little money left. I told them some good things. They deserved to hear them."

"I thought you couldn't use your gifts for pay," Malcolm said in a sour tone.

"This is for charity," Holly said, imperturbably. "I make my money writing computer-security programs at night. I support the ASPCA and Animal Rescue New Orleans, and it gets me out of the house." She shook the basket at him. It rustled, but he heard a few coins in the bottom. Griffen reached into his wallet and came out with a five. Malcolm did not produce any money. She studied him, then put out a hand.

"I'm Holly Goldberg." Malcolm shook hands with her. "I don't have to ask if you're a relative," she said. "You look just like Griffen."

Griffen didn't feel any more comfortable than his uncle looked at that remark.

"Malcolm McCandles. Griffen is my nephew."

"Welcome to New Orleans, Mr. McCandles. I know you'd wish for other circumstances, but it is what it is. Come on home with me."

Holly refused their offers of help in closing shop for the day. She folded up her table and tent, put it all on a two-wheeled cart that had been propped against the fence, and towed it behind her.

"Let me take that," Griffen said.

"Gallantry isn't dead," Holly said. "Thank you."

Griffen pulled the cart beside Holly and his uncle. Holly walked toward the river, talking as she went about the city. Malcolm still looked uninterested, but his eyes went to the sites she described. Griffen knew he did not miss a thing.

Six

A little to the west of the French market, Holly turned up the walk to a small wood-framed house painted blue, a single in between all the double shotguns on the street. In Griffen's opinion, it was exactly what a pagan would live in: wood furniture, natural fabrics, handmade rag rugs on the floor, dream catcher hanging from the window frame, slightly untidy but warm and cosy. The melamine-topped table in the sunny kitchen was as Griffen remembered it from his previous visit. The rest of the rooms were lined with bookshelves, all of which were stuffed beyond capacity with volumes of every size. Many, many more books stood in heaps on the floor around the feet of the overstuffed armchairs. At one side of the small living room hummed a computer terminal with a blocky monitor sitting on top of—what else?—more books.

Malcolm frowned at it.

"A witch with a computer?"

"Nothing in the rede that forbids it," Holly said breezily, setting out cups and saucers on the table. Fresh, fragrant brew dribbled into the glass carafe on the base of an ancient Mr. Coffee. "It still hurts no one, and I don't keep anything oathbound on my hard drive. My boyfriend Ethan's out at the moment, so what can I do for you?"

"Val," Griffen said.

"I know." Holly poured out coffee for all of them and offered cream and sugar and a willow basket of enormous peanut-butter cookies.

"Have you, uh, seen anything?" Griffen asked, after a welcome sip.

Holly shook her head. "I haven't tried since you called the first time. You can mess up the channels, so you don't know if you're looking at your hopes or the reality."

"Are you going to read my palm?" Malcolm asked. It was a challenge.

"You know, you don't have to believe in what I do," Holly said mildly, putting a palm on Griffen's chest to forestall an outburst from him. "I'm just trying to help. Why don't you sit right here?" She opened a hand toward a broad-backed chair upholstered in denim. "I've got *Wall Street Weekly* and *Smithsonian Magazine*."

"Don't patronize me!" Malcolm snarled. Holly shook her head.

"You know, you'd be better off saving your fire for the real attacks that are coming. I've been dreaming hard these last few weeks. The whole world's on the verge of change."

"Isn't it always?"

"Not like this," Holly said, gravely. "Not for a long time. Come on, then. You can critique my technique." She arranged four pots, each holding a burning charcoal tablet and a tiny pinch of incense at the four cardinal quarters of the room, and resumed her seat at the kitchen table. At her direction, Griffen took the chair to her left and Malcolm to her right. The sweet smell of sandalwood and myrrh flavored the air just a little.

Holly took their hands and held on to them tightly. She had a good grip. With her eyes closed, she began to croon softly. Malcolm pursed his lips. Griffen closed his eyes to shut out the sight and let himself feel. Holly's house always felt very safe. He sensed a cosy energy that was at the same time powerfully protective.

"We seek Valerie McCandles, for the good of all, according to the free will of all," Holly said, in a low, musical chant. "If it be her will, let her come to us from the other side."

They waited. Griffen peeked out of one eye. Holly's

forehead wrinkled, pushing her fair brows down. There was no interruption in the energy filling the room.

"Well?" Malcolm asked.

"She's alive," Holly said, opening her eyes. "I'm sure of that. Her spirit has not been set free. I'd have seen or felt something."

Griffen let out his breath with a whoosh. "Then where is she?"

For answer, Holly closed her eyes again and tightened her grip on their hands. "Val, we are your friends and family. We seek you with love. Send us a sign. Ooh!"

Her eyes flew open.

"What?" Griffen asked.

"Well, she's out there somewhere. I felt her just for a moment, then I got bounced back. There's a block around her."

"By evil or good?" Griffen asked.

Holly shrugged. "Magic's magic. The intent delineates good or evil according to your morals and ethics. The caster probably thinks it's good. But I'm not able to break through it."

"That leaves us no wiser." Malcolm was displeased. "What hard evidence can you give us?"

"We don't need evidence. She said Val's all right, but someone with powerful abilities is keeping her from us," Griffen said. "That's confirmation."

"It's not proof."

"I'm sorry, it's the best I can do," Holly said, a worried frown on her face. "She's all right. I can tell you that."

Griffen held out a hand. She gripped it.

"Thanks, Holly."

"Thank you for your time, Miss Goldberg," Malcolm said. He rose from the table. "I have an appointment later, and Griffen is coming with me."

Unapologetically, Holly reached for the basket and extended it to him. This time Malcolm unfolded his wallet. He put a twenty in the can. She smiled.

"The cats and dogs thank you, Mr. McCandles. Griffen,

I'll leave an intention in the ether. If anything comes through, I'll let you know."

As they were leaving, Malcolm's cell phone rang. He took it out of his breast pocket. The BlackBerry, slim and fangled to the nth degree, was much fancier than Griffen's simple flip phone. Griffen felt a pang of envy though he knew he could get any kind of phone he really wanted. He just had never indulged himself to that extent. Malcolm clicked the green button.

"Malcolm McCandles."

Griffen could hear a musical female voice on the other end.

"We'll be there," Malcolm said. A click sounded from the receiver. Malcolm looked up at him solemnly. "It's time. Do you know the Court of Two Sisters?"

Griffen left the car with the valet at the entrance on Bourbon Street. He knew the restaurant well. It was a favorite of visitors to the city but was considered a special-occasion venue by the locals because of the price of the jazz buffet. Griffen felt his mouth water in appeal for some of their famed curried chicken and salmon mousse. At least Holly's cookies had stilled the growling in his stomach.

"Let's get a table in the courtyard," Griffen suggested. "It's a nice place to discuss business."

"Our . . . associate is in a private dining room."

Griffen frowned. He glanced at the Fairy Gates attached to the walls of the entranceway, wrought-iron portals that had come from Spain and were decorated with tiny Christmas lights. They were supposed to bestow good luck and the gift of gab on those who touched both of them. He'd never noticed any difference. In case it helped, he angled out of his way to run a finger over the ribs of each one. He was nervous about meeting Malcolm's "connection." If his uncle was afraid of this man, how should he feel? What power could the man wield against a couple of dragons? Was he anything like Rose, Griffen's friend who had been a voodoo priestess in life yet still maintained a ghostly presence in the French Quarter? Griffen pictured a man dead for eight decades. He had seen plenty of horror movies. Was he a skeleton? Were the parts of his body rotting and falling off? Did he have maggots crawling out of his eyes? The images in his mind grew more and more disgusting until he was ready to back out and go home.

The receptionist was finishing up on the phone as Malcolm approached her.

"Yes, ma'am, two for ten o'clock Sunday morning. We'll see you then. Thank you." She hung up the phone and smiled. "May I help you?"

"My name is Malcolm McCandles. I'm expected."

She eyed him curiously, then glanced at Griffen. "Yes. Just one moment." She made a gesture. An old man in a waistcoat and bow tie over a pressed white shirt came over. She touched the list. He nodded.

"Right this way, gentlemen," he said.

Griffen hesitated. Malcolm put a hand on his arm.

"Come along, Griffen," he snapped. He peered into the young man's face. "Is this too much for you?"

"No! I see dead people . . . all the time," Griffen said, inadvertently quoting from *The Sixth Sense*, a movie he had enjoyed years before, never assuming that he'd ever emulate the Haley Joel Osment role.

"He's a little different than any other undead," Malcolm said. "Just take your lead from me . . . if you would."

Griffen was so unused to Malcolm's deferring to him even a little that he lost his poker face for a moment. "Whatever you say."

As they entered the high-ceilinged private dining room, a man in a blue business suit was leaving. Griffen caught a glimpse of pale blue eyes in the big, florid face. He looked as if he wanted to say something to Griffen or those remaining in the room but thought better of it.

He followed Malcolm inside.

It was dim in the chamber, but no more so than any of

the interior rooms of the Court of Two Sisters. Most people chose to sit in the courtyard, with its pergola of green vines draping lines of shadow, and spiral iron staircase in the corner that led to nothing. He had heard it was haunted but had never personally seen any of the ghosts that occupied it.

His imagination had wound him up to expect almost any kind of horror, so he was almost disappointed when the man at the head of the table extended a hand to him.

"Reginaud St. Cyr Duvallier, Mr. McCandles. Pleased to meet you. Have a seat. This is my secretary, Miss Nita Callaway. Best damn secretary in the whole United States."

"Uh, nice to meet you, sir, ma'am," Griffen said. "Call me Griffen." He gave a brief glance to the modest-looking woman with the laptop open before her on the table, then gave his whole attention to Duvallier. This was the man who worried Malcolm? He looked like half the visitors coming to New Orleans from Miami Beach, Texas, or Arizona. He had thick white hair brushed back from his forehead. He was thin for his big-boned frame. The cuffs of his snow-white shirt flared too widely around his wrists. His cheekbones and temples were filled with hollow shadows, and his skin looked weathered, not decayed. The nails on his knobbly, dry hands had been neatly cut and buffed. Only his eyes said he was anything but an ordinary man. They glowed. Literally. Internal fire lit them red and yellow. Griffen felt his mouth go dry. "Are you a . . . zombie?"

"Manner of speakin'," said Duvallier, grinning. His teeth were square and white in his brownish, leathery skin.

"Griffen!" Malcolm snapped.

"Don't take it out on the young'n," Duvallier said, patting the air with a hand. "I'd rather have honest curiosity than veiled assumptions and whispered rumors. Next time you visit me, I'll tell you all about it. I hope we can be friends, Griffen."

"I . . . hope so," Griffen said. The horror stories had nothing to compare with Duvallier. Unlike the brain-seeking monsters staggering around dropping body parts in movies, this was an intelligent and powerful man who just happened to be dead. Griffen saw why Duvallier might terrify others.

"'Course we will. You drink Irish, don't ya? There's a bottle of the good stuff on the sideboard there. Pour y'self one. Johnny Walker Blue for you, Malcolm? You got good taste. I'm a brandy man myself."

Malcolm folded his hands on the table and leaned over them. "Mr. Duvallier, you and I need to talk about Penny Dunbar."

"You know, that man who just left?" Duvallier asked, sitting back in his chair. "He just asked me if I'd kill her. Now, you want to tell me why I shouldn't do what he wants?"

Seven

The bleached blond male assistant straightened the flowers in the tiny crystal vase on the little table under the window. He pulled out the chair and set it at an angle, so it would be easy to get into. The curtains that covered the lower part of the window cut the glare coming off the enormous swimming pool outside.

"Will there be anything else, dear?" he asked.

Valerie McCandles set her magazine down on the wide arm of the padded chair under the reading lamp and stretched her feet on the damask-covered ottoman. Dishes of saffron chicken with rice, sectioned oranges, a green salad with perfect tomato slices on top, and a small cheese selection had been arranged on the tablecloth. A tall, pale blue china pot emitting the succulent smell of fresh, hot coffee steamed on a coaster beside its matching cream pitcher and sugar bowl.

"No, thanks, Henry. That looks great."

"Well, eat it before it goes cold," Henry said. "It's just not the same after that. And cover your feet! You don't want to catch the flu." He shook out a woven pink cashmere throw and flung it over her bare toes. "The troops are massing for your afternoon inspection."

"Are they ready?" Val asked with a wry grin.

"Are they ever?" Henry asked, with an impatient roll of his eyes. "I'll send Roxanne in in forty-five minutes to do your hair."

"I can do my own hair," Val said defensively. Her long blond tresses were still slightly damp from the shower after her morning swim.

Henry let out a pained sigh. Val relented. It was no good arguing with him. He had an ironclad opinion on how she ought to look in public.

"Okay," she said.

"Good. Your day clothes are laid out in your dressing room. See you later!"

With a quick glance around to see if anything else was out of place, he bustled out.

Val waited until the door closed behind him, then kicked off the throw. Henry was a mother hen. If she had let him, he would have fussed over her every minute of the day.

She heaved herself out of the armchair and sat down at the luncheon table. Her belly threw her off-balance even though it was still small enough that people usually missed the bulge under her customary baggy tops. The doctor who had examined her the previous morning declared that it was on schedule for a five-month fetus, and that the six months still to go on her pregnancy should be no problem.

Eleven months!

Sometimes, it sucked to be a dragon.

"How are you doing, kid?" she asked, patting her tummy affectionately. Her unborn child shifted inside her as if answering her question. She smiled contentedly.

When she had first discovered that a passionate night with a handsome man had resulted in pregnancy, Valerie was conflicted. She was then only twenty years old, with no career, no degree, and hardly any money. She hadn't finished college before her brother Griffen had swept her up and hustled her away from campus to live in New Orleans, where it was— safer. Since then, she had had a birthday, sandwiched in between a host of revelations. The first of those was that she was a dragon. There was no denying she and Griffen were different than anyone else she knew. The college infirmary had broken two needles on her arm before suggesting she take the flu vaccine by nasal inhaler. Her roommate had teased her about being too tense. Yet Val distinctly recalled getting inoculations as a child. The dragon characteristics must have been forming gradually. She couldn't yet breathe fire or transform shape, as she now knew she probably would one day, but she was immune to stab wounds or cuts.

That made shaving her legs a lot easier. No more nicks in the shower.

Apart from that, she saw little practical use for the trait.

A much-less-welcome piece of knowledge was that Griffen had held back on telling her about most of these cool things. Why? It wasn't like ignorance would prevent their happening. His mentor, Mose, had talked with him for days on end, teaching him how to be an effective dragon. Why hadn't he passed those lessons along to her? She wasn't that much younger than he was. Not even two years separated them. If he could handle it, so could she.

Val tried to shut out the nagging in her head, delivered in Melinda's voice, that they wanted to leave Val helpless and dependent on them. She doubted it. The one person she could rely upon to drop everything for her was Griffen. Had he not come to her college to get her away from the assassins who were stalking them? Didn't he help her get her own apartment, so she didn't have to share with him and could keep her privacy? Didn't he hire people to follow her around New Orleans to prevent her from being bothered by Melinda? Well, Melinda had gotten past them eventually. Only Griffen himself could have kept an experienced and determined lady like her away from Val. The baby in her womb was Melinda's grandchild.

Val found it a curious dichotomy that she had come to terms with Melinda, would happily die for the sake of her future child, and yet looked forward to killing the bastard who had impregnated her when she saw him next. Melinda was carefully keeping her son out of Val's way. It wasn't the fact that she was going to have a baby; it was that he had used another dragon skill, a kind of magical hypnosis, to get in bed with her. For robbing her of free will, she was going to beat him to death the first opportunity she could. Sometimes, when she had an odd moment, she fantasized about what heavy objects she was going to use on him.

As for the baby itself—Val carefully kept from trying to guess its gender—she had never loved anything so much in her life. She'd been of two minds when she first found out. She was glad she hadn't jumped at her first impulse, to get rid of it. Now Val wanted to be a mother. She was eager for the day in late September when her baby would be born and she could hold it in her arms for the first time. The joy she felt every so often when she thought about it made her feel good all over. Sure, there were going to be problems ahead. Handling a newborn and the rest of her future at the same time would need a lot of planning and plenty of help. She was luckier than many single mothers who had fewer resources to count on. The Quarter was not only her neighborhood, it had become her extended family. Hers and Griffen's.

She had few clear memories of their parents. Griffen and Val had been small when their mother and father left home for the last time. Still, Val recalled being held in strong arms and rocked. There had been a blue teddy bear with a yellow ribbon around its neck and amber plastic eyes. A mellow soprano voice and a deep baritone voice sang nonsense songs with her tiny treble. She had a mental image of a small blond woman and a very tall man. To her childish memory, they had been perfect. Now she realized how little she knew about them. Her uncle had never really sat down with her and Griffen to tell them what had happened to take their parents away, or to answer any questions they had had over the years.

How easily she had accepted the status quo. Immediately, she felt a pang of distrust. Had Malcolm done something like Nathaniel and compelled them not to be curious? No, how could he? He was never home, or hardly ever. She and Griffen didn't miss him when he was away during their childhoods. Val was grateful that he had taken them in, but she had no strong feelings for him. He hadn't called them in over a year since they had moved to the South. Maybe he was glad to be rid of them, like Melinda said.

Val tore off a piece of bread and played with it moodily. She really shouldn't trust Melinda. The older dragon was far more concerned about the well-being of Val's baby than about Val herself. Still, she treated Val like a real adult.

Maybe too much of one.

A rap on the door drew her out of her reverie.

"Come in!" she called.

A timid face peered around the doorway.

"Are you ready for me, Miss Valerie?" Roxanne was a petite woman with shining blond hair pulled back and folded against the back of her head. At six feet tall, Val felt like a giant next to her. That reminded her of her friend Mai, one of Griffen's girlfriends, petite with delicate bones. She missed Mai.

"Sure," she said. "Come in."

"Thank you."

Roxanne dragged in her rolling cart of hairdressing tools. Without another word, she went to work on Val's hair, gently combing out the tangles and drying it with a cylindrical brush and a blow-dryer with a huge diffuser attached to the mouth.

"How's it going?" Val asked, staring out at the dancing lights on the pool.

"Fine, fine," Roxanne said, clipping her words off hastily. Like everyone in this house—if you could call this sprawling resort complex a house—except Henry, she was terrified of Val.

"Do you have anything special going on this weekend?" Val asked in an encouraging voice.

"Oh, no. I don't, I mean."

Wow, Val thought.

She subsided in the chair and let Roxanne work on her. When the roaring of the blow-dryer stopped and the pulling at various tresses of her hair ceased, a hand mirror peeped shyly around the edge of her vision. Val took it and looked at her reflection. Behind her, the beautician was almost trembling as she held up a large, rectangular mirror so Val could see the back of her own head. Her long blond hair was parted on the side and combed out in waves like Cameron Diaz's.

"It looks beautiful," she assured Roxanne.

"Thank you. Shall I do your makeup now?"

Val opened her mouth to protest, then thought of facing Henry again. "Sure. Thanks."

At least she didn't look like a drag queen when Roxanne was through with her. In fact, she looked like the pages in the fashion magazines that touted "The Natural Look," finished and smooth without seeming to be made up at all.

"That's fabulous! Will you show me how you do that?" Val asked, turning her face from side to side to admire the effect. "I mean, tomorrow?"

"I . . . uh," Roxanne stammered.

"You have to get permission?"

"Yes. Um. Shall I help you dress?"

"No, thanks," Val said firmly, rising from the chair. "I'd rather dress myself. Tell Henry I'll be ready in five minutes."

Roxanne gathered her tools and shoved the cart hastily out the door. Val shrugged out of her robe and dropped it on the bed. The room was so tidy that the single rumpled garment stood out like a neon sign. Val grinned a little naughtily. She could make her own mark.

Before the promised five minutes were up, Val marched out into the broad hallway toward the grand staircase. The thick blue carpet swallowed the sound of her high-heeled sandals. The wrap dress that was tied just above her bulge almost matched the shade of blue. Not that the décor had been chosen to complement her looks, of course, but she could pretend that it had. All those programs on the Discovery Channel about royal palaces and mansions around the world that zoomed around to show those pilastered columns and frescoed ceilings didn't really tell how it felt to live in one. She could have told those fulsome voice-over announcers that it was daunting but comfortable.

When she reached the head of the stairs, Henry appeared out of nowhere and took her arm.

"Very nice," he said, looking her over critically. "Very understated. Come on. Everyone needs to get back to work."

"I don't have to do this," Val said. "They can work without having me check on them every day."

"Melinda always checks on the staff. She left you in charge, so you need to keep everything moving. Here's the day's itinerary." He opened up a little palmtop computer and handed it to her. The little gray screen displayed several columns, each headed by a single word: MAINTENANCE, SUPPLY, COMMUNICATIONS, DISBURSEMENTS, DELIVERIES, and so on. Val absorbed as many of the items as she could before Henry whisked it out of her hand and nodded toward the banister. She took hold of it, wary of her heels.

Normally, at that time of day, she would be wearing jeans and a T-shirt, cleaning up from the lunch crowd in the bar where she worked, and looking forward to reading a book while a few people wandered in for a Coke or a Bloody Mary. Her greatest intellectual exercise was figuring out if young-looking patrons were as old as the birth date on their driver's licenses said they were. In forty-eight hours, she had turned into Junior Miss CEO.

She wasn't sure yet if she liked it.

At the bottom of the stairs, nearly fifty people were waiting for her. Val was dismayed at the annoyed looks they shot her, expressions that vanished immediately when Henry frowned. Her, they feared. Him, they respected.

"Everyone!" Henry snapped. "Please give Miss Valerie a quick progress report, then you can get back to work. Vilus, kitchens, please."

A tall, thin black man in chef's whites with a gold kerchief tied around his neck cleared his throat.

"Got some nice pompano in this morning. Had to compost about twenty pounds of potatoes because they were going green. That's okay. I've got dehydrated potatoes in the pantry, and I gave Marcella the order for fresh spuds for

Friday's dinner party. The menu's on a disk if you want to check it over."

What dinner party? Val wondered, but Marcella, a sharp-eyed, round-faced woman in a tight suit-dress, took up the narrative without expanding on Vilus's statement.

"The two Spode plates are back from the china restorer, so the set's complete again," she said. "Nothing else to report."

"Good," Val said, since that seemed to be what the staff was waiting for. One after another, they gave their brief statements in noncommittal voices, the import of which went right over her head. She smiled and nodded, trying to sound encouraging. As soon as the last person, a Hispanic-looking gardener named Juan Pablo, named off the tulips that were sending up shoots along the front drive, the crowd seemed to explode outward. Val didn't have time to say "Thank you," or "Dismissed," before the room was empty. A vacuum cleaner started up in the hallway next door, and she heard distant clattering and the murmur of voices.

Henry stepped up alongside her, touching a key on the small computer's pad. "That went well," he said. "You should have asked about Agnetta's baby, but you can do that tomorrow."

"What about him?" Val asked, trying to remember who Agnetta was.

"Her. Lolita Arcadia. Six pounds, four ounces. She was born Monday. Michael told you yesterday. Michael from Housekeeping?" Henry looked exasperated. "He's subbing for Agnetta while she is on maternity leave. You still have to go to his office to sign the card for her."

"I don't remember all that!"

"After the briefing, you should have gone back to your room and written notes," Henry said. "It would look better if you had those facts at your fingertips."

"Look, they all know that I'm faking it. I don't have a clue what I'm doing."

"You aren't *faking it*; you're learning," Henry said, rolling his eyes. "And, yes, everyone knows you're new. Now, come on. We have a lot to do today."

"What's next? Posture lessons?"

"Close," Henry said, taking her arm again. "Fittings. What on Earth will you wear on Friday? You only have one dress. It's gorgeous, but it's just too much for this event. And you need to learn everyone's name and details so you can make chitchat."

Val halted, jerking him back a pace. "Wait a minute. This dinner party? I'm supposed to attend?"

"Good heavens, no!" Henry chuckled. Val heaved a sigh of relief. "You're hosting it."

She gawked at him.

"What? No!"

Henry ignored her protests and towed her away.

Eight

Even when he spoke to Malcolm, Duvallier kept his eyes fixed on Griffen. Griffen found his scrutiny nerve-wracking, something the old man surely knew. Malcolm was appalled.

"Mr. Duvallier, you can't be serious. Penny Dunbar is a bright new light on the political scene."

"Never met her," Duvallier said. He gave an offhand wave. "Maybe never will. And call me Reginaud if you like. I'm gonna call you Malcolm, so let's be friendly. You, too, Griffen."

Griffen shifted uneasily.

"Uh, thanks."

Malcolm frowned. "This country needs leaders, Mr. Duvallier," he said. "Leaders with a vision for the future."

"I know that!" Duvallier laughed. "This ain't the first dance I been asked to, Malcolm. Just that I also know that if Penny Dunbar don't run, there's a hundred others with similar qualifications standing right behind her, waiting their chance."

"She's the only one I am concerned with at the moment," Malcolm said. "Who was that man? Why does he want her dead?"

"Well, dead or outten the way. I don't think he cares a lot which one, himself, but the folks he's workin' with say they want her gone permanently." Duvallier chewed the end of his cigar. Griffen could tell he wanted to light it, but he held back. The only reason he could guess was that the secretary didn't like it. He doubted a man like Duvallier cared about most people's feelings, but having him concerned for Miss Callaway was a facet Griffen hadn't suspected.

"What can we do to persuade you not to hurt her?" Griffen asked.

"Persuade me?" Duvallier echoed. He tilted his head. "Try me. I would enjoy hearin' your logical explanation for why I shouldn't exercise my whim."

"If you really don't have strong feelings one way or the other, what's the difference?" Griffen asked, trying to sound casual though his heart was pounding in his chest. "I don't know Miss Dunbar, but I've seen her on television. She sounds pretty sensible. She might be a good governor."

The fiery eyes were unimpressed.

"Politicians are a dime a dozen," Duvallier said. "They all say what they think will get your vote. One's pretty much like another. I'm only interested in how any particular one benefits me in the long run."

"Ah," Malcolm said. "Then what benefits would you like to receive in exchange for backing Penny Dunbar instead of . . . interfering with her campaign?"

"Are you empowered to speak for the lady?" Duvallier asked.

"I . . . speak for the people who are helping to finance her campaign."

Duvallier waved the cigar. "That's not enough. If I don't interfere with her, like you say, I want access to her ear anytime I need it."

"I can arrange for that," Malcolm said.

"And there's the matter of my fee. It'll be sizable, I want you to know."

"Of course."

"And a position in her office once she's elected."

Malcolm swallowed. "I will see what I can do."

"Forget all about it, son," Duvallier said. He leered at Malcolm. "I just wanted to see how desperate you are. You know I can't sit in no office like I am. It's just fun to see if I could bargain you out of the last cent in your pocket. You'd agree to anything here and now if I would just take the threat off the table. Well, I won't do it."

"And why not?"

"Where's the pleasure in that? I love a good race. Miss Dunbar's just one of the horses. If she crosses the finish line first, well and good. If she don't, well, she's an also-ran. I put my money on winners, and winners only, because they're the ones who pay off."

Griffen sensed a challenge. "Do you like to back winners? I don't know if you were aware of my business . . ."

"Well, yes, I am, young man," Duvallier said, widening the glowing red gaze. "Y'all run Mose's gambling concern. Fine fellow. Played with him myself, back in years gone by. But penny-ante poker and three-dollar bets at the racetrack window don't interest this old man no more. I like the big races. Like this one. Governor of the state of Louisiana. Almost the biggest prize there is, and your girl wants to go that distance, too, don't she?"

"Yes, she does," Malcolm said. "I represent the people who want to see her reach it."

"That's just fine. But she's not alone in this race."

"Whom does your other client back?"

"That's none of your business. You can take a shot in the dark at guessing the name, but right now there's about seventeen potential candidates who'll be in the primary."

Malcolm lowered his brows. "I have no proof that the man who just left has anything to do with the coming election. After I made an appointment to meet with you, who knows what arrangements you made to impress me? For all I know, he was a salesman who hoped to interest you in a new coffin!"

"You think I'm *playin'* you?" Duvallier demanded. Miss Callaway huffed and looked outraged on her employer's behalf. Malcolm glowered.

"I *know* you're playing me. I simply wish to know to what extent!"

Duvallier's eyes glowed brighter.

"Uncle Malcolm . . ." Griffen began uneasily.

"I don't have to impress you, son. I didn't even have to see you. It was a matter of courtesy that I allowed this meetin' at all. You from out of state. This is a Louisiana matter."

"*I* live here," Griffen said.

"You ain't the one who's backin' Penny Dunbar, so why don't you hush for a minute?" Duvallier said.

Griffen felt his temper flare. The little spark of fire that was always in his belly began to dance with joy. With difficulty, he tamped it down and spoke more calmly than he felt.

"I'm part of this discussion now. What you're talking about is premeditated murder for hire."

Duvallier grinned at him. "You like to call things like you see 'em. Good for you. It ain't strictly accurate. But it don't change nothin' to give it a name."

"Well, what else do I call it?" Griffen asked. "Some other person offers to pay you to kill someone."

"I don't say I accepted the other fellow's offer, now have I?"

"But you won't accept ours?"

"I like to keep my options open."

"How can we change your mind? We are prepared to fund many initiatives to improve life for the citizens of this state: transportation, education, tax incentives . . ."

Duvallier waved a hand. "All talk. I don't care whether one lone person lives or dies. The world's crowded enough as it is."

"That's rich coming from you," Griffen said. "If overpopulation bothers you, why didn't you just lie down and die when *your* time was up?"

"Because I wasn't ready to go," Duvallier said. "Still ain't. I care that I'm here. It's the folks who came after me that are usin' up resources I might want for myself. Sure, it's pure selfish, but that's the nature of the human organism. Fine word, ain't that, organism? I got it outten *National Geographic.*"

"I'm not going to sit here and argue ethics with a zombie who reads magazines," Griffen said. "You're gambling with people's lives!"

"Ain't no finer currency, son."

"You think that you can take on every dragon in the state? If you take out one of us, you make enemies of a lot of powerful and dangerous people!"

"And what do you plan to do about it?" Over his unlit cigar, Duvallier's eyes glowed like embers.

"The first move is yours," Griffen said.

"So we shifted from poker to chess," Duvallier said, taking the cigar from his mouth. His leathery cheeks spread in a real smile. "You think an army scares me, son? All right, then, let's see how your strategy works. You know how campaigns are run in this state?"

"With or without your help?" Griffen challenged him.

Duvallier leered. "Oh, with, boy, with. For a long time now. They run what they call a 'jungle primary.' Now, you know what the law of the jungle is, don't you, son? Survival of the fittest. If you can keep your candidate alive until the primary, I'll let her run. 'Fact, I'll give her my support, and too bad for my other client. If not, well, then, it lays the question, don't it?"

Malcolm was aghast. "You can't do that!"

"Sure I can. It's all a game, ain't it? You better run along now," Duvallier said. He flicked a hand toward the door. "Nice to meet you, Malcolm. You, too, Griffen. Lookin' forward to seein' you again. We'll do lunch sometime." Duvallier chuckled and put the cigar back in his mouth. "I like that phrase, *do lunch*. Funny thing, language. Take care of y'selves, now."

Even with his long legs, Griffen had to scurry to keep up with Malcolm's retreating back. He caught up with him on the curb, where his uncle was handing the car's claim slip to the valet.

"I'm sorry for making things worse, Uncle Malcolm."

The elder McCandles regarded him gravely.

"They went very much the way I feared they would, Griffen. Actually, I appreciated your input. It was helpful."

Griffen stared at him. "How? I just challenged him to try to kill Penny Dunbar before the primary."

Malcolm sighed. "I and my associates grossly underestimated the importance of the local angle. Your presence gave me more credibility with Mr. Duvallier than I would have had alone. My associates and I felt that with the growth of the global community, we might be able to exert pressure as interested parties. But, as the late Speaker of the House Tip O'Neill justly said, 'All politics is local.' Mr. Duvallier is, perforce, old-school. I would further appreciate it if you remained involved."

"Sure," Griffen said, surprised. "As long as it doesn't interfere with my business. Or finding Val."

"I had not forgotten your sister. I have various investigators out in the field, following up leads as to her whereabouts. She is not likely to be harmed in her condition."

"There's a long way in between not being harmed and able to come and go as she wants," Griffen said.

"I know that, but we do not know if she was under duress or left of her own volition. Her life is not actively in danger, and Miss Dunbar's is. So, if you please?"

The valet brought the Toyota to a halt at the curb. Malcolm tipped the young man and received a half salute in return.

Griffen got behind the wheel.

Nine

Griffen felt shaken. He wished he could talk to Rose. He thought of the ghost of the voodoo priestess as his special advisor and sometimes guardian angel there in the French Quarter. She often sensed when he needed her though she seldom if ever appeared when there was anyone else around. He glanced at pedestrians on the sidewalks but saw only tourists going to watch the acrobats performing on the adjoining street that closed for the afternoon. Scarcely any locals, and none of them the distinctive, slender, African-American woman wrapped in colorful skirts and shawls. He sent out a silent plea to her to find him later.

"Where can I drop you?" he asked his uncle.

"Where are you going?" Malcolm inquired politely.

"Back," Griffen said. "I have to check and see how things are going. I have . . . responsibilities."

"So I have heard. May I come with you?"

Griffen gawked. He had thought he was done with his uncle Malcolm for the time being. "I don't think you would find it interesting," he said politely.

"I admit, I am curious," Malcolm said. "You went from a fairly unsuccessful college student with a less-than-responsible attitude, to a manager and owner of a going concern, however . . . illicit."

"It's a gray area," Griffen said, uncomfortably.

"Forgive me. It was not an opening to an argument. You have done well, or so I have heard. We need to talk more, and, if you would permit me, it would be a privilege to see how you have changed." Griffen growled inwardly at the thought of performing for his disapproving elder relative, but part of him suddenly craved showing off.

"All right," he said. He turned the next corner and headed for the Irish pub.

Few patrons sat at the scattered tables or hugged the dark-stained wooden bar when they arrived. The hour before dinner was often a good time for a private conversation. The room was dimly lit and just warm enough to be comfortable. The clack of pool balls at one of the two pool tables and the blare of the jukebox across the big, open room made for homey background noise. The Irish pub was Griffen's favorite spot in the French Quarter. He knew all the locals who frequented it and would look out for them, as he knew they would look out for him. The food was decent, the beer fresh, and the bartender knew everyone's favorite drink without having to ask.

Griffen took a seat at the rear of the bar, the "family" side, beside one of the pillars decorated with little white Christmas lights. Malcolm slid in beside him.

"This is a nice, quiet neighborhood," Malcolm said. "Where is your office?"

"I don't have one," Griffen said. He raised a finger, and the bartender poured him a Diet Coke. "What will you have?"

"Black coffee, thank you. I don't usually drink that much or that early in the day, but it seemed imprudent to refuse Mr. . . . our recent host."

Griffen understood from Malcolm's reticence that Duvallier's name was not to be spoken aloud. Griffen knew very well how easy it was for a stray word to be overheard.

He waited until the barman set a white mug before him, filled it with steaming, sable liquid, and turned away to give them their privacy.

"You run a tab?" Malcolm asked.

"I'm in here all the time," Griffen said.

"And you pay it off regularly?"

"Why do you ask?" Griffen inquired, keeping his face blank.

Malcolm nodded. "I see. None of my business, though you undoubtedly do keep up with your bill, judging by the bartender's demeanor. He showed no signs of impatience with you."

"Few people get impatient in New Orleans," Griffen said. "Life moves at its own pace here."

"So I see. It will take me some getting used to. But I am interrupting your day. You have responsibilities, and I have this excellent coffee. Chicory, isn't it? Proceed with your duties."

"Excuse me a minute." Griffen turned his back on his uncle. He took his cell phone from his pocket and hit the speed-dial number for Jerome.

"Hey, Grifter!" his lieutenant's soft voice murmured in his ear. "Where are you?"

"The pub," Griffen said. "How's it going?"

"Everything's fine, man. You sound like you need to detox."

"Later."

"Uh-huh. What do I need to know?"

Griffen glanced over his shoulder at Malcolm, who was pointedly not listening.

"Uh, I'd rather tell you when I see you."

"Uh-huh, company?"

"Yes," Griffen said. "My uncle's in town."

"I get it. No problem. Be there later."

The mellow clack of pool balls broke over the murmur of afternoon conversation. Griffen looked up to see who was playing.

At the farther of the two tables in the Pub, his girlfriend Fox Lisa waved an eager hand at him. Griffen wasn't surprised that he hadn't seen the little redhead over the heads of his barmates. She was worth noticing. Her long hair was pulled back in a ponytail, and she wore a skintight green T-shirt with a plunging neckline that showed off her generous bustline, and tight, faded jeans. Her companion, though, would have been difficult to miss anywhere. Her hair was red, too, but a pale strawberry blond that was struck gold by the Christmas lights. Freckles dusted her skin but only served to adorn it. Her figure was what the magazines called willowy, as if a strong wind would make her bend. Her mouth was wide, made for smiling—or kissing. Her pale blue eyes, though, had steel in them. She had on wide-legged, pale beige trousers and a soft top, an outfit more suitable for a fancy nightclub than a corner bar. She put down her pool cue and headed toward him. With a start, Griffen recognized her.

He stood up.

"Uncle Malcolm, isn't that . . . ?"

Malcolm looked astonished. "Indeed it is."

Fox Lisa scooted around her friend and reached up to give Griffen a hearty kiss. "Well, hey, there," she said. "I wondered when you were going to get here! I want you to meet my friend!"

"Penelope Dunbar. Call me Penny."

"Penny's running for governor," Fox Lisa said. "She belongs to my shooting club. She's been looking for campaign workers. I'm running St. Bernard Parish for her. She said she was interested in meeting local business owners, and I told her about you. She said she had heard about you."

"In more ways than one," Penny said. Her alto voice was musical. She shook hands with him. She had a firm grip. "And this must be your uncle." She took Malcolm's nerveless fingers in hers.

"Yes," Griffen said, belatedly and not a little lamely. "Penny, this is my uncle, Malcolm McCandles."

"I've been looking forward to meeting you, Miss Dunbar," Malcolm said.

"The pleasure's all mine, Mr. McCandles. Call me Penny."

Fox Lisa looked taken aback and a little disappointed. "You know him already?"

"Yes," Penny said, with a million-watt smile. "This is the man who is going to save my life."

Ten

Penny and Malcolm had been at a small table in the corner for hours. Their voices were shielded by the voices of the crowd that had built up in the bar. Neither of them ate anything. Penny smoked two or three cigarettes. She and Malcolm drank cup after cup of black coffee.

Griffen crumpled his napkin and pushed aside the basket of chicken bones. Fox Lisa held on to her tumbler of Jack Daniel's and toyed with the last of her french fries.

"I can't believe you know her already," Fox Lisa said for perhaps the eightieth time.

"I don't," Griffen said. "Uncle Malcolm said he was coming to New Orleans to meet her. I have never thought of her as anything except a name on the news until this morning. You know I don't pay a lot of attention to politics. I'm just too busy."

"What about your uncle? What does he have to do with political campaigns?"

Griffen was all too aware the conversation with Duvallier was off-limits, but he had gotten into a lot of trouble in the past for keeping important information from the people in his life who might be affected by it. "I'm not sure. Maybe he works for her party?"

"The Economy Party? I thought it was only in five states so far."

Griffen thought hard. He loved the debates among his friends in the Irish pub, especially at night over a friendly beverage, but politics was not one of his major interests. He could reel off the full cast of classic MGM movies, but he doubted that, if challenged, he could name his local councilman or both sitting Louisiana senators.

"I honestly don't know his connection, but he came here to talk with her."

"So what *are* they talking about?" Fox Lisa asked again. She challenged him with a look. "I'm not gonna let you drop yourself into a situation again, Griffen. Or me. I'm not even rested up from Mardi Gras. I know *you're* not. Does it have anything to do with Val? Have you heard from her?"

"No, and no," Griffen said. "Look, what if . . . ?" He shot a look toward his uncle and decided to take a chance on making the older McCandles angry. He knew he could trust Fox Lisa with his life, or any secret. "What if I had heard something, about some trouble that might involve Penny?"

Fox Lisa's large eyes went round.

"What kind of trouble?"

"Well, what if I had heard something about someone who might want to . . . hurt Penny?"

Fox Lisa threw back her head and laughed. "Oh, that old thing?"

"What old thing?"

"The assassination threats! Sweetheart, this is Louisiana! If a candidate didn't declare a blood feud against his opponent, you knew you couldn't take them seriously. It's nothing. Makes for a good news report. Sometimes I think they call in the threats themselves." She stopped and studied his face. Her expression became solemn. "You think this one's not pure bluster, don't you?"

"I . . . have reason to believe there's a legitimate menace."

"Who's behind it?"

"That I can't tell you," Griffen said, firmly. "Not until I've talked with Uncle Malcolm. Just . . . in the meantime, can you make sure she doesn't take any unnecessary chances?"

Fox Lisa patted her purse. Griffen remembered she had a loaded gun in it that she knew how to use. "We're both packing. I won't say Penny's a better shot than me, because she's not—but she isn't afraid to pull the trigger. And she's a brown belt. I've seen her throw some pretty big men across the room. That's how she keeps in shape. She's also got a head of security on her campaign staff. Maurice is a bouncer at a club near the Superdome. You want me to give him a heads-up?"

"This . . . might not be that kind of attack. I don't know what it might be or how to counter it. Not yet, anyway."

Fox Lisa nodded solemnly. "Griffen, I'll do everything I can to help her. She'll make a great governor. I believe in her. If that means blasting the shit out of some werewolf, it would be my pleasure."

Griffen shrugged. "When I know anything I can tell you, I will. You know that."

Fox Lisa grinned. "I don't mind. I stopped thinking I knew everything about the time I turned thirteen."

"Hey, Grifter!"

Griffen turned to see Jerome sidle into the pub. He was a tall, muscular, African-American who had been Griffen's best friend in college and was his second-in-command running the gambling operation. Griffen waited until Jerome picked up a chilled glass of beer from the bartender, then shoved a chair out from their table with his foot.

"Hi, Jer. How'd the games go?"

"No problem." Jerome glanced around. He caught Malcolm's eye and nodded to him. Malcolm nodded back. Penny Dunbar shot a curious glance his way, then returned to the conversation. Griffen watched this silent exchange with interest. It shouldn't have surprised him by then that Jerome knew Malcolm McCandles. Griffen was all too aware how many people had been watching him as he grew up. A prophecy about a powerful young dragon had come to be centered on him. Whether it was true or not, the focus of a lot of dragons was on Griffen. He would really have appreciated having it confirmed, so he could get on with his life, but that was unlikely. Instead, he had to settle for picking up clues and nuances where he could. "Any news about Val?"

"Nothing. Gris-gris called to ask me the same thing. It'll be a couple more days before they let him out, and he's jumping to start looking around as soon as he can."

"He really should not rush a belly wound," Jerome said. "But trying to keep Gris-gris down is like trying to stuff bees back into a hive."

"I know." Griffen frowned.

Jerome nudged him with the back of his hand. "Don't worry, Grifter. I'm sure Val's fine. I've got some ears and eyes looking for her, too. Hey, here's tonight's takings. We did okay. Doughboy asked me for a loan." He mentioned a runner who also helped with the catering arrangements. The nickname referred to his wide belly and high voice. "He's got child support to pay. I made a note of the amount. He never asks, so I made an executive decision."

He slid an envelope under Griffen's hand. Griffen slid it off the table and into a pocket.

"You know more about this business than I do," Griffen said. "If you think this isn't the beginning of a trend, I respect your judgment."

"He's as honest as anybody. He just got caught with empty pockets. It could happen to anyone." Jer lifted his chin toward the other table. "Anything I can help out with on this?"

"I don't know yet," Griffen said. He explained what he could. Jerome's face went blank as he listened, as if he was psyching out fellow players at a poker table. "I hope it's nothing."

"Rumors like that get started all the time."

"I've heard something . . . more substantial," Griffen said. "It's more than rumor, but I think less than fact."

Jerome nodded. "You can count on me, when I have time."

"Thanks, Jer," Fox Lisa said.

Griffen gave him a wry look. "If that's an obvious warning not to waste all my own time on it, I already know that."

Jerome put his hand on his chest. "Who, me? You're the big boss man. You make the rules."

"If I want other people to follow them, I had better do it, too. I get that."

Fox Lisa looked at her watch. "It's late. I better get Penny out of here. She has an interview on television tomorrow morning. They want us there about six thirty."

Griffen stood up and pulled back her chair.

"I'll drive you home. I have Brenda's car."

She smiled up at him.

"Thanks, but I have one of the cars from the campaign. A Lincoln."

Griffen raised his eyebrows. "I'm impressed."

Fox Lisa tossed her red ponytail. "Maybe if you're good, I'll take you for a ride in it sometime. This is the real thing, Griffen. Penny's a good bet to make the nomination. All kinds of people are throwing money at us. Do you think that's why Penny's being threatened?"

"It's got to be power, hate, or fear," Griffen said. He knew he was hedging. "Those are the classic reasons."

"Penny is the nicest person! I can't imagine who could be so mean!"

"Neither could I," Griffen said. "Do you want me to walk you out?"

"No need." Fox Lisa pulled his head down and kissed him soundly on the lips. "I'm warned. That's all you needed to do. You delegate. Not everything has to be you."

She sidled up to Penny and whispered in her ear. Penny nodded. Fox Lisa slipped out into the night. Penny waited until she was out of sight and beckoned him over. Griffen slid into an empty chair at their table.

"That was very diplomatic of you," she said, a glint in her eyes.

"What was?" Griffen asked.

"You managed to tell her to watch out for me without telling her more than she needed to know. I'm grateful."

"Happy to help," Griffen said.

Penny smiled. "I'm so happy to hear you say that! Because I am going to need all the help I can get in the coming months. Can I speak to you sometime tomorrow afternoon? I want to make use of your special skills."

Griffen enjoyed flattery as much as anyone else he knew, but it sounded to him like the run-up to a favor. A large favor. "May I ask what it is you need?"

Penny put a hand on his arm. "Let's not talk about it tonight. I am absolutely talked out. Malcolm, thank you. Will you tell our other friends I am grateful for all their support?"

"Of course," Griffen's uncle said. "I am to assure you that they are all in this for the long term."

Penny smiled. "So am I," she said. She leaned back and blew a smoke ring. "No matter what. I don't plan to let anything get in my way."

A car horn honked.

"There's my ride." She smiled. "So very nice to meet you both."

Griffen and Malcolm stood as Penny shouldered her gold-brocaded designer purse and went out into the night. Griffen thought her walk was halfway between a stride and a sashay, sexy but with power. They sat down. Malcolm looked toward the other table and gestured subtly. Jerome joined them.

"Malcolm."

"Jerome."

Griffen looked from one to the other. There was some history there, but it was obvious neither one was planning to enlighten him then.

"What do you think of her?" Malcolm asked them.

Griffen eyed his uncle. "Why didn't you tell me she was a dragon, too?"

Malcolm looked sour. "How did you know?"

"I'm starting to get a feel for when someone has dragon blood," Griffen said. "But the real giveaway was when she blew a smoke ring just now without taking a puff of her cigarette first."

Malcolm's eyes were hooded. "Then she meant you to know. It is not common knowledge outside certain circles."

"Does D— Does *he* know?"

From outside, a car horn started honking frantically. The roar of a powerful engine all but drowned it out. Griffen was on his feet before he knew it. He ran outside, Jerome and the rest of the bar on his heels. He was just in time to see a city garbage truck heading the wrong way down Toulouse straight toward a black sedan. He got one glimpse of Fox Lisa behind the wheel of the car, her face bleached white by the truck's headlights. She turned her head to look back over her shoulder. The car leaped backward with a refined roar, but the truck continued to bear down on it. Fox Lisa couldn't back away swiftly enough. Griffen dashed to catch up with the truck.

"Hey!" he yelled, trying to attract the driver's attention. "Stop!"

CRASH! The truck piled into the car, crushing the hood. The windshield burst, spraying chips of glass all over the street.

Griffen ran toward the car. He glanced behind him at the pale, shocked faces lit by the streetlamp.

"Get the driver!" he shouted.

Malcolm leaped up onto the step beside the driver's door. With a powerful wrench, he tore it open.

"There's no one in it!"

Griffen had no time to concern himself with the mystery. The car was bent into a rough W, with the hood mashed almost vertical. He tugged at the passenger door of the Lincoln. It was bent so much it couldn't open. Penny and Fox Lisa, their laps draped with deflated air bags, hammered at the handles, trying to escape. Griffen pulled at the back door. It popped open. He leaned in and grabbed Penny's hand.

"Unbuckle your belt," he ordered. She clicked it open. When it retracted, Griffen pulled her over the seatback and thrust her outside, into the arms of the waiting crowd. Jerome was there. He picked her up and carried her to the sidewalk. "Fox Lisa, are you all right?"

"I'm fine," she said. Her voice trembled. She undid her own belt and climbed over the seat by herself. She ran around the rear of the car to Penny and threw her arms around her. "You okay, darlin'?"

Penny looked shaken, but she stood tall, pushing both Fox Lisa and Jerome away. "I'm fine."

She regained her composure so swiftly, Griffen was astonished, until he saw pocket cameras appearing by the dozen in the hands of the crowd. Flashes popped off, making him wince, but he stiffened his expression into one of open concern.

Malcolm appeared at their side. He took Penny by the arm.

"You may need medical attention," he said. "This way."

"Yes. I'm all right!" she called to the onlookers.

Fire trucks crowded onto Toulouse from Rampart Street behind a city police car. Firefighters in heavy rubber coats surrounded the two vehicles and prepared to pull them apart. An ambulance siren wailed and clucked. The revolving lights splashed on Burgundy, and a couple of uniformed paramedics came jogging around the corner with a stretcher on wheels between them.

"Anyone hurt?"

"No," Griffen said.

"Yes," called a man's voice near the bar. "This guy's unconscious."

"Go," Malcolm whispered to him.

Griffen followed the paramedics through the wall of people to a spot just a few yards beyond the Irish pub. On the narrow sidewalk, a heavyset black man in green city coveralls lay on his back, eyes squeezed closed, an expression of horror on his face.

The medics knelt on either side of the patient. The elder, a tan-skinned beanpole of thirty or forty, pulled back the black man's eyelids and felt for a pulse in his neck.

"Got a flutter," he said. "Rapid but steady. Skin's cool."

The younger, a black woman in her twenties, applied a stethoscope to his chest.

"Shallow breaths," she said. Together, she and her companion rolled him onto the stretcher and pulled him toward the waiting ambulance.

Griffen ran alongside. "What's wrong with him?"

"Can't tell yet. Are you a relative?"

"No. I was in the bar over there when the crash happened."

The beanpole eyed the mass of twisted metal.

"He must have been thrown clear, or he might have jumped for it when the truck went out of control. We'll know more after we get him to the hospital and get him stabilized."

A couple of tow trucks attached themselves to the now-separated wrecks and prepared to haul them away. Griffen looked around for Fox Lisa and Penny.

"Miss Dunbar is over there holding a press conference on road safety," Malcolm said, suddenly at his side. "We need to talk."

"Do you think that was . . . him?" Griffen asked.

"I don't know," Malcolm said, looking worried. "But we must go on the assumption that it was one of his . . . efforts. We need to discuss safety measures."

Eleven

"I think it's fairly clear that was only an attempt at intimidation," Malcolm said, tenting his fingertips together in an armchair in his suite at the Sheraton. Griffen sat on the couch, feeling bleary. He was short on sleep. Jerome sat beside him, turning an empty glass around and around in his long fingers. The police had taken statements from everyone before letting them go. Penny was reluctant to tear herself away from the knot of reporters that had gathered to take notes and video the crash scene for the morning news, but a large-boned woman with a cloud of white hair and a no-nonsense attitude arrived to bundle her into a taxi.

"It might have been a warning," Jer said. "You might bruise a dragon in a car accident, but it'd have to be crushed completely to kill her. We ought to know," he added, with a nod toward Griffen.

"But a warning to do what?" Malcolm asked.

"To back off this election. But you talked with her all evening. Did she sound like the threats made her want to quit?"

"Er, no. In fact, they seemed to add to her determination."

"The accident doesn't have to have had anything to do with Penny at all," Griffen argued. "It might have been a city worker who went on a bender and decided to take the truck out for a midnight joy ride."

"C'mon, Grifter, you don't believe that? Turning up so conveniently just as Representative Penny Dunbar was going home from an evening out with friends, with plenty of witnesses on hand?"

A very unwelcome thought struck Griffen. "So she set it up herself?"

"They don't call her Bad Penny for nothing," Jerome said.

"*Bad* Penny?"

"She turns up all the time. You never noticed that she never misses the opportunity to appear in public? Ever since she started as a member of the school board back when she was still in college, she hasn't missed a store opening or an important funeral. She was real cute, too, with those dimples and that sunshiny hair, and she was born knowing how to talk to the camera. She must have a scrapbook bigger than the New York City phone directory. Sometimes events happen just when she needs a publicity boost. Normally, the campaign season doesn't get started till next month. She's jumping the gun a little, but it's pretty smart to show up in the paper at regular intervals. The driver wasn't hurt. The city'll repair any damage to the vehicle. Her car belongs to her campaign. Even if no one showed up, she wouldn't lose a thing."

Griffen felt his head start to pound. "But Fox Lisa could have been killed!"

"Doesn't she have dragon blood, too?" Malcolm inquired. "I thought I sensed it."

"Just a little," Jerome said. "Pretty dilute, but she's a tough girl."

"Well, we cannot take a chance that it was a stunt. It is undeniable that she is under threat. We must assume that Reginaud Duvallier was behind the crash. You had better escort Miss Dunbar to the television studio, Griffen." Malcolm consulted the heavy gold watch on his wrist. "They will need to depart in approximately two hours to arrive on time. You will need Miss Dunbar's address."

"I haven't had any sleep yet!" Griffen protested. "Why don't you go?"

"Griffen, I have other lines of investigation to follow up. You can rest after the interview is over. In the meantime, I suggest sustenance. Replenishment of blood sugar will help buoy you through the coming hours."

He'd given Griffen that same advice when Griffen was a boy. Griffen nodded.

"I know a couple of places that are already open for breakfast."

"I would prefer room service."

"This hotel's isn't running right now," Jerome said promptly. "They close every night for a couple of hours to scrub down the kitchens."

"Yes, you would undoubtedly know that for professional reasons," Malcolm said. "Then how do you supply provender for your clients during games that run into the predawn hours?"

"We got a great caterer," Jerome said, standing up and moving toward the door. Griffen and Malcolm sprang up to follow him. "They make these little cheesy things that would knock your eyes out."

"That sounds . . . rather upscale for such a seat-of-the-pants operation as yours," Malcolm commented.

"Well, you know," Griffen said. "You have to move with the times."

"It was terrifying," Penny confided to the female host on the *Eyewitness Morning News* show on WWL-TV. The woman, a light-skinned African-American in her thirties, kept her eyes fixed on Penny with an expression of concern. Penny sat bolt upright on the couch in the mock-library set facing the two hosts. Her slender hands fluttered in the air. The pearl gray two-piece suit she had on made her look even more ethereal than usual. "And then, if my campaign worker hadn't slammed the car into reverse and stamped on the gas the way she did, we might have been killed." She told the story in such breathless terms that Griffen found himself taking deep gasps of air.

"A big shout-out to her," the male host said. He was a genial man in his fifties, slim with fair hair. He glanced off camera to where Fox Lisa was waiting beside Griffen. Fox Lisa, dressed up for a change, wore a dark green dress and heels. After some persuading by his uncle, Griffen had promised to shave and wear a jacket over his customary dark blue silk shirt and khaki trousers. He found he was dressed more professionally than anyone else in the room but Fox Lisa and the hosts.

"Yes," the woman added. "We're so happy nothing happened to you."

"Apart from getting my wits scared out of me!" Penny said, with a coy little smile for the camera. "But I'm all right now. This morning I went to Charity Hospital to visit the poor man who was driving that truck. I want to add my voice to the campaign to make certain that our city workers are not scheduled for outrageous hours, so that they feel they have to make up the time late at night. Not to mention it violates local noise ordinances."

"Is that what he told you?" the female host asked.

"No," Penny said, a plaintive expression wrinkling her forehead. "The poor man's still unconscious. No one knows what's wrong with him. He probably needs some of those expensive brain tests, which Lord knows this parish can hardly afford."

"Very curious," the man said, with a photogenic frown. "But this gives us a chance to ask you about progress on your program to wipe out corruption in local government and free funds that might help to pay for medical treatments for the indigent."

"My campaign for governor is going well," Penny said, reframing the question without hesitation. "I have picked up endorsements from the school board, the fishing industry, numerous local corporations, and many of our leading citizens. All my generous contributors and sponsors are listed on my website. That's PennyForLAGovernor.com," she added, with a smile for the camera. "Everyone who funds my campaign, no matter how small a contribution, is listed. Every penny counts. 'A penny for Penny,' I like to say. For every penny, I promise you a dollar's worth of good government."

"Very cute." The woman chuckled, but she looked discomfited.

Beside Griffen stood the heavyset white-haired woman who

had taken Penny away the night before. In spite of the early hour, her pearl gray two-piece suit, subdued jewelry, perfect makeup, and carefully coiffed hair suggested lengthy preparation. She was mouthing the words along with Penny. So the answers were all well rehearsed. Griffen was impressed how natural Penny acted on camera. Jerome was right. She had amazing poise under pressure. She answered the questions she wanted to and in the way she chose. Since the program was going out live, the hosts had no choice but to smile and nod.

Griffen had never been in a television studio before. Through the video monitors that were everywhere, including attached to the rear of every one of the five cameras rolling around the bare concrete floor, it appeared that the set was a comfortable library in a gracious home, perhaps somewhere in the Garden District. Instead, peering over the shoulders of the camera crew, what Griffen saw was a well-lit island in the middle of a barren cinder-block room. The bookshelves were on heavy casters, hidden behind the angled sofas. The rest of the furniture was on a quartet of carpet-covered platforms, raised about eight inches off the floor. Cables snaked from them across the floor, ducking into long rubber bumpers that prevented an unwary toe from catching underneath them. Where they crossed walkways marked on the floor by yellow paint, they were secured with adhesive strips that looked like colored masking tape. The soaring ceilings were crisscrossed with long metal brackets from which hung enormous lights with shutters around the plate-sized lenses. Only a quarter of them were on, arranged to throw light behind and beneath the three people on the set as well as on them. It made the whole scene look more realistic. Far from being disappointed, he was impressed. The only thing he didn't like was the inescapable high-pitched whine of the machinery. It threatened to overload his dragon-sensitive hearing.

"Well, we look forward to hearing more on your campaign as the season kicks into high gear," the male said. "Thank you for being with us this morning, Representative Dunbar."

"We're so glad to see that you were unharmed in last

night's accident," the female host added. She turned to the camera. "And for those of you who haven't seen them, we have photos on our website of the aftermath of the crash. Representative, thank you for being with us."

"My pleasure," Penny said. She beamed vivaciously at the hosts, then at the camera.

"And we're on commercial," a disembodied voice said. "Thank you!"

Penny detached the small microphone that had been threaded up into her blouse and stood up. She shook hands firmly with the two hosts and came over to the white-haired woman.

"How was that?" she asked.

"Great, honey," the other woman said. "I can hear the phones ringing already."

Penny glanced at Fox Lisa, and the brilliant smile beamed out again. "Thank you once more for saving my life, Fox Lisa," she said. "It was above and beyond what I would ever ask of my volunteers."

"Quick thinking," agreed the other woman.

"It was nothing," Fox Lisa said, her cheeks reddening. "Um, have you met my boyfriend, Griffen McCandles?"

"Hortensia Peck," the other said, wrapping both hands around Griffen's and pumping it enthusiastically. "Call me Horsie. Heard about you. What did you think of our girl?"

"I think she was very brave," Griffen said. "Fox Lisa really came through for her."

"No one could deny that, honey," Horsie said. "And I assure you, we're all grateful for her. I mean, Penny thanked her right there on the set."

Griffen frowned. "I didn't hear her name mentioned."

"Oh, she must have said it. Penny wouldn't forget a little thing like that."

A tall man wearing a headset earpiece with a microphone extension, blue jeans, and a worn army green T-shirt came bustling up. He had a no-nonsense expression on his face. He beckoned them out of the studio and into the hallway.

The heavy door closed silently behind them. Griffen glanced up at the square ON AIR sign illuminated next to it.

"Representative Dunbar," the man said. "Pleased to have you here. I'm a little troubled that you ignored my instructions not to bring up the election this morning. It's against the fairness doctrine we broadcasters follow. All candidates for a public office receive the same amount of airtime. Finessing mention of the campaign into an unconnected interview like you did means we'll have to give equal time to your opponents."

Horsie put her arm through his and drew him close to her side.

"Now, Stewart, you know it ain't no law in this state."

Stewart pulled himself loose.

"No, but it's an accepted practice," he said. "And we intend to stick to it. We don't want to give the appearance of partisanship. All right. You got a gimme this time, but once we start airing campaign coverage, for every time you electioneer on the air, we have to give each of your competitors the same amount of time. Or we can air footage of you without sound. Your choice. We still run a seven-second delay. My soundman can hit the mute button anytime."

The two women exchanged glances.

"I'll get back to you on that," Horsie said.

"All right. Y'all have a nice day." Stewart put his headphones on and went back to the studio.

"Come and have breakfast with us, Mr. McCandles," Horsie said, leading the way out of the WWL-TV building. "I'd love a chance to talk with you."

Griffen felt desperate for sleep, but the fog overwhelming his brain cleared for a moment. He didn't know what kind of threat Penny faced, but until Uncle Malcolm investigated further, they were fumbling in the dark.

"Uh, sure," he said.

"I know just the place," Penny said, putting her arm through his. "You'll love it."

Twelve

The famous Brennan's was crowded with tourists even on a Friday morning. Griffen did his best not to get in anyone's way. He recognized faces, but the identities were muddled in his mind. He shook hands and slapped backs when someone called his name. The restaurant had a long waiting list; it always did. Horsie left the three of them a few feet from the desk and went to whisper to the maitre d', an elegant man in his fifties with silver touching the temples of his smooth black hair. He recognized Penny immediately, and his expression changed from nonchalance to expansive welcome.

"Representative! What a pleasure. I didn't expect to see you until Sunday! I can seat your party in just five minutes if you don't mind."

Penny kissed him on both cheeks.

"Of course I don't mind, Mitchell. You know Mr. McCandles?"

Mitchell favored him with a blandly pleasant look. "Yes, of course. You were in last with Mr. and Mrs. Nussbaum, weren't you? Back in August?"

"Yes, that's right," Griffen said. Mr. Nussbaum was a high roller from Ohio. His wife loved all the landmarks of New Orleans, and he loved to gamble. When he won, which he did often, he took his tablemates out for breakfast. "That's some memory you have, sir."

Mitchell shrugged. "A trick of the trade," he said. His

attitude became markedly warmer as he turned back to Penny. "We have your Community Awareness flyers on the hostess desk. People have been signing up for the program by the dozen since we started handing them out."

"Just making people aware of little things helps. We all have to work together," Penny said, fixing her gaze intently upon Mitchell. Griffen wondered if she was using mind control on him, but it could simply have been her charisma. She exuded palpable charm. She wasn't that attractive, but when she talked, it was hard to look anywhere else.

Mitchell was certainly caught in the spell, and so were a number of the other patrons. Griffen noticed that Penny was careful to pitch her words and speak clearly so she could be overheard. Tourists aimed their cameras at her. Horsie nudged her subtly in the side with a forefinger. Penny turned at just the right moment to aim a beaming smile at each lens. The tourists looked embarrassed and gratified. They might not know who she was, but they could tell she was important. Griffen, who had traded for years on flying under the radar, was a little uncomfortable under the intense scrutiny of bystanders, but he soon realized he didn't have to worry. Their gazes slid off him on their way to fix on Penny. She was good.

". . . I said, we can go this way, Mr. McCandles," Penny said. She threaded her arm through his and pulled him along behind the host. Griffen snapped out of his reverie.

"C'mon, Griffen, wake up," Fox Lisa said, teasingly. She nudged him in the back. Griffen shook himself. He edged between the tables, avoiding diners in their chairs. Penny held on to him and smiled like a bride fresh from the altar.

The host spun to a halt before a table for four spread with a brilliant white tablecloth and shining silverware. "Ma'am?" He pulled a chair out. Penny settled into it like a soap bubble alighting on the surface of a pond. Griffen hurried to help seat Fox Lisa. Horsie didn't wait for either male. She slid in toward the table by herself. The chair legs groaned as she dragged them over the floor.

"Coffee?" asked a young black man in a white coat, appearing at tableside. Feeling like a drowning swimmer seeing a life preserver, Griffen held up his cup to be filled. The server poured for the ladies first. The heavy, rich aroma tantalized Griffen so much he was almost salivating by the time he took the first sip. Clarity seeped into him with the hot liquid.

"This stuff ought to be illegal," Horsie said, echoing his own thoughts, "but thank God it isn't. Come back in five minutes, honey. We're gonna need refills right away."

"Sure, ma'am," the young server said with a brilliant smile.

"Penny, have you thought about who might have been behind the attempt on you last night?" Griffen asked. "Who knew you were going to be in the pub at that time?"

"No one but me." Horsie answered for her. "I have to know where she is at all times. She ought to have an aide with her, but she said she wanted to meet with you and your uncle in private." She gave Penny a reproachful look. "He could have sat across the room."

"I was there!" Fox Lisa said indignantly.

"Of course you were, honey. I meant someone who knows how to talk to the press."

"Well, I'm learning. I could probably have handled it."

"A major incident like that, we needed Walter Cronkite," Horsie said. At Fox Lisa's blank look, she waved a hand. "Before your time. So you think that crash was meant to take her out? Who?"

Penny must not have told Horsie everything about her conversation with Malcolm.

Griffen shrugged. "My uncle heard some rumors. It looks like at least some of them might be true."

"Do you have any proof of that? It was deliberate?"

"No. Nothing that I can say with any certainty. It might have been an accident."

"Honey, *you* ought to be a spin doctor," Horsie said, with a sly gleam in her eye. "Unnamed sources?"

"You could call them that. But it looks like it might be credible."

"Uh-huh. I'll make sure to keep an eye on her. Not that she always makes it easy."

Penny put her long hand on Griffen's and leaned toward him, her eyes fixed on his. "Griffen, in case no one else has bothered, I want to thank you on behalf of the state of Louisiana for coming here and becoming such a positive influence in our community. I know I appreciate what you've done in such a short time, and I hope you'll continue to be involved while you live here."

Griffen blinked. One cup of coffee was not enough to completely dispel the haze he was in. He must be hearing things.

"I don't know how much of a positive influence I've been," he said.

"Oh, but I disagree," Penny said. Her blue eyes twinkled at him. Griffen felt dazzled. He had never been around movie stars until recently, but a few of them joined the poker games he sponsored. He was getting over the glamour they exuded, mostly because they didn't choose to turn it on him. This must be what it was like to be in the full spotlight of their regard, and he wasn't sure how to handle it. "You may not have noticed what has been going on in this country lately," she continued. "The presence of terrorists on American soil is just horrifying to me and to all decent people. As yet, they haven't really taken a foothold in Louisiana."

"Yeah, but we have our own problems," Griffen said. "Drugs, gangs, and guns are everywhere in New Orleans."

"I'm glad you noticed that," Penny said. Her focus shifted from one of his eyes to the other, making him follow her eye movement. "I know you've been a force for good since you've gotten here."

"To tell the truth, that hasn't been my main intention," Griffen said. "I needed to make some money and get out of a bad situation, which I would prefer not to discuss here. I've just done what I had to."

"As you please," Penny said, smiling warmly. "I understand you want to keep some things private. But, from what I've heard, and especially from Fox Lisa, here, you have raised the standard of living for your employees, made peace with some pretty fierce folks around town, and done your best to help preserve one of the crown jewels of this state. Visitors who don't know anything else about Louisiana know the French Quarter of New Orleans. You've made it a better place for them to come."

Griffen shifted uncomfortably. He felt as if he was being held to some standard of behavior far above his normal lifestyle. Part of him, the altruistic part, wanted to live up to it, but the commonsense part said he was being snowed. He didn't have to have a quick-deal grifter switching cups around on a folding tray table, asking him to find the lady, to figure that out. Penny was canny. He steeled himself and decided to watch for pointers instead.

"Thanks," he said. He sat back to make room for the waiter to refill his coffee cup. He grabbed for it and gulped half the boiling liquid.

Penny must have sensed the change in his attitude. Her tone changed from soothing to businesslike.

"Part of being a responsible citizen is seeing the things that need to be done and doing them," she said, briskly. "That's my job. As governor, I intend to take a hard stand on corruption, both in government and in daily life. That means stamping out the bad practices that everyone has been winking at all these years. Now, you've seen a lot of things go on in broad daylight that are against the law, haven't you, Griffen?"

"Yes, I have," Griffen said, wincing as her voice rose to a level that could be heard at the near tables. They were already being watched with open curiosity. Penny was a public figure. Her presence was exciting attention, not only from the patrons but from the restauranteurs, who were themselves foodie royalty in New Orleans. Mitchell had almost certainly alerted the owners that Penny was in the house. Fox Lisa had to have given her chapter and verse on his business. He had never tried to hide any of the details from her, and now he was wondering whether that had been wise. "I try not to let anyone get hurt."

"And that is most admirable," she agreed. "But there's a long way between not letting anyone get hurt and helping, isn't there?"

And there was the stick, Griffen realized. Penny was capable of using any situation to further her own interests, up to and including throwing him under the bus. "I don't think I can be of much help. I'm pretty busy. I was planning to take a week off after Mardi Gras, but my sister has disappeared. Most, if not all, of my free attention has to be focused on finding her and bringing her back safely."

"I understand that," Penny said. "Fox Lisa informed me about your sister. Have you reported Valerie's disappearance to the police?"

Since Detective Harrison had been at his krewe's afterparty when Griffen discovered Val was missing, he could answer that with a clear conscience. "Yes, I have. They're looking into it, but there are no clear leads. I haven't heard from her since late Tuesday night."

"But she's a grown woman, isn't she?" Penny asked. "She might have just gone off on her own for a while. If she wanted to get in touch with you, she could."

"It's a lot more complicated than that," Griffen said, uneasily. Dragon or not, the situation was none of Penny's business. She understood that immediately, which made him even more uncomfortable.

"Well, I don't plan to take up a lot of your time, Griffen. I understand how vital it is that you find your sister, and you need to make a living. I won't ask for more than you are willing to give."

There was the velvet glove, slipping onto the iron fist again.

"I hope you're not looking for campaign contributions from me," Griffen said, lightly. "Mardi Gras cleaned me out, and I have some other debts left over from last year."

"Well, if you find a spare penny or two here and there, you know I would appreciate any help on that front you can give," Penny said, just as lightly. "No, I was speaking of your most admirable protective instincts. You all but tore that car door off to get us out of the wreck last night. If you can extend them to helping to watch my back when I'm in public, that would be my fervent wish."

"Uh, well, that sounds all right, but my uncle could . . ."

"Malcolm is an important man in my out-of-state fund-raising committee," Penny said sweetly. "He doesn't live here. You know the ins and outs of our culture here."

"Well, some . . ."

"But he knows none of it." Penny scooted her chair closer to him without making a sound. He could feel the warmth of her skin and smell her perfume. It was a spicy blend that tickled his nose and stirred his blood. "I'd feel so much safer. Between you and Fox Lisa, I know I'd be well protected." Her large blue eyes were all that Griffen could see.

A baby at a nearby table let out a happy gurgle and banged on his plate with a spoon.

Griffen blinked again. She kept her gaze fixed on him. He wasn't sure if she knew that she was trying to bend him to her will or if it just came naturally to her. In any case, it was a powerful sensation. He had to fight hard against it. All his senses told him he wanted to cooperate in anything she asked.

It had already worked on Fox Lisa. She looked at Griffen with a similar intensity, willing him to give Penny what she wanted.

That, as much as anything else, gave Griffen the steel to sharpen his mind.

"I'll do what I can for you," he said. "I'm sure you have a security detail already that stays with you at public events. I'll keep my ears open and let you know if I hear anything."

A tiny wrinkle of annoyance deepened between Penny's coppery brows. Griffen felt the compulsion redouble, but he held on to his will.

"I hate to hear you say that when I'm counting on you," Penny said. "But I did tell you that I would be grateful for any time you can spare me. But you don't mind if I call on you to help look after me at my appearances? If you're free, that is."

Griffen thought about it for a moment. He could see nothing unreasonable in such a request.

"All right," he said. "I'd be happy to do that."

Penny beamed. He felt a wave of happiness wash over him. The diners at the nearby tables smiled at one another and seemed to cheer up, even the ones who weren't listening in. She had some serious mojo. He needed to get away from her before he promised her his firstborn.

The thought reminded him of Val and *her* pending firstborn. He pushed back his chair and stood up.

"I really need to get out of here," he said. "I have to take care of some things."

Fox Lisa got up to kiss him. The other two women remained seated but extended hands to shake.

"Well, it was a real pleasure meeting you," Horsie said. "I've got your cell-phone number. Should I send you a copy of Penny's upcoming schedule so we can coordinate?"

"I'll get back to you," Griffen said firmly.

"Oh, c'mon, Griffen," Fox Lisa said. "Horsie, I'll bring it to him."

"Thanks, honey."

"I'd better go," Griffen said. He hurried away, just before a smugly smiling Mitchell escorted the restaurant's esteemed owner to greet Penny. She offered a gracious hand to him. Griffen was already forgotten.

Thirteen

Griffen made it out into the spring sunshine before he realized he still hadn't consumed anything but a cup and a half of coffee. He shook his head. Penny could make anyone forget their own name. He looked at his watch. It was too early for a burger at Yo Mama's, but Annette's served breakfast all day. He had a sudden yen for their grits grillade, a spicy cutlet served over light, creamy cornmeal mush. He strode toward Dauphine. Once he had some food in his stomach, he intended to go home and get some sleep. He glanced at his phone. No messages from Jerome or his dealers.

"No news is good news," a soft voice said.

Griffen almost jumped out of his shoes. Rose was walking beside him.

"I'm really glad to see you," he said. "How long have you been there?"

"Since Brennan's. You were making decisions. I didn't want to interrupt you until you had made up your mind."

Griffen had had to change his mind about a lot of things since coming to live in the French Quarter. One of them was his preconception about voodoo queens and ghosts. Rose was both. Instead of being a wild-eyed harridan calling down curses and sticking pins into cloth dolls, Rose was a lovely, slender, well-groomed African-American woman in her thirties. That is, she would have been in her thirties if she were alive. She wore a scoop-necked blouse, a long, colorful skirt tied tight at her small waist, and a scarf on her head, part of her Creole heritage. Still, she must have had a closet in the afterlife because she also appeared to him in a fancy ball gown.

"That last time I saw you, you were dancing with Detective Harrison," he said.

Rose's cheeks dimpled. "Thank you for that. It was good for both of us. I wish him to find closure and move on. If we are meant to be together again after his life's candle is burned out, that is one thing, but I do not want him to be lonely until then."

"Do you know something I don't?" Griffen asked.

She looked at him sideways out of her long eyelashes. "I know many things. Not eternal truths or visions of the future. I see the man I knew. I will watch over him, but he deserves happiness. You can help guide him in that way."

Griffen had a momentary vision of counseling the burly vice cop on his love life and quailed.

"I doubt he'd let me," Griffen said. "And it's really none of my business. We're not that close. I already know more about his life than he probably feels comfortable with."

"He trusts you in ways he trusts few others," Rose said. "That is why you must not lie to him. He is strong. He reacts against new knowledge and sensations, then he steps back to assimilate what he has learned. I have always admired his wisdom. That is one of the things I found attractive about him. And his tendency toward mercy."

"I've benefited from that," Griffen admitted.

"And you have taken advantage of it. Acknowledge the karmic debt. It is not harmful to owe another as long as you remember you must repay. The eternal balance must be maintained. Your portion in life is great. Be generous with those to whom not so much is given."

Griffen felt as if he had just opened a fortune cookie. "Whatever that means," he said.

"You will learn in time. But you said you wished to see me."

Griffen tried to stifle a yawn and failed. "I have to eat something. Can I buy you breakfast at Annette's?"

"I do not need earthly food," Rose said, "but I will enjoy absorbing the pleasure of others who dine there. David Harrison and I often had breakfast there. It has good feelings. And wonderful coffee."

Griffen wanted badly to ask her about her earthly life, but at that moment he needed her insight about other things.

The motherly waitress in the tight pink uniform set the menu down on the small corner table and left him alone with the coffeepot. For a weekday morning, the little diner was fairly crowded. Griffen sat with his back to the rest of the room, hoping no one would be able to overhear him. The city had numerous inhabitants that before he had come he would have called "supernatural," but he had since learned were just ordinary people. Basically, they got along as much as anyone else did. You couldn't call the loup garou, the shape-changers, or the local vampires good citizens, but they tended to live and let live—most of the time. Not only that, but New Orleans tended to have a greater-than-normal number of tuned-in humans like Holly, who could see the others for what they really were.

"Can anyone here see you?" Griffen murmured, glancing over his shoulder. Two elderly African-American men laughed and argued over their breakfasts. An intense young woman with straight dark hair and eyebrows bent over a book as if absorbing the words along with her coffee. Three young mothers gossiped while their children threw crackers and bits of toast at one another. Half a dozen obvious tourists consulted guidebooks and maps.

"A few," Rose said. "But they do not recognize me. All they see is a couple at a table. We can speak freely."

Griffen sighed. "Good."

She smiled. "You sound like you are setting your bag of troubles down at my feet."

"I could sure use your help," he said. "Do you know that Val is missing?"

"Yes, I do," Rose said. "You need to bring her home before she is changed beyond recognition."

Griffen felt his heart sink. "Is she in danger?"

"Not for her life," the priestess said. "She, too, has choices to make. They may not be the right ones. She is young and has much wisdom to gain."

"I want to find her, but a lot of people are demanding pieces of my time. I've hardly checked in on my dealers for three days."

"You must stand up for yourself, Griffen."

"I know! I don't want to get involved with Penny Dunbar. She tried to blackmail me into helping her. Fox Lisa believes in her. I don't know how much is her qualifications, or this . . . glamour that she gives off. It's like a drug. I had to keep pinching myself so I didn't promise her the moon."

Rose smiled. "A strong woman is a role model for a soul as young as Fox Lisa. She wishes to emulate her. I understand that very well."

"But Fox Lisa's strong in her own right," Griffen said.

"She may not feel that way. She is vulnerable while she works out who she is in this lifetime. Working for Penny Dunbar may give her some insights."

Griffen frowned. "I don't really like Penny. She sounds like a nice lady, but she's tough as a boot."

Rose laughed, a tinkling sound. "You have had limited experience as yet with Southern women, Griffen. We seem delicate and helpless, yet we must run our households and businesses as well as any man. Do I need to remind you how seldom things are as they seem?"

"Thanks for the philosophy lesson. She was in a major car accident that could have killed her, but it seems as if it didn't even faze her."

"Oh, it did. It shook the foundations of the spirit world."

"A car accident? Why?"

"It was an interference," Rose said, solemnly. "Malign influence that took over the soul of that poor man in the truck. It was one of the reasons I have not been able to come to you. Many of us found our way back to this world blocked."

"To kill Penny? But she's just a politician. Like Duvallier said, they're a dime a dozen."

Rose shivered. For a moment, he could see the chair rail through her body.

"It is not merely a person's profession that shapes the shadow he casts in the world. Penny Dunbar is a receptacle of power, as are you. To remove her would set that power free and cause a void that could easily be filled by evil."

Griffen felt a cold weight grow in his stomach, to the great annoyance of the point of fire that lived there. "So I should be protecting her?"

"To keep the balance of power, it would seem so."

"Why me?"

"Partly because she asked you. A person in danger has a right to choose a champion."

"What about my sister?"

"That is a choice you must make."

"Well, that's easy," Griffen said, firmly. "Val's well-being and her baby are my first priority."

"Is it?" Rose tilted her head. "The enigma of life is that we cannot make all things happen."

One of the other things that Griffen had had to come to grips with was that ghosts weren't always insubstantial. Rose gripped his arm. Her hand was warm.

"Don't look on the surface. Look beneath. Penny Dunbar is frightened. She is in danger. That is why she makes alliances she would normally avoid."

"Like me," he said.

"And others. Together they form a chain that can anchor her to this world when malign influences would wish otherwise."

"What does that mean?" Griffen asked.

"Your food's up in a minute," the waitress said, coming up beside him with a pot in her hand. "Can I warm up that coffee, honey?"

Griffen glanced up at her. "Sure," he said. He looked across the table. Rose was gone. It figured. She had left him with more questions than he had before.

He let the waitress pour.

Breakfast was, of course, on the house, the manager of Brennan's was pleased to inform Penny.

"We're always happy to have you here, Representative," he said, standing and bowing over her hand like an ancient courtier. Penny was pleased. She liked having her importance acknowledged. She had made certain that everyone in the restaurant could see and hear her during the meal. She ate daintily but with open appreciation. Horsie gave her a look of approval.

"Thank you, sir," Penny said. "Everything was superb, as always. All of the Brennan's restaurants are stars in this unique city. I just adore the bananas Foster. And that young woman made it so well—what was her name, Lucy?"

"Yes, Lucy," the restauranteur said, looking gratified.

"Well, thank you very much for a lovely breakfast. Just what I needed after my interview on television this morning. And such a grand antidote to my experience last night—I trust you heard about the incident last night?"

The gentleman's face immediately went solemn. "Yes, we all did. And we're all so glad that you came out of it safe and sound."

"Well, thank you," Penny said, touching him on the arm. "You are all so very kind."

Noblesse oblige offered and acknowledged, Penny sauntered to the door. She let her hips sway enticingly, giving the men watching her from behind a little thrill. They would remember it with pleasure. It ought to translate to a good memory at the voting booth.

Horsie held up her hand against the brilliant spring sunlight that met them outside the door.

"Honey, you're going to freckle like mad if we stay out here in this. I'll call for the car."

Penny stopped her from reaching for her cell phone.

"No, it's a fine day, and we're not too far from the local office. Let's walk there. I want to thank the volunteers who are giving up their days, like Fox Lisa here."

The little redhead soaked up the small compliment like the sunshine. Penny smiled. All these willing souls, all working for her. Barring any *unforeseen* accidents, she would make a good showing in the primary. Next stop, the governor's mansion. In her mind, Penny had already begun redecorating the office.

From Brennan's front door, she turned westward along Bourbon Street and set an easy pace, leaving the hip swing in operation. A good deal of foot traffic was abroad. Penny caught the eyes of people who recognized her. If they were across the street, she smiled at them. If they were on the same side, she greeted them and shook hands.

A man in a polo shirt walking with a woman carrying a large tote bag all but stopped to gawk at her. Penny gave them a cool but pleasant nod.

"Aren't you going to shake hands with them?" Fox Lisa asked, tagging at her heels like an eager puppy.

"Why, no," Penny said, with a quick glance over her shoulder. "They're from out of town."

"You can tell that quickly?"

Penny laughed.

"Oh, honey, you can tell tourists from locals. So can I! That man was just so transfixed by the sight of two gorgeous redheads that his wife is going to kill him. I didn't want to make matters worse."

Fox Lisa looked disappointed with herself.

"Oh. You're right."

That was one bad case of hero worship that Fox Lisa had. It made her doubt her own common sense. Never mind, Penny reminded herself. It just meant that the girl would never question anything Penny asked of her.

She could feel her skin warming in the blessed sunshine. It probably did mean she would gain a few more freckles, but it was so good to get out and walk. She had so much reading to do when she got back home before going back to Baton Rouge in the morning. She needed to check over the position paper she had dictated to her secretary on mandatory sentencing guidelines—the way the legislature was writing them, they were skewed racially, and Penny couldn't let that pass. Couldn't the boneheads see that they would screw their own chances for reelection and her chance to be governor? Most humans were just too dumb to live.

Penny weaved through the visitors on the sidewalk, smiling loftily at potential voters. A shop door opened ahead of them. Penny diverted slightly to avoid the man coming out. At first she only caught a glimpse of the dirty, flat, plaid cap on his head and the ragged scarf around his neck. The next moment, she took in the face between them. She gasped. His nose was a pair of vertical holes, and the mouth was lipless. Teeth in purple-gray gums grinned at her. The eyes bulged from torn sockets. The man, or what was left of one, started toward her, reaching for her with clawlike hands. A gray miasma rose from his body and coiled into the air like a foul smoke. Even though she was several feet away, she recoiled, right into Fox Lisa's arms.

"What's wrong, honey?" Horsie asked.

Penny turned to the other women. "That man! Do you see him? Coming out of that store!"

Horsie and Fox Lisa looked past her.

"Which store, darling?" the older woman asked.

"That one!" Penny pointed.

Fox Lisa let go of her and strode ahead. She stopped when Penny nodded. She tugged on the handle.

"Here? This one's not open yet. The door's locked."

"But there was a man! He was coming at me."

"Threatening you?" Horsie asked.

"Stay there," Fox Lisa ordered. As Penny watched, she searched the area for the man. Penny knew from bitter experience that he would be gone without a trace. The small woman returned, shaking her head.

"No one's here, I promise." Fox Lisa patted her purse. "If

anyone tries anything, I'll take care of them. It'd be self-defense. You don't have to worry at all."

"Thanks," Penny said. She did her best to control her nerves. She set off walking again, but without the sexy swing.

"Should I call for the car?" Horsie asked. "If there's a stalker out there, you shouldn't expose yourself."

Penny waved away the offer.

"No, no, thanks, honey. I think I must just have been seeing things."

But she knew she wasn't.

Fourteen

Val quivered with nerves as yet another thirtysomething man in a business suit took her hand. She met his warm brown eyes shyly.

"Ms. McCandles, glad to meet you," the man said.

"Welcome, Mr. Stern," Val said. She was glad of Henry's exhaustive briefing, including photographs and thick dossiers, of the people on the guest list. "We're very happy you could make it. I know you're very busy with the new memory project at NanoStream. You probably don't have much time off these days."

"Uh, yes. But I'm happy to get away on a Friday night."

Mr. Stern cast a curious eye toward her belly. A lot of people did glance at it, but for some reason this felt like a real violation of privacy.

"Hem!" Val cleared her throat with purpose.

Mr. Stern's cheeks reddened a little. "Well, thanks, ma'am," he said, and hurried into the room.

Unconsciously, Val smoothed the blue silk draping. The dress had an amazing cut that made her feel like a pregnant supermodel. The dressmaker, a tiny, wizened woman with apricot hair, eyed her without ever touching Val, laid out a pattern on a huge sheet of paper, and came back the next morning with a chic Grecian sheath on a hanger. She wished Val "mazel tov," and bustled out again. When Val tried the dress on, it fit like magic. The thickening at her waist looked becoming rather than ponderous.

Braided silk cords in the same fabric as the dress held up the shoulders and crossed underneath her breasts. The asymmetric hem danced around her calves. The garment felt light as air but was thick enough that her amazingly expensive undergarments were completely concealed. It was better than armor. Val turned to the next guests.

"Mrs. Green and Mr. Green," she said, shaking hands with the wife first, as she had been instructed. "Thank you for coming."

This time, the woman eyed her up and down before meeting her gaze. She offered a friendly smile. "We have three children," she said. "When's it due?"

"Late September," Val said.

"Boy or girl?"

"I don't know."

Mrs. Green gave her a conspiratorial smile and tugged her husband's arm. A server met them three paces away from Val and gave them drinks.

Val leaned back against the newel post of the elegant double staircase. She didn't realize she had been holding her breath. A slim male photographer in a brocade vest and a bow tie knelt before her to take her picture.

"Oh, don't," she said, petulantly.

"Mrs. Wurmley's orders," he said, with a winsome grin. "Besides, you look great."

"Thanks, I guess. Hi, Mr. Neville," Val said, straightening up to greet a large African-American gentleman in a dinner jacket that strained across enormous shoulders. Her hand was enveloped in a palm like a Ping-Pong paddle. "I mean, good evening. Thank you for joining us. I'm Valerie McCandles."

"Glad to be here," he said. His voice was hoarse, but it had a lilt to it. "And where are you from, pretty lady?"

"Well, I'm from Michigan, but I live in New Orleans."

"N'Awlins? Why, that's my hometown!" he exclaimed, pleased. "Wait a minute, you don't have anything to do with Penny Dunbar?"

Val squeezed her memory for a drop that contained the name. "Uh, the politician?" she asked.

Neville grinned, showing split front teeth. "I like the way you say that. Even more that you don't know who she is. Nice to meet you, Ms. McCandles." His eyebrows lifted. "I think that's Mike Burns."

"Yes, it is," Val said, following his gaze to the evening's guest of honor, a handsome man four or five inches taller than her six feet. From her briefing, Val knew Burns was a former professional baseball player, had graduated summa cum laude from Stanford in economics, and expected to raise funds that evening for a run for the Senate. Not from this state, wherever it was, but from Maryland. A thought wandered through her mind that it was strange she didn't know where she was.

"Well, I need to talk to him. Pleasure, Ms. McCandles."

Val almost collapsed with relief.

Thank heavens, that was the end of the reception line. Henry came over to take her by the arm.

"Nice job," he murmured. "Now, mingle. I'll let you know when you have to announce dinner."

"What do I say to them?" Val whispered desperately. She didn't know anything about financial debentures or Rolls Royces or whatever rich people liked.

"Why are you asking me?" Henry said, shooing her away. "You're in the hospitality business. Talk to them as if they were your customers."

Oh. Really? Was that all? Val took the glass of yellow juice offered to her by the thin girl in uniform and moved into the midst of the crowd.

"So, how is the economy treating you?" she inquired of Mr. Benjamin, a plump, short man who had arrived alone. According to Henry's dossier, he was the CEO of a technology company and held a majority of the shares. "Did the dot-com bust hit your company?"

"Not too hard," he said. "We had to close down a line I thought was promising."

"Where do you see expanding next?"

"Personal computers," he said, warming to his topic. He leaned a little closer to her. "There's a lot of room for light-weight machines. When the market recovers, people will want high-end gear. My niche consumer is white-collar work-ers. They have cash to spend, and they like having the latest and lightest electronics."

"Don't you want to go after the teen market?" Val asked. "Every kid I see is playing games on pocket devices."

"No, I don't see it," Benjamin said. "That's not where the growth is going."

"You're wrong," a slim, dark-haired man said, joining them. "She's right. The kids have all the money. I'd put my lines on turning out cheap, easy-to-use machines, and license every game I could afford."

"Mr. Novello publishes comic books," Val explained to Benjamin.

"Graphic novels," Novello corrected her with some heat.

"I'm sorry," Val said. "I haven't read any since I was little."

Benjamin laughed. Novello lowered his black eyebrows into a disapproving V.

"You'd find they've changed a lot. You might like them more now."

"Print is dying," inserted Mr. Green, joining them. "Sorry to overhear. Electronic books are the next big thing."

By asking a leading question here or professing the need for explanation there, Val was able to keep the men talking. She listened closely, as Henry had told her to, in case any of them sounded as if his finances were in a downward spiral. She hated the feeling that she was spying on them, but she didn't want to let Melinda down. Griffen would have finessed the conversation much better than she could.

How weird that Griffen hadn't called her. She had left a message for him on his cell phone that morning. Even al-lowing for a late-Thursday session, he ought to have listened to it by then. She was worried about Gris-gris. Every time she had called so far, the sweet-voiced nurse at the hospital told her he was asleep. How badly hurt was he? He had insisted he was going to be all right when she had seen him Tuesday night. If only she could talk to him.

She cringed at how much daytime calls must be costing on Melinda's house phone, but her cell phone was good for local Louisiana calls only. When Melinda came back, Val wanted to go home. She would pay her hostess back later. If her job was still there waiting for her.

Henry appeared behind the crowd and lifted his eyebrows at her. Val went up to Burns, took him by the elbow, and addressed the rest of the circle surrounding him.

"It's time for dinner. Would you all come this way?"

She steered her captive toward the double doors that led to the formal dining room. As she went, she touched guests on the sleeves or the back of their hands. Immediately, they broke off conversation and fell in step behind her. Val felt like the Pied Piper.

The doors ahead of them seemed to open by themselves. Val heard a collective gasp as the guests saw the brilliance beyond. Crystal glasses in clusters at each place on the table caught the light from the enormous chandelier. The china plates glowed like exotic pearls. The white of the linen napkins and crisp tablecloth was one Val had never been able to achieve in her own laundry. She wondered what the secret was.

She steered Burns toward the head of the table and took her place at his right hand. Little tent cards, handwritten by Henry in perfect copperplate, stood on each plate in front of the peaked napkins. A buzz erupted among the other diners as they bustled around to find their seats. Servers, some on staff but most hired for the evening, stepped from concealment against the inner wall to collect cocktail glasses and assist ladies into their chairs. A slim, good-looking man who might have been a flamenco dancer whisked Val's napkin off her plate and spread it over her blue silk lap. Marcella, severe looking in a black silk floor-length dress, directed two young women to pour chilled water into round-bellied glasses. She nodded, and dinner service began.

Val had adored the tiny silver forks Henry had shown her during her briefing on how to conduct a formal dinner until he informed her they were for eating escargot—snails. She cringed as the small plate was placed in front of her.

"Just eat one," Henry had commanded her. "You're the hostess. No one else can begin until you do."

The snails, decanted from their shells and concealed under a crust of bubbling, fragrant butter, looked like wads of gray chewing gum. With her heart in her throat trying to prevent anything else from going through it, Val smiled at Burns and speared a snail. It took all her self-control to chew and swallow the rubbery glob, but she did it. To her relief, as soon as she had taken a mouthful, the rest of the table dug in to their appetizers. In fact, they seemed to like it. Val would have been much happier with a roll to sop up the delectable garlic butter, but none was served. Honor satisfied, she turned to Burns.

"So what should I be worried about in this economy?" she asked.

He smiled at her. "Not much. The drop in technology was a natural downturn. Everyone should have seen it coming. If you didn't have investments in those companies, you should be all right for now. The market is coming back."

"That's good," Val said. She took a sip of water.

He had very handsome blue eyes. They twinkled with mischief.

"You're not eating your snails."

"I've heard they're bad for developing babies," she said.

"Oh." He knew that wasn't true, and his conspiratorial grin proved it. "It's a nice change to sit next to a woman as attractive as you. Where do you come from?"

"New Orleans," Val said.

"And what do you do there?"

No need to tell another fib. "I'm a bartender, Mr. Burns."

"Call me Mike. I thought you seemed too normal for this crowd. What's your connection with Melinda?"

"A distant relative," Val said. That was probably true, too. She bet all dragons were connected back to some reptilian Adam and Eve.

"Not a mother-in-law?"

"No," Val said firmly.

"Ah," Burns said, looking pleased. "Then you won't mind my asking what you're doing tomorrow evening?"

"I don't mind at all," Val said. He was handsome, and she liked the warm tones of his voice. She knew he was a politician, but she had had passes made at her by several prominent citizens of New Orleans. "And call me Val."

"I know a spot with a terrific band, nice for talking—and getting to know one another." The blue eyes glowed.

"That sounds great," Val said. "Just keep in mind I'm not much for late nights at the moment."

"No problem," he said. He glanced down at her belly. It seemed impossible for anyone to ignore it, but Val didn't find his attentions offensive. Quite the opposite. If he found a pregnant woman attractive, she had to like him for his open mind.

They chatted through the salad and the Asian consommé and into the perfect, blood-red tenderloin with a gigantic golden scallop perched beside it. Hers was served with a fantastic au jus instead of the wine sauce the others had. It tasted absolutely divine. Living in the French Quarter, she had learned an appreciation for fine food that she could never have dreamed of in her dorm years. This meal would have been a triumph in any of the best restaurants in New Orleans. In spite of herself, Val was filling up. She knew that dessert was a chocolate pot de crème with a thick, creamy texture like fluffy fudge. She wanted to save room for it, but everything was so good she was finding self-control difficult.

Henry appeared on the other side of the room and gave her a severe look. Val scooted her chair back with the help of the server who appeared there, and stood up. She tapped her water glass with the edge of her spoon. Henry mouthed the first words of her speech along with her. After a nervous hesitation, she was reeling it off as if it were a familiar song.

"Ladies and gentlemen, on behalf of Melinda Wurmley and the Economy Party, I want to welcome you all this evening. You've all come because you support the goals the Economy Party represents. Tonight, we're happy to have Michael Burns with us. He's hoping to be the next United States senator from Maryland. Please welcome Michael Burns."

"Mike," Burns said, as he rose. He touched her on the shoulder, and Val felt a tingle race through her body. "Thanks, Val. My friends, I appreciate your being here with me this evening. It's no easy task to bring the goals of a third party into this two-party system, but we believe the time has come for a way of true leadership . . ."

For the first time in her life, Val didn't find a political speech boring.

Fifteen

Griffen straightened the cards in his hand, then set them facedown on the green cloth. His opponents sorted their deals. A couple of them had easy tells. Albert Nieder, forty, married, and balding, an occasional client from Alabama, wrinkled his brow when he got bad cards, as now. Lacey Dominick, seventy-seven, rail-thin with flyaway gray hair, let the left corner of her mouth go up and straightened her shoulders slightly. She thought she had a winner. Griffen doubted it. Good thing she was loaded. She flew in monthly from Florida for business conferences and spent her evenings at one of Griffen's games. She liked to have a female dealer at the table and tipped generously. Griffen had assigned Phoebe, a forty-year-old widow supporting a couple of teen-age children. He watched Phoebe's short-nailed, amber-tinted fingers deal out the three river cards with deft motions. She set down the deck and folded her hands.

"You're the small blind," Griffen reminded Albert. The bald man grunted and pushed in a couple of chips.

The Hotel St. Marie, halfway between Bourbon Street and the Irish pub on Toulouse, had never allowed Griffen to host a game on its premises before, until the manager met him at a meeting for local business owners supporting Penny that Horsie had set up. They had charged him corkage for his catered buffet but allowed him to bring in whatever he wanted. It was the first good thing that had come out of his connection with the candidate. Otherwise, Penny was running him ragged. That afternoon, he had walked five steps behind her as she toured a community house's new after-school facility for middle-school children. She hadn't commanded so much as appealed to Griffen to be there. Fox Lisa couldn't make it since it was in the middle of her workday. Griffen had had to get up two hours earlier than he was accustomed. He hadn't seen so much daylight since he'd been at college. At least the event hadn't lasted long. Griffen had been able to escape to get together with Jerome for a late lunch at the pub. They had a chance to unwind and go over games scheduled for the upcoming weekend. This was the only table he planned to sit in on, but that was because a good friend had come to play.

The other two men at the table were local business owners. Bert Leopold owned several car dealerships. He had been king on the Nautilus Krewe float at Mardi Gras, two weeks before. He was a burly, balding man who had played high-school football. He and Griffen were friends, having recently shared a couple of experiences they would never discuss in front of the others. Griffen was inclined to go easy on him. Bert was shrewd though not much of a poker player. It was difficult to read him, but he tended to waste his opportunities. Bobby Hogan ran a funeral home in Metairie.

"You got no more expression than one of your corpses," Bert kidded him. He leaned back to grab a handful of tortilla chips and a bottle of beer from the snack table. "You got anything in there?"

"Put up some money and find out," Hogan said. He had a long, lugubrious face the color of mahogany, with three lines running across his high forehead. What was left of his frizzy hair around a polished dome was iron gray. "Say, Griffen, saw you at the Baptist Church on Sunday, when Miss Dunbar came to pray with us. You sang and clapped with the best of them. Didn't know you were in the faith."

"I'm not, Bobby," Griffen said. "My girlfriend works for the Dunbar campaign. She wanted me to come with her."

"You votin' for that girl?" Hogan asked.

"I haven't decided yet."

"Well, me neither. She talks good, but so do all of them. It's like they have a circuit, comin' around all the churches. Otherwise, we don't see 'em much."

"Well, that's when they have time for us," Bert said. "Twenty." He put two green chips in the pot.

"When they want money," Lacey said, her lined face alight with wry humor. "I get invitations to party events, dinners, auctions, you name it, with the coupon carefully filled out in my name, and suggested donations, if you please."

"Bad Penny hit you up for money yet?" Bert asked.

"Not yet," Griffen said.

"Well, she will. They see us as walking wallets: not too smart and full of folding cash."

"Lord God, if only that was true!" Bobby said. Albert laughed. His current hand was good. "It's the incumbents that are the worst. All of a sudden, they not sure if your zoning is clear, or if you need an ordinance variation, and if you just contribute to their reelection fund, they'll make sure it'll go your way."

"That sounds like asking for a bribe," Griffen said.

Bobby made a wry face. "Oh, son, it's all part of the game. You got to learn how Louisiana politics are played. They always talk about Chicago being the worst for corruption, but they ought to come down here to see how it's really done. You've got to feed the wolf at the door to keep him from eatin' you, but if you give him anythin', he never goes away."

"Damned if you do, and damned if you don't," Albert said with a frown. He had nothing, and Griffen knew it.

"Sixty," he said. Albert grimaced and threw his cards away. Griffen's triumph was momentary. Bobby was holding queens full and trashed the rest of them.

"Trouble is, Griffen," Bobby said, as he raked in the chips, "if you show up around the state with one of the candidates, people are gonna think you want her to be elected. You know how appearances are."

"I know," Griffen said grimly. "But I haven't decided for anyone yet, really."

"Well, spread your time with some other candidates. That's just my suggestion."

"Thanks, Bobby. I'll keep that in mind." Not that Griffen was going to have much of a chance: Penny had strong-armed him into agreeing to have her back during a tour of the industrial plants up and down the Mississippi, a school recital, and a store opening over the coming week. It was no use protesting that he didn't have the time. Penny would turn to Fox Lisa, who had trouble saying no to her idol.

"Lady Luck's your only favorite, isn't she?" Lacey said, with a sweet smile. "A pity she's neglecting both of us today."

Lacey was right, unfortunately. When the game ended about one in the morning, Griffen came away from the table with about 10 percent of the pot. If it hadn't been for the house cut, he'd have been down for the day. His mind wasn't on his job. He was worried about Val, but what Bobby said concerned him as well. The tables weren't as full as they could have been, even considering that Mardi Gras had only been a few weeks before. He wondered if running security for Penny *was* hurting business. He'd have to discuss it with Jerome. There was no way he was going to allow his income to be jeopardized by a political candidate, no matter how personally endangered she was. He still had the presence of mind to thank the players for coming.

"Would you like me to call you in a day or two to set up another game?" he asked Lacey and Albert.

"Oh, my, yes," Lacey said, with an exasperated wave. "I'm stuck here until Tuesday."

"Leave a message," Albert said, after checking his phone. "My wife's got us going on some bayou tour. Night, everyone."

Bert stopped to talk to him before heading to the elevator with the others.

"Say, what do you hear from your sister?" he asked in a low voice.

"Nothing," Griffen said uncomfortably.

Bert regarded him sympathetically. "I'm sure she's okay. I'll pray for her."

"Thanks, Bert. I appreciate it."

Bert started to turn away, then seemed to remember something. "Don't let this sound like I'm trying to hit you up like those politicians, but that Asian girlfriend of yours was talking to me during the Mardi Gras party about buying a car. I've got this little Ferrari she liked the sound of. Not trying to pressure you, but in this economy I'd love to move that vehicle."

"Mai?" Griffen asked. "Uh, I think she went home to visit her family. I'll make sure to ask her the next time she calls me."

"Thanks, Griffen. See you next week?"

Phoebe sorted all the unused decks into a case along with the boxes of chips. She had a cooler on a folding cart for the food. Griffen always made sure Phoebe took the leftover buffet home with her. With two ever-hungry boys, her refrigerator was empty more often than full.

"Y'all want me to take the card bucket to the men's shelter?" she asked. Mose had started the policy of donating the used decks, which were otherwise in good condition, for homeless men.

"Sure, if you're going that way," Griffen said. He had to admit that since Penny had mentioned his donation to the community, he had become more aware of the small things he did for others. Those that he had not inherited from his mentor had just come naturally to him. The altruistic streak they revealed surprised him. Before, when he had all his living expenses provided for him, he'd gleaned the maximum from every dollar and was always on the lookout for more. Now, though everything he had he earned, he found himself sharing money that was not needed for immediate expenses, and sometimes even those. It didn't bother him; in fact, it felt good.

Bert reminded him again that he had not heard from Mai.

He was concerned about her, too. Like Fox Lisa, she was formidable, but the two could not have been more different. Fox Lisa was tough in her way but a more approachable person, unlike Mai, who had much more dragon blood than Fox Lisa did. They had met during college, and like Jerome, she was older than she looked. How old, Griffen didn't know. She had connections throughout the dragon community but was part of the coterie called the Eastern dragons. That group was his enemy—their choice, not his. Dragons tended to fight for dominance of an area. As the dragon with the most undiluted blood heritage, New Orleans was his, deeded to him by Mose, and he intended to hold on to it. He wasn't sure where Mai stood. He wanted to know, but he no longer trusted that she would tell him the truth.

In all the fuss to find Val since Mardi Gras had ended, he hadn't seen Mai. Automatically, he opened his phone to look for messages, but the only calls were from Jer or his uncle. She had checked out of her luxury hotel suite, leaving no forwarding information. She had answered none of the messages he had left on her phone. As she had during college, she vanished completely.

He was still angry at her, knowing that she had kept information from him that he needed to survive the attacks by the Eastern dragons who had come after him. Griffen was shocked to find how little he knew about people he had known for years. He had always thought that Mai had his best interests in mind, but that wasn't true. He had cared about her. They'd had fun together. In his mind, he tried to separate the playful, spoiled girlfriend of his college years from the fierce, powerful Dragon Lady that he now knew her to be. It was a lot to take in.

Mai was an enigma. She had defended and helped him, but she had also betrayed him. He wondered if he would ever know where he really stood with her.

His phone rang.

"You said you wanted to talk," a chilling male voice said over the line. Griffen recognized it immediately.

"Where and when?" he asked.

"Now. How about Pirate's Alley?"

Griffen suddenly felt a frisson of icy fingers walk down his back. The narrow passageway was dark at that hour, and the high walls made him feel claustrophobic.

"How about the Café du Monde?" Griffen asked.

He could tell the speaker was smiling. "Well lit? More routes of escape? Fine. I'll be there."

Sixteen

Griffen placed his chair up against an interior pole in the enormous café and tried not to look as if he was nervous. A young waitress, clothing dusted with the inevitable powdered sugar, came to take his order.

"I'm waiting for someone," he told her, scanning the people who drifted in and out of the open-air building. He didn't see anyone he recognized, but under the circumstances, he wasn't sure if he would recognize his connection.

"Y'all want me to come back?"

Griffen calculated the benefit of having a cup of boiling liquid to hand, but decided that could be considered too hostile.

"Yes, thanks." The waitress turned to the next couple to sit down.

A large, heavyset black man leaned over and nudged him in the elbow. "Say, ain't you Griffen McCandles?"

"Yes, that's right." Griffen looked at him, trying to remember if he knew him from either of the Dunbar events or the Baptist church.

"My nephew Luc works for you," the man said, with a big smile. "Thinks the world of you."

Griffen grinned, relieved. "Glad to hear it. Luc's a good dealer."

"You don't need another employee, do you? My son's sixteen. He's got to get some work this summer."

"I don't have anything at the moment, but I'll tell Luc if I need anyone."

"Hey, thanks, man."

"Pass the sugar, please?" asked a middle-aged woman with diamante glasses and badly dyed brown hair at a nearby table. By the bags around her feet and the expensive camera on the chair beside her, she was a tourist.

"Sure," Griffen said. He offered the round sugar dispenser to her. She poured a long stream into her coffee, then handed it back.

"Well, nice talkin' to you," the black man said, getting up. He hitched his belt under his large belly. "Gotta take a break."

Griffen watched him go toward the café's restroom. He felt a poke in the back. He peered around.

"Do you know what time the Cabildo opens in the morning?" the tourist asked.

"Sorry, no," Griffen said. "I think the hours are listed on the door."

"Oh. Okay." She smiled and sipped her coffee.

A shadow fell over Griffen.

"It's a good thing I'm not hunting you, or you'd be toast," a rumbling voice said. Griffen looked up into friendly hazel eyes. The big man was back. Griffen tensed. The man's eyes had been brown before. Griffen's heart pounded loudly in his chest. The man smiled, showing large, brilliant white teeth. "How are you, Griffen?"

"Not so bad," Griffen said, keeping his voice level with some difficulty. "How've you been, George?"

Griffen should have expected a disguise of some kind. The George, as he liked to call himself, was a shape-shifter, capable of appearing in any guise. Griffen didn't know what he had looked like originally. He was no more human than Griffen himself. Most of the time, he seemed an ordinary, nondescript man with forgettable features. The George couldn't be killed by any means Griffen knew, though he had tried. But the dragon hunter and his potential prey had come to a détente sometime ago. Griffen was hoping now for an alliance of sorts.

"Busy, busy, busy," the George said, settling down at Griffen's table. The waitress took orders for fresh coffee and a couple of plates of beignets. "But you don't want to hear about my job."

"No, I don't," Griffen admitted. Success in the George's case meant a dead dragon. "But I have to."

George's eyebrows went up. He clasped the coffee mug with his big hand even though it was boiling hot, and took a deep swig.

"That's interesting. Why?"

"My sister is missing. She's been gone about three weeks. She hasn't gotten in touch with me, and I'm worried about her."

The George didn't console him with empty assurances that Val might have gone off of her own accord. "No contract is on file in our office about Valerie McCandles, I assure you. Her disappearance has nothing to do with us. Do you have any suspicions that this is an assassination or an abduction?"

"Uh." Griffen hesitated. He hated to inform George that another dragon was on the way, but he had no doubt that was at the heart of her disappearance. "I hope it's an abduction. Val's pregnant. She's gotten chummy with, er, the father's mother."

"Melinda Wurmley." George nodded. He cocked his head at Griffen's surprise. "She's about as subtle as a nuclear explosion. She hasn't been shy about spreading the news that she's going to be a grandmother. We keep tabs on as many of you as we can. I wondered why Nathaniel went to Africa. Mumsy sent him out of town."

"To protect him from me?"

"From Valerie, I would assume," George said. "You're formidable, but Val will one day be terrifying. She might be a target, but not at present. A baby opens the field further, though. A pure-blood baby, or nearly so. A tempting prize for many parties." He eyed Griffen speculatively. "Yes, you're right to be concerned, but she and her offspring aren't in any danger from us. We only work by contract."

"What if you had a contract?" Griffen asked, drawing pictures in the powdered sugar on the table.

"On your sister?" George's eyes widened.

"To find her," Griffen corrected him. "To get her back here safe and sound, with her child. You have resources I don't. At the moment, I have absolutely no idea how to track her. But that's what you do. You find dragons."

"And kill them," George reminded him.

"Not always. I'm still here. And I want Val back alive."

"What if she doesn't want to come?"

"I'd want to hear that from her directly. I would have to believe that she wasn't under any compulsion, magical or otherwise."

"Fair enough," George said. "Can you afford our rates?"

Griffen was frank. "I doubt it. I'd have to owe you. If you let me work out a payment plan, I will keep up with it."

"Well," George said, "we know where you live."

Griffen gulped. The George smiled.

"A little hunter humor there. No offense. I have to check with the office, but I see no reason not to take the contract. There's only one condition."

"What?"

The George leaned across the table, his assumed bulk menacing. "We have the right to defend ourselves if threatened. Collateral damage is possible. You are not responsible for it, but if we need to take measures, we will."

"Wait a minute, you'd kill . . . ?" Griffen had a mental picture of Melinda, Lizzy, and her brothers lying in pools of blood. In spite of his difficult history with them, he was horrified.

George held up his hand. "I told you, we don't freelance. But you do not get to warn our quarry. The idea is to go in and out, achieving the objective as swiftly and as accurately as possible. Nothing more, nothing less. If you feel you have to warn someone, I am your first telephone call. I'll take care of eventualities and changes in plan. Not you. This is life and death, Griffen. I expect to hear from you at once if Valerie returns on her own."

"It's a deal," Griffen said. He hesitated.

"Good enough. We will bill you." The George tilted his head. "Something else on your mind?"

"I've had . . . some intelligence from a source I can't tell you that another dragon is in danger," Griffen said. "Penny Dunbar."

"Are you asking me if a contract has been taken out on *her*?"

"Yes."

"You can't expect me to reveal confidential dealings that have nothing to do with you."

"They do!" Griffen said. The hunter raised one eyebrow. "I'm . . . obligated to help make sure nothing happens to her. I don't want to become 'collateral damage' if you're out to get her."

The George fixed his greenish brown orbs on him. They looked less human than ever. "I can't tell you if she is a target."

"But . . ."

"But it's none of my business if she's not a target," the George finished. He took a big, square beignet from the top of the pile and bit into it. He chewed slowly and deliberately, swallowing the first bite before taking another.

"Are you saying that's the case?" Griffen asked.

"In truth, I say nothing," the hunter said. He ate three beignets in a row, washed down with plenty of coffee, while Griffen puzzled that out.

"I think . . . maybe . . . that I have nothing to worry about," Griffen began, tentatively.

The George's poker face was almost as good as his. "That is your conclusion."

Griffen wondered just what cards he was holding. "I am going to act as if it is, but I take nothing for granted."

"Prudence is a wise course."

Griffen made a face at George's linguistic circumlocutions. He thought hard before asking the next question. "Have you ever heard of Reginaud St. Cyr Duvallier?"

That made the George's eyebrows go up. "Yes, indeed. We try not to deal with him."

Griffen almost whistled.

"That's a relief!"

"He doesn't need us." The George considered him carefully. "He is a resourceful man and a dangerous one. I don't need to warn you to look out where he's involved."

"No," Griffen said. "I've met him."

"Are you his target?"

"I'm not, but I know someone who might be."

"That acquaintance may be more short-lived than you think, then." The George cleaned his hands carefully with a paper napkin. "We're done for the time being. You won't hear from me again unless there is a development." He rose and dusted off his brown corduroy pants.

"Why do I feel as if I've just made a deal with the devil?" Griffen asked wryly.

The big man winked at him.

"You're in the right city for it. But I feel the same way, Griffen McCandles. This *was* unusual. But you are an unusual dragon."

The George stepped out of the brightly lit pergola onto the dark pavement. Griffen blinked. In between one step and another, the shape-shifter seemed to vanish.

"My!" said the voice of Dorothy Gale in his memory. "People come and go so quickly around here!"

Seventeen

The tiny Asian woman leaped over the head of the bulky, pasty-faced male enforcer and clung to the peeling brick wall with her claws. Her long, straight, black hair had been pulled out of its neat chignon into frantic strands. Mai hated Melinda for making her ruin her manicure and her hairdo. The other enforcer, a taller, leaner male with a shock of brilliant orange hair, leaped to grab her ankle. She scrambled up a few feet and kicked at his face. He dodged, but she caught him in the cheek. He hissed.

Only yards away, outside the mouth of the alley, thousands of New Yorkers weaved their way down the sidewalk, heading toward the subway to go home, that five o'clock look on their faces. The businesspeople, male and female, wore suits. The fashionistas wore designer labels. Those who wanted to be thought "in the know" wore black. Mai hoped one of them would stumble her way, perhaps to indulge in a little freelance mugging, and alarm her would-be assailants long enough for her to escape over the rooftops.

"What an unexpected gift," Melinda said, watching the battle from the entryway. She was a short, dumpy woman with nondescript brown permanent-waved hair, obviously dyed. Mai suspected it had long ago gone to gray. Melinda was too vain to let her age show. Those pointed Jimmy Choo heels she had on were far too young for her. If there was any justice, though Mai had long ago given up believing in justice, she hoped they hurt like hell. "Giving me a chance to kill you in decent privacy."

"If we were in Chinatown, you'd be the one up here," Mai growled.

"I am never foolish enough to go there," Melinda said, examining her nails. She buffed a red-painted forefinger on the sleeve of her coat. "Not without a sufficient escort. Something you should have kept in mind, dear. But it won't trouble you for long."

That's what you think, Mai thought, edging sideways toward a fire escape. Redhead clambered up the wall after her like a spider. Below them, Blocky sidled between the Dumpsters, keeping his eyes on them. Mai searched for an advantage. She had no fear of losing her grip. New York buildings were easier to scale than climbing walls in the gym. Their ancient brickwork, pipes, conduits, and rainspouts were such good handholds, she wondered that there weren't more burglaries. She admitted she had an advantage with her dragon strength and natural claws. A pity it was still daylight. In the dark, she could effect a full transformation and flit away on spread wings.

Bundles of black coaxial cables snaked up the side of the building she was climbing. Redhead was close behind. Hiding the cables from view with her body, Mai slit them with her talon. He should get enough of an electric shock to distract him.

Instead, she heard a bellow through a window.

"Goddammit, the cable just went out!"

"Call the super," a female voice shouted back. "This is the fifth time this month!"

Mai glanced over her shoulder. Her pursuer grinned at her. All right, so electronics weren't her long suit.

"Hurry up and finish her, Dean," Melinda said. "I have a dinner date."

"Take your time, Dean," Mai said, in a mocking tone. "She could stand to miss a couple of meals."

Mai was more worried than she sounded. The truth was, she couldn't afford to be caught. None of her people, the Eastern dragons, knew she was in town. They all thought she was still in New Orleans, where she was assigned. Her honored head of the family was already angry with Mai for failing to bring Griffen McCandles under their control. She had already had over a year to do it. The task wasn't as easy as she had first thought it would be, and it was growing more difficult all the time. Griffen was learning wisdom in that place, something he had shown little sign of gaining back in college. In spite of herself, Mai was impressed with his progress. She was fond of him, but clan loyalty was stronger than her individual wishes. Not to mention that if she wanted to continue to live on the very generous allowance she received, she would have to do what she was told. If she did not succeed soon, she would be superseded by another dragon, or team of dragons.

She had run into another snag that prevented her from taking more drastic action. Griffen's sister, Val, had become dear to her. She had never dreamed such a thing was possible. In all her long years, and Griffen would never learn the true total from her lips, she had yet to make a real friend. Val had reached out to her, offered her trust, and saved her life even at the risk of her own.

In all her long years, no one else had ever done that for Mai, not without expectations in return. Val had done it because that was what friends do. Mai was suspicious of such openness. In her experience, vulnerability equated with death. But she liked it. She had come to care for Val, and she felt innately protective of her.

When Val had disappeared Mardi Gras evening, only one person could have been responsible: Melinda. Mai sought for witnesses who could tell her where the elder dragon had gone. It had taken bribery, threats, cajoling, and some honest detective work, but she trailed Melinda and her minions to the Big Apple.

To her dismay, Mai had not yet found a trace of Val. She

wasn't staying in the extremely expensive suite in the Trump Towers with Melinda and Melinda's insane daughter, Lizzy. Val was not resident in any of the other suites nor in any other hostelry close by. A *very* nice young man in the New York public records office had checked for her, and Melinda owned no private homes in the five boroughs, at least under that name. Mai was reduced to tailing the other dragon through the city like a gumshoe.

Evidently, electronics was not her only short suit.

"You followed us like an elephant trampling through Bubble Wrap for the last week," Melinda taunted her, as she dodged and swung through the alley like it was a filthy jungle gym. "You couldn't have been more obvious if you had brought Macy's Thanksgiving Day Parade with you. I cannot imagine what makes you dog my footsteps like that. If you want to know where I'm going, just ask me. I would be delighted to tell you personally, to your face, to go jump in a volcano."

Mai bounded off the top of a Dumpster and grabbed for a rung of the fire-escape ladder. With a loud screech, it slid downward, taking her with it. The hair on the back of her neck stood straight out with fear. She let go of the rusty metal and dropped to the alley floor. More swiftly than she would have believed, Blocky closed the distance between them. He grabbed her around the body, trapping her arms at her side. She kicked for his crotch. He shifted her so both her legs were beside his hip, leaving her feet flailing at air. He grinned in her face. Mai hissed. Headbutting him would hurt. Instead, she bit him hard on the nose. He bellowed and squeezed his eyes shut.

Dragon skin, at least that belonging to those of nearly pure blood, was known to be impenetrable to anything on Earth. That is, with one exception: dragon teeth. Otherwise, a baby dragon's fangs would remain helplessly beneath the surface of its gums. It takes time for teeth to erupt, but they can and do work their way through the tough epidermis. Mai couldn't bite his nose off, but she was pleased to see that she had drawn blood.

He lost focus, and his grip slackened. Mai didn't wait for a second chance. She slithered downward, out of his arms. Redhead saw her move and went for her. Mai tumbled in a backward somersault on the sticky pavement, coming up on her feet. She sprang. She kicked off against an empty Dumpster. Before the metal receptacle finished ringing, Mai had her arms around Melinda's neck. She towed the elder dragon backward into the confined space between two Dumpsters. The enforcer dashed toward them.

"Back off!" Mai ordered Redhead. He windmilled to a stop.

"Don't be silly!" Melinda gasped. "Kill her before she kills me!"

"I'm not in the mood for this, Melinda," Mai said in her ear. "Today is your lucky day."

"What? What do you want?"

"A life for a life."

"Whose?"

"Yours for Valerie McCandles. Where is she?"

"Why is she any concern of yours?"

"She's my friend."

"Really." Melinda turned her head in Mai's grip to look her in the eye. "You? You have friends?"

Mai swallowed. It was a weakness. She was not accustomed to admitting to any. She had made an error. She kept her face as impassive as possible. A fellow Eastern dragon would have seen through her façade, but no ordinary dragon would have seen any emotional response whatsoever. She made her tone austere.

"We have our reasons for wanting to know her location. They may be similar to yours."

Melinda was under no such restraint on her feelings. Steam came out of her nostrils and ears. "You won't get her, Mai."

"So you do have her! Every dragon in the world knows you're expecting a grandchild. Of course you want to make sure it comes into your hands when it is born. But we doubt Val's safety. I need to see her."

"The Eastern dragons have no business with my grandchild!" Melinda said. "Strangle me if you can. I'll never tell you where they are."

Mai thought about it for a moment. She could snap the elder dragon's neck. She had killed before.

"So be it," she said. She tightened her grip.

Horrified, Blocky and Redhead hovered a few feet away, looking for an angle to attack, but she was too well protected in her niche. With a tremendous shove, she pushed Melinda forward. The elder dragon stumbled on her narrow shoes. The two enforcers rushed to keep their employer from hitting the ground. In that split second, Mai grabbed the handle of one Dumpster, pulled herself up, and scrambled up the nearest drainpipe. In seconds, she was on the roof.

Before she started running, she heard Melinda's taunting voice below.

"You're getting soft, Mai! I might actually believe you have learned to care! Watch yourself! It'll get you killed!"

Eighteen

Griffen sat between Penny and Fox Lisa in the rear of the black Lincoln Town Car. He dreaded the long drive to Acadia Parish. The vehicle was a replacement for the one that had been totaled by the garbage truck in front of the Irish pub. Horsie sat in the front passenger seat beside the driver, a man of approximately Horsie's age but in far better shape. Winston Parmalee was Penny's head of security. A thirty-year veteran of the Marines, he had a sapphire-hard glare and an iron gray crew cut you could have landed a jet on. He had made it clear on several occasions that he didn't approve of Penny's amateur guardians. Even allowing Griffen to sit in on the briefing for her visit to the bayou was a major concession. He didn't reject Fox Lisa since she was a devoted campaign worker, but he hated having Griffen, known to host illegal poker games, anywhere near his candidate. Behind the limo, an unofficial caravan of press vehicles pulled away from the curb.

"Be happy to drop you off anywhere," Winston offered, as he swung out of the parking lot of Penny's campaign headquarters on a drizzly Tuesday morning.

"Sure," Griffen said. He would have been glad of any excuse to get out of going, though his conscience would have slammed him. Winston could undoubtedly handle any physical attacks, but what if something supernatural jumped out of the woodwork?

"Oh, now, let's all just get along," Penny said. She leaned forward and patted Winston on the shoulder.

"The public is likely to draw the wrong conclusions if Mr. McCandles is present," Winston said.

"I think they will draw the right conclusions, won't they?" Penny said. Her tone was so bright it was almost brittle. "That he is a concerned citizen who has given up some of his very valuable time to support me. Isn't that right, Griffen?"

She clutched his wrist with her nails. Griffen suppressed a grunt. If he hadn't had dragon flesh, he would have looked like a suicide victim.

"I'm a concerned citizen," Griffen assured Winston. "I won't get in the way, and I will stay out of the cameras. I don't want to be on the evening news any more than you want me there."

Winston grunted. "There would be no chance at all if you weren't there."

"Now, stop it! He's coming along, and that's that!" Penny said, her voice rising almost to a shriek.

Griffen eyed her with dismay, but neither Horsie nor Winston seemed surprised by the outburst. Fox Lisa, dressed in a dark green business suit and a bow tied at her neck that hid all her tattoos, gave Griffen a nervous look. Her job at this rally was to introduce Penny to the crowd, which meant memorizing a short speech and speaking into a microphone before an audience. Fox Lisa had the speech down pat.

"But every time I think of opening my mouth in front of everyone, my throat goes dry," she had told Griffen.

"I'll be there with a bottle of water," he had promised her.

She clutched his hand in both of hers. Griffen squeezed her fingers gently.

Since he had spoken to George five days earlier, Griffen felt he could relax a little. The shape-shifter assassin and the shadowy organization behind him wasn't after Penny or Val. It wasn't easy to kill a dragon. Chances were that the people backing Duvallier didn't know about Penny's species. He wouldn't have given long odds on that since they did know about Duvallier. Griffen held out hope, though, because Duvallier hadn't said he intended to kill Penny. Penny was a fighter. She was armed, knew martial arts, and had alarms and bodyguards within almost constant reach. Griffen did not know how much more he could be expected to contribute to her safety. He hadn't yet seen any threats he could handle better than Winston or any of her other security agents, all of whom openly questioned his presence.

The man who had driven the garbage truck had come to two weeks ago with no memory at all of how he had come to be driving his vehicle the wrong way up a one-way street in the middle of the night. No trace of alcohol or drugs could be found in his bloodstream, so the police cited him for dangerous driving and left it at that. People with whom Griffen had discussed it either shrugged their shoulders as one of those inexplicable things that happens in New Orleans or put it down to bad juju. Since Rose had not reappeared to confirm the latter, Griffen was left with no answers. The worst thing was that he was getting bored. Fox Lisa might hang on every little detail of the election, but having seen some of the workings from the inside, Griffen no longer felt privileged. The next time he talked to his uncle, he was going to ask for a more fair division of labor.

Except to look up at them peevishly once in a while in a silent demand for quiet, Penny ignored the rest of them and spent the long drive west reading documents from a briefcase at her feet. With nothing else to do, Griffen couldn't help but read over her shoulder. Penny read the draft of a request for funding, ran down a checklist of school-board members, and read letter after letter from constituents. Those ranged from computer-generated form letters to scrawls on large-lined notebook paper that could have been written by schoolchildren but on close perusal had not. Griffen was grateful for the excellent education he had had and wished everyone could say the same. Penny was clearly in favor of better schools, as she said several times as she dictated answers to the letters into a pocket recorder. Whatever sharp comments she made on the side to the unknown secretary that would be typing these replies, Penny was kind and forthright in the body of the letters. She might speak fluent politicianese, but she never talked down to her correspondents. She was frustrated by the limitations on her powers to change their lives. Griffen developed respect for her, though he would have hated to work for her full-time.

After a few hours winding their way through the inevitable road construction, Winston turned into a gravel drive that led down a long road overhung with dark green Spanish moss and bright green lianas. On either side of the road, the ground sloped down into soggy wetland. The towering ranks of dark-trunked mangrove trees crowded the land. At the end of the winding drive stood a group of nondescript cinderblock buildings painted white, with tiled roofs. Several other cars were already in the parking lot around them. A sweating bald man in a white Oxford shirt and a bow tie waited until the car came to a stop and pulled open the door.

"We're honored, Representative," he said. "Just as honored as can be. Everyone's lookin' forwa'd to hearin' you speak."

"Well, that's so nice of you, Mr. Anton," Penny said, graciously, allowing him to hand her out of the car. Upright, she stood at least five inches taller than the bald man. "I'm pleased to be here. What you and your folks here have accomplished is a boon to the environment."

"Where's the ladies' room?" Horsie asked, interrupting. She glanced behind the Lincoln at the horde of reporters pouring out of their vehicles and hoisting their cameras and microphones. "Penny needs to freshen up a little."

"Well, right there," Mr. Anton said. He pointed to a recessed door with a screened vent near the top. "Please help yourself."

Horsie took the briefcase and recorder and pushed Penny into the ladies' room. She stood outside the door, heading off the handful of reporters who tried to follow Penny inside. Instead, she took a sheaf of papers from the briefcase and distributed copies to each of them.

"Just give the girl some privacy," Horsie said with an engaging smile. She gathered up the nearest reporters in both arms. "We've had a long drive. You wouldn't want her to say something wrong just because she's tired out, would you? Here are some talking points she's going to be discussing today. Now, if you'll just come with me, I'll give you some exclusive information that I am sure you all want to hear. Mr. Anton, come with me, and you can answer their questions, too!"

She persuaded them into a gaggle and led them deeper into the property. On the other side of the buildings, a crowd of about two hundred people waited, murmuring to one another. With the grove as a backdrop, a low stand had been erected and furnished with a podium and half a dozen folding chairs.

Fox Lisa and Griffen were left with the austere Winston in the parking lot. Griffen inhaled the heady scent of the trees, so different from the smell of the French Quarter but seeming just as ancient. The breeze off the brackish water of the swamp was chilly. Fox Lisa hunched her shoulders.

"I doubt there was any good reason to bring you along," Winston said, his lips pursed. He had donned a pair of dark glasses against the strong light, rendering him into an expressionless statue. He was approximately the same height as Griffen but seemed taller because of the breadth of his shoulders. The front of his dark suit coat draped against his chest revealed a boxy outline. Griffen knew he was carrying a large handgun in a shoulder holster and at least two other weapons concealed elsewhere about his person. Griffen had a knife, almost standard issue for someone who lived in the Quarter. Fox Lisa had her pistol. Winston lifted his chin as a couple of uniformed Louisiana State Troopers climbed out of their patrol car. "Stay here." He went to meet the officers.

It was eerily silent. Griffen could hear a few birds calling in the distance and a jet streaking overhead, but little else. Then his ears perked up.

"Do you hear that?" he asked Fox Lisa.

She strained to listen. "No. What is it?"

"I hear howling."

"Well, there's coyotes all over this state," she said. She eyed him mischievously. "There's also the loup garou."

"I know," Griffen said absently, peering into the shadows cast by the orchard center building's eaves. "I didn't think they went around in daylight."

Fox Lisa looked sour. "I suppose you're going to tell me you met some of them."

"I did," Griffen admitted. "A few of them came to that conference in October. I haven't been in touch with any of them since."

She put her hands on her hips in annoyance.

"You met the loup garou?"

With a wary look toward Winston, Griffen hushed her.

"When we have time, I'll tell you all about the people who were there," he promised. "For now, just help me watch out for Penny. I want to get back to the city before tonight. I have a couple of games running in two different hotels."

Fox Lisa let her mouth relax in a grin. "I guess I'm just nervous. And a little jealous. I've lived here all my life. My folks used to scare me into behaving with horror stories about the loup garou and the ghosts who live in the graveyards. You hang around with ghosts and all those other things."

"Believe me," Griffen said, "your parents were right to warn you. I wouldn't want you to run into one."

Fox Lisa patted her purse. "It'd have to move faster than I can pull the trigger."

"They can move . . ."

"Reeeeeerrrrrrrrrgh!"

The hoarse scream tore the air. Griffen cast around for a moment, then realized it came from the ladies' room. He slammed open the door and ran in. Fox Lisa was close behind him.

Penny had been shoved against the wall between two hand dryers. With claws spread at her throat was a lithe, hairy creature with a long jaw, triangular ears, and a long tail, clad all over with thick black fur. Red eyes glared out over a long muzzle. A loup garou! Its head whipped around in surprise. It snarled.

Griffen leaped at the beast. He grabbed it around the throat and belly, and pulled it away from Penny. It twisted nimbly in his grasp, coming up with jaws open. Griffen twisted his face away. It bit his shoulder. He headbutted it in the face. It flailed at his chest with its claws, struggling to get free. It shoved all its weight into his midsection. Griffen lost his balance. He fell backward onto the cold concrete floor. The beast fell on top of him, biting at his face and neck. Griffen rolled over, taking the beast over with him. It was smaller and lighter than he was. He used his weight to hold it down while he freed one hand to shove its mouth away. It snarled and writhed, emitting an unearthly squeal. It clamped its jaws on Griffen's wrist. The sharp teeth couldn't penetrate his skin, but it hurt.

Fox Lisa was suddenly at his side, feet spread, her pistol in both hands pointed at the creature's head.

"Lay off, or I'll blow your brains out!" she shouted.

The loup garou looked up at her in horror and lay flat on the floor, its arms and legs limp. Its eyes lost the red light and faded to pale brown.

"What the hell are you doing in here?" Penny shrieked. She drew back her toe and kicked Griffen in the ribs. "You should have stayed outside!"

"I heard you scream," Griffen gasped. He clambered to his feet. So did the lycanthrope.

"I didn't scream," Penny said, her eyes flashing with fury. She pointed at the loup garou. "She did."

"She?" Griffen asked, eyeing the lycanthrope in astonishment.

The door burst open, banging against the cinder-block wall. Winston and the state troopers burst in, guns drawn.

"What happened?" he demanded.

Penny recovered her wits at once and brushed back her hair. It had become slightly disarranged in the melee.

"Nothing. I was just having a discussion with a supporter here."

"This is one of your supporters?" Winston asked dubiously. He turned. Griffen goggled. In that split second while everyone's attention was turned away, the loup garou had changed into a woman with long dark hair and a deep mahogany complexion. Her ankle-length skirt and peasant blouse were black. She wore no shoes. Griffen supposed they were harder to manifest than clothing.

"How'd she do that?" Fox Lisa demanded.

The loup garou glared at them.

Penny found a smile somewhere and pasted it on her face. She looked so demure and coy that Griffen would never have guessed her life had been in danger a moment before.

"You see? It's all settled. Now, if all you gentlemen would remove yourself from this female holy of holies, I have to get ready for my speech."

Horsie appeared behind them with the entire press crew in tow. "Honey, what happened?"

Penny put a gentle-seeming hand on the transformed female's arm. Griffen saw the loup garou wince.

"Why, we just scared each other," she said. "I was coming out of the stall when this lady was trying to go in, and she made a little noise. I don't see what all the alarm is about."

"It sounded like a scream," said a man in a bright red Windbreaker with the logo of the local television affiliate on it. He had a camera balanced on his shoulder.

"Did it?" Penny said. "I am so sorry to alarm everyone. Why don't you all go and wait for me, and I will be right out!"

"Well, come on," Horsie said to the press corps. "That little run got my blood pumping. No one had better fall asleep during the speech now!"

The reporters fell obediently into line and trailed after her, with a few shooting openly curious glances over their shoulders. Winston loomed behind them, ensuring that no one dallied. Fox Lisa followed them. Griffen went as far as the threshold and stopped, arms crossed on his chest.

"You, too, Mr. McCandles," Penny said, sweetly.

"This is as far as I go," he said. "I'm not going to let you out of my sight, in case this lady decides to assault you again." Penny looked as if she was going to protest, but Griffen was adamant. "This is why you wanted me here, right?"

"All right! But not a word out of you!"

Griffen objected to the tone, but he nodded. Just when he was ready to give up on Rose's assertion that Penny was in danger, this happened. He wondered how Duvallier had managed to conscript the notoriously independent Louisiana werewolves into putting out a hit for him.

The woman glared at Penny. "So this is the way you keep fait' wit' the loup garou? You cheat us blin', t'reatenin' ouah ancestral groun's, den you get de big dragon out heyah to beat up a po' li'l woman?"

Little woman? Griffen thought indignantly, but when he opened his mouth, Penny held up a warning finger like Han Solo's. She turned a sincere face to the loup garou.

"I told you that legislation to protect land takes time. I have to lobby my fellow officials to get a bill drafted and passed. That can get to be expensive. I told you that."

"Yah, but six t'ousan' dollah? Wheah we get six t'ousan' dollah?"

Penny's face could have been made of stone. "It's just a suggested donation. If you and your people don't consider that to be a fair amount, then tell me what you can give, and I'll let you know what it will support."

The woman twitched her skirt from side to side as if it were still a tail.

"Times is hard. We can affo'd maybe five hun'd. I brung it wit' me," she added hopefully, touching a pocket in her skirt. Penny was obdurate.

"Sorry. That's just not enough to do what you are hoping for. I've told you, there are expenses involved in declaring your family's land as endangered habitat. Pulling any tax-producing territory off the rolls has to be balanced by cuts elsewhere."

"That's all we got!"

Penny smiled apologetically. "Then it sounds like you are not as committed to the project as I was. I'll be happy to accept it as a partial donation, of course. I am so sorry, Mrs. Lemieux, I have many calls upon my time. I need to concentrate on my local constituents, until and unless all citizens in the state become my constituents. When I'm governor. And I am sorry to tell you that then even six thousand dollars won't touch the expenses I would be accruing to persuade my fellow lawmakers to deal on your behalf. We have so many other pressing matters. You understand, I hope? A small investment now would pay off handsomely later."

The lycanthrope's head drooped. "See what we can do."

Penny beamed. "That's wonderful. Get in touch with my assistant when you have a more concrete answer." She took the woman's hand in both of hers and shook it warmly. "Very nice to see you, Mrs. Lemieux. Come on, Mr. McCandles. I can't leave those people waiting any longer."

Griffen was appalled. Not only wasn't Penny in danger from the lycanthrope, she was shaking her down! He started to speak, but Penny grabbed his arm and marched him toward the door.

The loup garou slunk out of the ladies' room ahead of them and vanished around the corner of the building. She strode away with an easy lope that rapidly covered distance. In a moment, she was out of sight among the distant trees. A lonely howl went up in the wetlands, echoed by other, more distant wails.

"You're extorting bribes?" he hissed.

"Is that what it looked like to you, Mr. McCandles?" Penny said, with the brittle smile on her face that he had come to fear. She patted her hair down with her free hand. "Why, you misunderstand what you heard. I was just explaining to that good lady the realities of introducing special-interest legislation in this state. That's all. There are indeed expenditures that I must incur in the course of my duties. I am always happy to discuss such matters. I only wish that I could do everything that everyone asks of me. It's just impossible. Once I'm governor, there will be more I can do. Now, you have the good sense not to discuss the private conversation you just witnessed, don't you? Revealing it will just lead to so many complications."

By the cold expression in her eyes, Griffen understood exactly what those complications would include. Penny let go of him just before the cameras turned toward her. She smiled and waved both hands at the waiting crowd. Griffen scooted out of the way, so he wouldn't be caught in the lenses. Penny sauntered forward into a barrage of camera flashes. He was already forgotten.

Standing alone in front of the microphone, Fox Lisa shot Griffen a nervous look. He gave her both thumbs-ups and an encouraging smile. Fox Lisa cleared her throat audibly and began.

"Ladies and gentlemen, citizens of the fair state of Louisiana . . ."

Beside her, Penny stood, not a hair out of place on her golden head. Griffen stared at her in astonishment.

No wonder she's called Bad Penny, he thought.

Nineteen

When Winston brought the limousine to a halt at Penny's New Orleans headquarters late that afternoon, Griffen could not wait to get out of the car. It didn't matter how much danger Penny might be in. If he stayed, he was going to say something to her he shouldn't. He helped Fox Lisa to her feet and steered her toward the sidewalk.

"Where are we going?" she asked.

"To get a drink," Griffen said.

"Wait a minute," Horsie called behind them. "What about our debriefing? I've got snacks and the makings for cocktails. You know I make one mean Sazerac."

"No, thanks," Griffen replied, with a casual wave. "I've got to get back. I have some things to check on. I haven't got any useful input, anyhow."

"But I do," Fox Lisa protested. "Hey, take it easy, honey. I can't move too fast on these heels."

"Wait a moment," Griffen said. He swept her up in his arms and carried her down the street. She laughed delightedly and wound her arms around his neck. "Whew! Good thing you're light."

As soon as they were down the street half a block and out of sight of the office, Griffen set her down.

"What was all that about?" Fox Lisa asked. She slipped off the tall green shoes and shoved them into her oversized purse. "Oh, my God, thanks be for all small mercies. I don't know how Penny does it, day after day, walking on those spikes. Her shoes are about three inches higher than mine."

Griffen eyed her bare feet. "Should I call a taxi?"

"Oh, no, I'm used to going barefoot. I'll just watch out for broken glass. No problem. Let's go. It's not that far."

Griffen grinned at her. One of the things he loved about her was that little ever seemed to distress her for long.

At the Irish pub, Griffen helped Fox Lisa onto a stool on the family side of the bar and sank onto the seat beside her. The "No shoes, no service," rule was relaxed for regulars. The bartender, a large, friendly man with a balding head, didn't say anything about Fox Lisa's bare feet. Instead, he took one look at them and poured an Irish whisky, neat, with water on the side for Griffen, and a beer for Fox Lisa.

"Thanks, Fred," she said.

Griffen took a grateful sip of his whisky. The warm liquid rushed into his system like a fresh breath of life. Maestro, a slim, tawny-skinned man whose long salt-and-pepper hair was tied back in a ponytail, toasted him with a similar glass.

"Hey, y'all, we've got famous folks among us," he said. He pointed up at the television mounted on a bracket high on the wall. The early-evening news was on. The announcer, an African-American man, looked over his sheaf of papers and said something Griffen didn't quite hear, then his image was replaced by a long shot of the mangrove farm.

"There's you," Maestro said, touching Fox Lisa on the hand. "They've been running this clip over and over again."

The scene changed to another angle looking up at her from the side only a few feet away.

". . . I'm proud to introduce a real friend to the environment and your next governor, Representative Penny Dunbar!" On the screen, Fox Lisa moved aside to make way for the politician.

The regulars in the bar cheered. Fox Lisa beamed in delight.

"She worked really hard on her speech," Griffen said. "She was letter-perfect."

"You sound pretty professional there," said one of the female regulars, a Creole woman in her fifties seated on the other side of Maestro.

"You wait, Ann Marie," Fox Lisa said. "Maybe one day I'll run for office."

"Watch it," Maestro said. "Lie down with dogs, get up with fleas."

"Lie down with Bad Penny, get up with a communicable disease," Ann Marie said.

"Hey!" Fox Lisa protested. "She's good people."

"Would you vote for her?" Griffen asked the others.

Ann Marie thought about it for a moment.

"Maybe. She's done some good things. What about you? Tell me why I should vote for her. You're working for her campaign."

"No, I'm not," Griffen said, hastily. "I'm just there to carry things for Fox Lisa. She's the real star."

"I heard some rumors that you're getting in bed with the girl, that's all," Ann Marie said.

"He'd better not," Fox Lisa said, patting her purse. Everyone on the family side knew about the pistol. They laughed.

"See?" Griffen asked. "Do I look suicidal?"

"No, but you look like you carryin' too much money," Ann Marie said with a grin. "Want to run some nine-ball?"

"Sure," Griffen said. "Fox Lisa, do you want to play, too?"

"No, thanks," she said. "My nerves are too rattled to hold the cue steady. I'll come over and keep score for you."

They ordered some food at the bar. One of the two pool tables in the room was open. Fox Lisa sat down at the table closest to it. Griffen set his drink down near her and racked up the balls on the green felt. Ann Marie had her own cue in the rack on the wall. Griffen didn't want to go home for his good stick.

"Can I borrow yours, Maestro?" he called.

"Certainly, son. No charge," the older man said. He came to sit by Fox Lisa. "You don't mind kibitzers?"

For the first time all day, Griffen felt at ease. "No problem." He turned to Ann Marie. "Your break."

The slim woman narrowed an eye at him. "You're so sure you're gonna get a turn?"

"I sure hope so," Griffen said, opening his eyes wide. "But you know, I'm just an innocent country boy, hoping not to get taken advantage of by those folks in the big city."

"Well, I'll take your innocence, country boy. How much? Fifty?"

"Sure."

Maestro took charge of the bets. "Just so the money doesn't get lost," he assured them. Griffen laughed. He would have trusted any of the regulars with a million dollars in cash or his life. They were as good as family. Better in some cases. No one questioned Griffen's working for the Dunbar campaign any more than they would object to an alternative lifestyle, and several were represented among the bar's denizens. He ran illicit gambling. Tick-tock, a small, thin man with high cheekbones knocking back a shot of vodka, made a living playing saxophone on street corners. Miss Mercedes Bends, enjoying an Irish coffee and having an animated conversation with two men at the corner of the bar, was a transvestite. One of the men with her was a stranger who was visibly succumbing to her charms. Griffen wondered whether he should slip the man a word as to the nature of the tall, attractive lady in the tight, aqua blue minidress, then hastily remembered it was none of his business. The revelation might be a shock or a pleasure, but it wasn't up to him to deliver either. He was wearing a disguise of his own if one looked at it that way.

The clatter and thump of the balls falling into the table pockets was as soothing as a lullaby. Griffen found himself getting into the rhythm. Ann Marie was good but not as good as he was. She scratched on the four and stepped aside to let Griffen shoot. He was feeling hot. The cue felt like a perfect extension of his hands. He ran the table twice, winning her fifty. Griffen retrieved his drink and had a sip of whisky.

"Nice job," Ann Marie said, refreshing herself from her own glass. "Again?"

"Same bet?"

"Maybe I'm a fool, but yes."

They racked up and she went first again. Griffen kept his distance while she lined up her shot. The unspoken rule of any pool game was not to crowd your opponent's elbow lest ye be crowded yourself during a key shot. He'd accomplished plenty of jostles in his college career, both deliberate and accidental, but the mood in the Irish pub was slow and easy. Bloodletting was for tournament play, not casual games with friends.

"Hey, why'd you drag me away from headquarters so fast?" Fox Lisa asked during the third round.

Griffen grimaced. "I apologize. I just couldn't take any more politics."

"I might have liked to stay." Fox Lisa tossed her head. "Penny seemed pretty pleased with my introductory speech."

"Well, she . . ." Griffen stopped. Maestro and Ann Marie were pointedly not listening, but it was a courtesy. They could still hear him perfectly well.

"Was it something that happened in the ladies' room? Did she say something that pissed you off? I noticed you didn't say another word to her all the way back."

"That's it," Griffen said, thankful for a plausible-sounding excuse. "I didn't like the way she treated that woman."

"The lo— I mean, her?" Fox Lisa belatedly realized they were not alone. "You didn't like how Penny treated *her*? I thought she was threatening Penny!"

"Well, it wasn't exactly how it looked on the surface," Griffen said. "Penny was pretty harsh with her. She went away . . . really unhappy."

The news did not have the effect that Griffen wanted it to. Instead of being appalled, Fox Lisa was enchanted. Her wide eyes sparkled.

"You mean Penny told her off? Wow! Really? Nothing frightens her, does it?"

"No," Griffen said, grimly. "I guess not."

Griffen realized he had made a tactical error. He had made Penny more of a heroine to Fox Lisa than she had been before. Instead of warning her off the candidate, he had made her sound more attractive than ever. He'd have to explain it more fully when he and Fox Lisa were alone. He played a couple of more frames with Ann Marie, keeping the conversation firmly on general topics.

"I hear Bad Beth's at Yo Mama's tonight," he suggested. Both of them liked Beth Patterson, a local performer with a warm, husky voice who performed Celtic- and magic-themed songs at her regular shows. Once in a while, though, she assumed the persona of Bad Beth, who sang raunchy numbers and openly reviled the "other Beth" for being a strait-laced bore. "You always enjoy her shows. Want to go over with me later?"

Fox Lisa yawned deeply. "No, thanks. I'd love it, but I'm going to make it an early night. I've got work tomorrow. My boss let me have the day off for the drive to Arcadia, but I'd better be on time in the morning. I don't think Penny ever sleeps. Maybe tomorrow night?"

Griffen ran through the calendar in his head and found a reasonably empty evening.

"It's a date," Griffen said. He felt a sudden craving for one of Yo Mama's peanut-butter-and-bacon burgers. "Let's go for dinner, too."

"Sounds great," Fox Lisa said. She finished off her drink and the last of her sandwich. Her eyes met his and twinkled mischievously. "You want to come home with me now?"

"I thought you were tired," Griffen said, with a wicked grin.

She returned it. "Some things are better than being tired."

He leaned over and kissed her. "I'd love to, but I'd better wait here. Jer is coming by for a last-minute confab before this evening's games."

"All right," Fox Lisa said. "See you tomorrow."

Accompanied by a chorus of farewells from the regulars, Fox Lisa went out into the night. Griffen checked the time.

"One more game?" Ann Marie asked.

"Can you afford it?" Griffen countered.

"Maybe *you* can't," she said. "Rack 'em up. I'm feeling hot."

Griffen bent over to settle the balls, then removed the frame from the table. He stood back. Ann Marie glanced at him. She touched her neck and nodded her head toward him.

"You afraid of something?" she asked.

Griffen looked down at his own neck. Under his shirt he wore a string of red and black beads that Rose had given him. It had become such a natural impulse to put them on that he never thought about them anymore.

"They were a gift from a friend."

Ann Marie lifted an eyebrow. "You have a good friend. He thinks you need protection."

"She," Griffen corrected her.

"Even better." She shook an armful of bracelets at him. He recognized some of the symbols from his occasional browses through the local occult and voodoo shops and knew those were not for show. "Don't forget to be grateful to the gods who look after you."

Griffen spread his hands. "I don't know how much of it I believe, Ann Marie. A lot of things have changed my mind about the supernatural since I was a child."

"As the saying goes, son, it doesn't matter if you don't believe in God," Maestro said. "He still believes in you."

"You've got to find answers to your own questions," Ann Marie said.

"I've got one if you won't be offended by it," Griffen said.

"Fire away, Griffen," she said, with a laugh. "I can always whack you with a cue stick if I'm offended."

"What do you know about zombies?"

"What we really believe or what we tell the tourists?"

"The real thing. I need to know."

"Mind slaves? You can read up on that. I can give you the

titles of some good books, and a practitioner or two who have had to pull a few unfortunate souls out of the hands of unscrupulous people."

"I might have to look into that kind," Griffen said. "You know about that truck driver who had the crash outside a few weeks ago. He doesn't even remember getting into the truck. I'm thinking of the other kind. The, uh, walking dead."

Maestro and Ann Marie burst out laughing.

"New Orleans is full of those, Griffen," Maestro said. "This town's too good to leave, even when your time is up."

"I'm serious," Griffen said. "Who can make that happen? I mean, life after death?"

"We're serious, too," Ann Marie assured him. "Personal matter?"

"Yes."

"You being haunted?"

"Not exactly. Not me."

"Okay." Ann Marie thought hard for a moment. She and Maestro exchanged a glance. Their expressions were grave.

"Let me get back to you, honey," Ann Marie said. "I have to ask someone's permission before I can even give you their name. Give me a couple of days."

"Thanks," Griffen said. "I appreciate it."

A trio of men came in, all African-American, all in their early twenties, wearing baseball jackets over the inevitable jeans and T-shirts. On the surface, they looked no different than any New Orleans citizens, but it was the way they held themselves, the way their eyes moved, that set them apart. Griffen recognized one of them. He put the cue stick down across the corner of the table.

"Hey, Anatole, where y'at?"

"Hey, Mr. McCandles." Anatole's mouth stretched in a smile, but it didn't touch his eyes.

"Everything okay?"

"Yeah." He pulled a cell phone out of his pocket and pushed the green button. "Okay," he said into the mouthpiece.

A few moments went by before the door opened. Gris-gris shouldered in. Griffen was shocked. The gambler was always thin, but he had lost more weight since Griffen had seen him last. His gleaming dark skin had a gray pallor. The whites of his eyes were streaked with red.

"Hi, Gris-gris," Griffen said. He offered a hand. Gris-gris looked at it in disgust.

"I don't touch the hands of traitors," he said.

Griffen blinked. "Come again?"

Gris-gris's intense dark gaze grabbed his. "You been stealin' my customers while I was dyin'. And to think I felt you was my brother."

Griffen realized that the men had surrounded him while he was speaking to Gris-gris. At the bar, the other regulars were watching. Very subtly, men and women alike reached into pockets or handbags for the personal weapons they carried, and armed themselves. Not as subtly, Fred the bartender reached underneath the counter and came up with a battered Louisville Slugger. Griffen was family. If he needed to be defended, they had his back.

Griffen looked deep into Gris-gris's eyes. Something was wrong there. The other man kept blinking, as if his thoughts troubled him. There was an odd smell on his clothes and hair, like a musty spice. It made Griffen cough.

"I haven't seen any of your customers," Griffen assured him, trying to remain calm. "Your guys have been running your games. If anyone came from your tables and didn't tell me he normally plays with you, I apologize."

Gris-gris almost spat. "Not good enough," he said.

"What's not?"

"You sayin' it. I know it's true. And you swept my lady away. I looked everywhere, and no one seen her."

"Gris-gris, I swear I haven't seen Val since Mardi Gras. I'm as worried as you are." He peered closely at the other mån. Gris-gris kept clenching his fists and jaw. He really wasn't listening to what Griffen was saying. "If she wanted to break up with you, she'd do it herself. She's not shy. You know she's been happy with you. I wouldn't interfere with that."

"Hold it," Ann Marie said. She pushed her way into the circle and took Gris-gris by the jaw. He batted at her hand, but she had a healthy grip. She stared into his eyes. "He's not right, Griffen. He the one you wanted help with?"

"No," Griffen said, grimly. "This is new. But I think it goes back to the same place."

Ann Marie looked up at Gris-gris's escort. "This man shouldn't be out of bed. You take him home. I have to call someone." She turned to Griffen. "Did you touch him?"

"Uh, no," Griffen said, alarmed.

"Then you go home. I'll take care of him. I'll call you later."

Twenty

". . . So there are no concerns from any department for you to address at the moment," Marcella finished, flipping her notebook closed. Her mouth sealed into a firm line.

She and Val stood alone in the front foyer at the base of the grand staircase. For the previous few days, Henry had stood at Val's shoulder as she took the daily report. Today, in her hand, she held a note in Henry's flowery but immaculate handwriting that she was ready to take the report alone and would be expected in place at 10:00 A.M. When Val had come downstairs, Marcella had been waiting for her. Alone. Val had hesitated a while, expecting the rest of the staff. As the minutes had ticked by, Val realized no one else was coming. Reluctantly, she had asked Marcella for her report. It was short and not at all sweet.

"May I go now?" the housekeeper asked with some asperity. "I have many duties waiting for me."

Val desperately wanted to regain the appearance of authority. She cleared her throat.

"Can I ask how Agnes is doing? And the baby?"

"They are well," Marcella said.

"Just well?"

"Well enough. That is all you need to know."

Val frowned at her.

"You don't really like me, do you?" Val said. "I don't know why. I'm a stranger here. You people don't have to be so unfriendly."

Marcella was unmoved.

"Mrs. Wurmley wants you to learn from us. My job does not require friendship."

"Do you think I'm trying to take something that doesn't belong to me?" Val asked. "I'm only here for a while. I'll be going home soon. I don't want anything from Melinda, except . . ." She let her thoughts drift. Marcella smiled thinly, as if her suspicions were being confirmed. Val finished her sentence very firmly. "Except for some baby clothes. And the crib. I really need a nice crib."

"I see," Marcella replied, her voice even. "Can you honestly say you don't want a portion of Wurmley Enterprises?"

"I can't run a business," Val said. "All I do is pour drinks. I still have to finish college. I'm struggling here. Cut me a little slack. All I did was conceive a baby. If you think that makes me some kind of criminal mastermind, I have news for you, honey. As far as I'm concerned, I got swept up in some kind of whirlwind and whisked away to Oz. I don't even have ruby slippers."

Marcella didn't laugh, but her stony face seemed to relax a tiny bit.

"Would you like a pair?"

Val did laugh. "Only if they will take me back to New Orleans. I'm just trying to fit in, okay?"

"All right," Marcella said. She hesitated. "I really need to get back to work."

"Okay," Val said. "Report accepted. Thanks."

Marcella left but not with the same resentful stride as she had in days past. In fact, if Val had to put a name to her attitude, it would have been "thoughtful."

From that day onward, it did seem to Val as if the staff eased off the pressure it had been exerting on her in subtle ways. Her breakfast juice was never again sour. The towels waiting for her as she climbed out of the pool were not only perfectly dry instead of damp, but warmed. All of the estate's employees greeted her with a little more friendliness and patience. Once she had reassured them that she knew her place, they treated her as a guest instead of an imposition. Privately, Val thought it was hilarious that they felt they needed to defend Melinda against her.

The only one who didn't give her any room was Henry. The blond secretary never ceased to try to incorporate her further into the household. He lost patience when she didn't remember business facts that he had thrown at her in passing. Val wanted to strangle him even though she was learning more every day under his tutelage than she had in college. He seemed unaware of the minor conspiracy to make life easier for her. Marcella made sure that Val got breaks when she needed them, gave her the household report succinctly and coherently in the mornings so she didn't have trouble remembering the facts, and never brought her a problem for which she couldn't supply an answer. Val doubted Henry suspected someone was helping her crib for her debriefings with him in the afternoon.

Marcella had eased up so much that she began dropping by in the morning when Val had her breakfast and sharing the pot of coffee. Fraternizing with Val was probably strictly against the rules, so neither ever mentioned the second cup on her tray. Val learned Marcella had worked for the Wurmleys since she got out of college with a degree in hotel management. Her dream was to run a boutique hotel someday. She thought she was getting good experience here. Val realized that the dour woman was probably only about ten years older than she was. She just seemed so much older.

The staff was clearly intrigued and tickled by the growing relationship between her and Mike Burns. Val found new clothes in her closet that fit her changing body but were undeniably sexy at the same time. Magazines were left in her room turned to articles that he invariably found interesting if she brought them up. They were trying to facilitate the romance. Val thought it was cute of them. It was like having Cinderella's little dressmakers working for her. It was hard not to enjoy herself. And Mike.

If she had invented him, she would have found it difficult

to devise a more perfect man. Mike always looked gorgeous but not fussy. His blue eyes just melted her. He complimented her on her clothes and laughed at her jokes and stories. When they went out, he took her to small, quiet restaurants and clubs where they could talk. He never pushed. Val found that intriguing. Most of the guys she had gone out with had tried to get her into bed on the first night. She liked being with him. Every time the phone rang in the mansion, she hoped it would be Mike, asking for an evening out.

After a few dates, they found themselves gravitating back to the jazz club where they had had their first date.

"My life? My life's dull," Mike said, pitching his voice over the sound of the blender. The slim male bartender had recognized the lovely blond woman immediately and threw pieces of cut fruit into his food processor and squeezed a lime over the top. He poured out the orangy mixture, popped a maraschino cherry onto the top, and placed it before her. Val sipped it. The silky mixture was tart, sweet, and tangy. Her salivary glands puckered for a moment, then relaxed.

"That's delicious," she said. "I could get some great tips if I served that at my bar. What's in it?"

The bartender grinned.

"Mango, peaches, fresh lime juice, a half spoonful of bar sugar, cantaloupe, and a handful of peeled grapes."

"God. That's fantastic!" She attacked the straw again, draining a quarter of the glass in two or three sips. The two men chuckled. Mike slipped a five over the polished wood counter. The bartender accepted it and moved away to serve another customer. Val made a face at Mike. "Don't laugh at me. Taste this. It's great."

"I'm not laughing at you," he said. "I like to see you enjoying things. I'm pleased that I can bring you new experiences. It's hard to compete with New Orleans."

The name brought a surge of memories of the city back

to Val all at once, especially faces. She thought of Gris-gris and felt guilty.

"You know, I have a boyfriend at home."

Mike's eyebrows went up. "Serious?"

"Pretty serious."

"Are the two of you exclusive?"

Val had to think for a moment. "Well, we have been up until now. We never really discussed it."

Mike looked reluctant, but he was always the total gentleman.

"Should I take you home?"

"No, you don't have to," Val said after a moment. She really hated to have the evening end. "I've been gone so long, he might have found someone else by now. He's a pretty amazing guy."

Mike's shoulders relaxed. He hadn't wanted to go, either. Val was glad.

"What does he do?"

"He runs a gambling organization," Val said. "Like my brother."

"Really?

Val stared at him and clapped a hand over her mouth. She had a momentary vision of horror: Gris-gris and Griffen being taken away in handcuffs. The guilt surged again, overwhelming her. She found a tiny voice.

"I don't know if I should have admitted that to you."

Mike grinned at her and drained his glass.

"Well, don't worry about it. I'm not an officer of the court. I'm just a businessman."

Val pantomimed wiping sweat off her face. "Whew! Sometimes I forget I'm not back home."

Mike smiled and signaled for more iced tea. "It's fine. I don't like to judge other people . . . Could you see yourself marrying this boyfriend one day?"

"I don't know. We're having fun together." That statement sounded lame even to her. It wasn't fair to Gris-gris, either. It didn't say anything about how gallant he had been, how protective, and how incredibly good in bed he was. Mike didn't comment. She guessed part of being a politician was diplomacy.

"Do you ever want to get married?" he asked.

Val smiled sheepishly.

"I suppose so. I've had the fantasy every girl does, with the big day, the big dress, the big cake. Then I have to laugh because I live in blue jeans most of my life."

"So do I," Mike confessed. "I have to wear suits in public, but what I really love is my old college sweatshirt, broken-in jeans, and a pair of Birkenstocks."

"I would never have picked you for a sandals guy," Val laughed.

"Well, I've got tough skin."

"Me, too," Val said, then stopped. She wasn't about to discuss her newfound dragon heritage with a total stranger. "I used to go barefoot most of the summer."

"I always did. I love the feel of grass between my toes."

Val laughed.

"You're not like any of the other politicians I've met," she said.

"I am so glad you noticed," he said. "I hope I can convince you I am a very different kind of man. So, what are your plans after the baby is born?"

"I don't really know yet," Val said. "I tend to wing things, but I know I have to make a plan of some kind. I know that my brother and I are going to raise it. Griffen is a good guy. We haven't been that close in past years, but I really love him. He's turning out to be Mr. Overprotective." Val looked around the big room. It was late enough in the evening that he would be out and about. She ought to be able to catch him, maybe in the Irish pub. If he had seen Gris-gris, he could tell her.

"What are you looking for?" Mike asked.

"A phone," Val admitted. "I haven't talked to Griffen in a month. I have a lot I need to ask him."

He smiled a little sadly. "Can't you wait until after you get home?"

Val was immediately contrite. It had to be pretty insulting of her to be sitting with him and want to speak with someone else.

"I'm sorry. I'm being rude." She changed the subject immediately. "So, when did you first know you wanted to run for office?"

"Student council," Mike said. Val looked at him in mock despair.

"Not really!"

"Really," he admitted with a sheepish smile. A dimple formed in his right cheek. "If anyone was going to be in charge, I wanted it to be me."

Val laughed. It was really nice to go out with this man. He was so different from Gris-gris—just as driven but less intense. Instead of being in your face demanding respect, he brought you around to believing that he should get what he wanted. He was thoughtful, always noticing what she wanted. She wondered what he would be like in bed. The fact that he held her at arm's length drove her crazy in a way, but she kind of liked it. He was waiting for her to ask him. She wondered how long she would make him wait. It added a tantalizing spice to what was becoming a comfortable relationship.

"Your glass is empty," Mike said. He signaled to the bartender. "Hey, Mel, make us both a couple of those fruit shakes."

Val smiled.

Twenty-one

Yo Mama's had some of the best burgers that Griffen had ever eaten. The small diner on St. Peter offered a wide menu with some pretty odd names, but they all tasted good. Though Griffen would never have considered the combination before Jerome persuaded him to try it, he had become fond of the peanut butter burger. With no games on the calendar to oversee, Jerome decided to join them for dinner and the show to follow.

"You never came by last evening," Griffen said, scooping up molten peanut butter and a crumble of bacon from his dish with a chunk of baked potato. "How'd the situation play out at the Days Inn?"

"Thom Masters got drunk, as usual, like I told you. On the way out, he started puking in the foyer. When the night manager, Nelly, came over to help him, he socked her in the face. Almost knocked out a tooth. I tell you, Grifter, you're going to have to turn down his money."

Griffen made a face. "He's a good loser, Jer."

"He's been hitting the bottle too hard at the games. It's impossible for the caterers to keep him from helping himself. That's not their job. If he only behaves at a game if you or I play, he's not worth it. You want me to phone him?"

"No, I will. And I'll send some flowers to Nelly."

"Make it a bottle of Crown Royal," Jerome said, with a grin. "She's got expensive taste. How's the election stuff going?"

"Pretty well," Fox Lisa said. "Griffen's getting tired of it, but I think it's exciting."

"I'm not tired of it," Griffen lied. Both of the others blew raspberries at him. "Okay, it's not first on my list of favorite activities, but it's interesting to see how candidates get elected."

"Like making sausage, or so I've heard," Jerome said with a wise grin.

"Worse."

"Now, that's not true," Fox Lisa said. "It's pretty exciting to see how those running for government office want to help people."

"Help themselves, more likely," Jerome said. "I hear it's easy to line your pockets in the name of those very people."

"That's not fair. Elected officials make far less than their counterparts in corporate jobs."

"They make that choice."

"I think most public servants are basically honest," Fox Lisa said. Both Jerome and Griffen made derisive noises. "

"Really, girl? How long you lived in this state?" Jerome asked. "The home of Huey Long?"

"All my life," Fox Lisa said. "The good people outnumber the bad by a hundred to one."

"But it isn't the good people with their hands in other people's pockets."

"Well, Penny's not like that."

"Yes, she is," Griffen said. Fox Lisa glared at him, then her expression softened.

"Is that what you wanted to tell me yesterday?"

Griffen felt terrible destroying Fox Lisa's illusions, but it was necessary.

"Yes. I'm sorry. I know you put her on a pedestal."

"She was really accepting a bribe from a loup garou?"

"She was what?" Jerome interrupted them.

Keeping an eye out for eavesdroppers, Griffen told them what had happened after Fox Lisa and the others had left the ladies' room. When he finished, Jerome threw back his head and laughed.

"She has balls," Jerome said. "I take it back, Grifter. I'd vote for someone that tough. Dragon or not, if Penny's willing to make enemies that powerful, she's got something going for her."

"I told you," Fox Lisa said happily. "I'd do almost anything for her."

"Watch out," Griffen said. "She might ask you to."

As the evening went on, the restaurant filled up in anticipation of the late show. The star attraction for the night, a slim, pretty, blond woman in her early thirties wearing a blue silk bustier and a leather collar, arrived with her backup musicians, and they began their sound checks. Griffen, Fox Lisa, and Jerome moved upstairs and found a table where they would have a good view of the small stage. The upper room was decorated with S&M equipment and a stripper pole.

For a Wednesday evening, the bar was full, a tribute to Bad Beth's popularity. Smoke, mostly tobacco, began to create a blue haze under the spotlights. Griffen caught the attention of a female server setting down a margarita for the blond woman next to them.

"Can we have a refill?" he asked, holding up his empty Diet Coke glass. The server made a note of their choices and slipped away between the seats. The blonde beside them leaned over and held up her drink.

"You ought to try the margaritas. They mix them nice and strong." She ran a finger around the edge of her décolletage. She wore a skintight tank top made of bright orange spandex that was cut almost all the way down to her nipples. Those showed prominently against the thin fabric.

"Thanks for the suggestion," Griffen said nonchalantly. He turned back to Fox Lisa. "Come on over tomorrow evening. I just picked up a copy of *The Candidate*, with Robert Redford. It's a great movie."

"Yeah, I saw that one," Jerome said. "It's good. You'll like it."

"All right," Fox Lisa said. "Maybe it'll give me some pointers on this election."

"I think you're doing fine," Griffen said. "Everyone was pretty impressed with your appearance onstage, and I know you've been working hard. How's it going in St. Bernard Parish?"

Fox Lisa was glad of an opportunity to talk about her organization. ". . . and that was how I found Norbert St. Clair. He was an assistant public-relations manager for the last senatorial election. He likes Penny and likes the chance to work for an independent campaign. He's taken most of the work out of my hands, which is great for me. We've got a lot of volunteers ringing doorbells and handing out flyers for Penny's law-and-order initiative. I'm trying to get young voters involved, the ones for whom this will be the first election in which they get to vote."

"I think this'll be my second chance to vote," Griffen said. "I know I voted when I was in college, but I didn't really pay close attention to any of the candidates."

"Well, this is my first time, and I'm pretty excited," Fox Lisa said.

"I don't know what number this is for me," Jerome said. "I know that a couple of times it was tough to get into the polls. Some people didn't make it easy for us."

"That's one of the reasons I volunteered for St. Bernard Parish," Fox Lisa said. "I want to encourage young African-American voters to get involved and cast their ballots. Even if they don't want to elect Penny, everyone has the right to have their voices heard."

"Hear, hear," Jerome said. He reached for the check as the cocktail waitress set down their drinks. "And in support of your efforts, I'll get this."

Fox Lisa smiled, dimples showing in her cheeks. "Thanks, Jerome."

"Don't forget, I want favors when your candidate's in office."

"Hey!" Fox Lisa protested, shoving him playfully.

"What?" Jerome said. "I'm a realist."

The musicians finished their warm-up. Bad Beth, guitar in hand, stepped up to the microphone and began to sing. Griffen recognized the tune as a classic rock song by Bryan Adams, but the words were all Beth's own. Her husky voice laid out the lyrics slyly, building up to the punch line at the end of the first verse, which she delivered with her finger stuck in her mouth.

The audience laughed appreciatively. It was prepared to enjoy itself. Most of the patrons sat with anticipatory grins, cheering especially naughty lyrics. Griffen could tell who was an old fan and who had never seen the show by the looks on their faces. A very young couple near the top of the stairs, probably visitors to the city, was openly shocked at first. The boy started to get into it almost right away, but the girl's face glowed with embarrassment. She stood up and tried to persuade her boyfriend to leave. He pulled her down and put his arm around her. Her shoulders stayed stiff for a while, but the raunchy good humor of the crowd and the fun of the music eventually broke through her reserve. By the end of the first number, she applauded as loudly as the others.

"This is a new song," Beth said. She took a drink from a tumbler balanced on a stool at her side and toasted someone sitting in the audience. "Inspired by a friend of mine. Hope you like it. If you don't, too bad. Frigging eavesdroppers."

She struck up a chord and launched into a rousing song. Griffen listened with growing admiration. He thought of himself as pretty open-minded, but he realized that there was a lot he didn't know about other people's sex lives that he probably didn't *want* to know. The audience let out bellows of approval at every verse. By the second, they joined in the chorus. When the last guitar lick died away, Beth grinned at them. She and her band stopped to take a drink and retune.

The blonde next to Griffen leaned over and ran her fingers down the side of his neck.

"That sounded like fun," she purred. "Want to go back to my place and try it?"

"Sorry, honey, he's busy tonight," Fox Lisa said, removing the blonde's hand from Griffen's shoulder between finger and thumb and dropping it like a wet rag. "I bet there're some other guys here who would take you up on it."

"Oh, you could share," the other woman said.

"No, thanks," Fox Lisa said. "I don't think you're my type."

"You don't know what you're missing."

"I don't know . . . chlamydia?"

"Ooh," Jerome said, looking as if he was in pain. "Score one for the foxy redhead."

The blonde looked like she wanted to throw the remains of her drink at them. Instead, she got up and stalked out. Griffen was glad to see her go.

Beth returned to the microphone with her signature Irish bouzouki in hand, a stringed instrument like an overgrown mandolin. "This is a number from the Old Country, where the winters are frigid but the women aren't." She gave the laughing audience a broad wink and swept her fingernails down across the strings.

Griffen enjoyed Beth's performances in both incarnations. His newfound sensitivity to dragons, gained during the Mardi Gras season, had told him that Beth had dragon blood. Maybe not much, but definitely some. He wondered if she knew it, and he wondered what the other patrons would do if they found out. Probably nothing different; New Orleanians were so easygoing that they might just start asking for dragon music. Whatever that was.

Fox Lisa's purse started buzzing loudly enough to be heard over the music. She gave an apologetic look to the annoyed people nearby and edged out of the room.

While she was gone, the sozzled blonde made her way back in and sat down between Griffen and Jerome. Politely but firmly, Griffen helped her out of the chair and into her own. She drank the rest of her margarita and signaled for another one.

Fox Lisa returned a couple of minutes later. Griffen held her chair for her.

"I can't stay," she whispered. "That was Horsie. She said Penny wants me to come to headquarters to work on a speech with her."

"At this hour?" Griffen asked.

The redhead made a face. "I told you, Penny doesn't sleep. She's always working. I wish I could keep up with her."

"Are you going?"

Fox Lisa nodded eagerly. "She wants me to help her."

"She has speechwriters. Professionals. Don't they write everything for her?"

"I know, but Horsie said she wants my input. She said I had some ideas that she wants to include in her next rally. Isn't that great?"

"I suppose so," Griffen said. "Do you want me to go over with you?"

"No, thanks. Stay. I'll take the bus." Fox Lisa glanced at the stage. "I hate to leave in the middle of the show. She is so good." The audience burst into applause. Fox Lisa stood up. "I'd better get out of here."

Jerome stood up, too. "I'll drive you over. I've got a date in about half an hour."

"Thanks, Jer," Fox Lisa said. She leaned over to kiss Griffen. "See you tomorrow. Too bad. I was looking forward to after the show."

Griffen mustered a leer. It wasn't too difficult, considering the subject matter of the show. "Come on by later. I'll be up."

"I'm counting on it," Fox Lisa said.

She and Jerome slipped out of the room. Griffen felt reluctant to remain, but he didn't feel like going back to his apartment just yet. It didn't make sense to go home alone, when the bawdy good mood of the crowd was so infectious. He decided to take the blonde's advice and indulge in a frozen margarita.

The drink's combination of sweet and salty went unusually well with the lyrics of Bad Beth's songs. Griffen leaned back to enjoy both. The woman next to him kept up her intake of tequila. She really got into the sing-alongs. Griffen was impressed that she knew all the words to "Show Me on the Doll," a shockingly funny song that had made him blush the first time he heard it. At the end, he applauded hard, offering a few claps to his neighbor for her enthusiastic rendition.

"Thanks, handsome," she said, leaning close. "Too bad your friends left."

"Yeah, it is," Griffen said. He leaned away, putting his drink between them. "They'll both be sorry to have missed the end."

"I love a good happy ending," the blonde said. Her blue eyes were huge, outlined with royal blue liner. She toyed with his drink. She ran her forefinger around the rim, then ostentatiously sucked it off. Griffen turned away to listen to the show.

The blonde was not that easily put off. She shifted closer. Her hand tiptoed onto his thigh and into his lap. Griffen captured her wrist and shoved it away.

"Hey, I'm flattered, but I'm taken."

"I hate to see you stay lonely."

"I'm not lonely," he said pointedly. "I'm enjoying the show."

"You could enjoy it more with me, Griffen. We could have such a good time together if you'd just relax." For a moment, her eyes changed in shape, lengthening and adding sea-blue highlights. It was Penny Dunbar.

Griffen started to stand up, but she grabbed him by the arm.

"Don't be shocked," she said. "I can't go to shows like this as myself. So I don't. That way I can have a good time, and no one will ever know." She wrapped his arm in hers and rubbed her breasts against his chest. "Doesn't the music give you some ideas? Hmm?"

"Plenty, but I'm saving them for Fox Lisa. You know we're seeing each other."

"I know." Her lips brushed against his ear and bit gently. "And another girl, too, I understand. So you're polyamorous. So am I. I'm sure Fox Lisa won't mind since she's already sharing you, and it's me."

"I mind!"

Penny smiled lazily. "You like to be the one in charge? I like that. I'll try anything you want me to." She snuggled up. Her fingers felt along his belt for the buckle. "I wasn't happy when you took off yesterday. I wanted to explain."

"I think I understood what I saw," Griffen said. He removed her hand from his waistband. She shifted her grip.

"You're taking the moral high ground with me?" Penny asked, laughing. "How pointless! And how hypocritical, Mr. Gambling Tycoon. Your uncle told you to take good care of me."

"This is not what he meant."

"How do you know what he meant? Can't you just let go and be someone else tonight? Look around you. No one is who they seem. Even Beth is being bad for tonight. This is the greatest city in the world because you can be whoever you really want to, and no one minds. In fact, they encourage it. You really should try it, you know." She gave him a wicked smile. "You'd probably like it. I'm told I'm very good."

"Thanks, but I'd rather not. I really care for Fox Lisa."

The blue eyes turned flint gray.

"You know what happens if you don't do what I say," Penny whispered.

"Go ahead," Griffen said. "I'm tired of your threatening me. Report me. I'll be an item on the evening news, something out of your law-and-order campaign, then everyone will forget about it. This is New Orleans."

"Not if I report Fox Lisa, too," Penny said.

Griffen was horrified. "For what?"

"I think they call it aiding and abetting," Penny said. Her eyes never left his. A tiny smile played along her lips. Griffen almost trembled with anger. Smoke drifted from his nostrils.

"You'd do that to her? She admires you. She looks up to you!"

"Cute, isn't it? But she's a child, and I'm a woman. A fellow dragon. Your equal. Come on. Let's go back to your place. Fox Lisa never has to know."

"*How* much?" Griffen demanded in outrage, raising his voice above the music. Penny's eyes widened in surprise.

"What?" she asked.

Hastily, Griffen shoved her away and stood up.

"Forget it! I don't pay for sex!" He sidled out of the row and all but ran toward the stairs. He had to get out of there.

Murmurs followed him, and Griffen was afraid Penny would, too. His fellow music lovers would think they just saw a local "businesswoman" stating her price and overestimating what she was worth to her john. Surprise should keep her in place long enough for him to get away.

Griffen thumped down the stairs and out into the street. Jerome had warned him that dragon females were "kind of wild." Griffen realized he'd had no idea what that meant until that very moment. Penny really had no limits on going after what she wanted. She was willing to sacrifice anyone and anything to get her way. She was dangerous.

He thought of going back to the Irish pub, to sit among friends, but he needed to work through his outrage in private. He had to stop associating with Penny, and he needed to extract Fox Lisa from her clutches. Who knew what Penny would do to her if she wanted revenge against Griffen for rejecting her?

It was time to call Malcolm and change the terms of their agreement.

Twenty-two

Val hung on to the phone receiver, counting the rings. Six. Seven. Eight. Gris-gris had to answer sometime. She had tried every day, two or three times, as often as Henry would let her. This time she was determined not to let up until she got through. She drummed her fingers on the sitting-room table. It went to voice mail. She hung up and tried again. Five. Six. Click!

"Hello?" Val said.

"Hello?"

"Gris-gris?"

"No."

"Isn't this his phone? Who is this? Is he all right?"

"Oh, yeah, he all right," the voice said. It sounded faintly familiar. "Dis Jean-Claude. Gris-gris cain't ansa right now. He busy."

Val ran through the faces she knew of Gris-gris's employees and friends. She couldn't place Jean-Claude, but that didn't mean anything. Her boyfriend knew a lot of people. She would have left a message at his home, but like many people in the Quarter, he had no landline, only a cell phone.

"Well, can you take a message?" Val asked.

"Uh, mebbe. Lemme see if I can find somethin' t' write on."

Suddenly, the connection clicked off. Val found herself listening to dead air. No wonder she hadn't been able to reach Gris-gris! It sounded like someone had stolen his phone, maybe while he was still in the hospital. The nurses there assured her he was fine when he had been discharged. There was no other reason why she hadn't been able to get a call through.

Gris-gris wasn't the only one she hadn't been able to reach. Griffen had never returned any of her messages. She couldn't get through to Mai. Her uncle Malcolm wasn't home. Why couldn't she reach anyone in New Orleans? Had the whole city moved while she was gone?

A tiny foot kicked her in the midsection. Val patted her belly.

"Nice to know someone is still with me," she said. "What do you think? Where is your uncle?" Was Griffen mad at her because she had taken off without letting him know? She'd left him detailed messages often since then. How immature to give her the silent treatment. It wasn't as if they spent every moment together when she was in town. In fact, the two of them had been closer the last year than they had since they were small children. She doubted Griffen would stay mad for long. He had already begun to sound like an overprotective uncle. She wouldn't be surprised if he was already filling up her apartment with baby toys.

The doctor had been by for a second monthly prenatal checkup. He had given Val high marks for taking care of herself. Her midsection had expanded somewhat, though the rest of her figure remained largely the same. She ran around the estate every morning, about half her normal distance because the baby's weight threw her off, but she made up the difference by doing lengths in the pool. She took vitamins. She watched her waistline though the food was great. Everyone was really nice. She had little to complain about other than feeling isolated.

"Too bad you're not much of a conversationalist," Val said. "Try me."

Val jumped out of her chair. Henry had glided in without making a sound. He stood there, his lips pursed, hands folded against the waist of his dark blue jacket.

"Don't do that!" she said. Her heart slowed to its normal pace. He waved a dismissive hand. As usual, he was impeccably dressed. His velvet blazer and soft, faille trousers made Val feel as though she had slept in a pigpen and woke up during a cotillion. Henry waved an impatient hand.

"Sorry, but you're late for our meeting. We need to get this accounting done." He brandished a ledger at her. She groaned. "You said you were an economics major."

"Second year!" she said. "We had only learned basic accounting and theory. I've never worked on a sophisticated budget before."

"It's just balancing numbers," Henry said. He eyed the small table. "Do you want to work on it here?"

Reluctantly, Val put the phone down. "All right. Let's do it."

"Good." Henry opened the book and shoved it in front of her. "We were going over the first-quarter input and output."

"Why doesn't Melinda have this on a computer?" Val said. "There are some really good spreadsheet programs."

"She does. But computers are vulnerable. Having a set of physical books is a backup that makes sense."

"Well, why aren't we doing this on the computer and entering it into the book by hand later?"

"Somatic memory," Henry said. "If you handle something, you will remember where it is. On a computer, everything is just pixels. You'll have a relationship with the keyboard, not the data. If you would really like, you can do the data input yourself later."

"No, thanks," Val said. She glanced at the intricate brass clock on the green marble console table near the wall. "Mike is picking me up for dinner. I want to have time to change."

"Then let's get on with it," Henry said. He opened the book and pushed it toward her.

"You talk about body memory," Val said, "but all this is still theoretical to me. What is this for?"

"One of Melinda's businesses. We thought we would start you off small."

"What does it do?" Val asked, suddenly curious. At the top of the first page, PREPPRO was stamped in gold.

"Machine-embroidered patches and clothing. Universities are its biggest market."

"Cool! Have I ever seen any?"

Henry turned to the back of the book, where she saw a three-column printout of three-digit numbers, names, and telephone numbers. "This is the customer list. And, yes," he added, as if bored with the subject already, "they are also already on computer."

Val ran down the list. She found her college, Griffen's college, and many other familiar universities, as well as some entries that sounded more like retail businesses.

"Okay," she said, flipping back to page one. She was dismayed by the endless columns of figures, but she refused to allow him to see how nervous she was. "What are we doing?"

"We're going over the expenses versus profit. Materials, salaries, office expenses, shipping, volume discounts, and so on." Henry produced a large calculator and a scratch pad from his pocket. Val was always amazed how much stuff he managed to carry without ruining the lines of his clothing. She couldn't hide a credit card without having the outline show. "What I want you to do is to familiarize yourself with the raw materials and the products they go into."

With the image of a real business in her mind, Val began comparing figures in the ledger. Beside the numbers were names, cryptic abbreviations, and notations, like "17.5 h" or "300 spls." After seeing them noted on page after page, she came to recognize the names of the seventeen employees. Pretty soon she noticed the discrepancy between the amount they were being paid.

"What's wrong with R. Stiller?" she asked.

"Hmm?"

"Well, he has the same salary as about five of the others

for a while, but during these pay periods, his income varies a lot."

"Absenteeism," Henry said. "They earn hourly wages."

"Uh-huh." Val worked in silence for a while longer. "You know, there are five suppliers of thread. Mercer and Boyes have the same note next to them sometimes." She pointed to entries that read "50 no. 17 black," on two different pages. Henry was right: Handling something physical made it easy to recall where things were.

"Good!" Henry said. "PrepPro buys standard stock from both of them."

"Is there a volume discount? Would it make sense to get a quote for all that we need of one color?"

"It might. It could take a little negotiation."

"Is fifty spools at a time a big order? Find out what their price breaks are?" Val said.

"I can put you on the phone to them tomorrow," Henry said.

"Me?"

Henry offered a bland smile in the face of her outrage.

"Why not?" Henry asked, then clicked his tongue. "Look at the time! You had better go get ready. Marcella laid out that red suit you like. You might need a wrap. It's going down to fifty tonight."

Val stood up gently. The baby had gone to sleep again. She pictured it curled up with a tiny fist in its mouth. "Thanks, Henry."

Roxanne helped Val into her dress. Val sat before the mirror, feeling as if it weren't completely her body, as the petite beautician combed her long blond hair, then applied makeup. They had had just enough time to pull Val together when Marcella leaned in the door.

"Mr. Burns is here," the housekeeper said. If she had been less dignified, she might have winked.

"Thanks, Marcella," Val said. She looked at herself in the

mirror. The red suit—rose-colored, really—had a tailored, knee-length skirt under a light jacket that was pleated slightly at the sides to allow for her expanding belly. A gleaming, round pearl the size of a gumball, set in a smooth ring brooch of gold, was pinned to the left lapel. Val had picked the piece from the jewelry box that sat on her vanity table. Henry had assured her that she was entitled to borrow any piece that she liked. Melinda would be pleased if she enjoyed them. The purse, instead of being matchy-matchy, was gold leather. Her shoes were rosewood leather with a slanted gold stripe running over the instep. The label inside identified them as Stuart Weitzman. Probably five hundred bucks. She had never owned a pair of shoes that cost more than thirty.

Fairy princess again, she thought. *It's not really real. Enjoy it while it lasts.*

"How do I look?" she asked Roxanne.

The little woman looked up at her shyly. "Very pretty."

Val gave her a one-armed hug.

"You did a great job. I'd better run."

". . . I guess I never thought about all the items you need to organize to run a business," Val concluded. She realized she had been babbling, who knew for how long? Mike Burns smiled at her. She blushed. "Sorry to run on like that."

"You sound like you grasped everything admirably," he said. "That's great." Val made a face. Mike looked apologetic. "Sorry. That sounded patronizing. I didn't mean it to. I know people who have gained and lost millions who never picked up on what you learned just going over a set of books. You could be a tycoon in five years with your acumen. That's an honest compliment."

Val toyed with her iced-tea glass. The maitre d' had noticed her figure when she walked into the restaurant beside Mike. Instead of bringing them the wine list, he offered them tea or fresh-squeezed lemonade. Val saw the glance that Mike sent toward the mahogany bar that ran along one side of the dining room. He would probably have liked to have an alcoholic drink, but he insisted on having tea, too.

"Boy, I can't pretend any longer that I'm not showing," Val said, as the busboy in bow tie and vest came over to top up her glass. The young man, probably about her age, smiled at her with a kind of avuncular approval she was beginning to see on a lot of faces.

"You are one of the most attractive pregnant women I have ever seen," Mike assured her. "Well, tell me. If you were going to open a business of your own, what would it be?"

Val dropped a couple of brown-sugar cubes into the tea and stirred it until they dissolved. The restaurant was dimly lit but not too dark. White linen tablecloths shimmered, and tiny candles in miniature hurricane lanterns on each table picked glints off the paper-thin glasses. The other diners were firelit faces with shadowy bodies. Red roses in low bowls bloomed in the middle of each table. Val inhaled the scent with pleasure.

"I never really thought about it," she said. "If I ran a business, I'd want it to be one where the employees enjoyed what they did, not just earned a paycheck."

"Not really an easy combination," Mike said. "The high-earning jobs are usually high-pressure and cutthroat."

"I know. Maybe a bookstore? I love the ones in the French Quarter. Everyone who works there seems to love it."

"Not much potential for high revenues," Mike said firmly. "Ask the proprietor sometime what kind of a profit he makes."

"I guess I'd have to think about it," Val said. "Most of the places that I like going into are fun for me, not the people who work there."

"True. Like a restaurant."

"Or a bar. I like my job, but it's a lot of hurry-up-and-wait. Some people don't tip, and some of the ones who do think they've bought me along with their drinks."

Mike smiled. "Ever have to throw a customer out?"

Val smiled back. "Not twice."

The waiter appeared at their side. Mike insisted that she choose for both of them. That surprised Val, but pleasantly. She combed her memory for what he had enjoyed at the fund-raising dinner and at the jazz club on their first date. The music had been so overwhelmingly good that she had concentrated on that, not her companion. She was determined not to make that mistake again. He had eaten red meat without complaint. Rack of lamb was listed as a special. That sounded good to her, too. The waiter listened approvingly and departed on silent feet.

"How'd you know I love lamb?" Mike asked.

"I guessed," Val admitted.

"Good guess. So, I know New Orleans is full of good restaurants. Where do you eat when you have the chance?"

The food in the restaurant was as good as the ambience. Val savored each bite, but she enjoyed Mike's company even more. He drew her out about her family, her favorite music, dreams, and aspirations. He listened closely to her, his deep blue eyes fixed on hers. Val was flattered that such a handsome and accomplished man would be interested in her. He didn't push her to be alone with him or make improper suggestions. Val thought it might have been nice if he had. She missed Gris-gris. It had been over a month since she had been with a man. Her uterus might be occupied, but the rest of her body wasn't. His hand, strong but gentle under her forearm as he helped her out of her chair, set her nerves wondering what it would feel like on other parts of her skin.

She wondered what he would say if she told him what she was thinking.

Twenty-three

"I could have eaten three of those chocolate-mousse things," Mike said, as they waited in line to pick up their wraps at the coat-check window. "Good thing I didn't. I might have fallen asleep behind the wheel."

Val eyed him with mock alarm. "Should I drive back?"

"No, I'm under the legal limit for chocolate. Sometime when you feel like real indulgence, my secretary said she visited a place about six miles from here that serves a chocolate buffet she loved."

"Sounds great," Val said. "As long as you don't call me a 'gour-moo' again. In my condition, that sounds like an insult."

Mike pleaded innocence. "It's not a judgment, I swear. It's a classification. It just means you like milk chocolate. Since you haven't read *Chocolate, the Consuming Passion*, I'll find you a copy."

Behind the wooden half door, a small Asian-looking woman in a vest and bow tie accepted the hexagonal plastic claim check and a folded bill from Mike. In moments, she brought out the correct hanger with his coat and Val's pashmina hanging from it. She handed Mike his jacket but came out of the cloakroom to help Val on with her shawl.

"Thanks," Val said, pulling the soft folds tighter over her shoulders. She felt something crisp in her palm. As Mike swung his coat around, she peeped into her hand. A note, folded small, was hidden there. Val frowned, but the woman gave her an urgent look of entreaty. Val shoved it into her purse and let Mike take her arm. They went out into the chilly night air.

Who was that woman, and why did she need to pass Val a message? Val was certain she was a stranger. Was there something about her date that she needed to know? Was Mike a known lecher or something more sinister? She couldn't look at the note without his seeing it. Mike respected her silence as they rode back to the house.

He ran around to help her out of the car and escorted her up the front steps.

"You're probably pretty tired," he said. "May I call you tomorrow?"

Val pulled herself out of her fog to smile at him.

"I'd like that," she said. "Sorry to flake out on you there."

"No problem," he said. He leaned over and kissed her on the cheek. "I really enjoyed the evening."

Val started to ask him about the coat-check girl, when the door opened, and Marcella peered out at them.

"Me, too," Val said. She returned the peck and hurried inside. The austere housekeeper took the shawl from her shoulders.

"Mrs. Wurmley called an hour ago. She wanted to know where you were. Would you like to speak to her?" Marcella asked, leading her up the double staircase toward her room.

"Sure," Val said, suddenly weary.

"I will put the call through to your room."

"Thanks."

Val trudged up the steps, no longer feeling like Cinderella but an actor in some weird, avant-garde drama. She realized once again that she had forgotten to look at the license plates while they were driving. She still didn't really know where she was. Henry always gave her a supercilious glance when she asked, and none of the others even did that much. It wasn't as if she could run off. There was only a ten-dollar bill and some change in her wallet. She didn't have her credit card with her; it was inside a package of frozen spinach in her refrigerator at home. She gave Griffen credit for one "I told you so." Not that she felt as if she were in prison, but she felt under constant scrutiny. She hated being judged. Mike was the only one who didn't seem to be evaluating her all the time, but now she wondered what she had missed figuring out about him.

The phone rang even before she closed the door. Val picked it up. The strident voice blared in her ear.

"Valerie? How are you feeling? Are you keeping your salt intake down? You don't want to risk pre-eclampsia."

"I had rack of lamb tonight. It was divine," Val countered.

"At Benoit's? That is the best—organically raised, home-grown rosemary. Good choice. Listen, Valerie, have you given up on a yellow nursery? I found an adorable purple quilt for the crib."

"Fine," Val said. "That would be nice."

"So you're going with purple?"

"No. I still like yellow."

"But it will clash!"

"The baby won't care. I certainly don't. By the time he's old enough to notice, he'll hate everything I ever picked out anyway. His room will end up papered in rock posters and skateboard decals."

"His? Is it a boy?" Melinda demanded.

Val groaned. She sat down and peeled off the Weitzmans. Her feet were ridged with red lines where the straps had crossed them. She wiggled her toes.

"I don't know, and I don't want to know."

Her dismissive tone finally got through to the older woman. "Whatever. So, did you have a nice time with Michael Burns?"

Val felt a resurgence of the pleasure of the evening. "Yes, I did."

"He's a very nice man. He has a great future, and his family is very wealthy."

Val looked at the receiver, shocked. "Melinda, are you trying to fix me up with him?"

"Why not? You're a great catch. I could tell he liked you from the first moment he spoke to you. He respects you. He'd be a fabulous mate for you. Almost your equal."

She felt her heart sink into her feet.

"Are you saying he's a dragon, too?" she demanded.

"Of course! So were most of the single men who were at the party. I thought you would like to meet some men of your own class—well, almost. You outrank all of them, but each of them has his good points. Michael is my cousin. A good boy. He has excellent prospects. Since you don't want to continue with my son. I'll admit Nathaniel likes things his own way . . ."

Val fumed. Nathaniel's "own way" had been virtual rape. "I'll pick out my own boyfriends, thanks," she said shortly.

"Whatever," Melinda said again, and changed the subject. "Henry tells me you're a quick study. I'd like you to look over some vendors for PrepPro and pick out the best prospects. I'll call you tomorrow night and get your opinion."

"Melinda, I don't work for you."

"And you have so much else to do in the meantime? I would appreciate your input. And you might learn something. How bad could that be?"

"All right! I'll take a look at them. Melinda, when can I . . . ?"

"Thank you, sweetie. I'll be back there in a week, and we'll go on that shopping trip I have been promising you. You are going to adore Paris. Talk to you tomorrow. Bye!"

Val threw the shoes against the wall. Melinda drove her crazy. She was manipulative and pushy. It took all her self-control to keep the older woman from taking over her life. She would accept only the gifts and assignments she wanted. After all, what would be so bad about learning more about business? She really didn't want to tend bar all her life.

Melinda's other revelation put a whole new light on the evening. Mike Burns was a dragon? Was that what the coat-check girl was trying to warn her about? How would she know? Val couldn't tell humans from dragons, or any of the other weird creatures that her brother had been hanging out with in the French Quarter. Until they changed, or did something magical, she didn't know the difference. Had the girl seen Mike do something wrong? Could he be dangerous to her?

She dove for her purse and retrieved the folded slip of paper. Before she opened it, she padded over to her door and locked it. For good measure, she lowered the window shades. Val hated to feel so paranoid, but there was so much going on under the surface appearance of normalcy that she was overwhelmed.

The note had been hand-printed neatly in heavy black ink, similar to the kind Mai liked to use on birthday and Christmas cards, though it didn't look like her writing. Mai usually employed a flowing script like Western letters transposed into Chinese calligraphy. Val, an average student of the Palmer school of penmanship, had always envied her skill. Mai could have printed the note to disguise her handwriting.

"Valerie McCandles. Request a private conversation with you tomorrow evening. If you will allow, fold this note and place it inside your window frame tonight." The message was unsigned. The formal wording didn't sound like Mai. Who was it from? Val was certain no one had any idea where she was. None of her friends or family had returned any of her calls, and she couldn't put a return address on a letter since she didn't know what it was. How strange that Henry and the others conspired to prevent her from determining her location, as if it were a trade secret.

She vowed not to let that last piece of information remain unknown any longer. The next day she was going to demand answers. In the meantime, she wondered who wanted a "private conversation." It might be a pretense to get close enough to attack her, but she was pretty certain she could take care of herself. If she had any trouble, she could scream for help. The mystery creeped her out somewhat, but she was intrigued as well.

Before she went to bed, she tucked the note, folded into a tiny wad, into the wooden sash. The corner just peeped up above the frame.

All right, whoever you are. Let's talk.

In the morning, the slip of paper was gone.

Twenty-four

Griffen frowned at his cell phone.

"What do you mean, 'politicians are like that'?" he demanded, his voice rising. "That's absurd. She's dangerous."

The other patrons in the Irish pub glanced at him but kept their faces neutral. If he was having an argument on the phone, he wasn't in imminent peril of getting into a fight. If he wanted help, he could ask for it. Griffen lowered his voice. They went back to their drinks and conversation.

"Penny Dunbar is canny, not dangerous." Malcolm's voice was calm. "Griffen, you called me out of an important meeting. Please give me a summary of your concerns."

Griffen had dialed his uncle's office number with every intention of being patient, but the dismissive tone roused his righteous indignation.

"Penny lied to Fox Lisa to get her out of the room the other night so she could hit on me."

He could hear the smile in Malcolm's voice. "I have never before heard of an occasion when you rejected female companionship, Griffen."

"This was not an ordinary pass. When I turned her down, she threatened to expose Fox Lisa by dragging her in front of the public with me on trumped-up charges of illegal gambling operations. I'll take responsibility for my own actions, but I refuse submit to blackmail of an innocent person. I just wanted you to know that I quit."

"Griffen, please! I cannot drop everything and take over

protecting Miss Dunbar at this moment. I implore you to continue as you have been doing."

Griffen glared at the phone.

"She's eating up all my spare time. She's not even nice about it. Every time I tell her I can't go with her to an appearance, she drags out her vague threats. This last thing was the tipping point. I'm through."

"And has she?"

Griffen blinked.

"Has she what?"

"Has she summoned the authorities or called a press conference as she warned?"

"No. I walked out. I haven't heard from her since."

"And no hue and cry has been raised over either of you, has it?"

"No."

"I believe you have your answer, then. Her bark is far worse than her bite."

Griffen crouched over the phone, trying not to snarl.

"Uncle Malcolm, I'm done with helping her, if you call it that. I still haven't found Val. I've got a business to run. I want my girlfriend to stay out of jail, and I'd like to stay out myself."

"Griffen, Ms. Dunbar would not do that. She knows how much she requires your help. And mine."

"I wouldn't trust her as far as I can throw her," Griffen said. "If it came down to a minute of publicity versus five years in jail for me, I'd better hire a lawyer now."

"The fact is that she would not cause you any permanent distress."

"The fact is," Griffen said, enunciating as clearly as possible in as low a voice as he thought would be audible on the other end, "that if she causes my girlfriend any problems, I will kill her myself, and to hell with whatever it is you hope to accomplish getting her into the governor's mansion."

"Please, Griffen, Ms. Dunbar needs you. Don't make hasty decisions."

The spark of fire that resided in Griffen's belly danced up and down, pleading to get out and cause havoc. Griffen tamped it down with difficulty.

"I'm not acting hastily. It's been weeks since you asked for my help. She's a nightmare to deal with. I've seen her use blackmail on a number of people already. My business may skirt the law, but I don't stoop that low."

Malcolm chuckled. "I never thought that I would be lectured on ethics by you."

That stung, but Griffen ignored it.

"Yes, well, things change."

"Indeed they do. Griffen, I am certain you can find a way to remain involved. Be diplomatic."

"I'm not a diplomat," Griffen said. "It's your turn. I was doing you a favor. I'm through with that. She's trouble. There's no way I could ask anyone to vote for her. I can't imagine what kind of problems she would cause if she actually became governor."

"Penny is part of a much larger picture, Griffen. I apologize for not taking the time to lay it out for you. We need fellow dragons in positions of power. She is willing, hardworking, and cognizant of the rough-and-tumble aspects of politics. Not many of our kind wish to put themselves into the public spotlight."

"Believe me, she revels in it."

"So I perceived. Griffen, I am in a bind. My time is limited . . . as I know yours is. Please continue to assist us."

"Nothing happens to her! She engineered the only trouble she's been in."

"The car accident?"

Griffen hesitated. "I'm not sure about that. She could have."

"For what reason?"

"Headlines. She'll do anything to get in front of a camera. But those two events looked staged. She probably did it for the publicity."

"I'm afraid that does not set her aside in any way from

other candidates. Such things are common in hard-fought political races. I will make a bargain with you, Griffen. Give me another week to complete my current business. I will come down myself, and I will see if I can broker peace between you."

Griffen wasn't satisfied, but it was as much of a concession as he was going to get.

"All right," he said. "She's got a debate at the end of the week. I'll go, but I'll let you know if she chooses the nuclear option with me."

Malcolm's voice was dryly sardonic.

"I fancy that I will see that for myself on the evening news. Thank you, Griffen. Good-bye."

Twenty-five

Mai struggled with her Patagonia tent. She wanted to go back to New York and take the Erewhon salesman by the scruff of his neck up to the top of a very high building. She would listen to him describe once again how easy it was to deploy—yes, his word—*deploy* the three-man dome tent, then she would drop him from the heights into the midst of Manhattan midday traffic. She yanked the skewerlike tent peg from the long grass and flung it down. Nothing to do but start over again. She flipped the misshapen bundle of cloth out like a bedsheet and felt for the grommets. Her hands were getting dirty, as were the knees of her expensive, zip-leg, tropical trousers. She longed for a leisurely soak in a nice, deep bathtub, and she resented hugely that it was impossible.

She wished that she could stay in a hotel, but there was only one in this pitiful village in the midst of rural Pennsylvania, and Melinda's party occupied an entire wing. She could not hope to go unnoticed. Nor could any kind of tracer spell be missed. Melinda had ripped apart the subtle threads that Mai had laid on the Lexus sedan and each of the Armani suitcases in the enormous trunk. That meant, to Mai's horror, that tailing her to wherever in the world Melinda had stashed Val had to be done by actually spying on her. Luckily, New York was full of dragons and other shape-shifters, so Melinda and her goons couldn't detect her. Mai was proud of how good she had become at blending into the scenery. In her guise as a Swedish tourist, she overheard plans for the elder female's departure by hanging out near the desk of the luxury hotel.

Mai had a rented automobile waiting on the curb when Melinda emerged. She longed to have a vehicle that she truly deserved, like a late-model Maserati, but in order to remain incognito, she had to pick something more nondescript. As she sulked over the wheel of the black Prius, Melinda waddled from the building and waited while the doorman helped her into the Lexus. Behind her, the two goons escorted Lizzy out. The young female dragon grinned drunkenly at the doorman and hotel guests as she was pushed into the backseat beside her mother. No one thought much about it. Between the *dernier cri* fashions Lizzy wore and the expensive car, she must be wealthy. Poor people were crazy. People with money were eccentric. Eccentricity was tolerated, if often with a forced grin. Mai had to smile at the thought. If they knew how dangerous Lizzy was, they'd have readjusted their thinking back to crazy, where it belonged.

Mai waited while a taxi and two cars passed before pulling out into traffic accompanied by the sound of screeching brakes. *Death before eye contact*, was the motto for driving in New York.

And thence had begun eight days of aching boredom. It seemed Melinda was not in a hurry to go home. Mai drove at a discreet distance behind her. If Melinda had detected that she had a pursuer, it appeared that she didn't care. Mai followed her into the Hamptons. Naturally, the Eastern dragons had five mansions there, but Mai could not stay in any of them without losing sight of Melinda. Instead, she was forced, at enormous expense, to take a room in a property adjacent to the sumptuous estate that opened its gates to the Lexus. Normally, such a humble car as a compact would have been refused with a sneer, but the trendy nature of the smart new hybrid gave it entrée in this trendiest of venues. Even so, her pride still ached.

In order to check in, Mai was forced to use a charge card

with a very high limit. Her honored ancestors couldn't miss a four-figure sum on the balance. Before she had unpacked her Louis Vuitton bags, the antique telephone on the bedside table sounded a whiny ring.

"Why are you not in New Orleans?" the male voice at the other end demanded.

"Most honored elder," Mai said humbly. "I am pursuing other avenues of fulfilling the assignment you gave to me."

"And how does a six-thousand-a-week villa in the Hamptons aid in that mission? Not to mention the camping equipment and wardrobe that you purchased in Manhattan? And why did you not go to visit your celestial grandmother in Chinatown? She was displeased at the slight. She even prepared your favorite delicacies."

Mai swallowed hard. Grandmother was a terrible cook, and she insisted on telling stories about long-dead relatives dating back to the fourteenth century.

"I offer my humblest apologies. My time was not my own. I must remain close to Melinda," she said. "I need to be prepared for any eventuality."

"Why? She is not Griffen McCandles!"

"She holds Griffen's sister in some place of concealment," Mai said. "Most wise father, Valerie McCandles is with child. A nearly pure-blooded dragon child."

"Ahhhhhh . . ." The voice exhaled and went silent. "And it is your intention to secure this child and its mother?"

"Yes," Mai said. "At the moment, Griffen is in thrall to Melinda, pending the safe return of his sister. If she was in *our* hands . . ." She let her voice trail off suggestively.

"That is unusually perceptive of you," the voice said. Mai made a face at the phone. "Yes, a pawn of that quality could prove very useful to us. Very well. Secure this child in any way that is necessary. But curb your endless hunger for retail purchases, Mai. To become a thrall to the physical is to ignore the wisdom of the infinite."

That was rich coming from him, Mai reflected, since his first gift to her had been a solid-gold teething ring. His own homes could have been object lessons in creative spending.

"As you say, honored ancestor," she said. "But I may need to go further to obtain possession of this infant."

"Do what you must," the voice said. "Results will defend you far better than the sound of your own tongue."

With that, the line had gone dead. Mai hadn't heard from him since. She assumed that he had gone away to confer with the other elders on the possibility of such a powerful child. Griffen might well be the young dragon of the prophecy her ancestors muttered about all the time, but he might not. What if this next generation brought the prophecy to life?

Mai was careful not to go *carte blanche* with her credit cards, but she felt freer to indulge in a few of the extravagances she had so missed during the long months she had spent in New Orleans. Fine dining was one. Cash advances for bribes was another. It turned out that her chambermaid was a friend of the receptionist at the villa next door. No, no tall, pretty woman, blond or pregnant, was staying in the mansion or any of its guesthouses, but the short woman with the many employees had excited a lot of interest.

A hefty tip each for the maid and the friend ensured that Mai would get all details of Melinda's comings and goings. The friend made a reservation for her at an exclusive restaurant in the small town at the same time as Melinda's party. Mai had gone in disguise and enjoyed the elegant-tasting fare at a table nearly back-to-back with Melinda's, but she saw no sign of Val; nor did Melinda mention her to the Tommy Hilfiger—clad dragon couple having dinner with her. In fact, they seemed to be discussing politics. Mai tuned them out and concentrated on haute cuisine.

The ensuing three days followed the same pattern. Melinda visited with other dragons resident on the island. She attended garden parties, to which Mai obtained access by disguising herself as a catering assistant or other kind of attendant but not actually doing any work. To a casual observer, Melinda was doing what any other visitor to the

Hamptons might: enjoying the springtime weather, dining well, and hobnobbing with the hoi polloi. Mai seethed privately, unable to similarly enjoy the good life as she would under her own face and name.

She was relieved when Melinda finally decamped—daughter, enforcers, luggage, and all—and headed south. To Mai's annoyance, Melinda, having enjoyed New England, took a leisurely tour of the nation's historic sites along the Eastern Seaboard. Val was not in Philadelphia nor in Colonial Williamsburg. This rural town was their third stop in as many nights. Mai hoped that Val was there in Virginia. She had to be, to make up for the horror of sleeping in a tent.

At last the khaki dome was erected. Mai surveyed it resentfully by the light of a Princeton Tech fluorescent lantern. Her Neiman Marcus titanium kitchen unit was set up and ready to heat a UHT package of Lobster Newburg. She unrolled the Integral Designs handmade custom sleeping bag inside her tent and hooked up her battery-powered lamp and cell-phone charger beside it. A bottle of vintage chardonnay chilled in a self-cooling bucket. Mai all but fell into the Hennessy hammock lounger and sighed. As the sun rolled behind the rounded peaks, she unwrapped the crystal tumbler and poured herself a welcome glassful of chardonnay. She sipped the wine and savored its fresh flavor. Even in barbaric circumstances, a good wine improved matters.

Suddenly, she heard a yell. Mai doused the lantern and rolled to a ready crouch behind the lounger. Fifty years and more of martial arts discipline had tuned her nerves and muscles to fine instruments. She set the glass where she would not step on it, and listened carefully.

The bellow was not directed at her. She peered downhill toward the guesthouse. Shrieking and crashing noises erupted at the end of the rustic building. Dogs began to bark. Mai tried to see what was happening through the windows, but sheer curtains obscured the view. She crept downhill, keeping low and silent in spite of her heavy Asolo boots.

She jumped as a dark-clad body thudded against a

window. Now she could hear crying and, above all, Melinda's voice tearing the air.

"How dare you call my daughter a freak!"

The body thumped against the window again, then disappeared. With lightning reflexes, Mai ducked aside just in time as a desk chair came crashing through the glass and landed on the gravel path alongside the building. Seconds later, a balding man in suit trousers and a short-sleeved Oxford shirt flew through the jagged opening. He landed on his shoulder and collapsed on the ground. He moaned. The arm had to hurt, but he didn't stop to tend it. He scrambled up and fled into the darkness. A heavy book and a brass bust flew out and thudded down where he had just been.

Melinda was not finished yelling. "You will be hearing from our attorneys in the morning! As if I would stay the rest of the night in this fleabag you call a historic hotel—you have no idea what a historic hotel was like! I was there! Now, get out of my way. Dean! Get the car! Lizzy, darling, calm down. The nasty man is gone."

Mai groaned. Not now! Not when she was ready to settle down for the night!

But Melinda was preparing to move on. Stocky pulled the car up to the side door and left it running as his employer shouted for him.

Mai ran silently up the hill. Without caring what damage she did, she bundled together all her camping gear and shoved it into the hatchback trunk of the Prius. The tent poles snapped. She hoped they were replaceable. Curse Melinda! Couldn't she even dawdle considerately?

Luckily, Melinda could be heard even by ordinary human ears at a distance of hundreds of yards. Mai pulled around the mountain road and was twenty feet behind the Lexus as it pulled out of the hotel drive and rolled southward. She poured herself another glass of wine.

"I refuse to let the whole evening go to waste," she said to her reflection in the rearview mirror. She lifted the crystal tumbler in a toast to herself. "Their next stop had better have a decent hotel!"

The doorbell of the New Orleans apartment rang. Penny Dunbar looked up from the mass of papers spread out across her desk. It was after eight—not too late for friends to come calling and certainly early enough for someone to come over from the campaign office. Still, it never hurt to be cautious. She picked up the holstered pistol from where it lay on the corner of the desk. She slipped her feet into the scuffs under the desk and padded over to the apartment door.

"Yes?" she asked, through the peephole.

The corridor was unusually dim. Penny peered out. A man with a baseball cap pulled down over his face stood there with a clipboard held tightly in his hands. The light made his dark skin look gray. His untidy dreadlocks spilled from under the cap and clumped on his shoulders. Penny opened the door but with her foot braced against the edge on the inside.

"Scuse me, lady, I takin' a suhvey. Who you votin' foh gov'noh dis Octobah?"

Penny sighed inwardly, but mustered a bright smile.

"Well, I'm going to be voting for Penny Dunbar," she said. She posed prettily in the doorway, waiting for the poll taker to recognize her.

The man leaned toward her, grinning, his eyes leering out from under the brim of his cap.

"You sure she gonna live to election day?" he asked.

Penny recoiled backward. The man's face looked as though a car tire had crossed it, leaving tread marks where the nose should have been and a mouthful of broken teeth. She choked with fear. But just as quickly, fierce indignation rose beneath it. She reached toward the man's throat with one hand.

"And just what do you mean, saying something like that?" she demanded, but to a blank wall.

In that split second, the man had retreated a dozen feet up the hallway, too fast for an ordinary man to move. Penny rushed out after him. He outdistanced her easily. The fire-escape door banged closed in her face. She hoisted the pistol in one hand and flung the door open.

Except that he wasn't going down the stairs. He stepped out of the shadow of the recessed apartment door ten feet away and smiled at her. Her heart pounded in her chest. She spun and squatted into a square stance, the gun pointing at him. He tipped a salute to her with a finger broken into a Z shape.

"Y'all keep in mind what I said, heah?" he said. "Have y'self a good night, now."

Twenty-six

Duvallier sat in the skybox and contemplated the open-air stage in the well-lit middle of the Superdome. That Penny Dunbar was a fine-looking woman. Spirited, too. He was enjoying the game mightily. She'd taken the last few attacks in her stride, no problem. This one ought to be ready halfway through her speech. He sat back in the elegant, padded armchair and put his thumbs behind his suspenders.

The arena, a modern white puffball of a building, its brilliant green Astroturf surface covered with a protective fitted floor, had filled up with people and equipment long before the debate was scheduled to begin. Nine of the declared candidates were present, including the two front-runners, Bobby Jindal and Kathleen Blanco. Their supporters, who must be numbering in the thousands, Duvallier estimated, waved banners and ribbons. The others, like Penny Dunbar, had fewer prospective voters present, but they all wore expressions that said they were the only people there who mattered. The multicolored seats in the stands were, for once, filled to capacity. Duvallier watched with interest as devices like small construction cranes trundled through the mass of humanity. Two or three technicians, mostly men, rode each device on tractor saddles, operating cameras and sound equipment that fed a central control room somewhere he could not see. A couple rolled around the perimeter of the arena, but most of them were right in the heart of the crowd, pointing straight at the main stage.

He also spotted men with cumbersome cameras on their shoulders racing back and forth between the moderator's table and the stage like squirrels trying to find the best nuts. It was quite a performance. Duvallier was enjoying it. He liked to see how things were done.

"I don't see how she stays in the race," Albert Sandusky said, sitting beside him. That man had a voice like a bad conscience, always haranguing. Duvallier snapped out of his pleasant reverie. "You must not be doing enough to deter her."

"You bother me enough, I won't be able to keep track of what I've got goin' on in here," Duvallier said, letting a little of his temper show. "I ain't got to be here to make this work, son. 'Fact, sometimes it makes my people a little nervous if I'm around, know what I mean?"

By the look on his face, Albert Sandusky knew exactly what he meant, but he was determined to watch Duvallier oversee the trip wires being planted in Penny Dunbar's path. Those weren't nothin' to brag about. Just another little reminder or two that there were forces out there that didn't want her goin' a step further in her political career than she already had. Tough girl, though. Big, strong men had died of fright facing what he'd sent her way. Duvallier was halfway inclined to let her go on and win, yes, win. He could make that happen. It'd take a little more effort than getting her to lose, but it might be worthwhile. He'd certainly enjoy seeing Albert's reactions. And maybe it would provoke Sandusky's reluctant partners into showing up and having a conversation with Duvallier at last. Duvallier didn't like the disrespect that the lack of such a visit showed.

At five minutes before eight o'clock, the nine candidates filed out onto the stage and took their places at matching podiums, probably brought over from Tulane University, only a few blocks from the enormous sports arena.

Each of the luxury skyboxes had been furnished with a gigantic television set built into the wall. The one to Duvallier's right came to life at that moment with a blare of sound.

Sandusky leaped for the silver-gray remote control and brought the volume down to a reasonable level. The whole Superdome was wired for sound, and pictures, which were brought right to one's easy chair. Duvallier had a superb close-up view of the candidates, one at a time and in groups, from several different camera angles.

The men were, except for hair and skin color, fairly indistinguishable from one another. Every one of them had on a dark blue suit with gray pinstripes, and a red tie. The two women wore two-piece suits like those Miss Callaway fancied, with a pale blouse underneath and a bow tied at the neck. Mrs. Blanco was an attractive woman, but she didn't shine like Miss Dunbar. Penny drew the eye. If beauty were the sole characteristic for success, she'd have won the race.

They had all had their faces made up for the cameras. A few had the grace to look embarrassed about it. Their managers and assistants bustled around, filling their water glasses, brushing imaginary flecks off the shoulders of their coats, handing them updated copies of their position papers. Sandusky's employer didn't seem unduly nervous. His manager, a fresh-faced, café-au-lait African-American man of about thirty, leaned in to murmur in his ear, pointing out lines on the papers in his hand.

"I been following your man in the newspapers," Duvallier said, lighting his cigar. Without Miss Callaway present, he felt free to indulge in tobacco. He blew a stream of fragrant smoke toward the ceiling. "Smart fellow, Congressman Benson. I remember when his daddy held the same post. Like it's been passed down in the family. Little on the dull side, ain't he?"

Sandusky's mouth dropped open in shock. "I've never told you his name, Mr. Duvallier!"

Reginaud shook his head.

"You didn't have to, son. I'm no fool. I guessed a long time ago. He's not one of the leaders, but he seems a little too plain. He has to get past Miss Dunbar's popularity to gather a large enough base to go all the way. None of the others need a face to step on as much as he does."

"Oh," Sandusky said. If a man could be said to look crestfallen, he did. "Please don't approach him, Mr. Duvallier. I implore you."

"I know, I'm your secret weapon. But when all this is over, I want to meet the man."

"I'll . . . make sure of that."

"You be sure you do." Duvallier said. He settled back to watch.

A distinguished man, a local celebrity with a great following in popular media, stepped forward to run the debate. Duvallier had seen him in the newspapers and on television now and again. The fellow ran a cooking show and an outdoor show as well as hosting news programs. Duvallier liked his folksy personality.

"Candidates, ladies and gentlemen, and members of the press," the moderator said, with a genial smile to each. His voice echoed out over the heads of the thousands of people standing around the stage. "Good evening. I'm proud to be able to present this gathering of highly qualified and intelligent people. These are your candidates for the office of governor of the great state of Louisiana." As he reeled off the names, each candidate gave a dignified nod. "Welcome and thanks to you all for being here. Now, I'll start out the first question with you, Lieutenant Governor Blanco. About environmental protection, it has been said that you don't support . . ."

Behind Penny Dunbar, Duvallier could see her manager, a lovely white-haired woman with some curves to her, and, he was delighted to observe, Griffen McCandles. Duvallier had received some more pleading notes from Malcolm McCandles. He had ignored them all, in spite of Miss Callaway's insistence. Making dragons sweat was good fun. He was about to do it again.

Sandusky fidgeted, but Duvallier relaxed. The psychological moment hadn't come yet. This was going to be a long process. He was in no hurry. He had nothing ahead of him but time.

The environment was too easy a subject. Each of the candidates wanted to be seen to be doing the most he or she could for it. No disagreement there except where the budget should be spent first. Duvallier could not have given a barrel of piss for any of their opinions, but to the moderator, who was an outdoorsman, it was catnip. He beat the subject half to death before someone made him call for a station break. The hot lights powered down slightly.

The candidates gulped water and had sweat patted off their brows by their solicitous staffers. Only a minute or so went by before the action started all over again. The assistants scooted back to their places, and the debate resumed.

The outdoorsman, deprived of his pet subject, got onto the topic of public education. Jindal trotted out his views, which he presented pretty well, about paving the way for improvements in primary schools across the state. The others didn't have much to add to the topic that was any more interesting. Duvallier watched the lights in supporters' eyes go out as the candidates started citing results from educational programs that they backed. It just couldn't be good for the television ratings to have them all quoting statistics. But mavericks were already breaking away from the crowd, speaking out of turn. One after another, the candidates interrupted each other, challenged one another on figures and grade-point averages. Penny Dunbar waded into the fray on this one, cutting off Congressman Benson. He looked peeved.

Sandusky let out a wordless exclamation.

"Are you going to let her get away with that?"

Duvallier smiled. "Still not the right moment."

This subject was best for Blanco, who as lieutenant governor had been involved in updating the school system, but she had some challengers.

Another break, to sell some more soap. Anyone could tell that the outdoorsman wasn't keen to break into the third topic on the agenda, law enforcement. This was Penny Dunbar's pet pony.

The moderator knew it and wanted her to speak toward the end. He kept holding her off with a stern finger, but Penny didn't take that kind of admonition seriously.

"Madam Lieutenant Governor, I think you're wrong about those figures!" Penny said, cutting off Mrs. Blanco in mid-sentence.

"I think if you'll let me get to the end of my remarks," the other woman said, with an aggrieved expression.

"Well, if you're basing your whole remarks on a fallacy, maybe you ought to rethink them."

"Representative!" the moderator said. "Please let the lieutenant governor finish." As Penny started to open her mouth again, he spoke first. "Please!"

"My dear sir, I can't stay silent when my honored opponent is getting everything so wrong!"

The moderator remained genial. "Well, Representative, if you'd just hold your fire until the end, I know all of us want to hear your views."

Duvallier grinned. He very much doubted whether anyone wanted her to pick their arguments apart, but he was looking forward to her trying.

She was fidgeting like a racehorse waiting for the starting gun. Before the words, "Representative Dunbar?" were out of the moderator's mouth, she was off.

"You all know my record on supporting law enforcement," she said. She brandished a handful of papers. "I have the latest documentation on the result of bills on crime prevention passed from laws I sponsored in the state legislature. A drop in crimes against property of over thirteen percent! A drop in crimes against people down by seven!"

Congressman Benson cleared his throat. "It would be a fine thing to attribute the reduction to bills, but don't you think the fine people of law enforcement . . . . ?"

Penny turned a smug look on him and returned her gaze to the cameras.

"Distinguished ladies and gentlemen, the safety of the people of the state of Louisiana is my very nearest and dearest concern," she began. She raised her arms, and her body began to sway gently.

Faster than you could say "leading economic indicators," the other candidates were in trouble.

Duvallier had not been born in time to see either of the ladies named Marie Laveau, but he'd heard from his own grandfather that the elder of the two voodoo queens could do a dance that would make people go out of their heads. Benson ought to have been afraid of Penny Dunbar, not just because of her dragon blood but because she had learned how to charm mankind without having to resort to her other natural gifts. Both together were a powerful combination.

Penny started that movement from her ankles upward. It was subtle but powerful. Before too long, every man in the arena was focused on her. Not on what she was saying, though the honeyed words melted into their ears and convinced them they were wise and profound, but the movement. It was something so primal that they couldn't have described what it was that made them pay attention so closely. She had them, had them all. Mrs. Blanco, four down from her on the stand looked puzzled, but the men were rapt. Penny's voice droned on, almost a hypnotic accompaniment to her dance. She spouted off facts and figures lyrically, like the words of a song. The men nodded, their faces blank. Her image was all that they could absorb.

Time to interfere. Duvallier spoke to the air. "Miss Daphne, honey, is Mr. Suskind in place?"

The ghostly voice of his late cousin wafted in the air like stale mist.

"Why, yes, Reginaud, he most surely is. He's enjoyin' the show. Always did like a spirited debate."

Sandusky's eyes went as wide as saucers. Reginaud grinned at him.

"You didn't really believe until this minute, now, did you?" he said. "What I look like, you could have had some of those Hollywood makeup men and special effects, too. But unless you think I snuck some of that electronic equipment into your own skybox overnight, you're just gonna have to take that step into the unknown. Daphne, darlin', get his attention. He's workin' for me today. He can watch television at the mortuary later."

"Now, Reginaud, you know he don't stay around that mortuary!" Daphne said, shocked. "Those days are over! It's not like it was in the old days. There's no one for him to meet. The nice people don't get brought there anymore."

Duvallier waved a hand. "Time's wastin', Daphne. Please boot Mr. Suskind in the behind."

"Oh, Reginaud!" She sounded exasperated at his crude remark, but the chill presence receded. Sandusky gulped.

"Suskind?"

"Oh, well, he weren't from my neck of the woods, but he obliges once in a while. Can't keep a good man down, no matter how much earth you pile on top of him." Duvallier grinned. "Now, keep an eye on our little girl up there."

Twenty-seven

Griffen stood at the back of the stage, his arms folded. Fox Lisa, beside him in a chestnut brown suit that made her red hair glow, radiated hurt. Penny had brushed both of them off the morning after the Bad Beth concert. Griffen's demands for an explanation as to why Penny hadn't been in the office when Fox Lisa had made the trip to do some work with her were ignored with extreme prejudice. Over the course of the next several days, Fox Lisa had yet to get an apology or any kind of acknowledgment that there had been some kind of misunderstanding. Penny's sweetly sarcastic tone made Griffen want to throttle her or walk out the door. At least, once she was in front of the cameras, she wasn't irritating either of them.

"I hope someone does throw a whammy on her," Fox Lisa grumbled, her arms folded around a clipboard she clutched to her chest. She stood rigid, refusing to acknowledge anyone else from the campaign. The hot lights shining at them from the foot of the stage made them both sweat and squint against the glare. Griffen felt the back of his long-sleeved silk shirt sticking to his back. "I will buy him a drink."

Fox Lisa had been so upset that night that when she finally had arrived at Griffen's apartment, he had had to spend hours consoling her instead of coaxing her into some mutual fun. Griffen blamed Penny for ruining his love life as well as the end of the concert. Fox Lisa was despondent, wondering over and over again if Penny had decided her input just wasn't worth her while and had left rather than wait for her. Griffen could not tell her what had happened at Yo Mama's. Penny knew he had kept the interplay to himself and kept shooting glances at him that were mockingly seductive. She knew anyone who saw them would misinterpret the expressions. Winston had imported a fresh set of indignant glares that he used on both Griffen and Fox Lisa. In the days since the slight, Fox Lisa had moved on from blaming her own short-comings to cold anger. From long experience, Griffen knew that mood was much more dangerous. He wished he didn't have to be there.

He had promised his uncle to stay with the campaign until Malcolm could relieve him. It was beginning to look as if Penny's fears were groundless. She was manipulating all of them. Griffen was getting tired of dancing to other people's tunes.

Horsie, in the thankless role of apologist for her candidate, caught Griffen's eye and offered him yet another friendly grin.

"I thought she was there," she whispered. "I swear to God. She called me on her cell phone. I'm so sorry, honey. I'll make it up to you."

"You can't," Griffen pointed out. "It has to come from Penny."

Horsie opened her eyes wide.

"Oh, but she's so busy. Don't mention it to her. She must have been somewhere else working and just flaked on that. It happens. Please, honey. This is a make-or-break event for her. Don't back out on us now." Horsie smiled, hoping to mend the situation. It didn't work. Fox Lisa's trust was broken. Griffen was relieved, but he was sorry her idealism had taken a hit. Horsie retreated, looking rueful.

He leaned over to Fox Lisa and put his mouth close to her ear. She shied away out of reflex, then made a face.

"I made us a reservation at Galatoire's for a late dinner," he whispered.

That managed to surprise a smile out of her.

"Well, thank you, Griffen," she said. "But you don't have to do it for her."

"I want to do it for *you*," Griffen insisted. "We haven't been there in a long time. You deserve it. Besides, you look so nice in that suit, I didn't want to waste the opportunity for you to show it off."

She leaned close and squeezed his arm. "I'll look forward to it. It'll give me something to think about beside talking points."

"I could recite them along with Penny," Griffen said.

"I hear them in my dreams," Fox Lisa admitted.

A man in a headset moved into Griffen's line of sight and gestured vigorously. When Griffen glanced at him, the man made a throat-cutting gesture with his finger. Griffen understood. He had to stop talking. Stifling a sigh, he shifted his feet and steeled himself to watch.

Griffen could have used a distraction. Politics were as dull as he had always believed. Having to smile and pretend to be supportive because of the television cameras was especially tortuous. The lights went up again for the third segment of the debate.

The moderator had reached the subject of law enforcement. Penny quivered at the podium, unable to contain herself as the other candidates took their turns speaking. Griffen knew it was only a matter of time before she interrupted one of them.

Yes, there she went.

"My dear sir," she began, her voice full of honeyed contempt, raising her voice over Congressman Jindal, "I am certain you have misstated the statistics. I have them right here . . ."

"Representative, if you don't mind," the moderator said, raising his voice to be heard over her. The person running the sound board was on his side. Penny's mike dropped to near inaudibility. The audience tittered. Her shoulders stiffened. Griffen could tell she was angry, and like the Incredible Hulk, no one was going to like the results.

To his amazement, she kept her silence. Griffen regarded her with suspicion. She was up to something.

He couldn't say later when he became aware of the motion, but by the time his conscious mind noticed it, Griffen realized he had been staring raptly at Penny. He thought that he was immune to her, after all her complaints and subterfuges, but something about the way she swayed behind her podium was fascinating. The movement came from her ankles upward, shifting her whole body from side to side like a snake. It was subtle, but he found it amazingly sexy and compelling. Penny aggravated him. He had to force himself to keep that in mind. But it was hard. Very hard. The longer he watched, the more he wanted to believe what she said. His will was bending toward hers.

Her shoulders, hips, and legs swayed. Blood pounded in Griffen's head. He wanted her. In his mind he saw her astride his hips, breasts swaying, writhing and tossing her hair. He couldn't concentrate on anything but her. He had to touch her, to draw that power into himself. The other men there might get to her first. She must be his and his alone. No one would dare challenge a dragon! He strode toward her.

Shriek! The platform creaked underfoot, snapping him out of the trance. Griffen stepped back into line. He realized he had been breathing hard. He glanced from side to side to see if anyone else had noticed him.

No one was paying attention to him. He scanned the row on both sides of him. All the campaign workers, whether or not they worked for Penny, had their eyes fixed on her. Most of the men had goofy smiles pasted on their faces. Most of the women frowned slightly, as if disapproving of what they felt. Some were as agog as the men.

Griffen knew that their fascination couldn't be because of what Penny was saying. He had heard the speech many times, with little variation. In it, Penny took credit for legislation that organized grassroots community policing and outlined bigger ideas for when she would be elected governor. Her answer to students' getting greater value out of the local schools was to make them safer. As a strategy, it was a can't-miss proposition. None of it cost very much to initiate, and it made for terrific photo opportunities for neighborhood leaders. It was dry stuff even to devoted followers, but he couldn't look away. He found himself eager for her next words. He wished she would turn around and look at him.

The huge audience cheered every time she finished a sentence. If she paused for breath, they broke into wild applause. Griffen had never seen anything like it. He wasn't close enough to smell pheromones, but it had to be some kind of phenomenon like that. Penny had a secret weapon, something magical. It worked on not just one person at a time, but dozens- —maybe hundreds. He had seen her speak in many places and she had gotten a good response from the crowd, but this was different. She compelled them to come over to her side and agree. Every camera in the room pointed at her.

The buzzer went off, indicating that her time was up. Without looking at it, the distinguished newsman automatically slapped it off with his hand, letting Penny continue.

"Our children are our future!" Penny said, raising her right hand to the sky.

"Yea, sister!" a loud baritone voice bellowed from the audience. Dozens in the crowd echoed him.

Penny shook a finger at heaven.

"We let them down every day we allow violent offenders to run our neighborhoods."

"Amen!"

"I will lead from the governor's mansion, but I need all of you to do your part! I need you to promise me two things!" Another finger joined the first.

"Name them!"

"One, that you'll blow the whistle on offenders in your neighborhood! Don't put up with their bad behavior one more day! And, two!" Penny was rising toward the climax of her speech. Her hands rose before her as if she was conducting an invisible orchestra. The audience was with her like a congregation. "That you'll go out on election day and vote! Punch that button that says . . . that says . . . !"

Her shoulders shuddered, and she fell silent.

As if someone had put a pin in a gigantic balloon, the energy burst out of the room, leaving it a deflated scrap. The audience groaned. Griffen felt the loss as if he had been deprived of something wonderful. He willed Penny to go on with her speech.

She didn't. Her shoulders were tense and shaking. Griffen realized she was staring at someone in the audience.

Griffen looked in the direction of her gaze. He ran his gaze back and forth through the rows of people. Nothing seemed out of the ordinary. Suddenly, he felt a cold ball of slime twist in his guts. In the midst of the murmuring populace was a man, or something that used to be a man. How was it that the crowd around him didn't see the horror Griffen beheld? His clothes, a parody of a business suit with a striped silk tie, were gray rags. Griffen couldn't tell what color his ridged skin used to be since it was a sickly gray mottled with purple and green, like old bruises. One eye hung out of its socket and bobbed on the leathery cheek. The face wore a rictus of a grin. The teeth looked outsized in the shrunken gray gums and shriveled lips. Griffen knew to the bottom of his soul that it wasn't a costume. He swallowed, trying to keep his gorge from rising.

"What's wrong?" Fox Lisa hissed. She, too, had broken out of her trance. "What's upsetting Penny?"

He pointed, trying not to make his gesture large enough to be picked up by the dozen or so television cameras. Fox Lisa followed the line of his finger and squinted into the crowd. She gasped.

"What is it?" she asked. "It looks like a zombie from the movies!"

"I don't know," Griffen whispered. "I'm going to find out."

He slipped out of the group of staffers and went down the stairs at the back of the dais. Fox Lisa clacked after him and kicked her shoes off at the bottom of the flight. She scooped them up and grasped them so the pointed heels could be used as weapons.

On the stage, Penny was still trying to recover her wits. The crowd, brought violently out of its reverie, roiled and muttered. Griffen shouldered his way into the mass of people. He dodged camera cranes and technicians in T-shirts and blue jeans. He kept his eyes fixed on the spot where he had seen the zombie. Why was no one else reacting to the creature? One look at it ought to have cleared the arena to the walls.

Fox Lisa had broken off from his side and doubled around to home in on the creature from the other direction. He could just see the top of her head in the midst of the crowd.

Something gray caught his eye. The rough texture looked like the zombie's sleeve. Griffen jumped toward it.

A hand caught him under the jaw and shoved outward. Before Griffen registered the mistake he had made, he was thrown roughly to the ground. A knee landed between his shoulder blades. The air whooshed out of his lungs. Griffen let out a pained OOF! He waved his hands to keep from being trampled by the forest of feet. The knee withdrew as suddenly as it had descended. The hand grasped a handful of the back of his shirt and hauled him upright. Griffen found himself eye to eye with Detective Harrison. The vice cop wore a heavy leather vest over a gray button-down shirt. His badge was on a strap around his neck. Harrison shook him roughly, then thrust him away.

"What are you doing, McCandles?" the burly man growled. "I was about to grab a troublemaker. You got in the way!"

"I was . . ." Griffen glanced at the stage. Penny stared down at him with a look of terror on her face. "I was, too."

Without the magic to sustain her hold over the audience, the debate could go on. The outdoorsman smiled genially at the camera and tapped the top of his clock. The melodious PING! sounded. The other candidates looked relieved.

"Your time's up, Representative. We'll get back to you on the next question."

Griffen returned his attention to Harrison.

Harrison eyed him sourly. "Your kind of troublemaker or mine?"

Griffen sighed. "Mine."

Harrison moaned, the lines in his meaty face angling downward.

"Shit, I hoped you weren't gonna say that. Do I even want to know what it was?"

"I don't think so," Griffen said. "I'll tell you what I can." He looked around. "Not here. I'll be at the pub later."

"All right. I want a full briefing."

Fox Lisa squeezed between two men holding JINDAL FOR GOVERNOR flags. "Hey, Detective, how are you doing?"

Harrison smiled down at her. "Been worse, Miss Fox Lisa. You look pretty fine in that suit. Running for office?"

"Maybe next time, Detective. Taking care of another candidate here."

Harrison glanced up at the stage. "Yeah, I've seen you on TV behind her. She was doing all right. Too bad she blew it." He pulled a palm-sized microphone off his shoulder and spoke into it. "I missed him, Larry."

A voice crackled out of the handset. "Got mine! Come on down by the forty-yard line. Ugh! Bring extra cuffs. He's a fighter, for sure."

Harrison punched Griffen in the shoulder. Griffen winced. Even in fun, the big man packed a wallop. "You owe me a drink later, McCandles. I'll be by to collect it."

"No problem."

The detective pushed away through the crowd. Griffen sought about for the zombie. No sign of their deteriorating prey. It had vanished.

"Why didn't anyone else see that thing?" Fox Lisa whispered, as they made their way back to the rear of the stage. The voices of the other candidates echoed from speakers over their heads.

"I don't know. Maybe no one who—who isn't like us can see it."

Fox Lisa's russet eyebrows went up. "Oh. So, it was definitely meant for Penny and no one else? It's that person that you heard was threatening her?"

Griffen nodded. This had to be Duvallier. He was playing with Penny's mind, to get her to resign. From the look on her face, he was succeeding.

Fox Lisa's resentment evaporated in sympathy. "I'm damned if I'll let that happen," she said firmly.

Mercifully, the debate was almost over. Penny steeled herself to answer the final question, but her reply was subdued, without the usual banter and veiled insults aimed at her opponents. The outdoorsman thanked them all. Penny waited until the lights went down for the last time, then strode immediately to Horsie's waiting arms.

The campaign manager enfolded her and stroked her golden hair as though Penny were a little girl. Griffen and Fox Lisa crowded close around her, shielding her from the reporters who streamed up onto the stage.

"Did you see it?" Penny demanded.

"Yes, we did," Griffen said.

Horsie was puzzled. "It's just the usual fans, honey. I don't know why you were so tense."

"That man, with the eye!"

"Everyone was eyeing you, honey. You're sexy as they come. They can't resist you." Horsie started to escort her toward the stairs.

"No!" Penny wailed. She reached for Griffen. "Stay with me, both of you."

"All right," Griffen said. Penny clutched his wrist with an iron grip. Horsie held on to her other arm. Fox Lisa trotted along behind, fluttering with sympathy.

"It's going to be all right," she assured Penny. "No one's going to hurt you."

Horsie waited until they had reached the underground garage, where armed guards let them into the enclosed area reserved for the VIP vehicles. She let Fox Lisa help Penny into the limousine and dropped back to speak to Griffen.

"What did she see back there?" she asked in a low voice. "She's never this rattled!"

"It was a warning," Griffen said. "She must have seen him before. I need to know where."

Horsie nodded. "When she's calmed down a little, I'll wheedle it out of her. Let's not bother her now. I'll make her some tea with whisky in it. She'll feel better."

"All right," Griffen said. Malcolm was going to have to know. He helped Horsie into the front seat beside Winston, then went to slide in the back beside Fox Lisa.

He took a cautious sniff of the air. Besides the usual smell of curing concrete, trash, and rainwater, he scented cigar smoke.

No doubt about it, Duvallier had been there.

Duvallier led the way back to the limo in the far reaches of the underground garage. The two frontrunners came out smelling like roses, but Congressman Benson also looked good. Once Penny Dunbar had lost her train of thought, the crowd snapped out of her spell. They didn't know what had hit them, but they all felt it and resented it. Duvallier grinned to himself. There had not been time left for Penny to undo the damage and leave them with a breathless memory of pleasure. No, it had snapped back on them like a rubber band. And all it took was a look at Mr. Suskind.

He stopped at the long black car, parked in the manager's personal bay, a special favor to an old, old, old friend, and glanced back at his employer's representative, breathless and wide-eyed.

"Gettin' your money's worth now?" he asked Sandusky.

"Yes, sir!" Albert leaped to open the door for him. "Yes, sir, Mr. Duvallier!"

Duvallier put his cigar in his mouth and took a satisfied puff.

"That's what I like to hear."

Twenty-eight

The ride back to the local campaign office felt like a funeral cortege, surrounded in darkness and silence, without any of the joyful noise that usually accompanied a New Orleans procession.

Once the Dunbar limousine pulled into the parking lot, and the office door was closed behind all but Penny's employees and her most devoted campaign workers, she allowed herself to go to pieces. She rocked back and forth in her office chair, sobbing, as Fox Lisa sat on a metal folding chair beside her and patted her back. The hands holding the wad of tissues to her eyes trembled. Horsie hustled to the antique wooden sideboard and poured a stiff shot of whisky into a tumbler.

"Knock this back, Penny," she ordered briskly. "You need it."

Penny took it. She gulped half the golden liquid and made a face.

"Burns," she said.

"Good. It'll melt the shakies out of you." Horsie poured one for herself and offered drinks around. Winston grunted his refusal. Fox Lisa accepted a glass but put it down on the desk beside her. Griffen shook his head. He wanted his wits clear. Penny's extreme reaction made him feel very uncomfortable. He knew there had to be more to the event than seeing a decaying corpse. She'd posed with uglier ones on her law-and-order beat.

"Penny, have you seen that man before?" Griffen asked.

"Now, let's just leave her alone for a while," Horsie said. "Come on, give the girl some privacy." She tugged on Griffen's arm. He stood up.

"No!" Penny said, alarmed. She stretched out a pale arm. "Don't let them leave!"

Griffen shrugged and sat down.

"Honey, what happened to you back there?" Horsie asked.

"She saw someone," Fox Lisa said.

"Are you being stalked, Representative?" Winston asked. "You should have informed me."

"It's not like that," Griffen said.

The big man's high forehead furrowed into deep folds over his clear blue eyes.

"If it's not like that, then what is it? If that kind of harassment is what she brought you in to prevent, you're doing a crap job."

"I didn't have anything concrete to go on before."

"You meant you didn't believe her?"

"No, I meant I had not seen what we're dealing with. Now I have."

"So, what are you going to do about it?"

Griffen rose. "I have to talk to a few people. I'll get back to you when I know something."

Winston frowned. "I don't like this mysterious stuff. Tell me what the hell you are planning to do to secure the representative's safety! I want details, not vague hints. Tell me the truth."

"Okay," Griffen said, exasperated. "I'm actually a dragon in human form. I have to go talk to a zombie about whether or not he ordered a walking corpse to go harass Penny while she was doing a magic dance to hypnotize the audience."

Fox Lisa giggled.

Winston's face went dark red. He threw up his hands. "I don't have to listen to this bullshit. If you're not going to give me a straight answer, then go to hell. When you get some results, I want to hear about it."

Griffen planted his palm on his chest with the greatest air of hurt innocence. "What makes you think I'm lying?"

"Get out of here!" Winston bellowed.

"No, I don't want him to go," Penny said, strength returning to her voice. "Fox Lisa, you stay here, too. You can come back and stay at my apartment with me. I have spare rooms."

Griffen shook his head.

"Penny, I need to get out of here. I will investigate for you, but I have other things I need to take care of. I have a business to run. You know that."

"Well, then, Fox Lisa will stay."

Fox Lisa opened her mouth, but Griffen spoke over her.

"She's got a job to go to in the morning."

Fox Lisa gave Griffen a dirty look, then turned to Penny.

"I'll stay, Penny. You don't have to worry."

"When's the next engagement?" Horsie asked. Winston took a tiny notebook out of his pocket and flipped through it.

"Five days. School visit in St. John the Baptist Parish."

"Can you come back then?" the plump campaign manager asked Griffen.

He looked at Penny's face, pale under its golden freckles, and nodded.

"I hope I won't have to. I'll get back to you."

"All right, honey. Thanks."

Griffen checked his phone. The display showed no messages, and the battery was fully charged.

"Call me if you need me."

"I will. Thanks, Griffen."

Griffen walked out into the night. A couple of newspaper reporters who had had the headquarters door shut in their faces were sitting on the hood of their car under the streetlamp, smoking. One of them spotted Griffen, ground out his cigarette, and rushed over, reaching into his pocket for his notebook. Griffen grumbled to himself. The last thing he wanted to do was give an interview.

"What caused Representative Dunbar's meltdown?" the first reporter asked. "Come on, Mr. McCandles. We saw you go into the audience. Who were you looking for?"

"I'm not at liberty to say anything," Griffen said. "Please, guys, don't quote me. Talk to the campaign manager. She's still in the office." He aimed a thumb over his shoulder. The reporters weren't going to give up on their bird in the hand.

"What's a gambler doing working for the law-and-order candidate?" the second reporter pressed, obviously hoping for an exclusive.

"No comment."

"How much money from your organization has gone to her campaign?"

"Not one cent," Griffen said.

"So, *more* than one cent?" the man pressed.

Griffen felt steam starting to come out of his nostrils.

"I have made no contributions to the Dunbar campaign. Thanks, guys. Good-bye."

He pushed between them and strode across the street just ahead of a passing taxi. The reporters followed, but he out-distanced them easily with his long legs. He lost them within half a block.

When he was certain he was alone, he flipped open his cell phone. Out of habit, he touched Val's number.

"The subscriber you have dialed . . ." The mechanical female voice came immediately. Griffen clicked the red button to hang up. He had to believe Holly's frequent reassurances that Val was all right. He tried the George's number. No answer at all. Griffen snorted, shooting two columns of smoke outward.

"Maybe no news is good news," Jerome said.

Griffen jumped.

"Jer! Where did you come from?"

"Right here in New Orleans," the other man said, a brilliant grin lighting his dark face. "You coming to find me?"

"No," Griffen said. "Just trying to get away from Penny Dunbar."

"Yeah, good luck with that, Grifter." Jerome pointed to a wall festooned with half-sheet posters of several political candidates. In the middle was one of Penny, looking seductive and efficient at the same time. Griffen wondered how she had managed that.

"Is everything all right?" he asked.

"Yeah, the game got called early because one of the players went into labor." Jerome grinned. "Never happened to me before. And she wasn't even losing."

Griffen felt a pang of concern.

"Is she all right?"

"Oh, yeah. Kind of lucky that two of the men there were dads. Both of them had been in the delivery room when their kids were born. They got her comfortable while I rang the front desk to call for an ambulance."

Griffen did some mental calculations on the cost of the hotel room, the dealer, server, and food, and whistled in dismay. "I hate to lose the money for the night. Would it help if I sat in instead?"

"Uh, no," Jerome said, quickly. "No trouble, Grifter. That was kind of a buzz kill, having Mama's water break right there. But everyone went away happy. They didn't get to play much poker, but having a baby on the way cheered them all up. We promise them a good experience. This isn't exactly the one they had in mind, but they'll never forget it."

"Did we send flowers to the mom?"

"Better than that: a basket with diapers and little rattles and things. The ladies in the hospital gift store gave me the rundown over the phone. Forty bucks. I put it on your credit card."

"Ouch," Griffen said, adding it to the mounting total in his mind. "I suppose it's good P.R."

"That's sometimes as important as profit."

"Yeah."

Jerome raised his eyebrows at Griffen's absent tone.

"What's on your mind?"

"Did you see the debate?"

"Nope. I was mopping up the floor and suggesting baby names along with the other guys."

"Penny Dunbar went into mental free fall. She was doing great until a walking corpse came up right in front of her."

"Whoa! Whose corpse?"

"I have no idea. If she does, she didn't tell me. She's pretty upset."

"I'm sure I would have heard about a riot in the Superdome."

"There wasn't one," Griffen said. "I think only dragons could see him. Fox Lisa and I did, but the manager standing next to me didn't."

"Duvallier?"

"That's my guess. You've lived here a long time. Do you know how to find him?"

"No. I've never had a reason to approach the political *eminence grise*. He's like the Shadow. You don't see him unless he wants you to."

Griffen poked the POWER button on his cell phone.

"Well, Uncle Malcolm knew how to find him. Are you up for a road trip?"

Jerome looked unenthusiastic, but he shrugged his shoulders.

"You're the big dragon," he said.

Malcolm McCandles did indeed know where to find Reginaud Duvallier. He refused to release the information until he had exacted numerous promises from Griffen to handle the matter with tact and caution. Griffen grew impatient with his elder relative and held the phone away from his ear until he had finished speaking.

"I won't say anything inflammatory, Uncle Malcolm, all right?"

"Report back to me after you have spoken to him. I wish you were not doing this without me, Griffen."

"Jer is coming with me," Griffen said, peevishly. "If I get out of hand, I'll let him take me out of there. All right?"

Malcolm sighed.

"If that is the best assurance I can get, then I will have to take it."

On the way along a darkened Canal Street to Odd Fellow's Rest Cemetery, Griffen rehearsed the speech he would make to Duvallier. Jerome understood that he was concentrating and listened to a blues station on the radio at low volume as he drove. The main thing, Griffen mused, was not to seem as if he wanted Duvallier's cooperation too much, but wouldn't it be more sporting either to come right out with an attack or let the election settle itself? He jotted down ideas in his notebook by the light of the dashboard radio.

They parked a block from the entrance to avoid drawing attention to the car. Jerome took a flashlight from the back-seat and put it in his jacket pocket. Griffen forced himself to walk in a casual manner. Few cars passed by at this hour. Anyone coming from the city was probably bound for US Route 10 or the country club on the other side of the highway.

A chain bound the black, wrought-iron gates at the entrance together. No streetlamps overlooked the graveyard. Griffen's dragon eyesight allowed him to see much more by the faint moonlight than a human could. Nothing appeared to move in the shadows between the ranked mausoleums. He glanced around for a foothold on the stone wall. It couldn't have been more than nine feet high.

"Sst! Grifter!"

He turned. Jerome beckoned. The gate stood open.

"C'mon!"

Griffen hurried to join him.

Except for the road noise coming over the wall from the expressway, their footsteps were the loudest sound around. The echo made Griffen want to tiptoe past the marble houses with their attendant statuary and urns. He knew intellectually that it was a warm spring night, yet he felt a chill in the air.

Murmuring like the wind in the trees rose around them. The crescent moon didn't cast much light, but even in that gibbous light, Griffen could see there were no glades within sight.

The cemetery long predated motor vehicles, and no roads existed to accommodate them, but they could still run into a police foot or bicycle patrol. Vandalism was a major problem in the ancient graveyards. In the moonlight, he spotted gang graffiti. Here and there, monuments had been overturned, and the yawning blackness of a mausoleum door wrenched off sent a chill down his spine.

Griffen counted rows and tombs, and nudged Jerome toward a white marble crypt overgrown on one side by twining ivy. The path under his feet was more deeply worn than those of the surrounding monuments—not surprising when he considered that the occupant came and went much more frequently than his neighbors. He nodded at Jerome. His lieutenant turned on the flashlight and shined it at the high lintel.

The name Duvallier in Lombardic capitals glimmered at them.

Jerome shut it off.

Griffen wasn't sure what to do. He tried the ornamental metal door. It was locked with a double dead bolt, an unusual accoutrement for a tomb. No light seemed to come from within. Griffen shook the door.

"Mr. Duvallier?"

He didn't hear the familiar raspy voice. Instead, whispering arose, dozens of papery voices like leaves rustling. Griffen listened, but he couldn't understand any of what they were saying. Having Rose as a friend, he wasn't really afraid of ghosts.

"Guess he's not home."

"I hear dead people," Jerome said. "You think they'll rat us out to Duvallier?"

"We'll have to assume they will," Griffen said. "We don't mean him any harm. All we want to do is talk to him."

"Well, leave a message. Maybe he'll get back to you."

"That's a good idea," Griffen said.

By the light of his cell phone, he wrote a note on a page of his notebook.

I would appreciate a meeting with you. Date and time at your convenience.

Sincerely, Griffen McCandles

He showed it to Jerome.

"Short and sweet," Jerome said. "Dragons go where angels fear to tread."

Griffen looked around. "I've met ghosts. I haven't met any angels yet."

"Neither have I. Saints, but no angels. They usually avoid New Orleans."

Twenty-nine

"I suppose," Detective Harrison said, staring down into the black depths of his coffee the next evening, "nothing ought to surprise me about this city anymore. Dragons playing cards. Faerie conventioneers. Dancing with . . . with ghosts. Now, zombies at a political rally."

Harrison looked as if he could have used a stiff drink but said he was still on duty. Griffen, in sympathy with Harrison, drank his Diet Coke. He signed to the bartender to keep their beverages filled. Griffen fished another fried shrimp from the basket between them, avoiding the traces of cocktail sauce and grease staining the paper napkin liner under the discarded tails. He chewed the crisp morsel, letting the rich oil of the flesh spread over his tongue. He thought of his conversation with Rose weeks ago, but he could tell by the frown of concentration on Harrison's face that now was not the time to mention it.

"As far as I know, there have been no physical threats since that car accident," Griffen said. "I'm not even sure that came from the same source."

"Uh-huh," Harrison said gloomily. "Publicity stunts. Dammit, I hate election season. They pull us off our normal beats and expect us to babysit overprivileged prima donnas who think that the servant part of 'public servant' only applies to us. The place fills up with crackpots and freaks—no offense."

"I don't consider myself a freak," Griffen said, evenly. "Though I'd have to agree with you about the . . . what Penny saw."

"Well, we had to stay around for the cleanup," Harrison said. "I didn't find any sign of that thing, not on the ground or in the videotapes."

"What were you expecting? A finger? A piece of nose?"

"Wish I had found something like that. Her campaign manager called up headquarters and read my captain the riot act on not keeping security tight enough. As if we're supposed to do something about supernatural bullcrap."

"Horsie doesn't know what was out there," Griffen assured him. "We're looking after Penny. I'm exploring some possibilities. I can't talk about them at the minute."

"I don't want to know!"

Griffen smiled. "I don't, either, but I don't have much of a choice."

"Huh," Harrison said, draining his cup and waving away a second refill. "I thought it was only in Chicago that the dead vote."

"I don't know if they do vote or not down here," Griffen said. "Think of them as just another special-interest group."

"Another pain in the ass," Harrison said. He eyed Griffen. "I don't like to ask favors." Griffen waited, not wanting to jump the gun on Harrison's thoughts. "You know what my city means to me. You just got here, but you're in deeper than any newcomer ever was that I know about."

"I'll do what I can," Griffen said. "It's not even a favor to you. My uncle dragged me into this. I gave my promise to him."

Harrison nodded, looking relieved. "All right. I'll take your word for it. I'm out of here. Half an hour, and I can sign off for the day. Dammit, I hate this season. Thank God it'll be over in November."

He pushed his barstool back from the counter and stood up. With one broad hand, he delivered a powerful slap to Griffen's shoulder.

"Stay out of trouble. I don't want to have to drag you and your 'employees' in. I don't feel like doing the paperwork."

Griffen winced inwardly at both the blow and the

thought, but he grinned. "Who'd notice me, Detective? I'm just an easygoing guy with friends who like to play cards."

Harrison snorted and stalked out.

Ann Marie came up and put an arm around his shoulders from behind. "You free, or you have to take care of business now?"

He turned and gave her a grateful smile.

"I'm free. How's Gris-gris?"

Ann Marie looked concerned. "That boy's meddling in things he don't know how to handle. Trying to do too much by himself. But his mental state is better. He's back to normal, which means he's bouncing off walls like a bat in a bottle."

"Can I see him?"

The Creole woman looked relieved.

"I was going to ask you. I was going to drop in on him. You want to come with me?"

Griffen glanced at his watch. About midnight. The two games he had going were nothing special. Jerome was playing in one of them. Brenda was dealing at the other. If they had any problems, he would have heard by now.

"Yes. I'd like to."

The first thing that would go through a visitor's mind when arriving at Gris-gris's home was that it didn't look as if it belonged to the head of a gambling organization. In fact, a little old lady from Pasadena could have moved in without changing a thing. The small, neat, painted wooden house had a lushly wild garden like one that might surround an English cottage. Two little glass lanterns with etched panels washed the painted front door with a warm golden glow. Griffen hung back on the concrete path and let Ann Marie reach the door first. From her pocket, she took a string of blackened sticks and shook them around the frame. Griffen realized that the sticks were human finger bones. He felt slightly sick.

The door opened from within. Griffen jumped back for a moment. A tall, lean woman peered out. It took Griffen a moment to recognize Estelle, the proprietor of the voodoo shop half a block off Bourbon Street. She met Griffen's eyes and nodded.

"All is well. You can come in."

On the other side of the threshold, Griffen sensed a presence, not of an intelligence but of a force. He had felt the same when Holly had warded her home to protect the sacred space from intrusion by malign energies. Ann Marie jangled the string of bones as she closed the door behind them. That sealed the entrance as tightly as an air lock. The air inside seemed warm and thick, and not just because of the candles he could smell burning. The sensation didn't alarm Griffen. He felt enveloped and soothed. He wasn't certain what he had expected, but the welcoming aura disarmed him.

Gris-gris sprang up from the blue-upholstered couch as Griffen entered. He stuck out a hand and grasped Griffen's long fingers in his own. His grip was powerful enough to make Griffen wince.

"Man, I'm glad to see you," Gris-gris said. "Sorry about the other night."

"No problem," Griffen said. He studied the smaller man. His nearly black skin had regained the healthy sheen that it usually had. The whites of his dark eyes were clear, not bloodshot and runny as they had been. Behind them, the quick, almost lightning-fast intelligence had returned. "Are you all right?"

"I'm fine! This is worse than the hospital." Gris-gris swept a hand around. "Least I was unconscious most of the time. Now I want to get out, but she don't let me."

Estelle shook her head. "It's just like being in the hospital. You think you're well, but you aren't." She pointed at a small plant in a blue container. "When that absorbs all your bad air, you can go anywhere you want."

Griffen glanced at the plant, a broad-leaf ornamental of some kind. It leaned to the left in a sickly manner. He surveyed the room. Against one wall were three parson's tables. On each were various esoteric-looking objects he couldn't identify readily. Above each was a decorated, crudely carved cross that seemed to go with the artifacts below. Candles in tall, narrow glasses burned everywhere: on the floor, on every table, and on the windowsills. In the middle of the room was what looked a little like an open beach umbrella with designs painted in neon colors on the handle. It seemed as if the room had been furnished with about half the objects from the voo-doo shop. Griffen tried to make sense of what he was seeing.

"Is this all part of the cure?" he asked.

Estelle snorted. "No! This is the problem."

"What do you mean?"

"Look around you!" Estelle shrugged her shoulders. "This is a jumble. No honest practitioner would sell a worshipper all this junk. This is the kind of things that a tourist would buy."

Gris-gris winced. "I needed help with a lot of things."

"Consultation is free to those in need," Estelle said. "If you had asked, I could have saved you a bundle of money, not to mention pestering the *lwa* so bad I had to call for help to pull you back."

"What's a lwa?" Griffen asked.

"Our gods," Estelle said simply. "They rule different parts of our lives, but with love, like parents. Voodoo is a family, Griffen McCandles. You have lived here long enough to know that our religion is not all bones and potions and Baron Samedi. You know Rose."

"But I haven't studied your beliefs," Griffen admitted.

Estelle shot an annoyed look at Gris-gris. "Neither has he."

"That's not true!" Gris-gris exclaimed. "I believe. I belong!"

"Then what's all this crap?"

Gris-gris looked as sullen as a little boy. "I needed a lot of things. I thought I could ask by myself."

"Of course you can ask by yourself. The *lwa* listen to all their children."

Griffen was interested. "But aren't you his priestess?"

"The role of a priest does not mean the same from religion to religion," Ann Marie said. "Our mother and father guide us, but we are given the tools to achieve goals on our own. We can make our own mistakes, but we ought to know when we are in out of our depth."

"Don't say it!" Gris-gris said. "Don't say it again! You both told me a hundred times. I get it."

"But will it stick?"

"Ann Marie, I know Estelle," Griffen said. "I met her before the conference last Halloween. Why did you say you couldn't give me her name?"

Ann Marie and Estelle exchanged glances. "When I saw Gris-gris, I knew he needed special intervention. You've met only a few of our number. Our congregation came to your conference, as did a few others, but not all the local voodoo queens and priests attended."

"I can understand that," Griffen said. "I was the only dragon there. Since then I've met dozens who live in the area."

Ann Marie smiled. "Some of those who follow voodoo don't want to be identified outside the religion. We aren't ashamed of our beliefs, but there are so many misconceptions. I had to go to one of the ones who stay in the closet, so to speak. I told Estelle, and she approved."

"May I know his name? Or hers?"

"It's not important right now," Estelle said. Griffen realized from the flat expression in her eyes that she was not going to argue with him about it. "But if you ever chair another conference, he and many others will come. They didn't realize that you were sincere in not promoting your own agenda."

"I'm never running another conference," Griffen said fervently. "I did a favor for Rose once. Someone else will have to step up next time. If I go, it'll be as a participant, not the master of ceremonies."

"Of those with great portion, great things are asked."

"I'm not Spider-Man. I'm just a guy trying to run a business and live my life."

"The important thing is that he came to help Gris-gris." Ann Marie gestured to the other dealer, who was pacing impatiently like a tiger in a cage. "Together, we performed a new ritual, a sorting-out, to bring things back to normal."

"What happened to Gris-gris?" Griffen asked.

"Voodoo is a family. This child tried to take the lead without knowing what he was doing. He did it with respect, but it's like taking everything in your medicine cabinet if you have a cold. You need guidance." Estelle shook her head.

"I told you why I did it," Gris-gris said. "I thought I had a lead on Val. I'm still weak in the gut. I wanted to get healthy fast, so I could go after her. I talked to a man, a weird guy. And there was a lady with him. I met him at the Court of Two Sisters."

" 'Weird' is a relative term in the Quarter," Ann Marie said, with a smile. "Define 'weird.' "

Gris-gris gestured. "He had a face like leather and eyes on fire."

Griffen's eyebrows went up in alarm. "I think I know that man."

"You do?" Ann Marie asked.

"His name's Duvallier. He's the one I wanted to talk to you about. The walking dead. What did he do to you, Gris-gris?"

"He only talked to me," Gris-gris said. "Said he had a line to the people who took Val, but he doubted I could handle them by myself. I don't take that from nobody. I went looking for what I needed. Next thing I know, I am in bed with my hands and feet tied together and a bunch of people chanting over me."

"We had to tie him up. He kicks like a shotgun," Ann Marie said. "But it's part of the ritual. You don't remember a lot of what happened in between, Gris-gris, because you were being reborn. Again."

"That sounds interesting," Griffen said, raising his eyebrows. "What else happens?"

Estelle made a gesture of impatience.

"If you're really interested in finding out about voodoo, come into the shop when you have time," she said. "I will lend you some books to read, and we will talk. I have no intention of setting another one like Gris-gris loose on the world with inadequate knowledge."

"Fair enough," Griffen said. "So, what is going on here?"

"A cleaning-out of the bad air this man made in trying to do good. You've met others who follow nature religions. Voodoo is similar." Estelle pointed at the numerous candles. "These have to finish their work. You don't ask the *lwa* to help, then turn your back on them. That's impolite. That power that Gris-gris does not need is being redirected to people who do need it."

"So, instead of being drained, he's too charged up?"

Estelle smiled. "Yes, that's a good way to define it. We have asked this rubber plant, as an analogue of this very energetic man, to take into it all the illness that he has suffered, absorb all his troubles. When it dies, then he is free to leave its presence."

"When will that be?"

"Not soon enough!" Gris-gris exclaimed, throwing his hands up.

"Can I do anything to help?" Griffen asked.

"Bring a bottle of white rum and a few cigars next time you come," Estelle suggested. "They will be offerings for the *lwa*."

Gris-gris dug in his pocket and came up with a fat wad of money in a gold clip. "Here," he said, peeling off a few bills. "Use this. Get good ones."

"It's okay," Griffen said. "You can pay me back when I bring the stuff."

"No, he's right," Ann Marie said. "The gift must be from him."

Griffen accepted the bills and folded them into his wallet in a separate section from his own money.

"What about Duvallier?" Griffen asked.

"The walking dead," Estelle said thoughtfully. "Yes, I will bring your question to our friend and let you know if you can meet."

Thirty

If it had been a movie set, Griffen would have assumed he was walking into the home of a mathematics teacher, not a voodoo priest. The house, in a small suburb of Baton Rouge, was like thousands in southern Louisiana: wooden frame, garden with stone ornaments outside, antiques and creaky floorboards inside. The dark-skinned man of Griffen's own height who had greeted him at the door and poured him a glass of iced tea completely filled the stereotype of a middle-aged professor who had been interrupted while grading papers. His tightly curled hair was mostly gray, and he had a potbelly. His long hands had buffed nails trimmed neat and short. Everything in the sitting room was equally neat. Even the altar set against one wall had more of the air of a Japanese tea ceremonial table than the overflowing chaos of the stands in Gris-gris's home. The man studied Griffen with calm brown eyes behind gold-framed glasses. He smiled.

"I greet you, Griffen McCandles. This is a nice change. It's not often I have a dragon stop in to visit. Usually you folks turn your noses up at mere humans like me. Our lives and experiences are unimportant."

Griffen grimaced. The reputation of dragons was going to have to undergo a renovation. Since he was the ranking "big dragon" in the area, it was up to him.

"I don't operate that way," he said. "I don't assume I know everything. I'd rather learn from other people than do things the hard way."

"Rare wisdom from a young man like you. So, what information do you think I have for you?"

Griffen hesitated. "I've been, uh, locking horns with a man—I mean, he used to be a man . . ."

The eyes glinted behind the bifocal lenses.

"Transsexual? Not my department."

"Uh, no," Griffen corrected himself. "I mean, he was a human being when he was alive. He's been dead a long time."

"Really?"

"Well, I have no proof of it, but he lives in a mausoleum. His skin is like leather, and his eyes glow red. He's spooky. He seems to have power, or influence, anyhow, over other, uh, undead beings. I think he's a zombie."

The man shook his head. "Zombies are under the influence of others, not the other way around."

"Well, he's the walking dead of some kind. He's threatening people that I have promised to help protect. How can I make him go away and leave us alone?"

The man nodded. He leaned back in his chair.

"If he has defied death, he could not have done it alone. You need to approach the houngan or priestess who created him. They must help you."

"Well, that might be hard. I understand it's been eighty years since he died."

That brought the man forward in his chair. His face was lined with concern.

"What is this walking dead's name?"

"Reginaud St. Cyr Duvallier."

The houngan shook his head.

"I know who he is. He's the kind of man who gives *me* nightmares. I have heard that he created himself, but he must have had help. It was a wrong thing to do. He propitiated many *lwa* to allow himself to pass into the land in between. Not one of ours though his power comes from all nature. He is what you call a self-made man. He believes that he has great influence, and it comes to him. It is in the spirit of voodoo, but he does not belong to our family."

Griffen felt a sense of desperation. The conversation was not going the way he had hoped.

"Can I propitiate them to take him back? I mean, he's been dead a long time."

"You would take a life?"

"Not willingly," Griffen said.

"That's good. You have a lot of power of your own. You could bring an end to his influence but not through force. You'd have to undermine his base of power. Is that the way you want to spend the rest of your life? He has all the time in the world. Do you?"

"No," Griffen said. "Then how do I get him to leave me and my friends alone?"

The man shrugged. "It sounds like you'll have to issue a challenge and have all your wits about you when you do it. Are you ready to face him?"

"I'm not, not yet," Griffen said frankly. "But I will have to be one day."

"When the time comes, you can ask for our help. We give it willingly."

Griffen smiled. "I appreciate that. I may not believe in your religion, but I believe in your people."

"That will do," said the houngan, with a smile. "Good luck."

Thirty-one

Val set her fork down on the empty plate and smiled at Marcella. The housekeeper had hovered beside her all the way through dinner, moving only to refill Val's tall glass of iced tea and remove empty dishes. Her presence made it difficult for Val to relax and enjoy her meal. It was a shame because it would have rated five stars in any fancy restaurant. If she had to go by food alone, hers was going to be the healthiest baby ever born.

The long, polished mahogany table in the enormous dining room was bare except for a pearl pink cloth. A shining silver candelabrum held three huge beeswax candles that dashed flickering light over the single table setting of Spode china and sterling flatware. Val looked regretfully at the last few crumbs.

"That was great," she said. "I didn't really think I liked asparagus, but that soufflé was amazing."

The dour housekeeper didn't change expression. "It is our pleasure to serve our guests," she said.

Val tilted her head. "Marcella, is there something about me that bugs you?"

The iron rod rammed itself back in the housekeeper's spine. "Of course not, Ms. McCandles."

"You know I'm just here temporarily, don't you?" Val said. A twitch between Marcella's dark brows made her think her guess was good. *You're not the only one who can read people,*

Griffen, she thought triumphantly. "I'm not trying to take advantage of Melinda."

That remark got more than a twitch. The corner of Marcella's mouth went up a perceptible quarter inch. "Anyone who thinks they can take advantage of Mrs. Wurmley doesn't know her."

Val laughed. "So I noticed. If you do or say something she doesn't like, she rolls right over you. It must be tough."

"Not really," Marcella said, then shot a hasty look at the dining-room door. "I just do my job. She notices when things run well. She doesn't really expect the impossible."

"Yes, she does," Val said, making a face. "She wants my baby's nursery to look like something out of a Laura Ashley catalog. I'm tempted to do the whole thing in Muppets and pirate ships. What do you think?"

"You may wake up and find it has been redecorated while you sleep," Marcella said, with a twinkle in her dark eyes.

Val was shocked rigid. Panic rose in her throat. She put her hands protectively on her belly.

"She'd do that? She'd sneak into my house overnight? What if she doesn't like the way I'm raising my own baby? Would she take him?"

"Oh, I'm certain she wouldn't do anything like that," Marcella said, but she looked uneasy. "Would you like some dessert? The chef made passion-fruit sorbet. It's delicious but very light."

"No. I *have* to get out of here," Val said. "I want to go home. No one has returned a single one of my phone calls or answered my letters. I think my boyfriend's written me off. No one cares where I am except Melinda, and she is only interested in my child!"

Marcella started to put her hand on Val's arm but withdrew it in haste. "I'm sure it's not that bad."

Val pouted. She hated herself for it, but her sense of pique had been rising unabated for some time.

"Well, my brother is ignoring me. That isn't like Griffen. He was turning into the original mother hen when he found out I was pregnant. I can't believe he is still mad I didn't call him for a week after Mardi Gras. It's as if he doesn't care about us anymore. It's been months!"

Another hesitation. Val almost leaped at Marcella.

"Is there something you're not telling me? Has Griffen called here to talk to me?"

Marcella relaxed one tiny bit. "No, he hasn't called here. No one has. I'm sorry."

"Oh." Val felt very alone. The baby kicked. Val didn't miss the irony that it was comforting *her*. "Listen, would you like to hang out sometime? I don't know what your schedule is like—well, I do, but I don't know what you do with your spare time. I mean, I can't go out drinking in my condition, but if you know a place with good music, or a cool shopping center, we could go there."

For the first time, the housekeeper smiled. "I'd love to, but I'm on call most nights except while I'm on vacation. I can't leave the estate." Val felt crestfallen. "I have a great sound system in my rooms. You're welcome to come down there and listen to music with me. The estate has an enormous CD collection. It has almost any artist or style you can think of. Some really rare old recordings, too."

"Great," Val said. "Maybe this evening?" Then she remembered her mystery visitor was due later. "Or tomorrow? I'm feeling kind of tired."

"I would be honored," Marcella said.

The door burst open suddenly, and Henry rushed in.

"There you are!" he exclaimed. He hurried to Val and took her hand. Marcella edged away, her eyes pleading. Val took that to mean that she wasn't to mention what they had just been discussing.

"What can I do for you?" she asked Henry, briskly.

Henry pulled her to her feet. "Melinda just called. She wants you to go over a different set of spreadsheets with me."

Val moaned. Melinda was running her life, and she wasn't even there!

"I told you, I don't work for her!"

"Well, that's going to change, too," Henry said, with a persuasive smile. "She wants to put you on salary."

"What?" Val asked, taken off guard.

"Exactly. You show a lot of acumen, and that doesn't come along every day. Why should you give away your talent? She thought sixty to start?"

"Sixty? Sixty what?"

Henry looked at her pityingly. "Sixty thousand, sweetheart. A year."

Val felt her eyebrows hit her hairline. "Dollars?"

"Unless you want to be paid in jelly beans. Dollars. Yes."

Val's knees went weak. She felt for the chair and sank into it. Sixty thousand dollars? A year? Why, that was an executive's salary. With money like that, she could buy a house with a yard, and a nice car. Her looming college loans would be no problem. In fact, she could start saving for her baby's education. She looked at Henry disbelievingly.

"Seriously? She thinks I can manage it? I have no experience."

"Melinda doesn't joke, as you may have noticed." Henry helped her up again. "Come on and look at the books for your new company."

Val looked over her shoulder as he ushered her out of the dining room. The housekeeper had vanished through the other door without a sound.

Thirty-two

The George waited about twenty feet outside Val's window until half past two in the morning. He was warm enough in spite of the light rain that was falling, but he was getting impatient. No shadows or sounds came from behind the light curtains. Had Melinda's fussy majordomo discovered the note she had left for him? George took the folded and creased square of paper from his pocket and brought it to his nose again. Female, definitely. The hint of perfume from toiletries was that of a fresh, light scent. Not the housekeeper, then, who favored woodsy spices. The beautician smelled of hair spray. The housecleaners, both male and female, wore no scented products at all, but anything they touched would have reeked of Lysol. No, Val had to have been the only one to handle the note. She had agreed to see him. So, where was she?

George longed for a cigarette, but he checked the wind first. The prevailing westerlies would carry the smell straight to the air intake for the household ventilation system. That would bring Henry and his minions out on the run. No one but guests were allowed to smoke.

The cell phone in the breast pocket of the camouflage army jacket vibrated. He eased it out, making as few motions as possible, and brought it to his ear.

"Yeah?"

"You wanted an update," Debbie said. The office manager

didn't waste time with meaningless niceties. "Melinda and her horde are about 140 miles from you."

Out of habit, George looked around him and took a good sniff of the night air. Nothing but bushes and trees and a few night-roaming animals.

"Are they on their way here now?"

"No. They're all tucked in at a fancy DC hotel, the Fairfax Inn. Very posh. No movement noted except the two big lugs walking perimeter."

George had seen the pair of enforcer dragons who worked for Melinda. They were big, tough, and well trained. It would have taken him maybe three or four minutes to kill them both. But better the devils he knew than fresh unknowns. If he or anyone else from the office wiped them out, Melinda would hire someone more dangerous. When the day came that he got a contract on the Wurmleys, as they were currently calling themselves, he would rather have easy targets.

"Sure they're not leaving?"

"My guess is no, unless Lizzy kicks up another fit like a few days ago."

"Good." George calculated. His car was in another lane parked among a dozen or so expensive numbers. One of Melinda's not-too-close neighbors was having a party that looked to be continuing well past dawn. He figured that the police patrols wouldn't notice his nondescript sedan among them. Once he made contact with Val, it should take no more than ninety seconds to get her outside the fence. Depending on how advanced her condition was, he guessed three to eight minutes to get her to the car. They could be on their way to New Orleans by three.

"When are you getting out of there?"

George poked the stud on the side of his watch that illuminated a minute LED. The digital numbers glowed dimly. "The girl hasn't been in her room yet."

"I think you've been stood up, honey," Debbie said dryly.

"I doubt it. Something else must be going on."

"Maybe she told someone about your note."

George thought about it. "From my observations, that's not her modus operandi. She keeps things as close to her chest as her brother does."

Debbie's voice held a warning. "Don't get attached! They're vermin. Just because they don't act like monsters doesn't change the reality! Do the job and get your ass back to headquarters. I have half a dozen assignments waiting."

It was no use arguing with her about the McCandleses. George couldn't say why he felt they were different from the other dragons he had stalked. True, it went against his instincts, let alone his training. Griffen McCandles struck him as a decent guy. He really didn't think like a dragon. Maybe this next generation would be different.

"I'll give it until three, then leave it for another day," he said.

"All right. Call if you need to."

"Got it." George clicked off the cell phone and stuck it in his pocket.

His feet were losing sensation from standing in one position for such a long time. He changed their shape slightly inside the light boots. Instead of flaplike human feet, they were inverted baskets of bone, balanced on five points. The cramping eased. The new structure was one he had used before when he had done a long stakeout in a tree. He couldn't run well this way, but he shouldn't have to.

He always wanted to disabuse the young punks who tried to join his organization of the notion that killing dragons was in any way *fun*. Like SWAT-team work, it required training, good armament, surveillance, protecting one's back, assessing the enemy, gathering evidence, and not moving in until one was certain of a clean kill with as little collateral damage as possible. The idea was to remove a dangerous pest and render the area safe for humanity to live, not to injure the sheep while taking out the wolf. Remaining alert for as long as one was close to a target was vital. What they hunted was smart, fast, incredibly tough, dangerous, and vindictive.

An unwary hunter was prey. You could only hope you'd be killed right away if you were taken prisoner without hope of escape. George always made sure he had at least five routes of escape planned and secured. He had such a long list of kills that he didn't stand a chance if he was intercepted in certain territories. That was one of the reasons it was so strange for him to have struck up an acquaintance with Griffen McCandles. Some of his relatives had been targets.

Maybe the boy didn't know that yet. The George sighed. Nothing good could last forever.

Melinda was taking no chances on a breach of security. It had taken George a good two hours to slink onto the estate, creeping past a dozen cameras and weight-sensitive pressure plates. God help the rabbit that landed on one of those hidden balances by accident. Two were wired with enough high voltage to fry almost anything smaller than an elephant. Five were dead drops into tiger traps filled with sharpened aluminum spikes. One near Melinda's bedroom window had been booby-trapped with military-grade C4 explosives and a hair trigger. At least that one had been sprayed with fox urine to keep the local wildlife off. He doubted the effort was out of basic decency; it would prevent unnecessary explosions. Melinda kept four huge black-and-tan dogs. They were loyal to their handler but to no one else on Earth. They'd refused every bribe George had tried on them. The net had been drawn admirably tight—against anyone who wasn't an experienced hunter, and a shape-shifter to boot.

Locating her country home had taken days of analyzing data from multiple public-records systems across America. Wealthy dragons generally hid their ownership behind a maze of holding companies and blind trusts. Melinda had been around long enough to leave property to herself in a couple of wills. This one had been really well hidden. It dated from colonial days, the property of an ancestor of hers who had come over with the first settlers. Its discovery had made the investigators and researchers in the office sit up with interest. They were going to delve into historic land grants and cross-reference them, but George had what he needed to start his mission. Posing as a journalist doing a puff piece on the Founding Fathers for a major news network, he had gotten the county assessor to open the plats of survey and show him the land boundaries. As they were a matter of public record, the names were printed in perfect block capitals on each property. "WURMLEY" spread out over numerous plots of land, but the largest and most easily defended had been this one. George had staked out the household's comings and goings over a week before. He had seen Valerie McCandles riding in a car, but he had not wanted to phone Griffen yet with the news. She seemed to be happy, not under duress. First impressions had to be followed up with a face-to-face meeting.

He liked the place. It was built on the kind of gracious, elegant lines prevalent before the Federal period. When it had been updated, which it had, the architects had kept the original lines but shored it up and made it more weatherproof and energy efficient. Melinda, or her ancestors, had spent money well.

It had not been spent only on physical alterations. George could sense spells of various kinds worked into the materials. There was a "forget me" sense imbued in all the doors and windows. Anyone who passed through them going out would forget how to get back to the house unless they had an amulet or a counterspell. Nice if you had in-laws you never wanted to have drop in again.

Five to three. The rain was coming down heavier. George's clothes were soaked through. If he'd been human, he would have been chilled, but all he did was change how his body stored heat. The pale night-light in the room hadn't yet been interrupted. George widened his pupils to admit a little more light, just in case he was missing a faint shadow. No. Where was the girl?

It was too late for a clean getaway this evening. He took another note, prepared in advance, from the side pocket of his jacket and slid the slightly soggy paper under the sash.

A siren split the night. George leaped away from the side of the house. He had tripped the alarm system.

Goddammit! he thought. That level of pressure hadn't done it the previous evening. The humidity must have made the paper swell beyond the tolerance of the unit.

The thunder of footsteps boomed down the stairs inside the mansion. George slipped into the trees and headed for his shortest retreat. He saw the terrain as protrusions and shadows. He ducked to avoid the former and trod carefully in the latter. He couldn't avoid every twig. A SNAP! made his heart pound with alarm. He drew a long Special Forces knife with a blackened blade from his pocket and slid it up his sleeve.

Behind him, the household had erupted from the front and rear doors. He counted the sound of six voices but at least twice that many sets of footsteps.

"Awwooooo!"

And, double goddammit, the dogs were out. George concentrated on re-forming his feet to fit the shoes. Trying to concentrate on too many things at once distracted him. He tripped and hit the ground on his belly. Not bothering to get up, he crawled, commando fashion. It was slower, but the humans were looking for an upright man. As he went, he lengthened his body and shortened his legs until he was more crocodile in shape than human. He put on a burst of speed and made for the fence.

The dogs found his scent easily. Bellowing like hunting hounds, they dashed into the underbrush. Deer that hadn't stirred a hair when George passed sprang up and dashed in all directions. The dogs were distracted, but only momentarily.

The handlers' voices fell far behind. He heard Henry's shout above all.

"Block the gates! Don't let him out!"

As if I were going to go out by either gate, George thought scornfully. He refused to underestimate the majordomo, though. If Melinda trusted him to maintain her castle—and her guest—in her absence, he had to be more perspicacious than the average human.

George slithered into a dip and discovered that rainwater had pooled there. His clothes, already soaked, picked up clumps of soggy debris. He spat out a decaying leaf. He grabbed hold of the nearest tree trunk and scaled it with his claws, hugging close to the bark. As soon as he reached a heavy branch, he slithered out along its length, then flung himself toward the next tree. Accompanied by a sharp creak and a crash, he made it to a branch two feet lower than the one he had been on. He halted there, clinging to the rough bark, listening closely. The dogs followed his scent to the first tree and surrounded it, baying. The handlers caught up. Out of the corner of his eye, George saw flashlight beams lance upward. He grinned to himself. Scrabbling down the trunk, he concentrated on putting as much distance behind him as he could.

The bittersweet, mixed aroma of soaked leaves and pine needles, mud and raccoon dung through which he was crawling filled his nostrils. He wiped some of the crud off along tree roots. His clothing was going to be a mess when he got out of there. Then he caught the whiff of a sharp scent. The acrid fume made his eyes water. It reminded him of ozone from an electric circuit, but it had an animal character to it as well. George yanked out all his mental file drawers searching for an analogue. Nothing matched. Had some innocent animal died burning on the electric wire running along the top of the walls?

No, whatever it was, it was alive. And, his hunter's instinct told him, homing in on him.

He slid to a halt and listened closely. His pursuer stopped, too, but not before George gained a fleeting impression of the direction from which it was coming. If he kept going toward the fence, it would intercept him from eleven o'clock. He wheeled around and took off at a right angle to his previous path. It put the other hunter behind him but made him pass through terrain that George had previously traversed. How it handled that would give him some more information.

It moved fast, a speed at which the rustling noises traversed from one side of his trail to another. The George kicked up his pace. He couldn't help being alarmed. What did Melinda have back there? A Komodo dragon? He hoped not. The giant lizard's poisonous bite couldn't kill him even if it did hurt like hell, but it would make him sick.

An anguished yelp and a howl told him the beast on his trail had come across the dogs. One of them might have taken a nip at it or just gotten in the way. The handlers' voices exclaimed in alarm. Henry shouted them down.

George neared the closest exit, then changed his mind about using it. The drain that led into the storm sewer under the street outside was too convenient. It was the roomiest and easiest to access of all the escapes. Once he left his scent in it, it would be useless to him a second time, and he needed a second time to get Val out. The next closest lay only ten yards to his right. The lanterns on top of the pillars abutting the entry gates cast some light on it, so George took a risk going there, but the passage between two fence sections was narrow enough that the creature on his tail couldn't overtake and trap him on the wrong side.

He made for the gap in the fence. It meant covering some fairly open terrain underneath mature evergreen bushes. No time to second-guess himself. He added extra muscle to his back legs and gave it all he had. Shadows of branches spotlighted by the handlers' flashlights made a chiaroscuro jumble ahead of him. He had to go by sense and memory. The bushes nearest the gap were juniper, the only ones in the front hedge.

A blast of lightning followed by a clap of thunder burst overhead. The George paused for a moment, taking advantage of the brilliant light to get his bearings. He could see a tiny thread of light peeking in from the gap. The rain pelted down harder now. George scuttled underneath the edge of a heavy bush.

Something caught his right pant leg. He jerked it forward, hoping to dislodge the bramble. Instead, a whole body shot forward and landed on his back. A cold, acid gust breathed in his face. Saliva dribbled down his neck.

Instantly, George flipped over on his back. His short, powerful legs flung the creature a couple of yards away. It lunged for him again. George drew his knife and stabbed at it.

In the faint light, he saw the creature's outline. At no time in his long career had he ever seen one like it. If the Hildebrandts had asked this monster to model for Gollum, there would never have been a second *Lord of the Rings* calendar. It was skinny, almost gaunt, with hollow cheeks in a faintly humanoid face, but its teeth were sharklike rows of filed wedges. Drool came out of both sides of its mouth as it tried to bite George. He fended it off his neck while looking for weak spots.

He didn't find many. The creature seemed as flexible and heavy as lead. Whenever it managed to scramble on top of him, George had to fight to pull himself out from under. Its skin turned away his knife blade.

"What the hell are you?" he demanded. Its impenetrable hide suggested dragon-kin, but its narrow skull, flat at the front, made the face protrude like a rodent's.

The next time it lunged for him, he wound his arms around its neck and forced the head upward. Back, back, back—George listened, waiting for the spine to snap. It never did. The flat skull touched the bony spine. It twisted its head and gave George a fierce grin. It wrenched out of his grasp, and George found himself hugging empty air.

A split second later, he was on his face, breathing rainwater and compost. The creature dug its teeth into the back of his neck. Well, two could play the contortionist game. He twisted his body. The teeth raked the flesh of his throat. Blood spurted. George ignored the pain and grabbed the creature's windpipe. He squeezed. It hung on, burying its fangs deeper into his flesh. George gritted his own teeth against the pain. He could feel something start to give . . . very slightly. A pulse under his claws juddered and sped up.

Howling burst out around them as the dogs caught up. The handlers surrounded him, kicking and punching at him. The dogs worried at his clothes with their teeth.

He could kill them all, but that would blow his cover. Three of the men had radios in their hands. They were in contact with others he could not get to and silence. Once Melinda learned that he was in the area, she would redouble security or move Val, or both. Painful as it would be, he had to take the punishment.

"What do we do with him, sir?"

George managed to twist his head to see the secretary arriving. Henry actually had on a safari jacket and pith helmet. Under its shielding brim, the blond human looked as imperious as a Victorian big-game hunter.

"Let it finish him," Henry said.

The head handler nodded to the others. They pulled the dogs back.

"No!" George pleaded, stretching out an imploring hand. "Let me go! I won't tell anyone . . ."

Henry shook his head.

I'll get you later, you cold-blooded son of a bitch, George thought. Dragons weren't the only vermin who could be merciless.

The beast let out a low, breathy chuckle, enjoying his pain. George decided to make the losing battle look good. He struggled against the fierce grip. With both hands, he pushed the jaws away from his neck. The beast snapped at his wrist, severing an artery. Blood sprayed them all. George bellowed in pain, no dissembling necessary. He brought up a knee into the creature's skinny backside. It let go for a moment, then hopped up on his belly with both back feet. As the handlers watched with growing horror, it dug through his clothes and skin like a dog excavating a hole. George could see his own intestines burst out like pink party balloons twisted into a French poodle. It hurt, though he had experienced worse.

He glanced at Henry, who seemed to be waiting for something.

Oh, yeah, George thought.

With a terrifying, sucking gasp, he died.

The handlers, silent with horror, leashed their dogs and

sent them back to the kennel with their leader. Henry himself stepped forward to take the creature by the ear. He clipped the leash to a ring in the fleshy upper lobe and tugged. The beast obediently stepped off its prey and sat on the ground to wash itself, as if it was an oversized, hairless cat. Henry nodded to the remaining men.

"Take it around back. Bury it under the compost heap. If anyone asks, we never saw him."

"Yes, sir," the men said. They sounded shaken. They hoisted George's body by his arms and legs, avoiding touching the tangle of bloody organs dangling over one side, and carried him through the now-driving rain around the perimeter of the house.

Once they had interred him under six or seven feet of rotting leaves and vegetable parings, George opened his eyes. No wonder no one ever broke into Melinda's estate.

Compost heaps, when well maintained, generated their own heat. Hence, it was nice and warm and, thankfully, dry inside. George gave himself five minutes to pull himself together and rearrange his shape back to that of a human being. Sound from outside was heavily muffled, but his "burial detail" did nothing to keep their passage silent. As soon as he was certain all the humans and dogs had gone back to the house, he tunneled his way out of the squashy, warm humus and made for exit number four.

He still didn't know what kind of creature had disemboweled him. Every detail of its appearance, including smell, was firmly entrenched in his memory. He'd have to put Debbie on it. If he hadn't been what he was, it could have killed him several times over during their brief fight. As it was, he was in some serious pain. His tissues were infinitely adaptable, but there was a limit on how much punishment he could take before he needed to crawl into a hole and rest. Now, however, was not the time.

Once out on the narrow avenue, George had to make certain to hide his trail. The rain was his friend. All trace of his scent was washed off the asphalt within moments of his

passage. He climbed hedges into less-well-patrolled properties, swam through three in-ground pools, and swung
through hundred-year-old oaks until he was positive nothing
except a high-speed movie camera in a helicopter could have
followed him. It was nearly sunrise by the time he felt safe
returning to his car.

It was small consolation, but some of the guests leaving
the mansion near his parked sedan looked worse than he did
as they staggered out to drive home.

"Debbie," he croaked into his cell phone as he pulled away
from the curb. "Bad news. They've got a demon."

"I'll double the fee," Debbie said at once. "You sound
awful. Go and get some sleep."

Thirty-three

Griffen stretched his long back as he walked along Toulouse toward Annette's at eleven o'clock in the morning. He had spent part of the night overseeing a poker game at the Hotel St. Marie, and almost the rest of it sitting up with Gris-gris. The slender gambler was crazy with impatience. The rubber plant looked annoyingly healthy. Gris-gris was ready to help it die by yanking it up by the roots and stomping it. Ann Marie had assured him that he was no more than a day or two from being liberated.

"We just want to make sure your soul is sealed up again where it ought to be," she said.

That comment had made Gris-gris fall silent for almost a minute. His nervous energy came springing back after that. All he wanted to do was talk about Val. Griffen absolutely did not want to know about his sister's love life. She had probably seen too much of his, and it was time both of them had their privacy. He challenged Gris-gris to a game of HORSE poker. The tournament comprised five different poker games, Hold 'Em, Omaha, Razz, Seven-card Stud, and Eight-High. Sometime during Razz, while Griffen was trying to construct a low enough hand to lose, Gris-gris had dropped off to sleep out of pure exhaustion. Griffen had quietly slipped out, waved the cluster of bones at the door, and left it in the flowerpot outside.

Griffen should have been exhausted, but maybe there was something in the voodoo magic that bestowed energy and clarity. Griffen's back was stiff from sitting in the same place for five hours, but he wasn't sleepy at all. Instead, he was roaringly hungry, and he wanted company. A heaping breakfast from Annette's kitchen filled his belly, and the Irish pub awaited to fulfill the latter need.

"Haven't seen you around for a few days," Maestro said, as Griffen swung into a seat and signaled for a Diet Coke from the bartender. The slim fencing teacher broke off from a conversation with a couple of regulars.

"I've been sitting up with a sick friend," Griffen explained. "You're not usually in here at this hour."

"Waiting for a student," Maestro explained. "He's a high-school teacher who wants to learn fight choreography. I told him it's better to know the basics of swordplay so you understand how to make fights look realistic but still safe."

"Sounds like fun."

"When are you coming back up for a lesson?" Maestro's studio was on the second floor of a nearby building. "You need to exercise those skills, or they'll go rusty."

Griffen made a face. He consulted his notebook. "I could use the workout. Do you have any time on Thursday?"

"Fine," Maestro said. "I have two other épée students coming in then. That will give each of you more bouts. Make sure you take the time to stretch before you come in."

"I will," Griffen promised. "Looking forward to it."

Griffen's cell phone rang in his pocket.

"Excuse me," he said to Maestro, and pushed the CALL button. "Griffen McCandles."

Jerome's voice came through the tinny speaker.

"Hey, Grifter, where are you?"

"Irish pub," Griffen said. "What's up?"

"Can I come and talk to you?"

"Sure. I'm just having a drink. Something wrong?"

"Rather talk about it when I see you."

Griffen was puzzled by his lieutenant's reticence. "Okay.

I'll be here." He put the phone on the bar and returned to Maestro.

"How's Ms. Dunbar?" the older man asked. "She looked pretty bad when the debate ended the other night."

"I don't really know," Griffen said. "I haven't seen her since then. Too much going on."

"I assume you haven't heard from Val because you haven't posted a huge 'Welcome Home' banner up there." Maestro pointed his own Diet Coke at the longest wall in the bar.

"No," Griffen said. He looked speculatively at his phone. Was it too early to call George?

Maestro patted his shoulder. "I'm sure she's all right. By the way, I have some pictures from the Fafnir parade last Mardi Gras that my cousin took for me. They were pretty spectacular. Do you want copies?"

Griffen had a mental flash of the condition of his float by the end of the parade and laughed. "Sure! Did you ride on our floats?"

"Wouldn't have missed it for the world," Maestro assured him. "I rode in a couple of others, too. The costumes are pretty similar. I must have tossed a thousand strings of beads. I love it. Halloween's better, though. That's just for us local folks, not for all the tourists."

"I'm looking forward to this year," Griffen said. "I was too busy last year."

"I hear you."

Griffen mused while the bartender topped up his soda. Had Mardi Gras only been a few months before? It seemed like another age.

"What's up, Griffen?"

He turned to see a man smiling at him. Griffen did a double take. The newcomer was a light-skinned black man with caramel brown eyes, wearing a handsome, lightweight gray designer suit and polished black leather shoes.

"Well, speak of the devil," Griffen said, putting out a hand. "How are you, Callum?"

Callum Fenway laughed. "I wasn't sure how well you'd remember me," he said.

"Are you kidding me? We were just talking about the parade." He gestured at Maestro.

"Must be something in the air."

Griffen introduced them. The two older men shook hands. "Yes, I remember you. Paid up in full, for 'The Pen Is Mightier Than the Dragon' float."

"Right!" Maestro said. "Nice to meet you again."

"Same here. Do you have a moment, Griffen?"

"Sure, Callum. Is something wrong?"

"Not at all." Callum glanced at Maestro, who tactfully turned away. "Haven't talked to you in a few months. We had a meeting a couple of nights ago, and you came up in our discussions."

"That sounds ominous," Griffen said.

"It's not. We just figure that now that we have a leader, we'd like to check in with you now and again."

Griffen knew exactly whom he meant by "we." Fafnir Krewe was made up entirely of dragons, from one who had a trickle of the blood in the midst of an almost completely werewolf heritage, up to just over half-blooded.

"I am not exactly your leader."

"Well, by virtue of blood, you outrank any of the rest of us. We don't mind. We kind of like having a clear chain of command. Etienne is good for running the krewe, and I'm good with the books, but as an overarching structure, we go by the old ranking. You're the big boss now."

"That's not necessary. I don't need to run anything. You're all doing fine."

Callum shook his head. "Son, you saw what a bunch of sheep the others were. We were ashamed to have human beings step up where dragons should have been out in front. I'm proud to know our fellow elemental krewes, but you're the boss. Even if you want to call it a nominal appointment, I suggest you accept it."

Griffen couldn't argue with that. "Just don't ask me to

adjudicate à la Solomon. So, what can I do for you, as big dragon?"

Callum pulled up the next stool and put his hands on the bar.

"Well, you know that the election is coming up in November. The jungle primary's October 5. Representative Penny Dunbar came to me and asked for a donation for her campaign for governor, on behalf of Fafnir Krewe. Since y'all were working with her, we figured it sounded like an endorsement, but I thought I should ask. She's the only candidate in the race who's one of us. Dragonkind has to stick together."

"She used my *name*?"

"Sure did. She told us that you'd consider it a personal favor if we threw our support behind her."

"I'm not working with her," Griffen said, feeling his temper rising. "That was a lie."

Callum gave him a strange look. "I saw you on television the other night, right behind her during that debate, where she had a fit of some kind? And I am sure that I caught sight of you when she made one of those speeches from a mangrove farm."

"My girlfriend is volunteer coordinator for one of the parishes," Griffen said, more calmly than he felt. "Penny has asked me to run security for her. She's had some run-ins that, uh, the police can't handle." He raised his eyebrows meaningfully.

Callum nodded. "I see. Anything you are going to need help on from any of us?"

"I hope not," Griffen said. "I'm waiting for a meeting that might clear things up."

"I see. Diplomacy's always a better option than confrontation. Well, it'd be good to have one of our own running the state. Never thought about it before. We were proud when she was elected to the state house of representatives. So, what do you want us to do?"

"Do?" Griffen echoed blankly. "No matter what my

feelings are about her, I have no intention of deciding for other people. Make up your own mind about it. Do you think that her aims are the same as yours? Will she support programs you consider worthwhile? Do you think she's honest?"

"Well, son, you know her better than we do. Is she?"

"Not really," Griffen said, lowering his voice, knowing Fox Lisa would take him apart if she heard him say so. "I've seen her take bribes."

Griffen got a cool look from the other dragon. "I've paid some of those myself, Griffen. That's just the cost of doing business in this state. Sometimes you need a little grease to make the wheels turn. But is Representative Dunbar effective? Does she take that money *and* do something, or just sit there?"

"She's definitely a doer," Griffen said, relieved to be able to give Penny kudos where they were merited.

Callum let out a gust of breath.

"Well, all right, then. I was going to throw my support behind Bobby Jindal, but if you like Penny Dunbar, then she's our candidate."

"That's up to you," Griffen said firmly. "I refuse to make up your minds for you."

Callum eyed him with a summing expression. "That's why you're the big boss around here, Griffen. You don't force your views on anyone. I never heard of a humble dragon before, least of all one with the abilities and talents you have."

Griffen was embarrassed. "Thanks, Callum."

"Like to sit down with you sometime, me and the rest of Fafnir. We want to know what plans you have for us all for the future."

Plans? But Callum looked so hopeful.

"Sure," Griffen said. "When this whole election thing is over."

"Sure thing. By the way, my wife Lucinda said to come to dinner on Friday. You free? Our housekeeper Edith promises to bring out some of her grandmother's best recipes. Brought up to date, of course. The cholesterol counts can kill anyone who's not actually out working in the fields. Her raised biscuits are good enough for a man to give up his hope of heaven."

"Thanks," Griffen said. "It would be a pleasure."

"Bring that pretty red-haired girlfriend of yours, too. There's always plenty."

Callum left. Griffen snorted the smoke he had been holding back. People kept putting him in charge of their lives when he didn't want them to! And how dare Penny use him to get to the krewe! She knew he was only helping her because Malcolm asked him to! The air around him turned gray. Inside him, the little spark danced for joy. Sourly, he tamped it down. Pouting, it subsided.

Griffen waved a surreptitious hand to clear the air. He glanced around. He hoped no one had seen him shooting plumes of vapor from his nostrils. To his dismay he spotted one pair of eyes on him. Fortunately, it belonged to Jerome. His lieutenant grinned and slid onto the barstool that Callum had vacated. He signaled to the bartender for a beer.

"Hey, boss, do those smoke signals mean a distress call? Anything I can help with?"

"Penny!" Griffen said, fighting to get his temper under control. "She's using my name to solicit donations. I am going to have to come down heavy on her. What's up?"

"Problem. Had a couple of dropouts for tonight."

"Does it leave us with enough for a table?" Griffen asked.

Jerome wrinkled his nose. "Not really, Grifter. And I had better tell you: two of them called to tell me they saw you on television Friday at the debate."

"Half of New Orleans did."

"Yeah, but they said they didn't know you were supporting Dunbar. They don't like it. They prefer their poker nonpartisan."

Griffen felt another burst of fury. The spark of fire in his belly kicked up against the breakfast he had recently consumed and crisped it to charcoal.

"I was afraid this was going to happen."

"It's *been* happening, Grifter," Jerome said patiently. "I've been running interference for you, telling them about Fox Lisa, but this time I failed the saving throw. It's not the first time. Remember the other night? I offered to bring you in as a substitute when the little mama went to the hospital, but they didn't want you."

"*What?*"

"I didn't want to mention it before. You've had so much on your mind. I thought it would blow over, but it's really turning into an issue. This election's got people polarized. It wouldn't have mattered in years gone by. No one wants to play nice with the other parties."

"What about tonight's clients?"

"They're both big-bankroll types, both of them have been at our tables before though not since before Mardi Gras. Trouble is, one of them works for the lieutenant governor, and he doesn't think it's prudent to be in the same room with you. The other, Penny, had his son busted at college last month for dealing a little dope from his dorm room. Made a big example of him. She was there for one of her speeches and got a tip about him. The roller thinks she has a snitch in the Vice Squad."

Griffen raised his eyebrows. "Harrison might like to hear about that."

"Yeah, but in the meantime, what do we do about the shortage?"

"How's the fill tomorrow evening? How about just canceling this one and bringing the remaining players in then?"

"No can do. Got a real whale from Florida, a new guy we were going to try and impress with our Big Easy style tonight. Marcel overheard him ask the concierge at the Sheraton where he could get a little action. He started a casual conversation and got him interested. Said we always have plenty of action. The three players who did stay are small-time, five-dollar chips. They won't impress him much."

"I'll have to sit in myself. Can you come in, too?"

"Got a date, Grifter," Jerome said, with a wink. "Sorry,

Grifter. I'd cancel, but we have tickets to a show. I am dead meat if I back out."

Griffen felt glum. "This is a real no-win situation you've handed me, Jer."

"Sorry, bro. I would help out if I could, but you don't really need me. Contrary to popular belief, I am not the only guy who is willing to sit at a table with you. There are a lot of good players in town who would jump at the chance to play a hot game with a powerhouse from Las Vegas. If you have to add a little lagniappe like some free table chips or a door prize, that just sweetens the pot. Why not give some of them a call?"

That struck Griffen as a good idea. He began to see a light at the end of what was becoming a longer tunnel than he had at first feared. *One problem at a time,* he told himself.

"All right. I'll hit the phones and see if I can dig someone up. Thanks, Jer."

Jerome felt in his pocket and came up with a square of paper with several notes block-printed as neatly as the type in a comic strip.

"Here's the details: hotel room number, dealer, catering menu. And take it easy, Grifter. This will all be over soon."

"Yeah. I hope I live to see that day."

Jerome stayed long enough to finish his beer and help Griffen calm down a little. They discussed ideas for the evening. Once he left, however, Griffen had no choice but to face an ordeal to which he was not looking forward. He dialed Penny's campaign office.

"May I speak to Horsie, please? This is Griffen Mc-Candles."

"She's not here at the moment, Griffen." He recognized the voice as one of the senior campaign workers, one who was coordinating the greater New Orleans area's volunteers. "Penny is here. She's waiting to do a press conference. Would you like to speak to her?"

"Thanks."

While Griffen waited, he drummed his pencil on his

pocket notebook, where he had written the salient points of the statement he was about to give. He didn't want to be provocative or hurtful, just straightforward, brief, and final.

"Hi there, Griffen." Penny's voice came on the line with honeyed vowels. "We haven't seen you around here in a long time. Hope you're coming by soon. I really appreciate all you do here. And Fox Lisa, too. She is here with me."

Griffen heard a faint "hi" in the background.

"Uh, thanks. I was happy to help." He cleared his throat. "Look, Penny, I am sorry to say that I have to back away from accompanying you to any more appearances. I really can't afford to be seen in public on your behalf any longer. It's cutting directly into my business. I told you that if that happened, I'd have to quit. And, I am sorry, but that is the case."

Silence fell on the line for a moment. Then, her voice returned.

"I see. Well, if you are sure, Griffen, then I understand. I am very grateful for all the time you have been able to give me. I will just have to do the best I can with the remaining resources I have."

"I'm not going to stop trying to solve that other problem for you, though. I'm just going to have to do it from a distance."

"Well, I really appreciate that," Penny said. "Let me know what you find out."

"Thanks. I wish you the best of luck. It's been interesting."

"Yes, it has," she said. "I'm sorry you won't see the rest. It's going to get more interesting."

She clicked off. Griffen expelled a long, slow breath. She had taken it better than he had feared. Now he had to work on saving the evening.

Before he could dial again, the phone rang in his hand. Penny calling back for some reason? No, the display showed an out of town number. Could it be good news from George? Griffen hit the green button.

"Hello?"

"Griffen, don't bark into the phone. It sounds childish."

Griffen felt as if he were eleven again. "Hi, Uncle Malcolm, what can I do for you?"

"I am at the airport. Where are you? I've been waiting nearly thirty minutes!"

Griffen groaned. He had forgotten that his elder relative was arriving that day. "I apologize. I've been busy. Among other things, I'm trying to get things set up for a game tonight." A thought struck him. "Uncle Malcolm, do you play poker?"

Thirty-four

Brenda cracked open a new red Bicycle deck, tossed the wrapper and the jokers in the bucket at her feet, and snapped the fifty-two remaining pasteboards into a complicated series of fans and arches. The players watched appreciatively.

The minisuite at the Royal Sonesta Hotel, decorated in soothing shades of blue, provided a comfortable setting for the game. Griffen had arrived early to make sure the hotel manager was comfortable with their presence. Neither of them, the manager assured him, wanted any interruptions.

Three players from Griffen's list had been happy to join the impromptu party. None of them cared whether he worked as a pole dancer, let alone as a temporary political attaché for a controversial candidate. They had shown up with their money. Griffen bought half a dozen bottles of different whiskies to hand out as prizes for point accumulation, number of wins, and designated hands. They sat on the highboy behind Brenda, glinting with amber points of light.

The whale, Douglas Jasper, a plump, balding man with a ruddy face and a double chin, sat at Brenda's right hand. He shook hands all around.

"Let me see if I have you all straight," he said. "David Saldez, Marcellus Latham, Scott Bellamy, Malcolm Mc-Candles, Tom McNair, Lee Goodrich, Griffen McCandles?"

"Great memory," Tom exclaimed. He was one of the original group slated for that evening, a small bankroller, as was

Marcellus. Griffen fully expected the two of them to drop out early. They were good company, though.

Griffen signaled to Marcel, who was acting as caterer that evening. As a reward for having brought Douglas in, it gave him the opportunity to pick up some extra tips during the game. Marcel sprang forward to start serving drinks and snacks.

"I watch people," Douglas said, pointing from one to the other. "For example, I can see that though we have two Mc-Candleses, they're not father and son. The interaction's wrong."

"Good call," Griffen said. "He's my uncle."

"Well, nice to meet you all." Douglas lifted his glass to them. Maker's Mark was his tipple. "Let's play cards."

Malcolm held his hand cupped just above the green felt of the tabletop. Brenda shot his two down cards directly into the low space. Malcolm raised his eyebrows. "Very impressive. You seem amazingly professional."

Griffen pitched his voice very casually to conceal his annoyance at his uncle's arrogant attitude.

"She is a professional, Uncle Malcolm. By the way, it was her car I borrowed the first time you visited."

"Ah. Thank you so much for the loan," Malcolm said, turning to Brenda graciously. "It was very kind of you."

"No problem."

"And no offense was intended."

"None taken, Mr. McCandles," Brenda said, with a saucy grin. Malcolm, slightly embarrassed by his gaffe, touched the plate of small delicacies beside him on the rim of the table.

"The food is good, too. In fact, your entire organization is well thought-out and well run. What do you think, Douglas?"

The big man grinned. "Cosier than I'm used to. Usually I'm playing in a room with two or three hundred other people at least, and cocktail waitresses leaning over my arm. This is really nice."

Griffen was on the small blind, so he concentrated on reading the cards for a moment. To his surprise, Malcolm opened the conversation.

"I see you as one of my fellow beasts of prey, Douglas. What do you do?"

"Mostly, I own a chain of restaurants. Dabble in this and that. How about you?"

"Investments," Malcolm said. "Fairly conservative, long-term strategy. Tell me about your corporation."

Douglas was all too happy to talk about himself.

"Well, my daddy started it with one little hot-dog stand in Tallahassee, Florida. I expanded it to a chain that reaches clear across the South. We're not as big as Crystal Burgers, but I believe in my menu and my customer service."

Griffen was pleased, more pleased than he thought. His uncle was an amateur player but a good judge of character. By instinct, Griffen could tell that he started to see players' tells. The whale had a habit of swirling the ice in his glass if his down pair was weak. But the more he concentrated and the larger the bets, the less body language he gave off. Malcolm made a couple of bad raises against him until he realized that something had changed. He played more cautiously after that. Griffen was happy with the way the evening was going.

As he had predicted, Marcellus didn't last past eleven o'clock. Tom surrendered his final stack of chips not too long afterward. He kept his last chip to hand off to Brenda as a tip. Both men were enjoying themselves too much to leave. They dragged their chairs away from the edge of the table and kibitzed from a distance. When play resumed, Douglas proposed a raise in the bets.

"Look at all those chips," he said, pointing at the stacks on the table. "How about let's play for some real money now? Twenty a point?"

Griffen collected nods from the others.

"Why not?" he said. He was only slightly behind Douglas in gains, holding about 23 percent of the chips. Brenda cashed in the fives and tens for twenty-dollar chips, and pushed a five-dollar bill toward Scott.

About one o'clock in the morning, fresh, hot food was delivered, courtesy of Leon, a young man, neat in a black leather jacket and new jeans, a busboy by day Griffen had met at Yo Mama's. Leon was a younger brother of one of Griffen's dealers and hoping to move up in the organization. He unloaded the two-wheeler he was pushing. Marcel arranged the covered trays on the table while Leon unpacked cases of soda and beer into the cooler at one end. Leon tidied up all the empties and stacked them up on the cart. He accepted a tip with a grin and left, but not without a hopeful look over his shoulder. Griffen made certain to lock the door behind him.

Less than an hour later, a knock sounded again at the door. Puzzled, Griffen looked at his watch. They still had plenty of food. No more deliveries were supposed to come unless he called for them. Maybe the hotel management was checking on him?

He set his cards down and went to see who was there. No sooner had he turned the knob than the door was shoved hard from the other side. Griffen blocked the door with his foot and leaned around the edge.

A big hand in a black leather sleeve was on the other side. The hand was white with a thick patch of hair on the back. That wasn't Leon. Griffen's gaze traveled up the arm to a short, beefy neck, with Harrison's face perched on top.

"Hey, there, Detective Harrison, what can I do for you?" he asked, trying to keep his voice down.

Harrison pitched his voice with unnatural clarity.

"I have a tip that there is an illegal poker game going on in here," he said. "Move aside, McCandles."

Griffen glanced down the hall. A sharp beam of light hit him in the eyes. He winced, squinting into it until he could make out its source. It came from the top of a video camera held on the shoulder of a man in blue jeans and a feed cap. Beside him, a woman held a black-topped microphone out toward him. Two uniformed police stood by, one black and one white, wearing bulletproof vests and helmets. Griffen looked at Harrison. The big detective's eyes were apologetic but firm.

"Brenda, honey!" Griffen called over his shoulder. "Can you hear me?"

"Uh, yes, Griffen," Brenda said, tentatively.

"The police are here, love. Please go and lock yourself in the bathroom. Don't let anyone in but me. All right?"

"Uh, sure, Griffen."

The news team looked at one another in bemusement. Clearly, that was not what they expected to hear. The two policemen grinned lasciviously.

Griffen held on to the door firmly and squeezed out through the smallest slot he could, then yanked it solidly closed. He leaned back against the door and folded his arms. Harrison had to move his hand in a hurry, so it wouldn't get slammed in the crack.

"Goddammit, McCandles, I haven't got time for this!"

"So, may I ask why you have decided to spoil my evening?" Griffen asked. He wore an aggrieved expression. "Do you know how long it took me to talk her into a date?"

Harrison's mouth dropped open.

"A *date?*"

"Well, why the hell do you think I would have reserved a suite at the Sonesta?" he asked, pitching his voice loudly enough so the newswoman couldn't miss it. "I have an apartment just a few blocks from here. I wanted this to be special for her!"

"Let me in, McCandles."

Griffen shifted so his back was against the doorknob.

"So you can embarrass her further? No way. Show me a warrant." He looked from one officer to another. "Is this random harassment? Or do you have a reason for invading my room in the middle of the night?"

Harrison looked over his shoulder at the reporters. "I was acting on information received."

"Uh-huh."

"It seems that my source was mistaken."

"No kidding. Can I go back in now? I have some serious apologizing to do."

The cameraman seemed to take the hint first. He put a hand on top of his apparatus and snapped off a switch. The brilliant light died away. Griffen felt the temperature in the hallway drop twenty degrees. The reporter put her microphone in her shoulder bag.

"Well, that was a bust," she said, stomping toward the elevator. The cameraman hurried behind. She slammed the elevator button with her palm and watched the indicator impatiently.

"Thanks for stopping by, guys," Griffen called after them, his voice sarcastic.

Harrison muttered to him under his breath. "I need to talk to you. I'll send my men away and come back. Wait for me."

Griffen replied without moving his lips. "Right."

"Hell with it," Harrison said, loudly. A few people had opened the door to their rooms and peered out. He gestured sharply at them, and they disappeared again. He went toward his men. "Let's clear out. Mackie, you can hit the streets again. Boulder, report in. Tell them it was a false alarm." Harrison aimed a thumb over his shoulder. "I'm going to try and talk this good citizen out of filing a report for harassment."

"Yes, sir!" they said.

"Hey, miss!" Boulder called. "Hold that elevator, okay?" He ran to catch up with the news crew. Mackie started to follow but turned back for a moment.

"Hey, McCandles, a piece of advice."

"Yes?"

"It's two o'clock in the morning. If you ain't got her naked by now, bro, you ain't gonna. Try a cheaper hotel next time."

"Yeah, thanks," Griffen said with a sour twist to his mouth.

The other officer laughed. They slapped each other's palms as the elevator doors closed on them.

Harrison put his thumbs in his belt and leaned backward.

"Haven't you learned enough to ask who it is before you open the door in this town?" he asked. "At least you were smart enough to block the peephole."

"Weren't *you* supposed to bang on the door and yell 'New Orleans Police'?"

"Maybe you just didn't hear me identify myself," Harrison said. "Although we've found in the past that giving perps a few seconds to hide the evidence screwed our cases in court. Not everyone remembers whether or not we identified ourselves when we entered the room."

"Aren't those reporters going to know?"

Harrison shook his head. "Video isn't worth keeping. I'd be surprised if that tape wasn't erased before morning. Nothing happened. They didn't get their big exclusive."

That brought Griffen back to the matter at hand.

"How did they know there was going to *be* an exclusive? Where did they get the information we were going to be here? Where did you get it?"

Harrison lowered his brows. His eyes turned wary. "Why?"

"Because I think we were both set up. I quit helping the Dunbar campaign this evening. Did you get a call after six?"

"No," Harrison said. "No call. One of my CIs came to me about an hour ago. Said it was a big game with thousands of dollars on the table. Maybe a couple of underage players. I brought it to my lieutenant. He said to go on it. Then the news crew showed up, said they were coming with us on the bust." Enlightenment dawned, and the big man's eyebrows went up. "Is that SOB informant working for *her*?"

"I have reason to believe that's true," Griffen said.

"Goddammit. I told you I hate elections. So I've got a double agent? Thanks for the tip. I'm going to go ream the little weasel a new one."

"I have to get back in there. Brenda's waiting."

Harrison smirked at him.

"It's not too smart to play around with your employees."

"I'm not playing a round with her. She's dealing the cards." Harrison pretended to be shocked.

"So you were lying, McCandles? To me? You promised you'd be straight with me."

Griffen saw he was kidding, so he played along.

"Harrison, I'd be a rotten poker player if I couldn't lie with a straight face, now, wouldn't I?"

"Well, it would make my job a lot easier. Go on back. Sorry to interrupt."

"No problem," Griffen said. "If you have time tomorrow, meet me for a burger at Yo Mama's."

"Sounds good to me. You can buy."

"Only if I make some money tonight! Good night!"

Griffen waited until the elevator doors closed on the chuckling Harrison, and he saw the indicator numbers begin to fall. He listened carefully to make sure no one was coming up in the concrete fire stairwell, then let himself back into the hotel room.

"You were a long time, Griffen," Malcolm said. "Any problem?"

"Nuclear option," Griffen said blandly. Malcolm's mouth opened slightly. It was the most shocked Griffen had ever seen him.

"What's that?" Marcellus asked.

"Ann Arbor term," Griffen explained. "It means the Queen of Spades is gumming up the game."

"Well, don't she always?"

"Whew!" Douglas exclaimed, puffing out his cheeks. "That was exciting! I thought for a minute we were going to get hauled down to the police station! The old NOLA hoosegow." He patted his pockets. "I'm not used to keeping bail money on me anymore."

"Well, it didn't happen," Griffen said.

"I knew it wasn't going to," Douglas said, beaming. "Malcolm here assured us that you would handle it."

"He did?" Griffen asked, surprised.

"Yes," Malcolm said, with an austere smile. It was the most relaxed Griffen had ever seen him. "You have always displayed a preternatural knack for self-preservation. I assumed it would extend to your clientele."

"Of course," Griffen replied, just as blandly. Douglas slapped his knees.

"Nice ruse, telling them you were here for a rendezvous. I can't wait to tell the fellahs back in Vegas. They'll howl!"

Griffen went to the bathroom door and knocked. "Brenda, it's safe. They're gone."

The dealer poked her head out. She emerged, clutching the rack of chips and the bank box in her arms.

"That was a close one," she said. "Kind of like the old days. When Mose was running things."

Griffen made a face. "I didn't know you missed them."

"I don't!"

She sat down at the table and began to set things up. Griffen broke his own rules and went to the bar. He poured a glass of red wine and set it down at Brenda's elbow.

"Just this once," Griffen said. "You deserve it."

"You bet I do," she said, flipping open a new deck and cracking the cards into an arch. "That was a good save, Griffen. Mose would be proud."

"It was great!" Douglas said. He turned to the young man behind the catering table. "Hey, Marcel, you were right! I never have had an experience like this one. You've got a permanent customer! I'll play with you fellahs anytime I'm in town."

"You'll be welcome," Griffen said. "Who's on the button?"

"You are," Brenda said.

She flicked cards to each of the players in turn. Malcolm reached for his tentatively. His eyes met Griffen's.

"I believe we will have to conduct an interview in the morning," he said. "With the Queen of Spades."

"Yes," Griffen agreed. Malcolm turned to their guest.

"Well, Douglas, do you ever have surprise visits from the

Health Department? I believe they enjoy appearing on-site without previous notice."

His conversation remained effusive, but his game became more cautious than before.

Griffen could hardly blame him.

Thirty-five

Val stared at Henry eyeball-to-eyeball. No matter how much she shouted at him, the blond man's face maintained all the emotion of a wax mannequin. She took a step back from him and inhaled deeply.

"What do you mean, I can't go out?" Val asked. "I have a date! Mike is going to pick me up at six."

"It's not safe," Henry said. "We found a prowler on the grounds late last night."

Val blinked her eyes blearily. She glanced at the clock. Seven. Normally she would have been awake by then, maybe even swum her laps, but not after a late night like the one she had had. She tried to react more like a responsible adult. The estate was out in the middle of nowhere. Break-ins had to be a genuine concern.

"Did he get in?"

"No," Henry said. "He tried, though. He attempted to break in through your window. When we looked over the site, we saw a lot of the same footprints in the same place over several days. Have you seen anything suspicious?"

Val couldn't help but feel guilty, remembering the missed meeting with her unknown note-writer.

"No," she said, tossing her head. "In case you forgot, you kept me up until three doing accounting."

"Come with me," Henry said. He took her by the arm and escorted her firmly toward the stairs.

"Where are we going?" Val asked, bumping down the steps beside him in her slippers. She grabbed for the banister to steady herself.

"The security center," Henry said. "This way."

On the ground floor beside the sweeping staircase, he took her to what looked like a plain wall with a large portrait of an eighteenth-century ancestor of Melinda's on it. He placed his hand against the white plaster. Val was deeply impressed when the whole panel swung out to reveal a corridor with carpeting on all four sides. Henry drew her into the tunnel. The door swung shut behind them, but they weren't left in the dark. Lines of tiny blue lights came on near their feet. In no time at all, Val's eyes had adjusted.

"I didn't know this was here," Val said. Her voice sounded muffled because of the padding on the walls.

"That, my dear, is the entire idea."

At the end of the hallway, they stopped at a plain door painted solid black. It opened to one side like the doors on the U.S.S. *Enterprise*, but silently.

"How does it know it's you?" Val asked.

"It doesn't. They do." Henry swept a hand forward.

The room before her was low and fairly small but jammed to the ceiling with racks of machinery studded with bright LEDs and video screens. Three men and women, all about her age, sat at the consoles, glancing from screen to screen, tapping on keyboards or adjusting knobs. The temperature was uncomfortably warm from all the electronics. Cool vents near the ceiling tried in vain to regulate the heat. The employees wore thin, short-sleeved white shirts, but they still looked hot. The room seemed to pulse with energy.

"Freaky," Val said. "Like the nerve center of a spy operation."

Her weariness faded away as she walked around the small room, trying to guess what all the devices were for. The center had cameras pointing to every part of the house. She peered at each screen, trying to see if there was one in her bedroom. To her relief, though there was a lens aimed at the hallway just outside it, none of the views showed the interior of any of the sleeping quarters.

Henry guided her to a seat at the end of the widest console beside a young woman with black hair pulled back from a broad, walnut-colored face with a high forehead.

"Pull up the footage from camera sixteen from last night," he ordered her. She tapped at a few keys, then slid her chair to one side to allow Val to get in front of the screen.

Val leaned in close to look at the black-and-white image. The edge of the pool was in the foreground. The water danced with tiny pinpricks of light, making it look like it had waves tossing. She remembered that it had been raining hard overnight. Beyond it, the ground sloped down toward the left, leading to the front of the house. In the background she saw a window. It had to be her room.

A stocky figure entered the frame. It approached her window. It raised a hand to feel along the frame. Then the figure leaned toward it, cupping a hand to help it see inside.

In the lower-left-hand corner of the screen, a set of white dot-matrix-style numbers ticked off, showing the time as 23:15:04 when Val first started watching. At Henry's direction, the woman reached over to tap another key. The video jumped slightly. The rain was heavy enough to be visible now, backlit by the faint illumination coming from the window. The figure approached several times to look inside. In the last instance, time-stamped 02:47:15, the person, hunched against the rain, raised a hand with something white in it and tucked it into the window frame.

At the right bottom of the screen, red letters burst into view: ALARM! INTRUSION WINDOW 16.

The dark shape moved away from the window and moved to the left. It walked more awkwardly than it had at first. Val wondered if it had hurt itself. The video stopped.

"What do you know about this?" Henry asked.

"Nothing!" Val said. "When that alarm went off, I was in the lounge with you. Those bells were so loud that my ears are still ringing. You just jumped up, said 'You're safe in this room,' and locked me in. I just sat there. I think I heard dogs barking and people yelling. I'm not sure how long it was before you came back and took me up to my room. That's all."

"And you remember nothing else?" Henry asked.

"No," Val said. "I didn't think I could sleep, but I dropped off as soon as I fell into bed. The first thing I remember after that is your pounding on my door to tell me that I can't go on my date."

Henry made a gesture, and the woman reversed the video. The dark figure reappeared near her window.

"You're sure that you don't know who that is?"

Val peered closely. "I can't make out any distinguishing characteristics, but he seemed to walk oddly."

"He? Do you know who he is?"

"No!" Val protested. "Of course not. I don't know anyone around here. I don't even know where I am," she added bitterly.

"Then how do you know it's a man?"

"He walks like a man," Val said. "That's what always gives away the female impersonators in the French Quarter. You can tell the ones who haven't learned to swing their hips yet."

"True," Henry said, thoughtfully. "Yes, it was a man."

"Do you think he'll try again?" Val asked.

"I doubt it," Henry said. "He had a rather bad accident when he ran into our . . . dogs."

Val's eyes widened. "A bad accident? How bad? As in killed?"

Henry looked sorrowful, but his voice was flat.

"Alas, yes. But we don't know if he was working alone. Our security is very tight, and we mean business. That's why I dissuade you from taking a walk around the grounds at night without letting one of us know. Marcella or I can arrange it so you will have nothing to fear. Please, don't go out after dark. Melinda would have my head on a pike."

Val trembled so much Henry had to help her out of her

chair. She made herself walk through the black door into the
carpet-lined corridor. Could she have been responsible for a
man's being killed? How horrible! She wanted to go home
more than ever. She was trapped in this monstrous house.

Henry hung back for one moment to speak to the
employees.

"We are on lockdown until further notice. Melinda will
be home tomorrow evening. If you have any questions, call
my number. Don't bother her."

"Yes, sir!" the three said.

Henry caught up with Val and tucked her arm into his.

"It'll be fine, dear," he assured her.

"How can it be? That man is dead! I want to go back to
New Orleans!"

Henry pulled her into the light and looked deeply into
her eyes as he stroked her hand.

"Darling, don't be so hasty. That man's unfortunate end
has nothing to do with you. It could have happened last week
or next year. We've had to deal with intruders many times.
You're too precious to risk, you know. Melinda really has
faith in you. And you've completely won over the staff. They
all love you. They would all be very sad to see you leave."

"But . . ." Val started to protest.

Henry's gentle voice was like a calming drone in her ears.
"At least wait until you have talked with Melinda before you
take any hasty steps. Then, I promise you, if you still want
to go, we will put you on first-class transportation back to
New Orleans. But you won't want to. You'll see. There are
too many opportunities here for you. Of all kinds." A twinkle
appeared in his eyes, and Val couldn't help smiling in response. "In the meanwhile, please feel free to confer with
Marcella and the chef about a menu for your dinner with Mr.
Burns tonight. Enjoy yourself. Everything in this house is at
your disposal."

Almost against her will, Val felt her misgivings ease. That
man *had* been trying to break into her bedroom window. He
looked as if he were waiting for her. She could have been hurt

or killed herself. Henry was right. They were only trying to protect her.

For a moment, she stood still, trying to decide what to do next.

"Why don't you go upstairs and have your swim and some breakfast?" Henry suggested. "You need to be ready for your day. Your swimsuit has been laid out—your new one. The old one wasn't big enough for the two of you. Go on. Meet me back in the lounge at two. We'll go over some of the corporate records. I promise I will leave you plenty of time to get dressed. Go on now!"

"All right. Henry, thanks," she said. "I feel better."

He smiled at her. "Just doing my job, darling."

Thirty-six

"**Firing** people," Val said, sprawled on her back on a lounger in the sitting room of Marcella's quarters, "is awful."

"It is," the housekeeper said. She sat cross-legged on a huge soft ottoman with a load of music CDs on her lap. "Did you have to let someone go today?"

"Yes," Val said. She shifted to one side. Her growing belly seemed to slosh over when she moved. The baby had gone to sleep during a mellow blues recording by Leadbelly. The jazz horns that replaced it had a rapid tempo but kept on a low volume so as not to stimulate him or her into a kicking frenzy. Val had already been to the bathroom four times since dinner. "I hated it, but he literally wasn't doing the job he was hired to do. The records go back for months. Half of the other people in his section were covering for him. He seems like a really nice guy, but he doesn't know what he's doing."

"Couldn't you demote him or lateral-shift him to another part of the company?"

Val shook her head. "There aren't any openings at the moment. I asked Henry a bunch of times. He would need more experience. He has no computer skills at all."

"An older man?" Marcella guessed.

"No. Thirty."

"Then he can get hired elsewhere. The market is terrible for older workers above fifty."

"The market's terrible anyhow," Val said. She sighed and threw an arm over her eyes. The music made her feel as if she ought to be doing something, dancing or walking, but she was too tired to get up. "Thank God I don't have to look for a job myself anymore."

Marcella smiled. "It's good that you have empathy for him."

"When I can't feel sorry for someone in trouble, I hope that someone will shoot me in the head, because I won't be . . . human anymore." Val hesitated. After all, she wasn't human, but she had been brought up to think she was. Did dragons really think and feel differently than people? She'd have to think about that later, when she was alone. "Of course, he was too upset to care that I did feel sorry for him. Ugh! Let's talk about something else! Your rooms are really nice."

"Not as nice as yours," Marcella said. "But I was able to choose my furnishings and color scheme—subject to Melinda's approval, of course. If I had wanted to paint the room black with neon sculptures, she might have had something to say."

Val scanned the low tables and smooth, porcelain lamps. The walls had been painted a faint sandy peach color, with the rest of the room in colors that reminded her of a beach sunrise. It was all very contained. The housekeeper's style was as neat and minimalist as her dress sense.

"Do you have to clean for yourself, do your own laundry and things?" Val asked, curiously.

"No. It would be a poor use of my time. I even have call on the stylist. You get priority, naturally. Like last night."

"What a waste *that* was!" Val said. "I hope your dates go better."

"My work is my life," Marcella said. "When I'm ready to move on, I'll start thinking about a relationship."

Val nodded. She'd heard many similarly dismissive statements over the bar.

"Bad breakup, huh?"

Marcella smiled sadly.

"The worst."

"Did you enjoy your dinner last evening?" Marcella asked. "You are dating such a dishy guy."

Val wanted badly to know if Marcella or anyone else in the household was a dragon but couldn't bring herself to use the *D* word. She suspected Henry was one of them. Marcella might not know. Or she might assume that Val knew which ones were what. It was weird not having a clue. She was happy to change the subject to Mike.

"He's amazing. I never thought I'd go out with anyone like him. He's classy, generous, funny, well educated, and not at all stuck-up."

"And a serious hunk."

"Totally. It's too bad we were marooned here last night. It was that all-important fifth date. I was seriously considering jumping him."

"You could have. You have privacy in your own quarters," Marcella assured her.

"Everyone would have known what was going on!" Val complained. "Talk about crimping my style."

"How did he feel about it?"

Val let the corners of her mouth drift upward.

"Oh, come on, he's been ready from day one. I think he knew."

Mike had been willing to wait until she was ready. That he let her take the lead was one of the traits that she found attractive in him. That, and that he was still interested in her in spite of her blooming body. Lately, when she had looked in the mirror, she had been appalled by her reflection. Accustomed to her usually athletic form, she found the growing bulges unsightly. But Mike found it sexy and found plenty of ways to show her without saying a word. When he helped seat her at the table laid in the small sitting room, instead of the huge and empty dining room, he had caressed the inner curve of her arm. He held her hand across the table and played with her fingers, drawing his own fingers over them until the tingling drove her crazy with desire. The shame was that one of the estate's employees was always just at their elbows, ready to pour drinks or clear the dishes.

"You could have asked us to go away," Marcella pointed out. "That's what Melinda does when she has a serious date here for dinner."

"TMI!" Val exclaimed. The mental picture of the gruff, aggressive Melinda pursuing a man around the table made her cringe. "No, that would have been too awkward. Next time, when we can go somewhere private." She smiled reminiscently. "We're starting to think about some things at the same time, like finishing each other's sentences. Weird."

"What's so weird? It sounds pretty normal to me. You two sound really compatible. Do you think it might work out to a permanent relationship?"

"Marriage?" *What would be so bad about marrying a guy like Mike anyway?* Val thought. He was her intellectual equal though far more experienced than she was. As he pointed out to her, she didn't need assertiveness lessons. Val believed that he liked having a woman who stood up to him. One of the things that held her back from really committing to a relationship with him was that it would give Melinda too much satisfaction to choose one of the men with whom she had set Val up. "I just can't believe he's not married already."

"Another one who is wedded to his job," Marcella speculated. "I think that politicians have to be more than a little selfish. They're on show all the time. Even potential spouses have to fit into what they think is the right public profile, the one they want to show."

"Well, I wouldn't settle for half of someone's attention," Val said firmly.

"When you go for a high-powered man like that, you might have to."

"No, I won't."

Marcella smiled slyly. "I think he's in for a shock."

"Maybe he is." The baby woke up and kicked her. Val put her hand on her belly. "Ooh. That one was right in the bladder." She looked at the clock. "I'd better go to bed. If Melinda is due back, I bet she's going to quiz me on what I've been doing. I had better get some sleep."

Marcella rose when she did.

"That is a good idea. And Val? If you do stay, I would be very happy. None of us would resent anything that you accept from Melinda. We know you aren't out to bilk her." The grin grew broader. "You might even shake her up a little."

Val smiled at her, feeling as if she had made a new friend. She put her hand on Marcella's arm. "Thanks."

When Val went up to her room, most of the lights in the house were out except for a few strategically located wall sconces. Everything felt so homey and warm. She felt amazed that the angst she had felt the day before had gone away. She could have a future here, a pretty nice one.

Her room glowed with soft golden light. One lamp, beside her bed, was lit. One of the house-elves doing turn-down service, Val thought, with a little grin. She reached for her nightgown and felt a slight draft of cool air. The window must have been left ajar.

Memory of that first mysterious note came to her. Automatically, Val felt along the window frame. There was no note, but the sash rested a hair higher in the frame than it should have. She felt the breeze coming from underneath and shoved it down again.

"I wish you hadn't done that," a voice said behind her. "Now you've engaged the alarm system on the sash. That was my only way out."

Val spun, balling her hands into fists. Her women's self-defense training from college flooded her mind in a split second. Unfortunately, the bulk of her abdomen kept swinging farther than her feet, throwing her off-balance. So did the sight of the other person in the room.

"Mai!" she cried.

Thirty-seven

Val closed the distance between them in two steps and wrapped her arms around her petite friend.

"Oof!" Mai returned the hug lightly, then twisted her shoulders. "Come on, moose, you are crushing my ribs."

Val let go of the little Asian woman. She stepped back and beamed at her. Mai had on a chic tan safari suit and soft boots. A black pouch was slung across her body on a strap, and a sheathed knife hung on her belt. Otherwise, she looked exactly as she had when Val had seen her at the Mardi Gras party ages ago.

"I am so glad to see you! Why haven't you returned any of my calls?"

"What calls?" Mai asked.

Val looked at her as if she had spoken in a different language. "I have been trying you from the house phone for, well, months! I don't have roaming on my cell phone. In the Quarter, who needs it? Haven't you seen messages from a strange number?"

"No," Mai said. "I have recognized all the callers I have received. Yours were none of them. I have been worried about you! Have you been here the whole time?"

"Just about," Val said. "Except for a day in New York to buy me some clothes. It was a big whirlwind. I saw three doctors, and we went to a show. Mai, was it you on the property last night? They sent out dogs and everything. They locked me in while it was all going on. Henry said that the person had been killed, but I don't know whether to believe him or not."

"No, not me. Some prowler, perhaps. A very unlucky prowler, I assume. This estate is locked up like Tiffany's vault."

Val suppressed nauseous images that sprang up. She had seen too many horror movies.

"How is Griffen?"

"I have no idea. I have been looking for you for months. You say you have tried to call me?"

"Yes!" Val said. "I left scads of messages. I heard your voice, so I know it was your line. I've called Griffen a dozen times a week, but he never calls back, either."

"It sounds to me like something is interfering with the calls," Mai said, her small face a smooth mask of concentration.

"Melinda?"

"That would be my guess. You would not think of her as subtle, but she employs subtle people."

"Henry," Val said, suddenly furious. "It has to be him. He runs everything here."

"But are you all right?"

Val suddenly wanted to show off. "I've been having a great time! Did you see that gorgeous pool outside? I have it pretty much to myself. Melinda has a gourmet chef who can cook anything though mostly I tell him to surprise me. The housekeeper is a really nice woman. We've been hanging out. And, oh! Melinda gave me a job!"

Mai peered at her. "A job?"

"Yes!" Val rushed to her desk to show Mai the books. "I'm running a company for her. She's paying me sixty grand a year! Henry gave me my first check yesterday. It was nearly a thousand dollars. It's unbelievable."

Mai handled the ledgers as if they had been dunked in urine.

"But why would you want to work, Val? You are a dragon female."

"I like to work, Mai," Val said. It sounded strange to say out loud, but it was true. "I really like doing things. I can't tend bar forever. When this little guy comes, I need to have some kind of income, and I'm not going to be able to work whole shifts for a while."

Mai pursed her lips in disapproval.

"So. She couldn't get you any other way, so she has bought you?"

Val felt her face grow hot. "She hasn't bought me! I like doing the work."

"And who was doing it before you came along? You never finished your business courses. Do you really know what you are doing?"

"Well, Henry answers my questions if I run into something I don't know . . . oh."

Val felt all her pride seep out through her feet.

Mai nodded sympathetically. "Spoon-feeding you the information."

"But I'm dating this amazing guy, Mike Burns. He's a candidate for the Senate. And he's a dragon."

"Don't trust a politician," Mai warned her. "They all lie."

"No, he's really nice! And handsome."

Mai's thin brows showed her skepticism.

"How's he in bed?"

"I haven't let it get that far yet," Val said a little sheepishly.

The brows rose higher.

"Really? You?"

"I'm trying to turn over a new leaf."

Mai shook her head.

"You have changed. A new job, a new man, a new attitude. I suppose you don't want to go home any longer."

Val burst into tears and threw herself into Mai's arms, nearly knocking the smaller woman off her feet.

"Yes, I do!"

Mai guided her to the ottoman, put her arms around her, and let her sob.

"We must get you home. How can we get you out of here?"

"I don't even know where *here* is," Val said, miserably. She reached for the box of tissues beside the lamp and blew her nose.

"North Carolina," Mai said. "We're not too far from the Raleigh airport. I could have you there in an hour. We will take the first plane going anywhere and make our way back to New Orleans."

The sudden plans took Val aback.

"I can't just leave!"

"Why not? You just said you wanted to go home. You are not making any sense, Amazon."

"It would cause too much of a fuss. Melinda's due back this evening. She expects to see me. I can't go missing right now."

"Why would you care? She swept you away from your home and friends without a backward glance. Everyone was worried about you. I was worried about you! I'll bet you have not thought of your boyfriend at home once."

"I have, too," Val said, the sense of guilt creeping back again. "I called for reports on Gris-gris from the nurses at Charity Hospital until he left. I heard all about his progress until he got well. They wouldn't let him use his cell phone in Intensive Care. Then someone stole his phone, so I ended up talking with a strange man." Val suddenly had a horrible thought. "Is he all right?"

"As far as I know, he is alive and well," Mai said. She had no idea if it was true, nor did she care, but Val did. The blond girl sighed.

"Thank God. So it wasn't you who left the note in my window the other night?"

"No, I just got here. Last night I broke into Melinda's limo and hit the HOME button on her global positioning system. *Finally.* I've been on her trail for weeks."

Val hugged Mai again, squeezing her so hard the small woman squeaked a protest. "You did all that for me?"

"For me, too. I have missed you, you oversized thing. Life hasn't been the same without you."

"Oh, Mai! I don't know how I could ever repay you."

She leaned over to hug Mai again. The smaller woman fended her off, guarding her ribs with her elbows.

"No! Wait until I actually get you home."

"First we have to figure out how to get me out of here," Val said, flopping down on the chair. "The security is insane. There are cameras everywhere. There's a computer room with more equipment than NASA."

"We will have to work on that. In the meantime, I am curious: Who left you a note? Show it to me."

Val was frustrated. She could see the folded card in her mind, the neat handwriting, even the color of the paper, but she couldn't reach into her memory and hand it to Mai.

"I can't. It's gone."

"Where did it come from? Who signed it?"

"No one signed it. When I was on a date last week, a coat-check girl at the restaurant passed it to me. All it said was that someone wanted to speak to me privately, and if I agreed, to leave the note in the window. I did. I thought at first it was you, but it had to be the man who the dogs were chasing the other night. Everyone has been very cautious ever since."

"I know. I had to sneak in when the garbagemen made their pickup from the rear of the property. It was disgusting. Do you think it was a private detective of some kind? Griffen might have hired one to find you. If I haven't heard from you, I will bet no one else has."

"I feel horrible," Val said, filled with guilt. "I can't imagine why I wasn't more worried when I couldn't reach anyone. I tried, but I never connected with a single person. I kind of gave up after a while."

Mai peered out the window. "I have some theories about that. I have had to fight against some unseen influence ever since I set foot on this property. I expect that there's something in the air."

Val frowned.

"Drugs?"

"No, more subtle than that. I can't put my finger on it. But do not tell Melinda you suspect she has been playing with your mind. Act as if you know nothing."

"Why? Why should I?"

"Because Melinda is dangerous. She has kept you here in ignorance for a long time, faking answering machines and busy signals so you will stop worrying and preventing you from going anywhere for months. She wants you here so you will have your baby in her home. She is doing everything she can to tie you to her. Snap out of it. Do only what *you* want to."

"I will," Val vowed, punching the chair cushion. "And I intend to have it out with her before I leave. I don't want to be looking over my shoulder for the rest of my life. Will you help me?"

"Will I help you?" Mai asked, scornfully. "After I have slept in a tent on your behalf? I would absolutely want to be here when you tell Melinda off. I would love to be a fly on the wall when you do. In the meantime, do you have anything to eat? I'm starving."

Val picked up the phone and hit the key for the kitchen. "Can I come down and get a snack?" she asked the sleepy voice who answered.

"I'll bring something up for you, Miss Val," the man said. Val remembered that his name was Esteban.

"Can't I just raid the refrigerator?"

"Oh, no, ma'am. I'll send up a plate."

"Send lots. I'm really hungry."

She could hear the smile in Esteban's voice. "Sure. Is there anything you have a craving for?" Val raised her eyebrows at Mai. Mai mouthed, "meat or cheese." Val nodded.

"Protein," she told the phone. "And fruit."

"Of course, Miss Val. On the way."

"Thanks, Esteban."

The voice sounded gratified. "You're welcome, Miss Val." Val put the receiver down. Mai smiled knowingly at her.

"I can see why you are reluctant to leave. You are treated like a princess. I would love that. I used to be." She sighed. Val felt a wave of sympathy for her. She didn't know much about her friend's history, but Mai had such elegant manners and very expensive tastes. In contrast, Val felt like a bull moose in snowshoes.

Within minutes, a soft knock came at the door. Val shot a look of concern at Mai. The Asian woman slipped underneath the floor length tablecloth of the glass-topped table.

Val opened the door.

"Hi, Esteban," she said.

She felt a shock. Instead of the friendly, stocky man with the splayed front teeth, it was Henry. He held out a tray.

"You called for a snack?" he asked. "My goodness, after tonight's dinner, I thought you might even skip breakfast."

"Not really," Val said. She threw back her head in defiance. "I'm eating for two now, you know."

"Of course," Henry said, setting down the tray with a clack. Val cringed in case the noise made Mai jump. He glanced around, then met Val's eyes. He winked. "Don't let the little one eat too much. We wouldn't want him getting fat."

"Her," Val said.

Henry raised his feathery eyebrows. "Is it a girl this week?"

"I think so."

"This child has changed genders more often than Eddie Izzard," Henry said. "I hope you decide on one before it's born."

Val controlled herself and smiled at him blandly. "Thanks, Henry. Good night."

"Good night. Just leave the tray outside the door."

Val closed the door after him and locked it with a firm hand. By the time she turned around, Mai had emerged from her hiding place. She smoothed her long, dark hair back into its shining waves and tied it into a knot at the back of her head.

"I dislike him already. He treats you like an idiot."

"He treats everybody like an idiot," Val said.

"He has power. Have you noticed?"

"No. I don't know how to tell."

"We will have to work on that, but after we get you home."

Mai pulled up the chair to the small table and dove into the food. Somehow in less than fifteen minutes, Esteban had put together a beautiful tray that would have been a hit at a fancy ladies' luncheon. A bunch of tiny grapes was flanked by fans of cheese slices and mounds of country pate. Near the bottom, like mystic glyphs, squiggles of three different sauces begged to be tasted. On a second plate, chunks of strawberries and melons ringed composed pillboxes of salmon and chicken salads. At the top of the tray was a selection of small pastries and slices of cake. Val's mouth watered. Luckily, there was plenty for two. She picked up the teaspoon from the right side of the tray and darted in to grab bites when she could. By the time Mai sat back and dabbed her mouth daintily with the linen napkin, all the plates were empty.

"I'll bet," Mai said, "that some serious attempts have been made to poach her kitchen staff."

"Wish I could take them home with me," Val said. "They could make a fortune in New Orleans."

Mai nodded. She put her hand over her mouth to stifle a yawn. "I am sorry, Amazon, but I have been up since before dawn. I really need to rest."

Val glanced at the clock. How inconsiderate of her not to realize how late it was!

"Take my bed," Val offered. Mai shook her head.

"Where will you sleep?"

"On the armchair. It's really comfortable. See the footrest? I can sit up and stretch out my legs on that."

Mai surveyed the chair and smiled. "Foolish giant. I'll take the armchair and ottoman. I can lie flat on that. You can't."

Val felt a rush of affection as well as relief. She had not

really looked forward to a night on the upholstered chair. Naps she had taken in its embrace usually resulted in back cricks. "All right."

Together they made up a small but comfortable bed for Mai. Val gladly sacrificed her crisp upper sheet, her quilt, and two of her three pillows to make her friend comfortable. She left Mai curled up and cozy with a cup of juice on the little glass-topped table beside her, reading a book.

Val cuddled down with the soft blanket and her remaining pillow, and had good dreams for the rest of the night. It was wonderful to know someone genuinely cared about her.

The sound of car tires outside woke her briefly. She heard the slam of metal doors and raucous voices like crows echoing in the darkness.

Melinda had returned.

Thirty-eight

When Val got up in the morning, the chair was empty and all the bedding had been returned to its normal location. Val wondered how it was she hadn't felt a thing. It was good to have such a talented friend. She searched the room, but Mai was not there. Where she had gone, Val couldn't imagine, but she trusted Mai's sense of self-preservation to keep Melinda from detecting her presence, even in this fortress of a house.

Breakfast arrived, brought in by Henry in person. He wheeled the cart in and started to put dishes on her small table. They smelled delicious, but Val kept resolve firmly in her mind.

"Her majesty is back," Henry said airily. "As soon as you're presentable, please come down to the sitting room. Melinda has a lot to discuss with you."

Val stood up, pulling her spine straight so she towered over Henry.

"Why wait?" she said, tightening the sash of her robe over her nightgown. "I have a few bones to pick with her myself."

How the staff communicated, Val had never been able to divine. As she strode into the formal lounge with Henry at her heels, Marcella pushed open the small door at the rear of the room that led to the servants' quarters and kitchen.

She drew after her a brass cart very much like the one that was used to serve Val upstairs but more than twice the size. On it Val saw two sets of dishes. Somehow, Henry had informed her Val was coming.

Melinda rushed out of her seat as if launched from a cannon and wrapped her arms around Val in a fierce hug. The elder dragon female wore a rust-colored two-piece suit with a texture like lizard scales and Salvatore Ferragamo shoes. She drew Val's robe tight over her belly.

"Valerie! You look wonderful, darling. My goodness, you've grown! But you are as beautiful as the goddess of the harvest. When I was pregnant, I looked like a hippopotamus. Sit down! Eat something. I didn't mean for Henry to interrupt you."

She bustled back to the little table and settled on one of the armchairs. Marcella laid out platters of ham, sausages, and eggs. A covered basket gave off the inviting aroma of fresh baked goods. In the middle, she set coffee- and teapots, pitchers frosted with condensation, and silver serving utensils. She unfolded a shimmering white napkin and put it across Melinda's lap. She flicked another one open and waited for Val to seat herself.

"I was afraid I woke the whole house up last night when I got home, but you must have slept right through the ruckus," Melinda said cheerfully. "Anyhow, I'm back! I have so many things for you, you will just scream with joy."

"I'm sure I will," Val said. She remained standing, her arms folded over her belly.

"Sit down already!" Melinda commanded, flicking a hand at the chair opposite her.

Val held her stance.

"No, thanks. I'm not too hungry."

Melinda looked mildly peeved, but the expression was fleeting.

"Yes, I heard about your late-night snack. But don't you want even a little something? My grandchild needs nourishment."

"He's getting everything he needs from me."

"He? Are you sure this time?"

"No!" Val said, shifting onto one slippered foot. "I just don't want to call him 'it.' Look, Melinda, why have you left me alone here so long?"

"Darling, I am not going to talk to you with my head craned back on my neck. It's uncomfortable. Sit down. We'll eat. Then we can talk."

"Come on, sweetheart," Henry said, winking at her. "Come and have some nice breakfast. We have all your favorites. Fresh strawberries." He lifted the cover off a china bowl to show her the ruby red berries sliced into bite-sized morsels.

Very reluctantly, Val moved toward the chair, fighting her own impulses all the way. Henry pulled it out and angled it for her. Val sank into it, feeling as if she were being pushed down. Marcella swept the white linen across her lap. It settled half-on and half-off her baby bump. It should have been nearly weightless, but it seemed to hold her down like a seat belt.

Marcella served coffee from the taller pot, then withdrew through the servants' door. Val watched her go with dismay. The housekeeper was her only ally.

She resolved to stand up for herself or, in the present case, sit. The knowledge that she knew where she was bolstered her confidence. *North Carolina,* she said to herself. *Just a few miles from the airport.*

"What would you like to eat, darling?" Melinda asked.

"She likes bacon, eggs over easy, and just scads of fruit," Henry said, just as she opened her mouth to reply. He dished plenty of all three foods onto her plate. "Sometimes we can talk her into a wee little cinnamon roll, but only if they're whole grain. Freshly squeezed orange juice, which we have right here. And coffee. Gallons of coffee."

"Is that much caffeine good for you?" Melinda asked.

"Well . . ."

"I did some reading," Henry interrupted. "It doesn't do any harm, apart from making us go tinkle more frequently.

I mean, piling caffeine withdrawal on top of a growing baby is just too much to ask of one girl."

Val looked up at him indignantly, but there was no more to add. She slashed through the rashers of bacon with her knife, making believe they were Henry's glib tongue.

"Why have you left me here so long by myself?" she asked.

"I wanted you to get acclimated, make new friends. I understand that you and Marcella have been enjoying some nice conversations."

Val feared for the housekeeper's safety. "Is that against the rules?"

Melinda chopped the end off a sausage as if staging an execution. "No, of course not. Marcella understands her place. She's not a dragon, of course. You've done very well incorporating yourself into the household. Some of the employees would rather go to you than Henry."

The smirk that Melinda and Henry exchanged told Val that the household workers were soon going to be convinced of the error of their ways. She felt sorry for them. Val held fast to the memory of Mai in her room the night before, and all the thoughts of her home. It might not be glamorous, but she wasn't a glamorous girl. Though she liked nice things, she refused to let them overpower her common sense.

"But why weren't you here? You said you had a lot you would teach me."

"And I will, Valerie. It sounds like you have been showing plenty of aptitude."

"I just feel like I've been wasting my time here waiting for you."

"Good heavens!" Melinda said, with a laugh. "I thought you'd appreciate the break. I kept Lizzy out of your way."

Val felt panic rise in her like a tidal wave.

"Is Lizzy *here*?"

"Of course she's here," Melinda said. "This is her home. But don't you worry: She's in her own rooms. She won't be in your way. If she has to come out for company, I'll give you plenty of warning."

Val stood up. "Melinda, you promised me I wouldn't have to deal with her."

"And you won't, dear. She doesn't even know you're here."

"She's not stupid, Melinda. She'll figure out that someone is staying here."

Melinda waved away the possibility. "I always see to it that she has plenty of distractions. How do you think I get anything done around here?"

"I don't know! When can I go home?"

Melinda shook her head.

"This is your home, Valerie. You can have whatever you want here."

"No, it isn't! My home is in New Orleans. I have an apartment in the French Quarter, if it hasn't been rented out from under me while I'm here. I hope Griffen's been paying the landlord. And why won't you let me call him?"

"Of course you can call him. You can call anyone you want."

"You've made plenty of phone calls, dear," Henry put in.

Val nearly sputtered her indignation.

"And none of them go through! You just make me think that I'm recording a message on their answering services. God knows who I'm really talking to. They must get a big kick out of listening to me babble. I don't appreciate it. I want to make real calls. And I want to get away before Lizzy figures out I'm here and attacks me again! She might kill me this time!"

"Call Dr. Drake," Melinda told Henry. "I don't know what's in those prenatal vitamins she's taking, but she's hallucinating."

"Immediately, Melinda."

Horrified, Val looked from one to the other.

"I am NOT hallucinating! You have me trapped here. I feel like a prisoner!"

"You're not a prisoner, sweetheart," Melinda said. "Come up with me. I want to show you all the nice things that I bought for your baby."

Val had a moment of temptation to see the items but did not want to let Melinda off the hook.

"If I had known she was in the house last night, I would have left!"

"It's just as well, then, that you didn't. Now, come with me."

Melinda grabbed Val by the arm and marched her upstairs. Henry stayed beside them all the way. Val could almost see him rub his hands together obsequiously to defer to Melinda.

She had little attention to devote to either of them. She listened hard as they went up the grand staircase and into the corridor on the other side from her room, hoping she wouldn't hear Lizzy's voice. Every little crack or squeak that the old house emitted made her jump.

"Now, you don't have to worry about her," Henry said, taking her other arm. He leaned in, putting his lips close to her ear.

"Lizzy hates me!" Val said. She knew she sounded like a petulant child.

"She doesn't really hate you. She doesn't hate anyone," Melinda said. "She's just . . . undirected."

"Undirected? She's homicidal!"

Melinda shook her head sadly.

"Valerie. Did you ever think in your selfish little life what it's like for me? Never being able to go anywhere without worrying about my daughter? Knowing that she can't ever live on her own? That I will have to make provisions for her if, God forbid, I predecease her? Did you ever think about *me*?"

"What?" Val asked, taken off guard. She was filled with contrition. "No, I never . . ."

Melinda sighed heavily. She took a large key from Henry and unlocked the door at the end of the hallway. "I didn't think so."

"Valerie doesn't mean to be inconsiderate, Melinda," Henry said soothingly. He patted Val on the arm. "She knows how many sacrifices you have made for her. And she's grateful for the comforts you've provided for her. Isn't that right, Valerie?" he asked. His voice fell softly on her ears. Val batted away the unfamiliar sensation with one hand. It caressed the outer pinnae and fondled her lobes. She started to like the feeling and relaxed. The voice stroked her gently and slipped inside. "You've had such wonderful opportunities. And the staff has been so kind to you. Everything has been provided for you. Why, it's like living in a palace, isn't it? You have everything here: lovely rooms, excellent food, designer clothes—and how well they fit you! Even jewelry to enhance your already stunning beauty. You *are* appreciative."

"Why, yes, I am," Val said. How immature of her never to say thanks for all the kindness that Melinda had shown her. What was the matter with her? She had been brought up better than that! "I am grateful. You opened your home to me. You were so generous to give me a job. I feel that I'm really learning something. I've met such great people, like Mike Burns."

Saying his name broke the mood for a moment. She remembered the last time that she and Mike had tried to go out for a date. She faced Henry accusingly.

"You stopped me from going out with him," she said. "It's like you're keeping me under house arrest."

"Not at all," Henry said, his voice like silk. His pale blue eyes seemed to enlarge as he faced her. "I only kept you inside for your own protection. You saw the videos. That man invaded the property! He could have been coming for you."

He might have been coming to rescue me, Val thought, but kept the words from reaching her tongue.

"But I like to go out once in a while. I'm going stir-crazy in here."

"It's a big house. How can you be stir-crazy?" Melinda asked.

"It's not that big!"

Melinda waved her arms impatiently.

"Henry, talk some sense into her."

Once the spell had been broken, Val realized that he had been influencing her to accept, even like, her captivity. She was furious. Mai had warned her that he must have had something to do with her not connecting with the outside world. And he probably messed with her mind so she didn't realize it! Couldn't the Wurmleys do anything without resorting to enchantment to get their way? Henry had, well, a manner about him that made her go against her better judgment. She was going to make her own decisions from then on.

She broke away from him and retreated partway up the hall. Henry bore down on her as inexorably as an avalanche rolling downhill. She was determined not to let him cloud her mind again. One way or another, she was going to keep her wits clear.

"Oh, no," she said. "Don't you touch me."

"Come now," Henry said, coaxingly. "Don't be like that."

Months of pregnancy might have changed her body, but she had kept in shape. Henry reached for her. She dodged him, keeping watch on his hands. The long, slim fingers seemed to weave the air between them. Did she imagine the glitter of sparks, or was that just light striking off a gem in one of his rings?

"I am not going to hurt you, dear," Henry said. "How can you even dream that I would harm a single hair on your head?"

"It's not my hair I'm worried about," Val said. She had reached the center hallway.

She heard footsteps and voices below. A quick glance showed her that Marcella had gone to the front door to sign for a delivery. She and the UPS driver were exchanging a few pleasantries as he clicked his pen against his clipboard device. The door was open!

Val didn't hesitate. She started down the stairs, taking them two at a time. Once she was out in the sun, she would be free! Never mind that she was in slippers and a robe. She would run naked if she had to. The nearest neighbor was about half a mile away. She regularly covered more distance than that in her daily runs on the Riverwalk at home. Once she was safely in someone else's home, she could call Mai. Her friend would get her on a plane and take her home.

"Valerie! Look! Isn't this beautiful?"

As her foot hit the last step, Val glanced up. Melinda stood at the top of the stairs. Beside her was the trim, black Britax stroller that Val had drooled over in the baby catalogs. Melinda pushed it temptingly back and forth a few times.

No! She was not going to let Melinda buy her! Val's slippered feet slithered across the marble floor of the foyer. She shoved between the surprised housekeeper and the UPS driver, and shot out into the sunshine. The warm light hit her like a beacon. She felt strength surge. She opened up her stride and dashed out into the gravel driveway.

One side of the iron gate stood open. It began to close as she neared it. Someone in the house saw her going and meant to cut her off. She could still slip through! Eight paces! Six!

A hand grabbed her by the shoulder. Val was dragged back by the very force of the grip. She looked over her shoulder to see Henry's grinning face inches from hers. How had he moved so fast? Coolness, like ice water, ran from his hand into her body. Val shivered. He really could do some kind of magic.

"Now, now, now, you don't want to go out there like that," Henry said.

Defiantly, she put one foot out, trying to force the other to follow. It wouldn't move.

"Yes. I. Do." Val gritted out the words. She strained to make her limbs move. Her feet were glued to the ground. Henry put his arm around her waist. Val's feet came unstuck, but they wouldn't move toward the road, only back in the direction of the house. Henry guided her along the drive and up the front steps.

"Oh, come back in, darling. You should see the wonderful things that Melinda has for your baby! You will be just thrilled. Marcella, help me with her. So sorry."

Henry apologized to the UPS driver, who stared at the sight of the pregnant woman in her pajamas. Val sent a pleading look his way, hoping that he would see that they were taking her back against her will. She tried to ask for help. Her mouth wouldn't follow her instructions. She was furious, even more so because her lips formed into a smile. The last thing she wanted to do was smile! Marcella saw her distress. Val knew she wanted to help, but the housekeeper was just as helpless as she. She put her arm around Val from the other side. As if it belonged to someone else, Val's body stepped in over the threshold.

"Good! Come on back and see all the things for your baby."

Henry and Marcella led her inside and up the grand staircase. He guided her toward the stroller. Melinda pushed it into her hands. Val couldn't help it. She stroked the handlebar. Henry smiled.

"Look, isn't it wonderful? It has every safety feature you can imagine," Melinda said. "And I have beautiful clothes, from newborn on up. Bring her this way."

Val had no choice but to go. With every step, she felt her resolve fading. They led her into Melinda's rooms, which were piled almost to the ceiling with boxes and bags of baby things.

"Look, darling," Henry said, opening up a backpack with dangling straps. He clipped it around her chest. "A snuggle pouch. Your little one will be nestled close to you, hearing your heartbeat. He'll be so cosy and safe. Don't you love it?"

Henry's voice slunk into her ears, praising each of the gifts as Melinda handed them to her. Wasn't she thrilled with the tiny garments? Didn't the handmade furniture fulfill every possible wish she had for equipping her baby's nursery?

Once again, Val felt like a princess, being overwhelmed by gifts from her fairy godparents.

After all, what was so bad about staying with Melinda? Where else could she get room service at all hours of the night? A sensible part of her brain said that most of the restaurants in New Orleans delivered, at any time. Melinda was making her a full partner in a growing business. And Mike was such a nice guy. She wasn't sure how much longer she could go without jumping on him. And, after all, Melinda was her baby's grandmother.

By the time Melinda opened the box containing a beautifully made three-in-one car seat with a plaid quilt that matched the washable upholstery, Val wondered what she could possibly have been worrying about.

George's phone rang. He reached toward the nightstand. The phone fell off into the gap between the bed and the table. It kept ringing while he chased it with one hand. The rest of him didn't want to get out of bed. Everything hurt too much.

"Yeah?"

"George? Are you all right?" It was Debbie.

"Just taking five," he said. "What have you got on that creature?"

"Finally got a bite or two. It's coming in now." George heard the computer printer grinding away on the other end. "Run the description past me again? Just to make sure."

"Gollum with shark teeth," George said. "Flexible as a rubber band. It's a hell of a good hunter, but I wasn't in a position to judge whether it's primarily a sight or scent hunter or if it homes in on emotions or body heat or what."

Debbie whistled. "Melinda can sure pick 'em. This thing is strong enough to kill dragons. It can't bite through their hide, but its jaws can snap an iron rod. In fact, it doesn't LIKE dragons. We ought to have one in the office if it wasn't so uncontrollable. How's she keeping it from killing everyone in the family?"

"The secretary. A gay guy named Henry. Lives on the premises, like the housekeeper, cook, and gardener. He was carrying its leash. Or at least I thought it was a leash. Could have been a whip."

"He's got to be a warlock or at least an alchemist. There are some compounds that are supposed to calm it down."

"Guaranteed?" George asked.

"Are you kidding? If magic worked the same way every time, it would be science."

"Can you send me some?"

"I'll put it into overnight, but you'd be better off concentrating on getting Henry out of the way. This creature's bonded to him. You're going to have to distract it to get it away from your exit point, or you'll never get the girl out."

"I know, I know!"

"You still thinking this contract was a good idea?"

George nodded, even though he knew she couldn't see him. "More than ever."

Debbie sighed, a gusty noise on the other end of the phone.

"Just promise me you'll never take a job like this again."

"I promise," George said. "If any other female dragon gets pregnant, she's on her own."

Thirty-nine

Griffen woke up to someone's pounding on his door. He felt for his bathrobe and put it on as he walked to his door. The clock said 9:00 A.M. Griffen moaned. It had better be an emergency to get him out of bed that early. The poker game hadn't broken up until after four.

"Griffen! Are you there? Griffen, answer me!" Fox Lisa's voice came through the ancient wooden panels.

Griffen disengaged the double dead bolt and the security chain. No sooner had he pulled the door open than Fox Lisa threw herself into his arms.

"Oh, I'm so glad you're all right!"

Griffen frowned. "Why wouldn't I be all right? What happened?"

Fox Lisa's nose was red, and her long hair was disheveled. She wore a skirt and blouse, but instead of matching heels, she wore battered sneakers.

"When I got up this morning to go to work, Penny asked if I'd talked to that no-good boyfriend of mine. When I said no, she told me that if I wanted to speak to you, I should go down to the police station. I did, but they said you weren't there! I came back here to see if I could find you."

"Why didn't you try calling me?" he asked.

Fox Lisa gave him a look that called him stupid. "That was the first thing I did! It went straight to voice mail. I figured they had it with your other things in Properties."

Griffen hadn't really needed the confirmation that Penny

was behind the appearance by the police and the press the night before. She had set him up to be arrested. But it hadn't worked.

"I'm fine," Griffen said.

"Oh, I'm so glad!" She squeezed his ribs tightly. Griffen hugged her back.

Once he held her in his arms, he realized how long it had been since they had been together. He had missed the feel of her skin and her scent. He put his face down in the waves of her hair and took a deep breath of her warm, spicy aroma. She giggled. He kissed her earlobe, then nibbled it. Fox Lisa brushed her lips along his collarbone and followed the line with her tongue. Griffen started kissing her seriously. She kissed right back, let out a deep sigh as he bent to continue his gentle bites down the side of her neck. He started undoing the buttons of her blouse. Fox Lisa untied the belt of his robe and began to fondle him. Griffen could no longer ignore the urgency he felt. He swept her up and carried her, still giggling, into the bedroom.

He couldn't hold back from rushing the first time, but Fox Lisa met him with the same desperate energy, thrusting her hips against his. He pushed between her legs. She wrapped her ankles around him and held on. Their bodies rocked together, faster and faster, until Griffen felt his hot tension release.

Once his immediate need was sated, he took the time to caress her in the ways she enjoyed. She moaned and writhed under his hands. The sight of her pleasure aroused him again, but he waited until she pulled him toward her. He was glad of his dragon-hard skin as her nails raked down his shoulders.

"I've missed you," he said afterward, with her head nestled against him. "Looking after Penny has made us waste too many nights apart."

Fox Lisa toyed with the hair on his chest with a thoughtful forefinger.

"So, what really happened last night?" she asked. "Why did Penny think you were in jail?"

Griffen hesitated before he answered.

"Because she set me up to get arrested."

"You're pulling my leg!"

Griffen told her about the events of the night before, including his private conversation afterward with Harrison. She looked dismayed.

"And you think it was Penny who sent them after you?"

"I'd bet on it. I quit her campaign yesterday. You were sitting right there when I called her. I could hear your voice. Didn't she tell you what I said?"

"No," Fox Lisa said. "She said you were still investigating about that zombie, and you'd get back to her. She lied to my face! I am going to go down there and give her a piece of my mind! *I'll* quit."

"Don't walk away just because of me," Griffen said. "She's still in danger. I don't have to like her vengeful attitude, but I recognize that she needs protection. I said I'd help out with that. I just said I refuse to come to any more of her rallies."

Fox Lisa shook her head as if to clear it. "I don't know what to do. I really believe in her, Griffen. She could do such great things."

"Where is she now?"

"I don't know," Fox Lisa admitted. "I suppose she went to the campaign office. I didn't care. I walked out of there. I was so angry. I just couldn't believe it. All this time you've been trying to pull me away, I resisted because I just hate having anyone tell me what to do. Are all dragons bossy like you?"

"I don't know," Griffen admitted. "I only know about me."

"Well, I was being stubborn. I knew you didn't believe in Penny, and I did."

"I just don't believe in any politicians," Griffen said. "More now than when I got involved in this election."

Fox Lisa started to sit up.

"I'd better go talk to her. Afterward, I'll decide whether or not to continue."

"I'll come with you."

She sprang out of bed.

"Beat you to the shower," she said, grinning over her shoulder.

Griffen scrambled up to follow, but she had too much of a head start. She stood in the tub, fending him off with the back brush. He joined her under the hot spray. Their laughter echoed off the walls of the bathroom.

In a much better mood, Griffen walked Fox Lisa to the campaign office. The small lot was full of cars, including a few he recognized as belonging to news reporters. To his surprise, the reporters were in them.

"What's going on?" he asked the man from the *Times-Picayune* through the window of his car.

"Some bigwig arrived, and they tossed us out," the reporter said. "He looked pretty mad. They locked all the doors, including the back."

"They'll let us in," Griffen said with determination.

"Well, if you get something, give us a break. My editor wants copy in by two."

"I'll see what I can do," Griffen promised.

He marched up and rapped on the door. At first he didn't get an answer, then the door crept open about an inch. Behind it was Neil, a dapper black man in his fifties, a staffer from Penny's legislative office. His tense face relaxed a little when he saw them.

"Hey, Griffen. Hey, Fox Lisa."

"Hey, Neil," she said. "I have to talk to Penny."

Neil looked over Griffen's shoulder. The reporters began to get out of their cars when they saw the door open.

"I'll let you in, but keep those reporters outside. We can't let them hear this."

"Hear what?" Fox Lisa asked.

In lieu of answer, Neil pulled them inside and shut the door firmly. The reporters banged on it and yelled to be let in. After a short time, they gave up. The shouting went on, though. Griffen realized it was coming from Penny's office. Winston stood in front of it with his arms folded. Griffen could hear two voices, a man's and a woman's. The phone banks in the outer office were quiet. All the other staffers, about thirty young men and women, most of them young, sat wide-eyed at their desks.

"What's going on?" Griffen asked.

"Your uncle arrived here over an hour ago and asked to see the representative. They started arguing right out here in the phone room. Horsie herded them into the office and told Winston to guard the door. Horsie's been trying to make peace between them, but it hasn't done any good. They've been bellerin' at each other ever since."

Griffen felt astonished. "I've hardly ever heard him shout before. He's always been kind of cold. In fact, the madder he was, the quieter his voice became."

"Well, he's been the opposite of quiet since he got here," Neil said. "And they're going round and round on the same argument."

". . . Outrageous behavior!" Malcolm bellowed. "Putting my nephew in jeopardy out of pique! Not to mention almost causing ME to go to jail because you are angry. An undignified, unwarranted nuisance! Is that any way for a potential governor to behave?"

"How dare you accuse me of taking revenge? I campaign on a platform devoted to law and order! When I hear of a crime in progress, I turn that information over to the authorities! All good, law-abiding citizens should do the same."

"Don't try your rhetoric on me! You received a tip? At two o'clock in the morning? How convenient that a news camera should also appear on-site to record that show of legal force!"

"The public should see crime being stopped!"

"And there weren't enough muggings or thefts last night to provide fodder for the news? Instead my nephew and I were nearly seriously inconvenienced!"

"You let me down," Penny said angrily. "Everyone lets me

down. There isn't a single person who has stood by me
through this whole miserable mess!"

Fox Lisa looked stricken at the last remark. Griffen put
his arm around her. "It's nothing personal. She strikes out
like a rattlesnake. You've seen it. She's just angry."

She gave him a grateful glance.

"I know. It's not me. I really never should have gotten as
involved as I have. I should have stuck to seeing her at the
shooting club or at a bar. She's a good pool player."

"I saw," Griffen said.

"Treating your staff and volunteers like traitors will en-
sure that they will behave like traitors!" Malcolm snapped.

Penny burst into furious tears.

"Now, honey, don't cry," Horsie said. There were some
muffled endearments.

"He doesn't care!" Penny wailed. "He's watching my campaign fall apart around me, and all he does is complain about
one teeny little mistake! Y'all aren't helping me!"

"I wouldn't have tried crying if I were her," Griffen said
thoughtfully. "It never worked for Val. Uncle Malcolm is the
original immovable object."

It didn't work.

"It seems to me, Representative, that all the problems
stem from you yourself," Malcolm said coldly.

Penny let out a scream of fury. A crash against the wall
that separated the offices made everyone in the outer room
jump. More crashing noises followed.

"You're so unreasonable!" she shrilled.

"You are behaving unreliably," Malcolm retorted. "You
need more focus."

"I'm desperate!" Penny said. "The field is too crowded!"

"Then set yourself apart! Give the public reason to follow
you and you alone!"

"I can't! My campaign is outgunned by every other one out
there! I can't compete on television, print, or radio advertising.
I can't afford to sponsor any kind of event, and I've tapped all
the local sources as much as I can. You promised to help!"

"I have been helping!"

"No," Penny snarled. "You sent me your good-for-nothing nephew to do your work for you. He's been there, getting in my way, interfering where he shouldn't!"

It was Griffen's turn to feel as if he had been sandbagged.

Fox Lisa gave him a hug back. "See? Rattlesnake."

"Yes," Griffen said weakly. "It hurts a lot more when it's aimed at you, isn't it?"

"No lie."

Penny wasn't finished inflicting her verbal abuse. "It isn't as though I could count on YOU for anything better! This campaign can't run on promises! You have not sent the money you promised! What happened to all those deep pockets you said you had access to?"

"Meltdowns do not inspire confidence in contributors!"

"It wasn't a meltdown! I lost focus. I couldn't get it back. You try delivering a coherent speech under those lights! See if you do any better."

"But that would be an everyday event for you if you are elected," Malcolm said. "You could be giving briefings on complex matters every day."

"Oh, so now it's *if*? Not *when*?"

"If your election were a foregone conclusion, you would not need me or my backers."

"Well, I need them now! This campaign is broke! I have a thousand expenses coming due, and we can't pay them. What would I do if that little piece of news got out?"

Griffen met the eyes of the man near the door. Neil nodded very slightly. He looked embarrassed. Griffen was astonished. Penny seemed to be raking in money from everyone she encountered. How could they have run through all those contributions—voluntary or otherwise—in such a short time?

"This mutual scathing is of no use to either of us, or our many concerns," Malcolm said.

"No! It isn't."

"In that case," Malcolm said, "allow me to propose the following . . ."

His voice dropped to a murmur. After a couple of angry exclamations, Penny quieted down in response.

"Oh, yes, honey," Horsie exclaimed. "This is good sense! Listen to the man!"

The level of conversation behind the door sank still further. The entire room of volunteers craned in wide-eyed curiosity. By the exchanged glances of puzzlement, no one could hear a thing. Even Griffen, whose dragon hearing was incredibly sensitive, picked up only who was speaking but not what they were saying. It went on so long he felt like breaking in, despite Winston's forbidding presence.

After what seemed like hours, the door opened. Winston sprang out of the way. Malcolm leaned out through a narrow crack. He scanned the room, spotted his nephew, and beckoned.

"Griffen, will you come in here, please?"

Griffen glanced beside him. Malcolm nodded.

"Yes. Ms. Fox Lisa, won't you come, too?"

Winston stood by reluctantly as Malcolm shut the door behind Griffen and Fox Lisa. Inside, Horsie sat in a chair with her head thrown back, looking exhausted. She clutched a tumbler with two fingers of liquor in it. Penny paced back and forth like a big cat. Her cheeks were flushed. Malcolm looked completely at ease, tidy, businesslike. He directed the newcomers to a pair of vacant chairs, then sat behind Penny's desk. She didn't protest. The walls bore a few new dents. On the floor, a vase lay shattered, its flowers scattered. Inscribed plaques presented to Penny for various distinctions had been torn off the walls and rested askew on tabletops and windowsills. No one drew attention to the debris. Malcolm interlaced his fingers and rested his elbows on the desk.

"We have had a small discussion regarding tactics and strategy for the coming campaign. Representative Dunbar and I have reached an understanding. Representative?"

Penny held her back very straight but nodded sharp agreement.

"It would seem that there are some matters that need rectifying. First, Ms. Dunbar has some things to say."

She came over and took Griffen's hands in both of hers.

"Griffen, I am very sorry if anything I have done has caused you any trouble at all. You have been a genuine pillar of strength for me. You've been just so good to come out whenever I've needed you. I hope you understand that anything out of turn that I might have said is because I have been under so much pressure. I need to handle it better. Thank you for your patience and good sense."

Griffen raised his eyebrows. Whatever had been said behind the closed door had knocked a little humility into her. She squeezed his hands before releasing them and turned to Fox Lisa.

"Sweetie, I haven't been as nice to you as you deserve. I appreciate your being so protective and sticking by me all this time. You have been a real shining light to this campaign, and don't think I haven't noticed."

Fox Lisa was touched.

"Oh, Penny, thank you! You know I'd do anything I can to help you. I believe in you."

"That's so kind of you," Penny said. "Now, there's no need to stay with me overnight anymore. I'm sure I'll be all right."

"But what about the attacks?"

"There have been no attacks," Malcolm said.

"What?" Griffen demanded. "What about the garbage truck?"

He glared at Penny. She smiled at him sweetly.

"Well, honey, I just have to confess. It was me."

"You did that?"

Penny looked a little sheepish, but she continued to meet his eyes.

"Well, yes. I, uh, convinced the driver to be there at that time, driving the truck he takes out every day."

"That dance you did? Like during the debate?"

"Yes. It's a voodoo thing. You wouldn't understand. He had to obey my bidding. He did it a little too well, though. He wasn't supposed to hit us. I don't know how he fell out of the cab. But I did make sure he was all right. He got Workman's Compensation for the accident."

Griffen felt his temper rise.

"You could have killed Fox Lisa!"

Penny waved a hand. "She was fine. I knew how good she was behind the wheel. We did an off-road run for charity last year, and she flattened the competition."

Fox Lisa looked embarrassed but proud. "That's true. We came in a flat sixteen seconds before the competition. We drove Penny's Jeep. About three-quarters of the way through the race, we jumped through a hedge that no one else would try."

Griffen raised an eyebrow at her.

"Made the Kessel run in less than twelve parsecs?"

"Yeah," she said. "It cut a hundred yards off the course."

Malcolm cleared his throat sharply.

"To return to the matter at hand . . . ? The accident was not part of the attacks that concern you."

"No," Penny acknowledged.

"That zombie at the debate?" Griffen asked. "Have you seen him before?"

"There've been several others, not just him," Penny said. "I'm terrified of dead people!"

"But they are just people," Griffen said. "Only . . . not alive . . . exactly. I've seen you on television at murder scenes, sometimes looking right at the corpse. What's different about these, uh, people?"

"I'm afraid that someone's cursing me. I know those zombies will get me soon. When I dance, I stand in two worlds at once. I'm vulnerable." She swallowed. "You wouldn't understand."

Griffen thought of the nights sitting up with Gris-gris and feeling surrounded by an invisible underworld.

"Maybe I would."

"No wonder you were freaked-out!" Fox Lisa said, her large eyes sympathetic.

"That is something that will have to be handled with a meeting," Malcolm said. "Since the gentleman who set those up failed to respond to you, Griffen, in spite of your local connections, then I believe it falls to me to make arrangements. In the meanwhile, we have devised a manner to raise both awareness and capital for the campaign."

"What?" Fox Lisa asked eagerly.

Malcolm turned to Griffen.

"Relying on the greatest talents around us, I believe that the most money can be obtained through organizing a poker tournament."

"Wait a minute!" Griffen protested.

"That's a terrific idea!" Fox Lisa said.

"Oh, no," Griffen said, backing away with his hands up. He had a sudden vision of a roomful of angry card players all clamoring for his attention, money, or blood. "Not a chance. I'm having trouble making ends meet with my own business. Sorry. I have already had regular customers refuse to play with me because I'm tainted by my involvement with Penny even though I'm not working for her. I'm done organizing things for other people. I have responsibilities. I need to make a living, and I have employees who rely on me for a paycheck."

"We can't argue with that," Malcolm said, stroking his chin. "That was our agreement."

Penny grasped his arm.

"No! I need you, Griffen."

"Sorry," Griffen said. "No poker tournament. Talk to the casinos if you want to do something like that."

"No," Malcolm said. "They will demand too large a portion of the proceeds."

"How about pool?" Fox Lisa piped up. "Penny's really good. She could do an exhibition."

"No one would pay to see that," Griffen said. "No offense,

Penny. Pool fans won't come to see a politician shoot pool. They'd want to see professionals. You could set that up a lot more easily. The pool halls would love the bump in business."

"Do you know who they would pay to see?" Malcolm asked. Griffen thought for a moment.

"Yes, there's Eddie Brown. I saw him in an exhibition last year. He's the best—if we can get him to come. And there are a few other players I've seen."

"That's a great idea," Horsie said.

Malcolm rose to his feet and dusted his hands together.

"Pool, then. Griffen, you will make all the arrangements. Er, Horsie, the advertising and promotion are up to you."

"No problem," the campaign manager said with a cheerful grin. "We'll plaster the state with it. We could get hundreds of entrants."

"Then that's settled."

"No!" Griffen protested. Malcolm frowned at him.

"But, Griffen, you know those who would be the biggest draw, don't you? And you know the ins and outs of the games and who has a facility that might donate its time for our event in exchange for favorable publicity? I think it is a splendid solution."

"So do I. Thank you, Griffen," Penny said. She kissed him on the cheek. "I am so sorry to have caused you all that bother."

She strode to the door and flung it open.

"Well, what are all of you staring at?" she asked the staff in the outer office. "Hit those phones! And could someone come in here and sweep up? We had a little mess."

"Yes, ma'am!" The volunteers sprang to work. Fox Lisa bent to gather up the spilled flowers. Malcolm took his cell phone from his pocket and began to dial a number.

Griffen found himself standing alone in the middle of the room. He stared at his uncle.

"How is it when you have an idea, I end up doing all the work?"

Malcolm put his hand over the microphone.

"Delegation, Griffen. Someday you will understand what that really means. Ah, yes, Miss Callaway, good morning!"

Forty

Griffen left the third pool hall with a handful of papers, including menus, the history of the hall, and a sample contract for holding an event. The owners, two men in their sixties, Griffen was grateful to discover, were indifferent to politics.

"If your money's green, you can vote for Martians," the older one said.

"How about dragons?" Griffen had asked. They laughed, but he felt as if he had gotten in the last word.

The fee to rent the hall for an evening was lower than the other two halls he had visited but still higher than Penny's depleted campaign purse could easily afford. He wasn't at all surprised to discover, with a major election coming on and candidates for almost every office looking for an angle, that no one would offer a break on their facilities. The same went for the professionals. Jamie Dewar, a pro Griffen had seen and admired, said he would be happy to appear, for a three-thousand-dollar fee plus expenses. They might have to fall back on Penny making trick shots and three-bank caroms for the cameras.

Griffen still had to come up with prizes, too. Malcolm's instructions had been clear: They must speak to the character of the state, they must not cost the campaign money if possible, and they must be "presentable." Griffen cringed at that adjective, but he understood. He couldn't ask for sponsorship from any of the gambling associations or titty bars along

Bourbon though they had the money and would have loved the publicity.

He strode back toward the Quarter. In spite of feeling railroaded, he enjoyed walking around the city, getting to know people. New Orleans had several districts, each with its own personality. The quiet, residential streets in between the economic centers, with their wrought-iron balconies dripping with flowering creepers elicited comparisons with the Mediterranean cities from which the city's European founders had come. People gave him a smile or a wave as he went by, and he returned the salutes. He couldn't imagine that happening up North, where making eye contact with strangers made them worry what it was you wanted from them.

The election was inescapable, no matter where he walked. On the tiny lawns in front of the wooden houses, clusters of campaign signs sprouted. Griffen didn't have to look far to see DUNBAR FOR GOVERNOR banners, but those were outnumbered heavily by the front-runners, Jindal and Blanco, and, surprisingly, by the candidate who had been neck and neck with her in the polls, Congressman Benson.

A few houses down, Griffen saw why.

"Hey!" he yelled.

A young black man wearing a vest over a T-shirt stood up to see who had addressed him. He had just yanked a Dunbar sign out of the ground in front of a property near the street corner. Griffen loped toward him. The young man backed away in alarm and took off running.

Griffen was fast on his feet, but the youth had distance on his side. He disappeared around the corner as Griffen reached the yard from which the sign had been displaced.

Griffen windmilled to a stop. He saw no point in continuing the chase. What would he do if he caught him, anyhow? Instead, he went to replace the sign in the ground.

It wasn't there. Amid a pile of Benson signs, the bracket lay on the grass, but it was empty except for a few charred scraps clinging to it. Griffen frowned. He had not seen the youth pull out a lighter or anything else with which he could have burned it. It seemed that Benson had his share of supernatural assistance. That was going to make the race more interesting.

He took the remaining Benson signs into a blind spot between two houses. To the utter joy of the fire spark in his midsection, Griffen let his temper build to the boiling point. A gush of fire rushed out of his mouth. The signs in his hands crisped and blackened. With a feeling of satisfaction, he dumped them in the next trash can. No sense in making it easier for the opposition.

Griffen sauntered around the corner. A screen door slammed beside him. He glanced through it at the small diner. It looked as if it was doing good business. He pulled the door open and found himself a seat at the counter. The stout black woman in the pink waitress uniform behind it came over to smile at him.

"Coffee, honey?"

"Yes," Griffen said. He moved his hands so she could pour the hot, black liquid into the stoneware cup. "What's good?"

"Everything, else we wouldn't serve it."

Griffen squinted at the menu, written in chalk on a peeling blackboard above the hatch to the kitchen. "Shrimp po' boy."

"You got it." She almost did a double take. "Say, didn't I see you on the television with one of them politicians?"

Several of the diners glanced up and gave Griffen a suspicious glance.

"Yes, you did," Griffen acknowledged, cringing for the inevitable discussion of Penny and her policies.

"Well, you cain't do no politickin' in here," she said. "You let my customers eat in peace."

"Believe me," Griffen said, gratefully, "that's all I want."

"Well, good. That's the rules: no hand-shakin' and no baby-kissin'."

Everyone relaxed and went back to their meals. Griffen sighed. The jungle primary was a little more than two months away. He couldn't wait for it to be over with. It sounded like most of his fellow N'Awlinians had the same feeling.

Griffen took the paperwork from the three pool halls home with him, along with a videotape he had ordered at Tower Records. It had been years since he had seen *My Fellow Americans.* He put the tape into his machine and threw himself onto the couch with his notebook and his cell phone. Enjoying the antics of Jack Lemmon and James Garner maneuvering to become the next president gave him a break from the real campaign but kept him in the mood for his task.

He figured that in order to make money, he needed at least eight tables for the contest, with plenty of room for onlookers and the press. The largest hall was up a flight of stairs, tough for disabled patrons, but it had twenty-three pool tables and a great kitchen. In Griffen's opinion, it was the best prospect, but it also had the highest price tag. No amount of persuasion had moved the owners to knock down their fee. He even brought up Penny's promise that half the proceeds would go to school programs for kids. They correctly countered with the fact that the event would rob them of a day's revenue from the entire game room. Not only that, but it was a publicity event for a politician. If she wanted to make a large donation to charity, the owners pointed out, she could write a check. Griffen could hardly argue.

All three had offered suggestions for prizes. One was a month of free play in the game room, with the equivalent in cash for out-of-towners. Another wanted to spot the winners to a fancy dinner for two at Commander's Palace. That wasn't bad, but the second- and third-place prizes were only T-shirts. He'd have to seek out local merchants who were willing to donate better gifts, probably in exchange for getting their names on the posters and in the flyers. Horsie would have to handle that.

Griffen groaned as he scribbled notes in his pocket pad. He felt as though he had been railroaded into helping, probably because he *had* been railroaded. He could have walked out of the meeting, but Fox Lisa was so enthusiastic about the idea that he didn't have the heart to do it.

His cell phone rang. He didn't recognize the number. It might have been one of the halls calling to let him know they had changed their mind about the fees. He put on his most professional voice.

"Good afternoon, Griffen McCandles."

"Hey, Griffen, I'm sprung!"

"Gris-gris!" Griffen said, delighted. "Where are you?"

"Down near your front door, brother. Want to buzz me in?"

Griffen went out to unlock the street door to the courtyard himself. Gris-gris was waiting, bobbing from foot to foot like a little boy. He sprang over the threshold and grabbed Griffen by the hand. He looked healthier than he had in weeks. The dull matte of his cheeks had become shiny and clear again. His eyes gleamed like onyx. Griffen felt his spirits lift.

"Man, it's good to see you," Griffen said.

"It's good to see anybody outside my parlor," Gris-gris said. He seemed almost wild with unspent energy. "You probably used to it, with the connections you got, but I never had such a rush. I *felt* that plant die. It just let go, and I got hit by this wall of energy, all but knockin' me down. I sat beside a couple of deathbeds in my time, and I never felt anythin' but sorry for the person who was passin'. This was different. Way different."

"When did it happen?" Griffen asked.

"About five minutes ago." Gris-gris darted from one side of the sunny courtyard to another. "I couldn't wait to get out of that house. Had to put that place behind me, at least for a while. I think I ran all the way here. Say, you got anything to drink, man? My mouth feels like the Sahara."

"I have some pop upstairs. If you want something stronger, we'll have to go out."

"No, man," Gris-gris said, a little grin raising the corners of his mouth. "I mean, I'm just thirsty. It's like all my senses come back to life at once!"

He followed Griffen toward the door of his garden-level apartment, then darted up the stairs to Val's. Griffen followed him, taking the steps two at a time. The smaller man flipped a key ring out of his pocket and let himself in.

It had been over a month since Griffen had gone inside his sister's apartment. After she had been gone more than a week, he had cleaned out her refrigerator and turned the air-conditioning off. The air in the small flat felt stale and still. Gris-gris walked through each of the rooms in turn. He turned to Griffen forlornly.

"She really gone."

"Yeah," Griffen said. "I hope you didn't think I was hiding her from you, did you?"

"No. You had a right to, if she ast you—you her brother. I knew you'd tell me the truth if she didn't want to see me. Just had to see for myself. Any news on her?"

"No. I hired a . . . kind of private detective. No news yet, but he has more of a chance of finding her than we will."

"Somethin' special?" Gris-gris asked. "Like you?"

"Yes, but not like us. George is different from anyone else I know."

"Let me know if you hear. Is that Mrs. Melinda involved?"

"Probably," Griffen admitted. "I can't prove it one way or the other yet."

Gris-gris pounded a fist into his palm. "If I ever get my hands on that lady . . ."

"I'd leave her alone if I were you," Griffen said, alarmed. "She's dangerous."

"So am I!"

Griffen gave him a wry grin. "I know. Come on down and have a drink."

In his apartment, Griffen popped a couple of cold cans and poured them into glasses. Gris-gris threw himself impatiently onto the couch, dislodging all the flyers and notebooks.

"Hey, sorry," he said, bending to pick up the papers. "What's all this?"

Griffen shrugged. "More stuff for the campaign. Penny wants to run a pool tournament. I'm trying to find a venue, but they all want too much money. Between you and me, she's out of cash. We need a place that can hold a couple of hundred people, but the fees are too high."

"I can help," Gris-gris said. "I got some connections myself. I know a couple of good places. They'll knock some money off the fees as a favor to me."

"Really?" Griffen asked, feeling the tightness in his belly ease. "Thanks, Gris-gris."

"Huh. Least I can do since you been sittin' with me, keepin' me from going out of my mind. I just wasn't right."

"Well, now you are," Griffen said.

Gris-gris was never one to linger in the past. "But you was lookin' for a pool hall. What could be in it for the owners?"

"In terms of cash, the bare minimum," Griffen said. He found the paper with the figures on the floor and handed it to Gris-gris. "Pretty much everything she has left at the moment has to go for publicity. When we get some donations in, I can put down a deposit. We'd offer a percentage of the gate and all the catering profits."

The smaller man couldn't sit still any longer. He sprang up onto his feet and started pacing restlessly.

"Okay. Let me call some people. Who you talked to so far?"

Griffen gave him the flyers from the three halls he had visited.

"Oh, yeah, that's one of my cousins," Gris-gris said, pointing to the second flyer. "I'll see what I can get him to do. Meantime, I got to get some games organized for tonight. Thanks, man. See you later."

He gulped half the glass of soda and set it down. Griffen had to hurry to open the door for him.

Forty-one

Duvallier pushed Griffen's note toward him across the table.

"It's a mighty polite letter," he said, enjoying the dismayed look on the young dragon's face. "You just forgot one little thing: I didn't have no way to get back in touch with you to give you an appointment."

"What?" Malcolm asked. He snatched up the slip of paper. His eyebrows rose as he read the brief message.

Duvallier clamped his cigar in his mouth. He was not allowed to smoke a stogie in Antoine's private dining room, not that he would with Miss Callaway looking on. The order for a dozen oysters had already been put in the moment he walked in the door, and shrimp étouffée for the two of them was waiting until he decided whether he needed a second dozen oysters or not. But business first.

"He ain't in the book, and seein' as how he was the one who was askin' me for a favor, I didn't see no reason to go lookin' for him."

"Griffen, this is unacceptable!" Malcolm said. "In such a delicate matter!"

The younger McCandles glowered.

"Don't be so hard on the boy," Duvallier said, grinning at them. "I bet you weren't so perfect back when you were a tadpole. But how'd you expect me to reply to you, son? Telepathy?"

"You could have sent one of your ghosts," Griffen said, his face expressionless.

That Griffen probably was nearly as good a poker player as he thought he was. The boy was trying to keep his temper, but he wasn't going to roll over and play dead just because he was at a disadvantage. Duvallier could feel the fear radiating off the youngster. Brave. That was admirable, though fruitless. He relaxed in his chair. He preferred it when they fought back.

"Now, that's not nice. Makin' my friends and acquaintances do the work when you were the one who was careless like that? I didn't say I couldn't find you. I just said I couldn't be bothered to find you."

Griffen had to be pretty embarrassed, but he continued to cover it well. Malcolm had expressions, just not too many of them. Just then, his long face showed carefully modeled contrition.

"I apologize for my nephew," Malcolm said smoothly. "He is unaccustomed to undertaking high-level negotiations."

"Not necessary here, son. Politics is pretty low-down stuff."

Malcolm, as Duvallier knew he would, assumed a position that looked like authority, resting his elbows on the table and tenting his fingers. Appearances weren't everything, as Duvallier could have told him, but he let him talk.

"Mr. Duvallier . . ." he began.

"Reginaud, Malcolm! Last warning."

"Reginaud, then. Have you given any more thought to my proposal? The group that I represent has a good deal at stake in the Dunbar candidacy. We would be grateful for your assistance. We are fast reaching the point at which Penny Dunbar can or cannot remain a viable contender for the office of governor."

"Running out of money, ain't she?"

"I won't ask how you know that."

"Everybody does, son," Duvallier said, enjoying the

moment. He didn't have to refer to the notes that Miss Callaway had in her laptop thing, though she had it open and facing him for his use. "When you are runnin' somewhere between eighth and seventeenth in a race with nineteen contestants, you have to stand out in one way or another. This state has how many representatives? And how many state senators? And how many of them are tryin' to better themselves by goin' for higher office? Well, that's not her best suit. She stands on law and order, but who don't? Even the politicians who are takin' money under the table—and I know she is, too—stand for law and order. So that leaves makin' headlines in some way. She hasn't broken no big scandals about any of her fellow candidates on television or in the papers—just the opposite. Congressman Benson's been trying to drum up dirt about Penny, isn't he?"

"Yes," Griffen said.

"He tries hard, but, trouble is, he has no bait on his hook. That girl annoys a lot of people, but it ain't nothin' out of the ordinary. And the last thing she might do: appealing to other people's greed and good citizenship at the same time by hostin' an event for charity."

Malcolm paused. Duvallier jumped on the hesitation.

"So that's what she's up to. What kind of grand gala is she trying to run?"

"I bet you know that, too," Griffen said. He glanced at his uncle. Malcolm paused, then nodded. "I've spent the last several days trying to line up a pool hall. I know they're not all busy between now and October, but for some reason they just can't find a date for a charity tournament. A bunch of pros I've asked to participate say the same thing. They can't make it no matter when it is. I think you've been talking to them all."

The boy had perspicacity. If he had had the chance to take him under his wing, Duvallier could have made a great man out of Griffen. Too bad about the dragon blood.

"I got friends," Duvallier admitted, with creditable modesty. "I made some phone calls. Maybe I suggested they had better things to do with their time on those days."

"Why prevent such an event?" Malcolm asked. "If indeed it only prolongs the inevitable, what harm does it do? You said if she survived to the jungle primary, you would back her."

"She's finished. She just don't say so yet, but she will."

"I doubt that very much," Malcolm said. "So much is at stake—why not let her try her best?"

"What's her best if we haven't seen it yet? She hasn't got the credibility to go on. You could tell her that for me."

"I won't," Griffen said, maybe a little more forcefully than necessary. "You can try and throw her off her game all you want. She will finish this primary. Maybe she will even become governor."

"She can try," Duvallier said, putting his cigar in his mouth and clamping it with his teeth. "She is mighty welcome to try. Well, gentlemen, it's a shame we didn't get nowhere today. It was nice to see you." He picked up the menu to the right of his plate and read down the list of the day's specials.

"What will it take for you to back off your contract on Penny's life?" Griffen asked.

Duvallier raised his eyebrows. So he dared to mention the elephant in the room. Good boy. He glanced up. The fear was still there, deep inside that façade, but the youngster was bolstering it with courage. He spoke around his cigar.

"Make me an offer. I'm still open to negotiation."

Griffen extended his hands, palm up, across the table, his face open with appeal.

"We'll have the event, with or without your interference. Name an amount. If we raise more than that for her campaign, you let her live. After that, winning the election is up to the voters."

"And if you don't?"

"I'll fight you for her," Griffen said simply.

"You don't even like the gal," Duvallier said with a shrewd smile. "I got a better idea. I don't like to step into the ring. That don't make for a very fair fight. You sound like a knight in shining armor. You meet my champion. You beat him, you win. Miss Penny can go on and do whatever she wants. Meantime, I might stir the pot a few more times. I'm havin' fun watchin' all of you jump."

Griffen leaped to his feet. The smooth negotiator was gone. Steam shot out of his mouth and nose.

"Fine," he said. "Send whatever you want. I'll take him on."

Duvallier laughed up at him.

"Spoken like a true hero," he said, enjoying the fury on Griffen's face. "But, son, remember the definition of a hero is pretty often a dead soldier."

"That was unprofessional, Griffen," Malcolm said, as they walked out of the restaurant onto the sidewalk under the colonnade that fronted the building.

His uncle could not chide him any more severely than he was chastising himself. Griffen kept the words of the houngan in his mind. Duvallier had time on his side, and he knew it. Who knew what kind of monster Duvallier was going to call up out of the blackness of hell to face him? He had just agreed to fight for Penny's life. Duvallier was right that he didn't even like Penny, but Griffen had promised Rose to look out for her. He could get killed keeping a gubernatorial candidate in the Louisiana race. Maybe he was too stupid to live. He thought that he was good at observing human nature and making use of it, but Duvallier just ran rings around him. He wanted to kick himself. The zombie had drawn him out and made him lose his temper as if he were a toddler late for his nap.

"I know," he said.

"It was childish."

"I know!"

"You were vulnerable. You let him get under your skin."

"I know!" Griffen exclaimed. "I want to kick myself!"

"Don't," Malcolm said. The slightly amused tone in the

elder McCandles's voice made him turn to face his uncle. "Your father would have been very proud of you."

Griffen was taken so far aback he stopped walking.

"He would?"

"Eminently. He always championed the underdog. It was one of his least dragonish characteristics. I rather hoped you wouldn't inherit it, but as you have, I am happy to make use of it. I want to put you by Miss Dunbar's side until Duvallier repeals his fiat."

"What?" Griffen asked. "No!"

"Did you mean any of the heroic bravado that you spouted at our leathery host?"

Griffen had to think about it. As much as he did dislike Penny's behavior, he was outraged that Duvallier could be so cavalier regarding whether she lived or died. And he had promised Rose.

"Yes, I did," he said.

"You really have changed, Griffen," Malcolm said. He let out a weary sigh. "We must continue as if we believe Miss Dunbar will proceed all the way to the primary, at the very least. What have you got on a venue for the fund-raiser?"

Griffen pulled out his small notebook and flipped it open to the well-thumbed pages of notes regarding the proposed tournament. He didn't want Malcolm to see how many entries were crossed out. He kept the notebook cupped in his fingers as they walked.

"Well, I've been to a bunch of places and talked to the owners," he said. "Every one of them wants a fortune for the day's rental, which we don't have. If we can raise the deposit, I have three pool halls that will let us make up the remainder out of sign-up fees. All three have dates open within the next couple of weeks. That was the range Horsie wanted in order to make strategic buys from the media outlets with the proceeds." He described the three prospects, from the worst to the best; perhaps not coincidentally, the fees rose with the desirability of the venue.

Malcolm looked disapproving. "Those are most assuredly not ideal. What about catering?"

"Each of these places has its own kitchen," Griffen said. "I have menus at home I can show you."

"Pool-hall food? That will hardly do, Griffen. We'll have to pay a caterer. What about the one you use for your games? That food was more than palatable."

"We'll have to pay another fee to bring in outside food. All of them were firm on that."

"Can't you do anything right?" Malcolm asked, sourly.

Griffen felt his temper rise, but he didn't let any of it show on his face. "You want me to look after Penny and set up this tournament, on top of my business? If you aren't satisfied, I'd be happy to step back and let you handle it."

"Hey, Grifter!" A slim, energetic figure dashed out of the sun and swung around one of the verdigris-stained posts of Antoine's balcony like a teenager. Despite the warm sun, he wore a jacket.

"Hey, Gris-gris, looking good!" Griffen greeted him with a slap on the back. Under the coat, the other dealer was still painfully thin. "Uncle Malcolm, you remember Gris-gris? Val's boyfriend?"

Malcolm was by no means as pleased to see him as Griffen was, but he grudgingly summoned up a gracious smile.

"Glad to see you up and about, sir."

"Yeah, thanks," Gris-gris said with a lightning flash of his teeth. He turned to Griffen. "Hey, man, got you a place for your tournament."

"You did?" Griffen asked.

Malcolm looked appalled. His expression turned dismissive.

"I am sure we don't need the place that you have found, my good sir. Thank you for your efforts. I know that Ms. Dunbar will appreciate all the effort—"

Griffen turned to his uncle and fixed him with the same cold glare Malcolm used to use on him when he came home late.

"Uncle Malcolm, remember our first conversation when you arrived here?" Griffen said, letting his voice rise peevishly at the end of the sentence.

Malcolm let his dudgeon deflate. "I do. Well, Mr. Gris-gris?"

"No mister needed," Gris-gris said majestically. "You can call me Your Grand Excellency. Lookie here." He whipped a sheaf of flyers from the pocket of his jacket. Pictured on the front of the thickest one was a handsome building of mid-nineteenth-century vintage with ornamented doors and grand pillars surrounding the entrance.

"This is the Fairmont Hotel, up on Baronne. You seen it, Grifter? Well, the special-events coordinator happens to be one Ms. Opal Ferris. Back in the day, she used to be my fifth-grade teacher. They have next two Fridays and Saturdays open for four-hour stretches in the afternoon or evening in either the Crescent City Ballroom or the Astoria Ballroom, your choice depending on the day. The hotel'll donate the space, but you have to pay for food and personnel, plus gratuities. Be generous, or Ms. Opal will have my balls on a skewer."

Malcolm was astonished and impressed. "This is marvelous, Gris-gris. This will be an excellent choice. Er, will you want your name listed in the program flyer?"

It was a concession, and all three men knew it.

"No, thanks," Gris-gris said, showing his teeth in a fierce smile. "Not too good for my rep to be involved with a politician. Call me an anonymous contributor. Yeah, I like that."

"We will," Malcolm said.

Gris-gris pulled out a shiny new cell phone and looked at the digital readout on the face. "Got to go. Got a game revving up in an hour. See you around, Griffen."

Griffen grasped the other dealer's hand firmly.

"Thanks, Gris-gris."

The smaller man grinned. "One miracle down, next to go."

He shot away down Saint Louis as if he had been launched from a gun.

"That is a most unexpected person," Malcolm commented, watching him go.

"You don't know the half of it," Griffen said.

Malcolm cleared his throat.

"Well, let's go take the news to Ms. Dunbar. We can soften the bad news with the good and make plans. I would say the sooner the better, wouldn't you?"

"I agree," Griffen said with relief. He strode after his uncle. "I can't wait for all this to be over with."

Forty-two

The George still felt as if he had been run over by a couple of freight trains going in opposite directions, but he had to get back to his mission. Not only would the agency not get paid if he didn't accomplish his goal, but he would feel a personal sense of failure, and that he did not wish to experience. His hotel was one step above a fleabag, but it had one amenity that meant more to him than clean sheets or quiet neighbors: great water pressure. He stood underneath the shower, letting the hottest possible water pound down on his bruised tissues.

His midsection didn't show any of the abuse that he had undergone, but he could feel it in his tissues. It was a good thing he didn't scar. Over his long lifetime of dragon hunting, there was not a square inch of him that hadn't been scratched, scraped, hacked, burned, cut, punched, broken, or stabbed. He had been electrocuted four times—no, five, twice on a wire fence, once with lamp cords, and two he preferred to forget altogether.

His clothing had had to be replaced entirely. Debbie had shipped a package to him so he didn't have to waste time shopping. He actually enjoyed shopping but rarely had time for it. When he had a break, which was an infrequent occurrence, he usually spent it stalking dragons for practice. He knew where the rich and famous hung out. To have Melinda's country home go unnoticed by the office for generations was a red flag. Who knew how many other secret cabals of the scaly vermin were hidden around the nation?

The new canvas cargo pants had been broken in for him, having undergone who knew how many machine washings to a supple softness like moleskin. He was grateful that the support staff back home were so efficient. George felt in the pockets of his new camouflage jacket for the brackets that would short the electrical contacts in the fence. The people in the house would never know that the fence had been breached. Many other nice gadgets were arrayed among the nineteen hidden pouches and caches, handy to grab but un-detectable unless you knew where to look and what to look for. Also in the package from Debbie was an amulet and a can of spray that smelled so noxious George had wrapped it in the plastic laundry bag he had found in his hotel room drawer before putting it in his pocket.

George looked at himself in the mirror before departing. He knew he wasn't up to 100 percent yet, but the sooner he could put North Carolina in the rearview mirror, the happier he would be. He put on the face he had worn the first day until he pulled out of the motel parking lot, then re-formed his features and let the light brown hair flood with black. If he were unlucky enough to be spotted by the security system in Melinda's mansion, they wouldn't recognize him as their previous victim.

George planted two of the breakers at either side of Val's window and engaged the circuit. A tiny blue LED inside a black plastic cover lit up to show the system was working. He closed the cover and withdrew into the bushes behind the swimming pool to wait. As soon as Val came back to her room, he would speak to her and see how much preparation would be needed to perform the extraction.

The overhead light came on. George crept toward the window and peered in. The girl had arrived, all right, but she wasn't alone. A man even taller than she was had his arm over her shoulder. The two of them looked pretty lovey-dovey. In fact, as soon as they closed the door to the hall, they were all over each other. Before they'd taken two steps inside, she was unfastening his belt, and he was clasping her buttocks in both hands. The kisses they exchanged were so fierce they looked as if they were devouring one another's faces.

George grinned. He could wait a while.

"Mike?"

The girl's voice had the long, languorous tones of someone who was relaxing after great sex. The shadow of a slim arm stretched out to him in the dim room. The man had left about twenty minutes before, donning his clothes and blowing a kiss to her. George waited until the man's car had popped down the gravel drive and into the night before he activated his overrides and slipped over the sill into the room.

"No," George said in a low voice. "You're expecting me, though."

Before he finished speaking, Val was on her feet. She grabbed the phone off the table. He wondered if she was going to throw it at him or make a call. He closed the distance and pushed his finger down on the receiver with one hand and grabbed her wrist with the other. The dial tone ceased. Val glared for one second before bringing her knee up to his groin.

George was too old a hand not to have seen that move coming. He shifted to one side and twisted. Her knee connected with his rear end. He bent her arm upward, making her bow over it. She didn't know the countermove to his and flailed helplessly. She scratched and bit at his wrist with her free hand. Ow! Those damned dragon teeth were sharp! George felt for the light switch and flicked it up.

"Please, Ms. McCandles, I'm a friend. I wrote to you several days ago."

"You did?"

Val raised her head. The pupils of her big blue eyes had shrunk to pinpoints. She studied him curiously. Drops of his blood stained her mouth, but she looked innocently childlike.

"That's right." George gestured to her hand. "I'll let you go if you stop attacking me."

"Oh, sure," Val said. She relaxed. George let her go and helped her to sit down on the bed. She hadn't seemed to notice that she was stark naked. He pulled the coverlet from the foot of the bed and wrapped it around her shoulders. He dabbed the blood from her face with a tissue from the box on the table. When she was clean, he put the tissue in his pocket, to avoid leaving any unnecessary traces of himself in the room.

"Were you expecting someone else?" he asked.

"A friend of mine," Val said. She glanced around for Mai. The small Asian woman had sneaked out of the mansion a couple of days before. Val wondered when she was coming back again. It had been nice to see her. Mai had warned her to keep her presence a secret. She was having a hard time remembering why, but she fought to keep her sanity. It wasn't easy.

After their discussion, Melinda had brought in the doctor to examine Val. Her baby was fine. Val was fine, too, and she knew it, but the doctor had insisted on giving her half a dozen medications. They made her feel a little woozy, but she was still able to keep from blabbing about Mai. She couldn't mention Mai to Melinda. They didn't get along. She bit her tongue to make sure she didn't reveal the secret to this man. But who was he? A memory forced itself to the front of her mind. She peered at him.

"Are you . . . are you the person . . . ?"

"Who left you the message? At the coat check?" The man understood what she was seeking, a means of establishing some kind of bona fides. Val felt an immense rush of relief.

"It was you!" She smiled at him. He smiled back. "You didn't come that night. I thought they killed you. I felt terrible."

"They tried to kill me," the man said. "I got better. My name's George, by the way. I'm a . . . friend of Griffen's."

"Is he all right?" she demanded. "Why hasn't he returned any of my phone calls?"

"He is doing just fine. He sent me to get you."

"Oh, thank God!" Val said. She stood up. The coverlet fell on the floor. She looked down at herself. Her burgeoning breasts, tipped in pink, spilled out over the smooth expanse of her rounded belly. She looked at George in horror. He regarded her with calm eyes.

"You might want to put something on," he said. "We have a lot to discuss."

Val fingered the pendant that George had taken off his neck and fastened around hers. For the first time in days, everything made sense. She clutched the silk robe around her body. Val did her best to absorb all the information that the man had given her. It wasn't easy. Everything that had gone on for the last few months seemed to have happened to someone else. She felt betrayed that the Wurmleys had hypnotized her again into compliance. Melinda's assurances that Val was staying of her own free will melted into the sludge of reality. She couldn't believe anything that Melinda had told her, not ever. The pretty surroundings proved to be nothing more than draperies concealing the iron bars of her cage. She felt trapped and alone.

"So, something in this house makes you forget you're here?" she asked.

"That's one of the effects," George said. "Unless you have the training to cope with it, or an amulet like that one." He nodded toward the necklace. "I think Melinda installed it to help cope with Lizzy."

"You know about Lizzy?" Val asked. George nodded. "Are you a dragon, too?"

The man grimaced. "No, but I know a lot of them. Even among other dragons, Lizzy is a byword for dangerous insanity."

"No argument here," Val said, remembering the night she

had fought for her life against the crazed girl. "So you can get me out of here? Tonight? Please! I have to go home!"

"Not tonight," George said with a rueful expression. "I have to make some preparations. No more than a couple of days."

"Aargh!" Val said, looking at the ceiling. Who knew what kind of machinery or magical apparatus was concealed behind it? "I need to get out of here now!"

The man put a hand on hers. "You have to be patient. I won't take chances with you. You know these dragons. They're dangerous. Melinda still believes you are willing to stay. You need to keep up the pretense until I come back for you. Otherwise, she might hide you somewhere so remote no one can find you. You need to act as if nothing has changed if you want to protect your baby. Melinda wants it safe."

"Well, it's mine, not hers," Val said. "I'll do it."

"All right," he said. He reached for the cord around her neck. Automatically, Val recoiled. Once the amulet was gone, she would revert to Stepford Daughter-in-Law-Elect. She couldn't lose her mind again.

"Don't!" she said. "Please!"

George looked sympathetic.

"I'm sorry, but I have to take it. I need it to get in and out. I will bring you one when I come back."

"Soon, please!"

"As soon as I can," George assured her. He checked his contacts on the window before sliding it open.

"Tell Griffen I'm fine," Val said.

"Tell him yourself when you get home," he said, with a brief smile. "Be ready to move when you see me again. The clock will be ticking. We'll have to hustle. Can you remember that?"

"Hustle," Val said, resolutely. She could feel the sense of clarity fading away. "Yes. I will try. But, please, hurry!"

With one rueful glance, George slipped over the windowsill and vanished into the night.

Forty-three

Val sat in her room, paging through *Parent* magazines and books on child rearing. Once in a while, she looked up to survey the piles and heaps of baby gifts that Melinda had insisted she keep in her room. It made things a little crowded, but the presents were so pretty, Val couldn't object.

She thought she would have to go over the books for PrepPro, but Henry told her that it wasn't necessary any longer. It was more important that she learn to be the best mother that she could. Melinda wasn't much help, except as a bad example. Val would be better off turning to the experts. Henry had a reading list for her and came by in the evenings to quiz her on what she had absorbed. He was a tough taskmaster, and she hated to disappoint him.

Marcella no longer joined her for breakfast. She told Val apologetically that with Lizzy in the house, she didn't have the time. Val felt it was just as well. She needed to keep her inner feeling of rebellion alive. She did not want to endanger Marcella by involving her. George would be back soon. In that moment, she would put Melinda and this crazy house behind her forever. Only the thought of that escape kept her from losing her mind completely.

After George's visit, she had felt as though she could handle anything Melinda threw at her, but the feelings faded. She was at war with herself. Her innermost thoughts belonged to her, but they were buried underneath the complacent girl who cooed over Baby Mozart tapes and bottle warmers. Melinda had gone crazy buying things for her first grandchild. By actual count, Val had 162 bibs, 16 onesies for newborns, and 40 in larger sizes up to a year. That was just casual attire. The kid would have more designer clothes than Posh Spice, whatever gender it proved to be. Nine infant quilts, patchwork, silk, polar fleece, and Egyptian cotton, were stacked up on a shelf in her closet. Val felt as if she had been given a huge baby shower in one sitting. It was a shame that she hadn't had a bunch of girlfriends to coo over the gifts with her.

At the moment, all she needed to do was gestate. No one was pretending any longer that she was really in charge of the business she was supposedly running. Mai had been right about Henry feeding her all the information. Val thought it was just as well. She preferred not to have to leave her rooms. She felt nervous walking through the house without an escort now that Lizzy was back in residence. Occasional visits from Mike were one of the few things that kept Val from going as insane as Lizzy. George or Mai had better come soon.

"Good grief, Amazon! This place looks like a BabyMart! Is there one single thing that she didn't buy you?"

Val sprang up. Mai slipped in the door and pulled it closed behind her. Val gave her a big hug that lifted the tiny woman off her feet.

"How did you get in?" Val asked.

"I followed the mail truck. Special delivery. I had to arrange it myself. Melinda just received a box of summer sausage from Swiss Colony. From a secret admirer. My goodness, Melinda cracked open the vault, didn't she?" Mai glanced around. "These are all very fine things. She spared no expense at all."

"Beautiful, aren't they?" Val dragged her over to see the changing table. "Look at this. It's my favorite. Hand-carved walnut. Amish made."

"Very pretty if you live in a Louis XV mansion. But it will be a trifle upscale for your apartment."

"But it looks good here, doesn't it?" Val said.

Mai frowned at her. "If you were staying here, that would be fine. You aren't thinking of giving in and living here, are you?"

Val forced her real self past the imposed obedience and managed to shake her head. She tapped her ear. Mai's light brown eyes widened. She nodded.

From the knee pocket of her cargo pants, she took a tiny crystal lantern. She wrapped Val's hands around it and touched the top. It turned red. Heat surged through Val's body. Her mind cleared. She let out a sigh of relief.

Mai removed a silver ring from her finger and put it on the ground between them.

"Okay, now she can't hear us. Are you all right?"

"I'm fine, but I'm ready to go. When can we leave?"

Mai shook her head. She sat down on the armchair and shrugged her slim shoulders.

"I've been working hard on it, Val, but I'm not sure how I can get you out of here. I could enlist my family, but that would cause an open war between Melinda's clan and the Eastern dragons. I can't afford to start that. We need help."

Val beamed. "We have help. I met the private detective. He's the one who left me the note. Just as you thought, Griffen sent him. He'll help us."

"Wonderful," Mai said. "He can slip in and out of here?"

Val nodded, glad to have some good news for her friend. "George has done it twice already."

Mai's pencil-thin brows soared toward her hairline.

"George? He said his name is *George*? What does he look like? Never mind! It doesn't make any difference! You can't go anywhere with him!"

Val gawked at her. What upset her friend so much?

"Mai, he's just a private detective. Why does he scare you?"

"He's not a detective, he's a dragon hunter! St. George—he's one of them!"

Val couldn't believe it. That nice man?

"Oh, come on, St. George lived a thousand years ago!"

"They're not human," Mai said, her eyes wide with fear. "They can live hundreds of years, maybe thousands. They're enemies of all dragonkind. He just told you Griffen sent him so you'd let down your guard!"

Val was terrified but practical. George had not seemed to want to hurt her. He was avuncular, kind, patient, and practical. He even had a sense of humor. Val felt certain he was telling the truth about coming from Griffen. Why would he lie?

"Are you sure it's the same guy? A lot of people are named George."

"Maybe it's not." Mai drummed her fingertips on the table. "All right, I'll check it out. If he's legitimate, I hope he can do what he says he will."

Thankfully, not all of Melinda's servants lived on the grounds. Mai hovered in the overgrown garden near twilight until she saw a tall, dark-skinned man leave the rear exit of the mansion and get into a green Dodge Rambler. She hoped that the dogs were not out yet. She didn't want to kill innocent hounds just because their mistress was a homicidal maniac.

The Rambler bumped over the rear drive toward the back gate. It operated on the inside by the use of a card-swipe reader. Mai allowed herself to assume her dragon form. As soon as the car was within thirty feet of the exit, she took wing. The driver rolled down his window to swipe his identification card. Mai edged into his blind spot and trotted out beside him to the rear access road. The Rambler turned left. Mai angled right.

As soon as she was certain she was out of range of any of Melinda's cameras, she flew straight up. Cell-phone coverage in this backwater was absolutely horrible amid the thick forests. Once she spotted a tower, she hooked her cell phone out of her purse. She could have transformed it along with her clothes, but it was her favorite designer handbag. With delicate claws, she touched a series of numbers. The phone rang twice."

"May I help you?" a woman's voice answered.

"Is this Debbie?"

"Yes, it is. May I ask who's calling?"

"It's Mai."

"How are you?" the voice asked, adding forced cheerfulness to its tone.

"No pleasantries, if you don't mind. Where is George?"

"I'm sorry, but he's not in the office right now. May I take a message?"

"No. I am in North Carolina. I know he is close by. I need to speak to him."

"That isn't possible."

"Debbie, I am an old customer. Your office has done research for me in the past. I am trying to figure out if a dear friend of mine is in danger."

"A friend?" The voice sounded incredulous. Mai was getting tired of that reaction from people. Was it so rare a thing as to invite astonishment? "Who?"

"Valerie McCandles," Mai said. "I expect that anything I say to you will be kept confidential."

"You're not looking for revenge against George?"

"For what? He has been helpful to me now and again. I am trying to prevent a situation in which I need to seek revenge. Where is he?"

"Just a moment, please."

Mai flew in circles, listening to instrumental versions of "The Girl From Ipanema" and "The Theme from *Peter Gunn*." She gave a disgusted grunt. They had not changed their HOLD tape since the 1960s.

After a few more vintage favorites, Debbie came back on the line.

"Bisby Motel," she said. "Do you need me to spell it?"

"No, but directions would help."

"No problem. Are you driving?"

"Flying."

The Bisby Motel had the sort of old-fashioned charm that would have made Mai drive all night to avoid having to stay there. A painted wooden butter churn and a three-foot crank-driven coffee grinder flanked the entrance. Tole-painted plaques covered the exterior walls, along with framed country adages and a large, peeling, gray sign that said VACANCIES.

Mai went around the corner of the building and up the concrete steps to the third floor. Debbie had said George was staying in room 318.

She stopped several doors down and listened closely. The room to her right had a DO NOT DISTURB sign on the knob. The occupant snored raucously. Mai tuned him out and fixed her keen hearing on each room in succession. A mother and small children, a peevish-sounding woman on the telephone, then three empty, including the George's room.

She walked the rest of the way and peered in through the picture window. The sagging slats of the Venetian blinds left just enough gaps for her to see inside. A pair of twin beds flanked a battered wooden night table. Facing them was a long melamine-topped credenza with a large television perched on it. At the rear of the room, a mirror reflected her eyes back at her. She could just see a sink to the right. No lights were on, but the beds had been neatly made up. The room stood empty. He was not there.

Mai always believed in letting the fight come to her. She spotted a chambermaid pushing a cart full of towels and sheets along the walkway.

"Can you help me?" she said. She pretended to fumble in her purse, making certain to let the Hispanic woman see the roll of greenbacks in her wallet. "I think I left my key in the drawer. Could you let me in?"

"Sure, ma'am," the maid said. She pulled a large ring of keys out along an elastic tether on her belt. Mai stood by while she unlocked the door, then slipped a ten-dollar bill into her hand.

"Thank you so much. My husband always makes fun of me for being absentminded."

"Men are like that," the chambermaid said. She tucked the bill away and pushed the cart toward the elevator. Mai waited until she was out of sight, then tiptoed into the George's hotel room.

Suddenly, a noose dropped around her neck and tightened. Mai grabbed it with both hands and tried to tear it away. She gasped as she was yanked back against a hard body. Warm breath washed her cheek.

"This may not kill you, but you'll wish it did."

Forty-four

George held Mai tight. He knew that he was stronger than she was, but she fought dirty. So did he, for that matter, but no sense in taking chances. He fished another long, looped wire tie from his pocket and captured both hands behind her back. He ratcheted the strap out until she moaned in protest.

"I'll take the rope off your neck if you promise nothing but words are going to come out of your mouth."

Her hooded eyes flashed, but she nodded. George loosened the cord. It was spelled to be strong enough to strangle dragons. He hated to use it, but he always carried it. Mai took a deep gasp of breath.

"Ow!" Mai protested. "You didn't have to do that!"

"When a dragon like you pays me an unexpected visit, you had better believe I take all precautions until I know where it stands."

"Don't call me 'it.' Check your messages! Debbie told me where to find you. I need to talk to you."

"Really? About what?"

"About what you're doing here."

He guided her roughly to one of the beds and made her sit down on it. He crouched at a distance but kept hold of the long end of her manacle tether.

"What I am doing anywhere is never any of your business."

Mai tossed her hair out of her face. "That is not true. I have used your services in the past. You never seem to mind taking my money for surveillance or research."

"True. But you can't hire me for anything at the moment. I'm on a job."

He had never seen such raw fear in the eyes of any of the Eastern dragons.

"What job? What is it you intend to do to Valerie Mc-Candles?"

George didn't let his surprise show. Of course, the Eastern dragons would be interested in a pure-blooded dragon baby, not to mention a fecund and reasonably sane mature female.

He had just returned from his final surveillance of the Wurmley estate. He had planted caches of supplies and weaponry in various locations inside the fence. On his checkthrough he had seen no signs of the Gollum-demon, but he could smell it. He was surprised that the dogs didn't go crazy at the scent of such an indiscriminate predator. Henry must have trained them not to freak out. Dammit, all he needed was one more obstacle to his goal. Interference from Mai could cause him to lose his concentration. That could prove fatal to his target.

"You know I can't discuss open contracts with you."

"What will it take for you to back off the McCandles girl?"

George regarded her with exasperated patience. "If I were working on a job for you, what would you think if I took a bribe from another interest? You know we don't work that way."

Mai stood up. George followed suit. He towered over the petite Asian female, but she was not intimidated.

"I'll stop you," she said. "Unless you kill me right now, I will keep you from taking her anywhere."

"Don't try, Mai. We don't freelance, but I'll protect myself."

"Bring it, tough guy," Mai said, holding her chin high.

George shook his head wearily. "Not now, Mai. Sometimes I like your sparring, but it's inappropriate at the moment."

"Really? *Why?* Tell me why! You have no idea what you're walking into over there."

"Sure I do." George snapped the wire tie off her wrists. He went to the door and held it open. "Get lost, Mai. I'll buy you a drink sometime once this is all over."

She rose, looking surprised. The way she gathered herself, George sensed that she was going to spring at him. He held up a hand.

"Would you mind not trashing my room? The staff has been really nice to me. And after you gave the hotel maid ten bucks, I'd hate to have her waste her tip scrubbing blood off the walls. It won't do any good anyhow. I might have to hurt you, and I still won't give you any details."

Mai halted in her tracks. Her lip curled, showing her sharp little white teeth.

"You'll be sorry, George."

"I'm already sorry. See you around."

He stood silently by the open portal and waited. Mai stared at him for a long time, then stalked past him. He watched her go around the front of the building, then kept watch until he was sure she wasn't coming back around the other side. With a sigh, he closed the door and took out his cell phone. He held it to his ear while he started loading his pockets with supplies and weapons.

"Debbie, we have a problem. I have interference. Mai is here. She just left. She wanted to know what I was doing here."

The secretary's voice squawked from the speaker.

"What? You haven't broken confidentiality, have you?"

"Give me a break. She's got a nasty sense of humor. If she knew I was saving a dragon instead of stalking one, she'd phone the news services. I can hear her laughing about it now."

"You have to get that girl out immediately."

"I know, I know. Putting together my kit now. I'll call you once I'm safely on the road with her."

Mai dashed into the trees. She held her handbag in her teeth as she ran. Transforming on the fly wasn't as easy as it looked in the movies. Better to complete the alteration as she went. As soon as her wings were clear, she opened them and flapped hard. She cleared a picnic table, only registering too late that it was occupied. She and a couple who had decided to sneak off for an afternoon quickie both got an eyeful.

"Oh, my God!" the woman cried, pointing over her lover's shoulder. "A demon!" The man rolled off her and gawked upward.

"Dragon, curse you," Mai muttered to herself. "Why do they always think scaly wings mean demon?"

She had no idea when George was going to make his move. She had to hurry. Val firmly believed that George was a benevolent rescuer, not a killer. Mai had three hard tasks ahead of her: convincing Val that George was a monster; convincing Val to leave the mansion now, at all costs; and finding a way past all of Melinda's insane security protocols.

At the mansion, she circled impatiently, staying out of range of the cameras, waiting for a vehicle to pull through either gate so she could sneak in. Twilight was coming. She didn't have any bribes for Melinda's herd of mutts. Damn George! He had made her forget details! Drink, hell! If she ever saw him again, she was going to tear out his guts and eat them.

At last, she felt a break in the security spell near the back. She flitted down onto the access road in time to see a car exiting: one of Melinda's day staff going home for the night. Mai closed her wings and swooped down toward the gate.

Curse it! Before she could reach the gate, it swung down again. All the security cameras lit up. Mai swore colorfully in Cantonese, Mandarin, Thai, and several ancient dragon dialects.

The only way in was with an ID or an invitation. She had neither. But the man in the car did. She turned on a wingtip and arrowed after him.

As the brown auto stopped at a T-intersection on the overgrown lane, Mai landed on the hood. The stocky, dark-skinned man in the driver's seat threw up his hands to shield his face. Mai reached in through the open window and grabbed him by the throat.

"You forgot something in the house," she said, dragging him eye to eye with her. "You need to go back and get it. Right now. It's a matter of life and death: yours."

"Yes, sir!" the man said. His eyes were so wide that they looked as if they might pop out.

"It's *ma'am*," Mai said. She shoved him back into the front seat, and slid in the window to the rear. She kept one claw at the back of his neck. His skin twitched. "Turn this junk heap around. Move it!"

"Yes, ma'am!" Though his hands were shaking, the man threw the car into reverse, executed a Y-turn, and raced back to the house.

Once they were through the security gate, Mai hauled the driver out of the car and tied him up with his own belt and a set of jumper cables. There was just room for him in the trunk, among the usual detritus humans accumulated in storage places. She unfurled a strip of duct tape from the roll she found there, pasted it over his mouth, then slammed the trunk lid down over his frightened eyes.

No alarms or lights went off, so her presence must have gone undetected. As twilight began to fall, a few more employees emerged through the rear door, chatting to one another in loud voices. Their noise covered Mai as she slithered in past the cars parked at the rear of the house. No one paid attention to a serpent the color of the gravel.

Once past them, she grew legs again to race along the edge of the house toward Val's window. Thank all the ancestors, it was open! Blessings on the Amazon's proclivity for fresh air. She rolled in over the sill, gathering her wings in and assuming human shape again as she stood up.

"Put your things together, Val. We have to get out now!"

To her horror, Val was not alone. A slim woman with black hair jumped up from the table and backed toward the door. After crawling over the dirt to get back, Mai was in no mood to have a mere human interfere with her plans. She dashed to slam the door closed and put her back against it. The other woman dropped to a crouch. Mai was surprised. The woman didn't look like a typical student of krav maga. Mai struck a karate stance, then relaxed.

"What am I doing?" Mai asked, appalled at herself. "I know what you just saw. Scream and I will kill you long before anyone can possibly come to your aid. Very painfully, I might add."

By then, Val was between them, hands holding them back from one another.

"Don't hurt her, Mai. She's my friend! Marcella, this is Mai. I told you about her."

Marcella stood wide-eyed, but she swiftly regained her aplomb.

"Pleased to meet you," she said. Mai laughed.

"I should have known that anyone who worked for Melinda would be made of steel," she said. "You are surprising for a human."

"Thank you," Marcella said.

"Enough pleasantries. Well, Amazon? Grab your purse! We have no time! The George is coming!"

"Who is the George?" Marcella asked.

"He's an assassin!" Mai cried. "He is here to kill you. I do not intend to let that happen. We need to go, now. Val, you say you do not believe me, but I just saw him. He is preparing to make a strike here. We must get away from here. Now!"

Val wore confusion like an itchy sweater. "I can't believe it; he seems so nice!"

"Forget nice," Mai said. To her great annoyance, Val had

fallen back under the house spell. "If I am wrong, you can apologize to him and to Griffen once we get you home!"

"Griffen!" Val's face brightened. "I want to see him."

Mai grabbed her hand. "Come with me."

Val pulled back.

"I can't."

"Why not?"

Val beamed. Her smile brought out the dimples in her cheeks and made her large blue eyes shine. Mai deplored the brainless expression she wore. "Marcella just came to tell me that Mike is on his way to have dinner with me. Isn't that great? I want you to meet him."

Mai waved her hand impatiently. "No one is supposed to know I'm here, remember? You can invite Mike to visit you when you get home."

"I *suppose* so."

Mai glanced at Marcella. "What about her? I hate to leave witnesses."

Val seemed startled, but Mai knew she understood what she was saying. Instead of vapid complacency, her expression changed slowly to one of resolution. She appealed to the housekeeper. "Marcella, please, we need your help. I don't know how much you know about Melinda and her family, but . . . we're like her."

Marcella took her off the hook at once.

"You're dragons. I knew that. I'm not."

"What about this Henry?" Mai asked.

"Oh, he's not a dragon, either, but he's different," Marcella said. "He controls almost everything on the property, even when Melinda is here."

Mai pushed impatiently between them.

"This place has almost Pentagon-level security. Can you get us past it?"

"I don't want my baby born here," Val added, crossing her arms over her belly protectively. Yes, the spell was broken now. "I want her born at home, where she belongs!"

For the first time, the housekeeper looked frightened.

"I'd do anything I can for you, Val, but Melinda will have my head, maybe literally, if I let you leave the house."

"If you get us out, then you can come with us," Val urged her. "My brother knows dozens of people in the hotel industry in New Orleans. He could find you the kind of job you've always wanted."

"Val!" Mai protested. Val glowered at her.

"We can't leave her here to die."

"We're not," Mai said. She eyed the housekeeper up and down. "You're in good shape. If you slow us up, it's your own problem. What do we have to do?"

"Nothing," Marcella said, showing as much resolution as Val. "I don't need to leave. It will be a harmless diversion. How could I know you were going to run away? I'll go and distract the security detail for a little while. Just be ready to head for the front gate." She glanced at her watch. "Give me ten minutes, starting from . . . now."

Val looked at her own watch, a round Patek Philippe slip of gold that Mai immediately envied.

"All right," she said. "Thank you."

Marcella gave her a grim smile. "No thanks needed. It may not work, but it is your best chance. Good luck."

She opened the door and peered out to make certain no one was in the hall.

The doorbell rang.

All three women looked at one another. Val threw back her head in dismay.

"Mike! I forgot about him!"

Forty-five

Marcella gathered herself and went down to answer the door. Val and Mai watched from the hallway, just out of sight.

"What should we do?" Val whispered.

"This is a gift," Mai whispered back. "He can get you off the grounds. If he is not an utter creature of Melinda's, have him take you out and drop you somewhere, then wait an hour to call me. If I am not off the property by then, I am dead. Go home to Griffen."

Val hugged her. "I don't want anything to happen to you!"

Mai shook her head. Val was so young! "I should be all right. I am not without defenses, and your housekeeper friend may help me because she wishes to please you. Are you ready?"

Val swiped at her hair. She wore no makeup, but she never needed it. Mai envied her that bright, clear complexion and that sun gold hair. Val looked down at her sapphire blue sweat suit.

"This wasn't what I was going to wear, but it'll be better for travel."

"Shhh!" Mai tapped her lips for silence.

Marcella opened the door. A tall man stepped over the threshold. The sun framed him from behind, giving him a halo of gold. He had a nice shape, though it was somewhat obscured by the faded army jacket he wore. Mai liked lean men with wide shoulders. Marcella shut the door behind

him, cutting off the glare. Mai nodded with approval. Black
hair, blue eyes, that jaw! She pushed Val's shoulder.

"Mmm! Very nice, Amazon. Now, go! I'll see you as soon
as I can!"

Val straightened herself up and shook her hair back over her
shoulders. The two people at the door looked up as she came
down the stairs to join them. Mike smiled warmly at her.

"There's the beautiful lady," he said.

"Hi, Mike." She smiled at him, feeling shy before Marcella. He swept her into his arms and kissed her. When he
let her go, Val sensed a tentativeness about him. Maybe he
didn't like having a date with so many observers. That was
good. He ought to go along with her plans—if she could get
away with it.

"What's wrong?" she asked.

Mike seemed surprised. "Nothing. You look lovely."

"Come in, Mr. Burns," Marcella said. She stood aside to
let him in.

"I have a better idea," Val said brightly, hooking her arm
into Mike's. She smiled up at him. "Let's go out tonight
instead."

"Uh, all right," Mike said. "Where would you like to go?"

"How about the jazz club?" Val asked. She knew that
building well by now. The ladies' room was down a blind
hallway. She could sneak into the kitchen and go out the rear
door if she had to.

"Why not?" Mike said. "I'm dressed a little casually for
it, aren't I?"

"Well, look at me," Val said, impatiently. She gestured at
herself. Her belly looked like a velour dome under the jacket.
"If they don't mind me, they won't mind you."

"You look fine," he said. "No one will notice your clothes,
as beautiful as you are."

Something in the way he said that struck her as forced.

She searched his face and tried to guess what he was thinking.

"What's wrong?" she asked again.

"Nothing's wrong, Val. Come on."

He hooked his arm in hers and drew her toward the door. Val held her breath. The sunshine felt so good on her face! She was going home. A pity about all those gorgeous baby gifts, but she didn't need much. Her baby kicked at her belly, as if telling her to hurry up.

"And just where. Are. *You* going?"

Val felt as if a sword of ice had plunged into her back. She turned and favored Melinda with a casual smile.

"Out for dinner," she said. "I thought it would be a nice change."

Melinda put her plump hands on her round hips and glared up at Mike, though her voice was as sweet as saccharine.

"What about all the work that my chef has gone to, to make a delicious dinner for you two?" she asked. "What am I going to tell him? He will be so hurt!"

"I'm sure that he will understand," Mike said. His eyes were innocent. Val could have jumped him right there out of sheer gratitude.

"Now, you remember the conditions that I gave you for seeing the mother of my grandchild," Melinda said. Her muddy brown eyes flashed into polished agate. "They did not include making plans without consulting me."

"Wait a minute," Val said, natural outrage flooding her for the first time in days. "Conditions? I'm the one who decides who sees me and where. I want to go out. Are you really going to stop me?"

Melinda eyed her up and down with a rueful expression. "Darling, you sound completely out of sorts. Your hormones must be so out of balance that it's a wonder you're not standing on your head. That's why I've been acting as your guardian for these months. You need me." She reached for Val's other arm. "Come on into the lounge and sit down. Where's Henry? Marcella, get him."

Val backed away.

"Don't you dare, Marcella," she said.

The housekeeper looked torn. Her hand went to the phone on her belt, but she didn't open it.

"Hurry!" Melinda barked.

"I . . ."

"Humans! They're useless!" Melinda bore down on Val, moving much faster than Val thought she could. She tried to pull her arm away, but Melinda clamped her hand on it with the strength of a bench vise. She fixed her glare on Mike.

"It was so nice of you to come over tonight, Michael, but as you can see, Valerie is out of sorts. She really needs to lie down. That little one must be giving her a bad time. I remember when I was carrying my Lizzy, sometimes I didn't know how I was acting. So, if you'll excuse us, I'm going to put her to bed. Come along, Valerie."

"No!" Val said. She tried to shake loose. Melinda held on.

"I say yes. You don't know what's good for you, darling!"

"For me?" Val asked. "You kidnapped me from my home. God knows how many lies you have told me over the last few months. I should be behind the bar, listening to Shriners tell me that their wives don't understand them. Come on, Mike. Let's go out and . . . get some food."

Val felt her voice die in her throat. She knew it was obvious to everyone that this had stopped being about going out to eat. Melinda understood that if Val made it over the threshold, she wasn't coming back. She clamped her other hand onto Val's wrist and barked an order over her shoulder.

"Marcella! Now!"

Val couldn't blame the housekeeper for being cowed. Marcella opened the small phone and dialed a number. Val thought she could hear ringing in a distant part of the house.

Val refused to wait for Henry to come and fuzz her brain again. A tiny kick under her diaphragm reminded her why it was so urgent to get out right away. Her women's self-defense teacher had told her that anything that let you run away from a mugger was the right action. She swept her leg under Melinda's feet. The older dragon dropped on the black-and-white tiles, but she didn't loosen her death grip on Val's arm. Val fell heavily on her knees.

"Dammit, let me go!" Val shrieked.

"Never!"

"Ladies, please," Mike said, trying to help them up. "Aren't you both overreacting?"

In unison, they chorused, "No!"

"Mike, help me," Val pleaded. She pried at Melinda's fingers. Undoubtedly against his better judgment, Mike got on his knees beside them. He pulled one hand loose. Before he could get the other one off, Melinda put her fingers around Val's windpipe. And squeezed. A red halo sprang up around Val's field of view.

"It's all right if you deliver from a coma, darling. Easier for us all."

Her vision narrowed into a diminishing disk of light, with Melinda's face in the center. Before she blacked out completely, Val summoned what was left of her wits and swung her left fist into the only thing she could see.

The grip on her hand collapsed. Val sat on the floor for a moment, panting. Her sight cleared. Melinda lay spread-eagled on the floor, eyes closed, mouth agape. She was unconscious.

"That was one hell of a punch," Mike said admiringly. "Come on, let's go!"

"Right," Val said. She still couldn't believe that she had knocked Melinda out. "Hurry."

Mike helped her to her feet. Marcella gave her a quick hug.

"I didn't call Henry, but he knows everything that happens in this house," she said. "Run. I hope I see you again someday."

Val returned the embrace warmly. "Me, too."

Swallowing hard in her sore throat, Val staggered a little unsteadily toward the door. Mike held her arm to steady her. She looked out to the driveway. The only vehicle on it was a dark green sedan with North Carolina plates.

"Where's your car?" she asked.

"Right there," Mike said. "Mine needed service. This is a loaner."

"Not your style at all," Val said.

"It was what they had. It drives just fine. Come on." He put his arm around her and urged her forward.

Val hesitated. Something *was* wrong.

At the top of the stairs, Mai saw Val balk. She peered over their heads toward the driveway. The green sedan didn't look like the kind of car dealerships lent out to repair clients. It was nondescript, almost a junker. In fact, she was almost certain she had seen it before.

Mai probed hard at Mike. A guy that good-looking had to have a few secrets.

He had. It was a big one. Mike wasn't a dragon. In fact . . . She stood up and screamed.

"Val, it's George! Run, Val!"

George could have ripped Mai's lungs out. He almost had the girl out the door! He reached for Val. The girl backed away for him. He extended his arm into a muscular tentacle and wrapped it around her wrist.

Her shattered nerves had put Val's reactions on full red alert. When his hand touched her, Val turned, raised a leg, and gave him a hard side kick in the stomach.

"Oof!"

He staggered backward, his rubbery extremities flailing for a handhold. The doorstep caught his heel. He tripped and fell on his back. He rolled over and sprang to his feet. With more presence of mind than most humans had, the housekeeper sprang forward and slammed the door on him.

Marcella spoke into her cell phone and took Val by the arm. "Come with me!"

"Mai! What about Mai?"

The small Asian woman appeared at her side almost as if by magic.

"I am here, Amazon. What now?" Mai asked Marcella.

"I'll take you through the back door. Where is your car?"

"In the road out front. It will be a run. Can you make it, Val?"

"Yes." Val had caught her breath by then. Melinda was starting to stir. She moaned loudly. Marcella took both young women by the arms. She hustled them into the dayroom and through the servants' door. Behind it, Val inhaled the warm, moist, mixed scent of drying laundry, insecticide, and cedar. Once they were through, Marcella pushed the door closed and snapped a bolt into a bracket just above the knob.

"That won't hold her," Val said.

"Yes, it will," Marcella said. "It's made to withstand Lizzy. Come on!"

They ran through parts of the house that Val had never seen before, much more humbly furnished than the grand rooms in which she had been living. The floors were polished flagstones with heavy, rectangular, woven rag rugs four feet wide down the center of the corridor. Narrow tracks worn into the fabric in parallel lanes told Val that they had been there a long time. Their intention, for which she was very grateful, was to keep the footsteps of those below stairs from being heard by the gentry above stairs. They passed heavy wooden doors with old-fashioned wood-and-iron latches fastened by very modern padlocks. Some of the rooms stood open, and a few even had large windows facing the corridors, like a sewing room where a plump Hispanic woman sat at a gently humming Bernina machine with folds of teal blue cloth in her lap.

"The kitchen is this way."

An alarm blared from the ceiling. *HONK ah HONK ah HONK ah!* Val tensed, clenching her fists, but kept moving.

Marcella's small phone started buzzing. The housekeeper lifted it to her ear and answered it in a supernally calm voice.

"This is Marcella. No, I am not in the front hall. What do you need done? What?" She sounded shocked. "Should I call the doctor? No, I will be there immediately." She glanced at Val. "I have not seen Miss McCandles, but I will go up to her room if you require it. Very well."

She holstered the phone. "Henry. The security room called him."

Val felt a jolt of panic, remembering how easily he sapped her will.

"Where is he?"

"He said he's upstairs. He's on his way down to the front hall."

"Good," Mai said. "Let us hurry."

"Right in here," Marcella said, guiding them through a pair of stainless-steel swinging doors. She pushed inside. The kitchen, like everything else in the house, was spotless and expensively furnished. Esteban and a few of the other kitchen staff turned away from a long metal table as they entered. The stocky little man set down the knife and the onion in his hands and scooped up a package wrapped in white paper. He ran to meet Val. She braced herself for a fight.

He smiled at her and pushed the parcel into her hands.

"Here is food for your journey. We guess something was up, Miss Valerie. You have been very nice to us. We appreciate. And we say nothing."

Val took the package and kissed him on the cheek.

"Thank you. I'm going to miss your cooking, Esteban. I've never eaten so well in my life."

"Makes healthy babies," the small man insisted. "Make strong boys!"

"And girls," Val said. "Whatever this one turns out to be."

"Out here," Marcella said, darting between the metal fixtures toward a block-glass window. Beside it, a painted steel door waited, latched closed with a steel bolt. The housekeeper flung it open.

On the other side stood Mike Burns. Or, rather, George. Val gasped.

He grabbed Val by the wrist. "Come on, Ms. McCandles. I'm taking you home."

"No!" Val screamed. She fought to plunge her fingertips into his pressure points. He didn't seem to have any. She pulled back. His grip was stronger than anything she had ever felt. "I don't want to die!"

Just like that, Mai was between them, her hands around his throat. "She's not going anywhere with you, assassin."

The George batted her away as if she weighed no more than a paper doll. She went for him again, but he held her at arm's length. A roar behind him almost rattled the windows.

"Do you really want to have this argument now? We both want the same thing! Security's been alerted. Any minute now, that monster's out. It's killed me once already."

"It did what?" Mai asked.

She looked genuinely shocked. The tall man—Val couldn't bring herself to think of him as Mike any longer, even though he looked just like him—grimaced.

"It tore my guts out."

"Why are you still alive?" Val asked.

"Shape-changer," Mai said with an offhand shrug. Explanations would have to wait. "What is it?"

The man shook his head.

"No idea. This thing hates dragons, but it will attack anything that moves. Come on, Ms. McCandles, we haven't got much time."

"Why? Why should she trust you?" Mai demanded.

"Mike" fixed his sapphire blue gaze on the small Asian woman.

"Because her brother did. And he didn't trust you. You sneaked in without telling anyone you were coming here. Griffen McCandles doesn't know you've made contact with his sister. He would lose his lunch if he knew you were fronting for the Eastern dragons. A double bonus. Nice prize for them, a baby like that, and one in the eye for Melinda?"

Baffled, Val looked from one to the other. Her heart

pounded in her chest, almost choking her with fear and anger.

"What does he mean, Mai?"

The small female tossed her head.

"You don't know what you're talking about!"

"Don't I?" He let go of Val, who retreated several feet from him. "Ms. McCandles, we have to go. That thing kills dragons. It likes killing."

Val heard Henry's voice in the distance. A flash of gray-white appeared between the trees, angling this way and that.

"I . . . I don't know what to do."

George made the decision for her.

"Go with her, then," George said. He plunged a hand into his pocket and came up with a set of keys. "Go out the front and take my car. It's closer. Don't stop even if they close the gates. The car should be able to knock through." He held out a hand to Mai. "Give me the keys to yours!"

Mai gawked.

"Are you crazy?"

"Go! My car has a full tank of gas. You should make Charlotte, no problem. Hurry!"

Mai looked grudging, but she handed George a key with a paper tag.

Val hugged Marcella. "Thanks for everything. If Melinda throws you out, come and stay with me. You'll love New Orleans."

"Now, Amazon!"

Mai grabbed Val's hand, and they set off running.

Forty-six

George watched them disappear into the long corridor, then turned to the slim, dark-haired woman in the neat shirtdress.

"Do I need to get you out of here, too?" he asked. "My usual job is rescuing humans from dragons, not the other way around."

She shook her head and gave him a rueful smile.

"Mrs. Wurmley is too lazy to replace a good servant herself. She'd probably tell me to engage my own replacement. I'll have plenty of notice to leave the house before I experience an unfortunate 'accident.'"

George felt in his inside breast pocket for his card case. "Take my card. If you ever need help, you've got a freebie coming."

Marcella tucked the pasteboard into her sleeve.

"Thanks. I hope I'll never need it."

"I hope so, too. Better give the hounds something to chase," he said. Drawing a deep breath, he plunged out into the garden.

The demon-beast was bellowing like thirty couple of hounds questing, to coin a phrase. Even at that distance, George could smell its dry, mildewy, dried-blood odor over the thick, fresh scents of plant and soil. He made as much noise as he could, kicking through rose trellises and knocking over garden statuary.

The distant noises all ceased, then came on again in full,

growing louder. George ran in place for a moment. The dogs came into view, about twenty yards away, followed by Henry and his pet monster. George flattened his back against an enormous tree, and made a show of fear and dismay. The secretary, wearing a panama hat and a flawless linen blazer, gloated at the sight.

"Well, what have we here?" he asked.

"Run, Val!" George shouted toward the kitchen door. He knew they were a long way off in the opposite direction, but Henry didn't.

The hairless skull of the demon rose, revealing those insane eyes. It bared its pointed teeth and laughed.

George let the entire party get a good look at him, then took to his heels. Exit point two was ready for an emergency egress. He intended to make use of it but not before the women had a chance to get to the car.

He dashed into the woods, feeling the Gollum-creature getting closer and closer. The creature knew the terrain better than he did, but he had the advantage of being able to lengthen his legs to stay ahead.

Ducking behind a broad elm trunk, George sprayed his last five feet of tracks with the can from his side pocket. A pale blue cloud spurted out of the nozzle. George recoiled, coughing. P.U! Whatever Debbie had sent him smelled disgusting! But it had better work. Knowing he was covered for a moment, he changed direction. His internal time sense said he needed to lay one more false trail to give Ms. McCandles enough time to get on the road.

"Yeeee-ipe!"

The bellow behind him told George that the demon had just run into the first cloud of spray. He angled left, grabbed a low branch, and swung himself upward. His chest broadened and grew more muscle so he could brachiate into the next tree.

The barking dogs spread out through the heavy undergrowth, searching for his scent. He leaped from branch to branch until he was within sight of the open expanse of gravel near the rear gate. Deliberately, he kicked at the bushes as he dropped to the ground, making as much noise as possible. Escape point two was within five yards of the exit. He bounded toward the gate, running over a car to make certain he was heard.

The Gollum-creature came hurtling toward him. Suddenly, it stopped, sniffed, and let out a bellow that chilled George's blood. The hounds tumbled to a halt around it, baying in confusion. The demon leaped over their backs, leaving claw marks in its wake, and headed toward the kitchen door.

"No!"

The demon hadn't been fooled. It sought Val's scent, and it knew that she had not come outside. Henry opened the door for it and followed it inside.

George dashed down the slope past the swimming pool. If the girls had not gone out the front by now, they were doomed. His legs, now almost eight feet long and with three knee joints apiece, covered the ground in a few seconds.

A roar split the air. George was just in time to see a rooster tail of gravel as the big sedan did a quarter donut through the open wrought-iron gates and sped off to the left. He couldn't tell through the dust which of the two females was at the wheel, but she sure could drive.

Almost at the same moment, the front door slammed open. The demon galloped out on all fours. Henry hauled back on its leash, but it towed him like a Newfoundland taking its owner for a morning drag. The hounds boiled out behind it, howling. In their wake came the grounds staff and Melinda.

"She's gone!" Melinda wailed.

"We'll get her back," Henry said, his pleasant face set in a grimace. He let go of the leash. The demon never looked back. It galloped out the gate and turned to follow the green sedan. "Get the car," he ordered.

Two of the groundskeepers dashed away. The rest rounded up the dogs and hauled them around the opposite side of the house.

George was horrified. The humans had been fooled, but the demon hadn't. It was going after the dragons. He had to catch up with them and warn them. He loped back toward escape point two and plunged out onto the road.

As promised, he spotted the white compact a few hundred yards away. George retracted the extra length of limb until the hems of his trousers touched his shoes. He couldn't afford to be stopped now.

He floored the accelerator. No answering rumble came from the Prius's engine. To his dismay, the small car pottered forward at a gentle pace. No amount of stomping on the gas made it accelerate any faster. In a hundred yards, it had sped up past sixty. Forcing himself to be calm, he drove after the demon.

The thick forests surrounding the twisting, hilly roads made it almost impossible to see anything but the few hundred feet ahead or behind the car. On a tight turn after a high climb, he found himself looking down at hairpins in the road. He spotted the green Dodge far below, sandwiched between a blue compact and a white pickup. At least it was making speed. Most of the road was concealed by overhanging branches. He peered around, trying to spot the pale-skinned demon.

Birds flew up from a spot two turns below him. By the snarling, he guessed that the demon had left the road and was cutting overland. George floored the Prius, growling in frustration at the lack of pickup. The hybrid might be the way forward for the American automobile industry, but it was an albatross around the neck for hunters of pale-skinned all-terrain demons.

George fished out his cell phone. No signal. Dammit! The mountains might have been beautiful to drive through, but in an emergency, travelers were on their own.

He left the phone keyboard side up on the tiny dash. As soon as he had a signal, he had to phone Debbie. Mai had a cell phone. The number had to be on file in the office. They had to know what was chasing them. He hoped he could catch up with them before it did.

Forty-seven

Ms. Opal, as she insisted Griffen call her, a stout, elderly African-American woman with a taste for fancy eyeglass frames and chintz dresses, had very short legs and a wide behind. Nevertheless, she stumped along before Griffen and Gris-gris, making them run to keep up. They took the stairs from the ground floor up one flight to the mezzanine level.

"The Fairmont Hotel is very proud that y'all chose us for your nine-ball event. Y'all gonna love what we have set up for y'all," she said. Her voice, a deep contralto, boomed off the paneled walls. She had a clipboard with well-thumbed pages in one arm. "Everything is ready for day after tomorra. You can review the menu before I send it to typesetting. How many copies will you need?"

Griffen pulled the notebook from his hip pocket and flipped through it to the notes he had made.

"Five hundred should do it. That will handle the entrants plus the press."

"Y'all better make it a thousand, at a minimum," Ms. Opal said. "Got to have some to stack on the check-in desk. Get a few curious folks coming in, might collect some extra donations." She came to a halt at a set of paneled double doors with bronze handles set in Beaux Artes plaques. "Come and take a look."

She unlocked the doors and swung them open. Griffen peered into the room over Ms. Opal's head.

The golden-hued lights of the ballroom shone down on

three rows of pool tables. Scoreboards on easels stood beside each one. At either side of the play area, six portable bars had been set up amid rows of chairs. The far end of the room was set up for the media. Sound and light boards stood ready for their technicians. Four-foot-tall speakers were placed at the corners of the room plus the midpoints of each wall. Near the doors where they had just entered were the judging tables plus game registration. All of these had printed and laminated tent cards lying on their bare surfaces.

"We don't put out tablecloths, barware, or paper goods until the last minute," Ms. Opal said. "Those things have a tendency to walk away, I just don't know how." She favored Gris-gris with a knowing look.

"No, ma'am," Gris-gris said, with more respect than Griffen had heard him use with anyone else. His thin face was earnest and open. "Couldn't say myself."

"So, was Gris-gris one of your more challenging students?" Griffen asked, keeping his face straight.

"You might say that," Ms. Opal said with a quelling stare at him. Griffen shrank back. The "teacher look" worked on him, no matter how many years out of school he was. "He was one of the smartest boys I ever had in my class. Mathematics comes as natural to him as breathing. Gettin' him to turn in his homework was the difficulty. I don't know why—it was always one hundred percent correct when I did get to see it. Now, have you finalized the number of players?"

"Eighty-two have pre-registered," Griffen said. "I'm leaving fourteen slots open for walk-ins. I have a single-elimination chart set up." He would have liked to run a double-elimination tournament, but he doubted that the public would have the patience, especially if they had a hundred players.

"Good. I have arranged for an easel here beside the judges for that purpose," Ms. Opal said with a nod toward the empty stand. "If you'd like to go down your checklist with me, I'll make sure we haven't missed anything we discussed."

Griffen nodded and turned to the middle of his note-book.

Gris-gris made a circuit of the room. "Can't see nothin' that I would add," he said.

"Are you two playing?" Ms. Opal inquired.

"Yes, ma'am!" Gris-gris said. "Been sharpening my cue for the purpose."

"Yes," Griffen said. "That was one of Ms. Dunbar's requests."

"I like that girl," Ms. Opal said. She gave a decisive nod. "Her programs for young people are turning shoplifters into customers. I think she'd make a fine governor. Not that I am political by nature."

"Neither am I," Griffen said. "Thanks, Ms. Opal. This all looks great."

"My pleasure, young man," the former teacher said, her eyes glinting behind her diamante glasses. "You had many good suggestions for this event. Are you certain you wouldn't like to take your talents into a full-time profession? Intelligent party planners are scant on the ground."

"No way!" Griffen said, hastily. "Ma'am."

Ms. Opal smiled. "If you change your mind, Mr. Griffen, come on back. I'd like to claim first call on your services."

"If that ever happens, ma'am, you have my word."

Once they had escorted Ms. Opal back to her office, Griffen and Gris-gris stopped in the hotel's coffee shop for afternoon refreshments. The waitress brought them Diet Cokes and slices of chocolate pecan pie.

"She's formidable," Griffen said, going over his notes. "I would never have forgotten to turn in my homework."

Gris-gris's dark eyes flashed. "You know I ain't afraid of no one, Grifter. Ms. Opal's the exception that proves the rule. Truth be told, I was afraid she'd find something wrong on my work."

"But she never did. Sounds like she knew you better than you knew yourself."

"I was only a kid then! Hope to God someone knew me better than I did!"

Griffen's pocket buzzed, followed by ringing. With an apologetic look at the patrons in the coffee shop who glanced up in annoyance, he fished out his phone.

Before he could get out a hello, Holly Goldberg's voice interrupted him. She sounded frightened.

"Griffen! Have you heard anything from Val?"

"No, I haven't," Griffen said. The spark of fire in his belly ricocheted off his internal organs. "What's happened? Is she . . . ?" He couldn't say the word.

"She is alive," Holly assured him, "but she is in mortal danger. The word broke through while I was reading someone else's palm in Jackson Square. The gods know what he thought when I started babbling about monsters and aliens."

"Is that about Val?" Gris-gris asked. Griffen nodded. "Where is she?"

"Monsters? Aliens?" Griffen asked. "What does that mean?"

"I have no idea," Holly said, apologetically. "I just know what I saw."

"Monsters? Chasin' my lady?"

Griffen waved a hand to quiet him, but Gris-gris didn't pay any attention. He snatched the phone out of Griffen's hand.

"Who's this?" he asked. "Uh-huh. This is Gris-gris. You doing okay, Ms. Holly? Me, too. What about Ms. Val? Say that again? Bald and white-skinned? Anything else? I KNOW it ain't like a telephone! I got to know what you saw! I been worryin' about Ms. Val for months! Well, of course she is. Yeah. Thank you, Ms. Holly. God bless you. Uh-huh, yeah, and your goddess, too."

He clicked off the phone and handed it to Griffen.

"She's comin' home, Ms. Holly don't know from where, but there's somethin' chasin' her. Ain't no . . . what you are.

Skinny, pale, and dangerous, like one of the Little Gray People. That's all we got to go on."

"Not all." Griffen frowned. He clicked on the small cell phone's directory listing and poked the number. He gripped the table's edge with his hand while counting the rings. After the fourth buzz, a pleasant female voice answered.

"May I help you?"

"This is Griffen McCandles. I have to talk to George, right away!"

"This is Debbie, Mr. McCandles. What's the problem?"

"The problem is . . ." Gris-gris waved a hand in his face. Griffen realized his voice was rising to a shout. By their peeved expressions, the other patrons were growing restless at his repeated interruptions. He brought it down to a stage whisper. "The problem is that my sister is in danger!"

"Has she contacted you?"

"No! I . . ." Griffen felt foolish saying it, but he got the words out anyhow. "A witch told me that there's some kind of monster after her."

"I see," Debbie said. He could hear keys clattering. "A reliable witch?"

"I would say so, yes."

"All right. Thanks for the heads-up. Let me try him right now, and I'll get back to you."

Griffen listened to the click in his ear and put the phone down. He and Gris-gris stared at one another.

"That your private detective?" Gris-gris asked. He could hardly sit still.

"Yes," Griffen said. "I wonder what went wrong?"

"What can we do? I got to save Val!"

"I don't know!" Griffen said.

"Well, I ain't no good at just waitin' around!"

"We have to," Griffen said. "We don't know where to go."

The phone between them rang. Both of them snatched for it, but Gris-gris was faster.

"Hello? This is Gris-gris. What? No, tell me! Oh, all right." He handed the device to Griffen.

"Hello?"

"I'm sorry, Mr. McCandles. Our confidentiality rules are strict. We only give information to the client."

"That's all right. What did George say?"

Debbie sounded frustrated.

"I can't reach him. The message says that he is out of cell-phone range at the moment. I have left a message to have him notify you as soon as he can."

What more could he say? Griffen thanked her and hung up.

"What do we do?" Gris-gris asked. "No way I can raise enough people to watch all the roads until she get here. We'll just have to drop out of the tournament."

"I can't!" Griffen said, torn. "I promised my uncle. He's got a lot riding on Penny."

"You have any other way to find Val?"

"No," Griffen said. "We'll just have to defend her when she reaches us."

Gris-gris nodded and patted the inside pocket of his light jacket.

"Yeah. That monster better be ready to run. I'll be loaded for grizzly bear."

Griffen didn't reply. He worried that guns and a protective brother dragon might not be enough.

George hugged a tight curve coming down the steep country road. Once he got it up to speed, the Prius did pretty well. Mai must have gassed it up right before she went to get Val. The needle had hardly left the F side of the gas gauge.

Ahead, he spotted a green route marker. He let out a huge sigh of relief. He had studied the area map and a topographical chart, so he knew that a left would take him to the city and the airport. Mai might want to fly back to New Orleans, but Val had no identification with her. After 9/11, she couldn't get past security, especially not with tickets bought on the spot. They would have to drive.

He waited for a semi to pass, then swung into the lane behind it. The screen of his mobile phone lit up. He noticed the name of a local carrier and four blessed bars of signal. He grabbed it and hit the autodial.

When Debbie answered, he blurted out a report of what had just happened.

"I lost sight of the demon about fifteen miles back, but there just aren't too many through routes out of here. Mai had a cell phone. Call her, Debbie. Keep calling her until she answers. Warn her about the thing. Give them all the data we have. Warn them!"

"Where are you going?"

"Toward the city. They're going to want to get on the interstate ASAP. We know they'll be heading toward New Orleans. Get me some backup!"

"I'll send every available demon hunter to the area," Debbie said. "Griffen McCandles wants to talk to you. He got a warning from a local witch. She saw the demon in a vision."

"Oh, great. Now we're getting news flashes from the great beyond. Did she say how to defeat it?"

"No."

"Dammit. That's why I hate séances. They're always unspecific about details. I'll do what I can to catch up."

George hung up. The words "I told you so" hung in the air, even if Debbie had left them unsaid.

Forty-eight

Mai hugged the wheel of the enormous car. She was unchar-acteristically silent. The argument they had had almost all the way through the mountains was the first serious fight they had ever had.

Val glowered out at the gray asphalt of the highway. She couldn't decide if she was more angry than frightened, or more confused than either. She had been dragged out of the house where she had lived for months, with nothing but the clothes on her back and some food. They had left behind her wallet, her cell phone, all the baby clothes, and that wonderful crib, but they had also ditched Melinda and Henry. She didn't know whether George was a monster or not. He said he was from Griffen. He had given them the car. Her mind spun in circles, but all of it pivoted on one single point.

She couldn't help herself.

"Why did he say that you probably were after my baby for your family?" she burst out.

"I told you, Val," Mai said, tight-lipped, staring at the road, "that is a lie. I came only to rescue you from Melinda's clutches. You are my friend. I would never harm you or your child in any way. The George seeks to put a wedge between us, to get you for himself. It seems as if he is succeeding."

"What about his saying he came from Griffen?"

Mai felt beside her for her purse and fished out her cell phone. "Call Griffen yourself and ask. We are more than far enough away to be out of Melinda's dampening spells and hacked technology."

Val seized the small phone and dialed Griffen's number. A series of tones came out of the speaker.

"Dammit! No signal," she said. She peered through the back window. Any minute, she expected to see Melinda drive up in a tank, or something, and carry her back to the estate. This time Val doubted she would be housed in a luxury room. They would probably lock her in a dungeon right next door to Lizzy. She couldn't decide whether to be more furious at Melinda and Henry, or at herself for being tricked into complacency over and over again. She had lost months! She should have stuck to her distrust of Melinda. Though the elder dragon had been a good ally during Mardi Gras, Val knew she had an agenda. To know she had walked into it like a mouse into a trap left her feeling disgusted with herself. She clapped the phone down on the seat between them.

"Damn!" Mai said. "This countryside is absurd! Val, how long have we known one another?"

Val pulled her attention away from the rear window and plumped her back against the seat.

"Well, really since I came to New Orleans. You and Griffen were at college. I didn't visit him much, so I hardly ever saw you."

"Right. But since then?"

"Well, I honestly thought we were getting to be friends."

"We ARE friends," Mai snapped. "Curse it! I knew it would be trouble if I let my guard down."

Her vehemence puzzled Val.

"Why?" she asked.

"Because dragon females scarcely ever make friends. We are protective and territorial and very competitive. I had never really had a friend before. You and Griffen are a very different kind of dragon. It has been hard for me, but I have been trying. Having you doubt me makes me wonder whether I am wasting my time!"

Val glanced over and saw the trails of tears glistening on

Mai's cheeks. She found a fast-food napkin between the seats and reached over to dab Mai's face. At first, Mai swatted her hand away, then let her dry the tears.

"I'm sorry," Val said. Her heart went out to the other woman. "You're not wasting your time. I love you, and I'm glad to have you as my friend. It's just that living with Melinda for months has made me paranoid."

"It's good to be paranoid," Mai said.

"I am," Val said.

"Good."

"Thank you."

"Don't mention it."

"I mean it."

"I *said*, don't mention it!"

"Okay. Um, I see a gas station up ahead. Would you mind pulling over?"

"*Again?*"

"I can't help it!" Val said. The capacity of her bladder had shrunk with the increasing size of her pregnancy, but she had been able to cope with it while she was living in one place. Riding in a car jostled her baby up and down on the beleaguered organ. "Please?"

"Of course," Mai said with a sigh. "That only makes the ninth stop since we left Melinda's. Never mind. I will top up the tank. This car is not nearly as economical as the Prius."

Val climbed out of the passenger seat and squeezed life back into her muscles as she walked toward the gas station's office. Her tailbone felt numb. How lucky it was that Mai and George had had to swap cars. She couldn't imagine making the trip in her condition in a compact, no matter how roomy inside Mai said it was. She stretched her back while waiting for the gas-station attendant to unhook the ladies'-room key from the wall behind the cash register.

As she walked around the small building, Val marveled at the landscape in that part of the country. She was so intent at staring at the mountains around them that she tripped on a pebble. She kept her balance, but the stone skittered away from her foot. It came to rest in a tuft of grass, but the scratchy sounds kept on.

Rattlesnake?

Val scanned the grass for movement. She was too ungainly to leap as she might have before. Besides deploring how it had come about, her temporary but increasing clumsiness was one of the only things she really disliked about being pregnant. She took careful steps, scanning all around her. Griffen had said her skin couldn't be penetrated, but she didn't want to trust his assurance out there in the middle of nowhere.

After her visit to a blessedly clean though dimly lit restroom, Val emerged into the sun and tiptoed back toward the car. The scratchy noises were growing louder. The rest stop was so quiet she could hear the radio playing inside the office. Could those noises be the tires of a distant truck?

Melinda had to be behind them somewhere. Val knew the senior dragon wouldn't let her go so easily, not after she had gone to so much trouble to trick her into leaving Louisiana, then letting Henry put the mellow on her so she wouldn't want to go home.

The big laugh was that if Melinda had been straight with her, she might have enjoyed her experience and wanted to stay longer. Knowing it was temporary would have let her appreciate the luxurious surroundings all the more. It would have been awesome to have her friends visit her in that mansion. The food was fabulous. She had been a little lonely, but there had been Marcella . . . and Mike.

Val felt torn. She had never dated what they called a "suave, sophisticated man" before. He wasn't anything like the well-dressed, high-tipping, visiting businessmen or conventioneers who piled into her French Quarter bar who tried, often obnoxiously, to get a piece of ass to go with their drink. Of course, she reminded herself, Mike wasn't like them—he was a dragon. Like her. If Melinda had done anything for her, it had been to widen her horizons and made her think about her future. Gris-gris was fun to be with, generous, passionate, willing to let her be who she was, but could he handle what she might become? People cringed at the mention of Melinda's name. Would the sound of "Val" one day elicit that same response?

The car parked beside the pump was empty; Mai must be in the office, paying. Val hoped she would keep track of the expenditures. She fully intended to repay Mai all the money she had put out to find and rescue her. Val straightened her back, releasing one more kink, and tried to look formidable as she walked back to the car.

Hail to me, Queen Dragon.

Then something grabbed her ankle.

Val tumbled heavily to the ground. She became aware all at once that the scratchy noises had stopped, and so had all the other ambient sounds. A naked man with gray-white skin held on to her left leg with both arms. She kicked at his ear with her right foot. He raised his head to snarl at her. His pupils were slitted.

This was not a human being.

Val screamed.

"Val!"

Mai ran out of the small building, with a rangy, balding man in greasy gray coveralls at her heels. The monster growled a warning. They wheeled to a halt.

"What in hell is that?" the man yelped.

"Hell is correct," Mai said. Leaving him gawking, she sprang at the creature. It let out a hiss and bit at her. She dodged, kicking it in the ribs. Val punched at its arm, trying to free her leg. The pale creature pushed Mai off. She tumbled head over heels over the gravel. She jumped to her feet. The monster started to drag Val toward the bushes. Mai leaped on its back, trying to pull its head back.

"This must be Melinda's guard dog," Mai panted.

"How did it find us?" Val asked. The creature wasn't hurting her, but she couldn't break its grip. She gagged on its moldy aroma.

"Heads up, ladies!" a deep voice cried.

Val dropped flat against the ground just in time to see a shadow swoop down.

CLANG!

The garageman swung a huge red metal canister into the creature's head. It fell limp. Val kicked free and scrambled away from it on all fours. The man helped her to her feet. Mai rose with more dignity. The monster lay unconscious on the ground. Val got her first good look at it. It seemed to be a cross between a human and a lizard, with fine, tiny scales where people had vellus hairs. Its fingers and toes ended in curved claws instead of nails. She shivered.

"What is it?" the garageman asked. "Is that Bigfoot?"

"No," Mai said. "It's a dangerous lunatic."

"I'm gonna call the police," he said, heading for the office. Mai caught his arm.

"Don't," she said. "They won't be able to handle him."

"The cops around here are pretty good, ma'am," he said. "Besides, I knocked it out cold. It ought to be down for a while."

A moan interrupted them. Val and Mai spun to look at the creature. It was coming around. Mai grabbed Val's arm.

"Hurry!"

The two women hurried to the car and jumped in. Mai fumbled with the keys for a moment, then revved the ignition. The engine roared mightily. Mai threw it into gear.

The creature jumped to its feet like a gymnast and ran to intercept them. Mai set her jaw grimly. She planted her foot hard on the accelerator. The car leaped forward. It hit the monster and knocked it twenty feet in the air. Val twisted around to look as Mai peeled onto the access road and headed toward the highway. The pale creature got to its hands and knees just as Val lost sight of it.

"How could I have lived in the house all that time without knowing it was there?" Val asked, horrified in retrospect.

"Damn Melinda and all her ilk!" Mai said. "I have seen that creature in the bestiary my family keeps. It hates dragons! How can she control it?"

"Henry," Val said. "It has to be Henry."

"Then both of them are chasing us, running behind their unspeakable hound," Mai said glumly. "All those switchbacks delayed us enough that it was able to catch up. It will be easy for it to follow us on the highways."

"Should we take smaller roads?" Val asked.

"No. It is following our scent. We would only be slowed down going through all those small towns. We had best continue on the fastest roads we can take, at maximum speed. Can you still drive? If we spell one another, we can continue day and night, stopping only for gas."

"I can drive when you get tired," Val said.

"Good. We should reach New Orleans within two days. We have food, thanks to your friends. I don't know whether to thank or curse George. He has all my camping equipment and supplies in my car, though I cannot deny that this is a more comfortable vehicle for long travel."

Val was grateful for her friend's quiet confidence.

The car thumped along the road. Val stared out the window. Through endless miles of pine trees and hanging vines, she spied a river. Her eyes followed the blue expanse, and she thought of swimming, water-skiing, inner-tubing . . .

"Uh, Mai?" Val asked.

Mai didn't shift her gaze from the road.

"What?"

"About those stops? Could you pull over at the next gas station?"

"Already?" Mai asked, outraged.

"It's not my fault!" Val said, feeling defensive.

"Curse it!" Mai said. "Why did our species ever stop laying eggs?"

"Please?"

"We don't stop again unless we have to," Mai said. "I don't care if you wet the seats. It's only a rental."

Mike rang the bell of the Wurmley residence. He tugged at his collar to make sure it was straight. It had been almost a week since he had last seen Val, and what a memorable night that had been! If an opportunity presented itself, he wanted to be alone with her again. She was a little vigorous, almost violent, in her lovemaking, but that made her all the more exciting to be with. The love bite that she had left on his chest, just above his left nipple, had healed into a circular bruise. It made him laugh ruefully to see it in the mirror.

The door was ajar. Mike pushed it open in time to see Marcella run toward him. Her arms were full of ladies' undergarments. By the size, they couldn't have been her own. Behind her, he heard shouts and other sounds of busyness.

"Oh, Mr. Burns!" Marcella said. "This isn't a good time . . ."

Mike smiled. "I'm here to have dinner with Val. Can you tell her I'm here?"

"You know perfectly well she isn't here! You helped her escape!"

Melinda bore down on him with righteous fury, her secretary in her wake. Mike knew Cousin Melinda had a chancy temper. It was what had made him reluctant to enlist her as a potential patron for his run for the Senate, but he had kept the relationship open because of Val. Now he wondered if he had made a terrible mistake. Female dragons were dangerous.

"I don't know what you're talking about," Mike said, keeping his voice calm. "What do you mean, escape? I thought she was visiting you of her own accord."

Melinda glared at him.

"But it was you! We have the security tapes to prove it! You were here less than an hour ago. You led my security staff on a chase around my gardens to distract them, and Valerie departed in the confusion."

"I just got back from my other house in Maryland," Mike said. "I was home for almost a week."

"Prove it!"

Mike straightened up so he towered over her. "Cousin Melinda, I don't know who you think you are speaking to. I don't need to prove anything to you."

Henry, the secretary, tapped her on the arm.

"A shape-changer, Mrs. Wurmley," he said. "She had an accomplice. Someone who could come and go without challenge."

"How did she make contact with anyone? You have been careless!"

"Not I." Henry raised his nose haughtily. "Perhaps you should ask your lovely housekeeper?"

Melinda turned on Marcella. "Is. This. True?"

"I don't know what's going on here, ma'am," the woman said. She was being very brave, but her voice shook. She knew more than she was saying. Melinda sensed it and brought her face close to the young woman's.

"Tell me!"

"Don't hurt her," Mike said, fiercely. If Val wanted to get away from there, all she had to do was ask him for help. He wondered why she hadn't trusted him.

The answer was simple: Melinda.

"She can't tell us anything more," Henry said, dismissively. "My little pet is on their trail. All we need to do is follow him."

Mike looked from one to the other.

"Pet? What kind of pet? Is that what killed the burglar the other evening? It'll kill Val!"

Henry shot him a triumphant glance.

"No, but it will kill anyone near her. Collateral damage. Regrettable but inevitable."

"I'm going with you," Mike said at once.

Melinda and Henry seemed to share an unspoken conference.

"Why not?" Melinda said. "Perhaps you can talk some sense into her. Dean! Get the car!"

Forty-nine

At 2:19 in the morning, Griffen's cell phone rang. He pulled it out of his pocket without taking his eyes off the cards in his other hand. Pocket rockets, two aces, lay facedown on the table before him. He could not lose. The kitty held at least five thousand dollars. He had cajoled, teased, and trash-talked his fellow players into raising against him. He was about to crash their dreams of avarice. Jerome grinned at him. Griffen had no tells to speak of, but his friend could discern when Griffen was setting other people up to lose.

"Griffen McCandles," he said.

"Griffen?"

"Val?"

He stood up, knocking his chair backward to the floor. The other players exclaimed in alarm. He patted the air with his hand.

"It's okay," he said. "I fold."

"You what?" asked the high roller from Springfield. Griffen gave him an apologetic smile.

"Sorry. I have to take this call. Family emergency. Your two queens can win the hand." He turned away from the table. Behind him, the other players threw in their cards with mixed groans and laughs.

"Is he a mind reader, or what?" one of them asked, as the whale hauled the chips toward him. Griffen didn't care.

"Val, are you all right? Where are you? This isn't your number. Whose phone is this? Where the hell have you been?"

The connection was poor. Griffen strained to hear over the crackling. He moved around the room, seeking the strongest cell-phone signal.

". . . On the road . . . following . . . ! Coming in . . . east. Damned mountains!"

"Wait a minute, I can hardly hear you!" Griffen said. By then, Jerome had left the table and was standing at his elbow. He mouthed the question.

Val?

Griffen nodded enthusiastically. She was alive. Relief, anxiety, and anger battled it out for dominance in his belly. He shouted to be heard over the static.

"Listen, Val, I have a warning for you. Holly said to look out for a bald . . ." He glanced back over his shoulder at the other players, who were listening avidly to his side of the conversation. "A bald, white guy. He's following you. It sounds like trouble. Bad trouble."

"I know!" Val's voice trumpeted suddenly from the speaker. "That's what I've been trying to tell you for the last five minutes!

"Where are you?"

"What?"

"Where are you?"

"I don't know! Somewhere in North Carolina!"

"North Carolina? Where are you coming from?"

"Melinda's house." She kept her answers short and repeated them until Griffen shouted an acknowledgment.

"Let me talk to George."

"He's not here." She sounded puzzled.

"Where is he?"

A roar interrupted Val's reply. Griffen heard a shriek, then the connection cut off.

"Val? Val?" He stared at the inert handset for a moment.

Val didn't call back. He tapped the RECEIVED CALLS folder. The number from which Val had called was Mai's.

What was going on?

Griffen thumbed the green button to dial the number. No answer.

He looked up at Jerome.

"Can you finish up here?"

Jerome glanced at the table. The dealer had gathered up the cards and was counting chips. The players were chatting among themselves, clearly curious.

"Looks like we're all done, Grifter. Hey, everyone, no need to rush off."

"No problem," said the whale from Springfield. "We can see you've got a problem."

"Sorry about that," Griffen said.

The player pointed a playful finger at him. "Just don't cop out on the tournament. I'm looking forward to taking that first prize. Five grand would be a nice going-home present."

"You can try." Griffen tried to look playfully predatory, but too many thoughts were playing bumper cars in his mind. "You'll have to go through me, first."

"It'll be my pleasure to leave you in the dust." He shook hands with Griffen and the other players. The room cleared out in moments.

"I have to find her," Griffen said as soon as the door closed. "She's in danger. George isn't with her, and it looks like Mai is. Where did she come into this?"

"No idea," Jerome said. "How do you plan to find them?"

Griffen thought hard for a moment. "Harrison. Maybe he can trace the call."

Jerome looked at his watch. "It's after three."

"If he's on duty, he'll still be up."

The burly Vice cop looked as weathered as his leather jacket. He chugged down half of the first cup of coffee, though it had to be boiling hot, and set the pottery mug down on the diner counter. The eyes he fixed on Griffen were bloodshot.

"This had better be important, McCandles. I was about to sign off. It's been a hell of a night."

Griffen explained about the call from Val. He held out his cell phone to Harrison. "So, could you trace where it was coming from? I have to find her before that thing gets her."

Harrison gave him a weary glare. "Is this the trouble you didn't want to tell me about?" he asked. "Your kind of trouble, not mine?"

"No," Griffen said. "This is something more."

"Do you have a court order? An FBI notification?"

"No."

"Are the people involved suspected of any felonies?"

"No, of course not."

"Are you still on the line with her?"

"No." Griffen frowned. "You can see that. She screamed, and the phone went dead. I've been trying to reach her ever since."

"Then how the hell do you think I can call out the NOPD to put a trace on a nonexistent call? We don't get to use that technology unless we have legal permission. You watch too many movies, McCandles. We don't have the magic grid sweepers Hollywood gives the TV cops. We can't guess when the perps are going to commit crimes, but we have to catch them doing it. Jesus, sometimes I think we score arrests as much on dumb luck as on slogging police work."

Griffen stood up. "Then I had better get out there. I'll drive until I meet her coming the other way."

Harrison raised his eyebrows.

"Are you kidding? What highway are they coming west on?"

"I don't know."

"Do you know how many roads there are between here and North Carolina?"

"No."

"Five good ones, plus dozens of dirt tracks, side streets, and dead ends."

Griffen felt hopeless. He had a mental picture of Val at the mercy of some kind of maniac with long teeth and a battle-ax. He plumped down on the cushioned stool. It exhaled a gust of stale air.

"Then what can I do?"

"Delegate," Malcolm said.

Griffen jumped. He turned to see his uncle, sleepy and peevish, wearing an open-necked polo shirt and khaki trousers. He had his arm through Holly's, escorting her as if she were a princess. Gris-gris, in his lightweight jacket, danced impatiently beside them.

"I called them, Grifter," Jerome said, in answer to Griffen's unasked question. "You can't do anything alone."

"You cannot do anything about Valerie, period," Malcolm said, fixing Griffen with an austere look. "We are nine hours before an incredibly important event, at which you will occupy a position of prominence and responsibility. Ms. Dunbar still requires your guidance, and your protection."

"Uncle Malcolm, Val is my sister," Griffen said.

"If I infer from what I just overheard, you do not know her whereabouts. There is nothing you can do, apart from being ready to respond when and if she comes within range of your aid."

"I know, but . . ."

"You heard from Val?" Gris-gris interrupted. "Why didn't you call me?"

Griffen felt contrite. "I should have, Gris-gris. I *don't* know where she is, just that she's on her way here."

"She's all right so far," Holly said. She took a faceted crystal the size of Griffen's fist from her shoulder bag and held it out to him. He peered at it but wasn't surprised that all he could see through it was fragmented views of her hand.

"Thank goodness for that."

"How do we get her home?" Gris-gris asked.

Holly looked grave. "I have no knowledge of that,

Gris-gris. We just have to do the best we can and hope she can outrun her pursuers."

"Pursuers, plural?" Gris-gris looked as if he would explode with impatience. "Or you just seein' mirror images in that crystal?"

"Don't be like that, man," Jerome said. "She's giving us the best she has."

"I know that, but I want my lady back!"

"Come, then," Malcolm said with a weary sigh. "Let us lay the facts on the table and try to make a plan that will cover all possible contingencies." He glanced at Harrison. "Detective, I appreciate your assistance. I am sorry my nephew interrupted your night."

It was a clear dismissal. Harrison took a breath all the way down to his potbelly, but he matched Malcolm's baleful mien with easy authority.

"Thanks, Mr. McCandles, but I'm okay. I need to know everything that's going down. Maybe I can help."

Malcolm studied him, then nodded.

"Very well. I appreciate your time." He surveyed the diner. The glaring fluorescent light spilled down on an array of melamine, chrome, and vinyl padding, and a few late-night customers. "Let us take that table in the corner. It is more private."

Griffen signaled to the waitress. They were going to need a lot of coffee.

Mike kept the speedometer needle at a steady sixty-five. Melinda had wanted to go faster, but he had refused.

"I still want to run for office next year," he said. "It would look bad if I had multiple interstate violations on my record. That is, if I still have your support."

"We'll see," she said. She sat back in the rear seat and refused to speak to him again. Mike was left alone with his thoughts.

He had taken over the wheel after both bodyguards had

driven for four-hour stretches apiece. They both insisted they could go on, but Melinda didn't want them to make stupid mistakes. They needed to be alert once they found Valerie again.

At the moment, all of them were asleep. Mike wished he could doze off, but he was almost afraid to. He was alone with his thoughts, which were so conflicted he thought he was seeing things. Not long after Charlotte, they had passed a white Prius on the road. Mike had to do a double take. The man behind the wheel looked exactly like him.

No, that had had to be an illusion. Mike shook himself again. He was playing in a game out of his league. Melinda might be his cousin, but she was certainly not his ally.

Until that afternoon, he had never really considered how dangerous Melinda was. She had led him to believe—no, she let him believe—that he had impressed her and was worthy of her backing for his Senate run. She had even allowed him to think that he might have found a suitable mate in Valerie McCandles. She gave him permission to woo Val and made the girl available anytime he was in the state. He and Val were compatible in so many ways, but Mike was wondering how much of that was genuine and how much influenced by Henry and his machinations.

As a dragon, he dismissed magicians and humans in general as an inferior race. It seemed that he had underestimated at least this one. To render Val as complacent as she had been was an amazing feat. He had known from watching his parents that he would not rule the roost when he mated. No male dragon ever really controlled a female. All he could do was convince her to allow him to form a household with her and help protect any offspring they might have. Val had made it seem like such a relationship would be easy.

He hoped she was all right.

An exit for Louisville loomed out of the darkness. If he took a wrong turn, he could delay Melinda's pursuit until Val was safely back home. He glanced at his mirror. Yes, all four of them, including the two bodyguards, were asleep. He eased the car slowly toward the turn.

He felt a sharp prod in his neck. A wave of flowery gentleman's cologne wafted around and tweaked his nose.

"Don't even consider it," Henry said, a menacing whisper in his ear. "Treachery will be met with death."

Mike glared at the windshield. "Do you always talk like a cheap movie?"

"Only when I am dealing with cheap politicians," the warlock said. "Drive to New Orleans. Perhaps you'll get to live."

Fifty

Griffen took a deep breath to compose himself. Though every red blood cell in his body wanted him to look hard, he did his best to ignore the curvaceous black woman sliding the zipper of her skintight red dress down between her breasts. She leaned forward. Her ripe breasts surged, so close to popping out. Griffen squeezed his eyes closed. *She's not there. She's not there.* He slid the pool cue forward. With a gentle CLACK, the cue ball rolled eighteen inches over the smooth green felt and tapped the nine ball. He found himself holding his breath. Almost in slow motion, the nine edged toward the far-side pocket. It began to slow down even further. Griffen exhaled, willing the ball to fall. Two inches. One inch. Then it vanished into the dark pocket as if a conjurer had made it disappear.

The crowd around him burst into polite applause.

"Well, damn you to hell, Griffen McCandles," Penny said. She leaned on her cue with an insouciant smirk. She was framed fetchingly against the haze of smoke filling the ballroom of the Fairmont Hotel. "That's four racks!"

"Going for five," Griffen said. Jerome stood up and handed him the glass of Diet Coke that he had been carefully guarding. With cash prizes on the line, a number of local Louisiana pool clubs had signed up teams, hoping to bring home some of the loot. That meant dirty tricks were not only possible but expected. Adulterating drinks was the least obtrusive distraction. A player might find his innocent beverage spiked with a healthy dollop of Everclear or flavored with something less palatable. Maestro, third on their roster, raised his own glass to him.

"You good," said the elderly dark-skinned man in sunglasses and a porkpie hat, the fourth player at Griffen's table. His paste-on badge identified him as ELMER. Griffen smiled.

"You don't make it easy."

"Not supposed to, my friend. Not supposed to." Elmer smiled back, showing crooked, yellow teeth. "All's fair in love and war, and this is war. In a genteel sort of way, y'understand."

"Yes, I do," Griffen said. Penny racked the balls. Griffen sighted the one ball, leaned forward, and shot. The cue ball bounded off two cushions and hit the diamond of pool balls, nipping the one from the rear of the pack. The onlookers let out a pleased exclamation as it skittered into the side pocket. The white ball came to a rest at the bumper an inch from falling in.

Anything that broke concentration was fair game. Not even the presence of television cameras, of which there were many, deterred experienced contenders from bringing their A game. One well-known pro, now playing somewhere across the room, had brought along his three "girlfriends." These well-endowed women, dressed in skintight dresses, flashed a hint of breast or bottom when the other men at his table were lining up tricky shots. The first time he had spotted a striptease in progress, Griffen had marched over to put an end to it, but Gris-gris, Jerome, and even Penny assured him that such subterfuges were normal.

"Sorry. I don't mean to be so snappish. I'm just worried about Val."

"Enjoy it," Jerome said. "You'd pay fifty dollars to see some of these ladies shake it in the clubs on Bourbon Street. I think I recognize the one in the blue bra."

The woman in question, a lushly figured African-American with hair dyed bright gold, threw Jerome a kiss. After that, Griffen had let the visual displays go ahead. The crowds loved them. The happier the onlookers were, the more likely they were to drop donations in the collection boxes arranged near every table. The cash prizes, represented by wads of fake hundred-dollar bills, lay on silver platters under glass domes beside the registration table. That had inspired other entrants as well as donors.

The event had been going smoothly. Griffen could almost forget his personal concerns in satisfaction for the way the elements had fallen together. He kept checking his cell phone for calls from Val or Gris-gris.

He had no way of knowing where Val and Mai were. At 5:40 in the morning, they had called one more time to say they had crossed the line into Alabama. Mai's phone battery was nearly empty. They had no charger and were too afraid to stop and buy one. Both of them were unharmed. Neither of them had seen the bald demon since their last fill-up. Griffen had just enough time to give her the hotel address before the connection had gone dead for good. Malcolm felt there would be greater safety in numbers, and in a building with several entrances and exits. The apartment complex might prove a trap for Val as well as her pursuer. They couldn't risk that.

George had called in. He was in a similar fix with regard to his cell phone. It seemed that he and Mai had switched cars. He refused to give Griffen any details as to how that had come about. George didn't know if he was ahead of or behind Val, though he suspected he was trailing her. He informed Griffen that four demon hunters were on-site in New Orleans and would help Griffen catch the dragon killer when it turned up. He told Griffen its name, but Griffen couldn't make sense of eight syllables of nonsense that weren't English or any other language he had ever heard.

Malcolm had not been pleased to hear that a demon capture might occur during the high-profile event. He stalked the hall like a private detective looking for evidence, as he tried to identify the demon hunters among the throng of players and onlookers. He was even more of a distraction than the girls, coming almost within elbow's reach of the tables to survey the action. After a few complaints, Ms. Opal had set a young porter to walk beside Mr. McCandles and keep him back out of the players' sight lines.

The elder McCandles had to be satisfied with the take the event had made so far. In addition to the players who had signed up in advance, a few dozen others had shown up just before noon to play. Griffen's chart was not only full but overflowing. He had had to calculate a rotation for additional newcomers. Malcolm checked the ledger from time to time and collected excess cash from Jerome and the campaign volunteers at the tables. Griffen had done the math in his head. The seed money from this tournament would kick-start Penny's campaign again. She could go the distance. To his own surprise, he felt excitement at the prospect.

Horsie seemed to be everywhere at once. She brought local luminaries over to shake hands with Penny. Griffen caught glimpses of her on the sidelines giving interviews to the press. He even saw her chatting with the dour producer from his visit to the local morning talk show. The glare from television cameras strobed over the tables like searchlights as the camera operators sought interesting angles. Horsie was thrilled with the way the event was running. On those rare times that Griffen caught her eye, she beamed at him and gave him a happy thumbs-up. Griffen and Malcolm had not told her or Penny of Val's imminent arrival. It might turn out to be a nonevent. In the meantime, they saw no point in adding to her concerns. To Winston, on the other hand, they had given a full briefing. The security agent accepted the confidence with a stony face and a curt nod. Since then, he had remained close to Penny, present but unobtrusive. Griffen had to admire him even if he didn't much like him. He had also approved hiring three off-duty Vice cops, Harrison among them, as extra protection.

Penny was on her brightest public behavior. She greeted everyone with a warm handshake and smile, and posed for dozens of pictures. She saved her normal vitriol for her volunteers and Griffen when she couldn't be overheard by reporters. He had made a point to avoid her, until they had ended up at the same table in round five.

Griffen had handicapped her in the middle of the pack so she would play against more than just visiting professionals. She dazzled the less-skilled players with her skill as well as her banter. She, Fox Lisa, and another redheaded volunteer from the campaign office had on tight, bright, aquamarine T-shirts printed with LUCKY PENNIES. They went well with other team shirts, such as the black-clad Agents of Chaos, the blue-shirted Ball Hogs, and many others based on puns or in-jokes. The roar of conversation in the hall was cheerful. As players were knocked out of competition, they started scratch games at available tables, half the (official) bets going to Penny's fund. Griffen had spotted a few of the local oddsmakers and had shaken them down, gently, to put in a portion of their winnings at the end of the day.

Griffen lined up his next shot, trying to ignore the antics of Maestro, an Agent of Chaos, who kept flicking a cigarette lighter just in the corner of his peripheral vision.

"So, do y'all know what it means to have 'savoir faire'?" Elmer said suddenly, just as Griffen prepared to shoot. Griffen lowered his head. At least it hadn't caught him in midstroke.

"Why, no," Penny chirped, smiling over her shoulder at a photographer from the *Times-Picayune*. "What does it mean?"

"Well, say you have a man in bed with a lady who is not his wife, and the husband comes home unexpectedly. The husband stops at the door of the bedroom. Then he steps back and turns away, pretending he doesn't see a thing. Would you say he has savoir faire?"

"Yes, I would."

The old man leaned back and put his thumb in his belt.

"Well, you'd be wrong. How about if the husband stops at the door of the bedroom, sees what's going on, then says to the man, 'Sorry to interrupt. Keep going.'"

Griffen tried not to chuckle. He took that moment to shoot. The three rebounded off a corner cushion. It slowed, then crept toward the side pocket. If he blew on it, it would drop. Instead, he stood up and leaned on his cue. The ball ambled along the felt, then dropped with a clatter.

"Sounds like savoir faire to me."

The dark glasses turned his way. "Not so fast, my friend. That still ain't it."

Griffen sighted the four ball. It was in a tricky position, next to the eight. If he sank the eight, he'd scratch. He could do it with a two-bank shot. He leaned over the cue.

"No, if the husband came home, saw the man, said, 'Keep going,' and the man *can*, then *he's* got savoir faire!"

Griffen couldn't help himself. The cue skidded out of his fingers. The white ball snicked right into the black eight ball, and both of them fell into the corner pocket.

Elmer smiled at him. "Like that one, huh? Well, looks like it's my turn."

"Now, was that nice?" Penny asked, sidling into Elmer's sight line.

"No, but it's a good story, ain't it?"

Maestro racked up the balls. Elmer leaned down. His cue was a beauty, hard maple, shiny with age. Griffen watched as he sighted down the diamond of balls, then moved the cue ball four inches to the right. It wasn't where he would have placed it.

Snick!

Elmer stood back. The balls leaped away from the white intruder in their midst. Griffen watched in amazement as the balls bounded off their fellows. The one, two and three, dropped into the left-hand pockets in order, one after the other.

"Well, damn," Maestro said, with open admiration.

"You just got to know where to stroke 'em," Elmer said. "Now, watch the four and five. They don't get along so good, but I can make 'em behave."

"That I have to see," Griffen said.

The old man took his time lining up the shot. The four and five sat a couple of inches apart near the rear-right cushion. An amateur would knock the five into the corner. Elmer seemed to take it as a challenge.

"I like to clear more than one ball at a time, if there's even a chance at sinking them. Makes the game more exciting, don't it?"

The physics that must have been going on in his mind made Griffen's own mind whirl. Elmer angled his thin body to aim his cue at the rear-left edge of the white ball.

Clack!

The white ball banked off the left, shot straight across the table. It narrowly missed the eight ball and nipped into the narrow space between the four and five.

As if stung, the four ball zipped down the back side of the table. Griffen held his breath. The colored sphere dropped with a clatter into the left-rear pocket. Almost at the same time, the five, caught by the backspin of the cue ball, rolled lazily up the right side, teetered, and plunked into the right-center pocket.

"Damn," Maestro said. "I think I paid my entry money for a master class."

"You too kind," Elmer said. "You could buy an old man a drink."

"My pleasure. What are you having?"

Griffen felt his phone erupt. He pulled it out of his pocket and stepped away from the table.

"Griffen McCandles."

"Grifter, I got 'em!" Gris-gris said triumphantly. "Melvin spotted the car comin' in on Route 10. He's been followin' 'em, and I just joined the parade. We're on Canal Street, comin' toward the central city."

"Any sign of a bald white guy?"

"Nothin' but a lot of traffic," Gris-gris said. "You want us to come right into the ballroom?"

"No, bring Val to the lobby," Griffen said, glancing

around at the tables. "If that thing turns up, I don't want it to be right in the middle of this crowd. How does she look?"

"Beautiful. See you in a few."

He put the phone away.

"Gotta take care of something," Griffen said. "I'll come back if I can. You get to fight it out for who advances to the semifinals."

"Well, that'll be me, of course," Penny said, with an exaggerated wink. Elmer missed a shot in his third frame and ceded the table to Maestro. Griffen left them to it.

Val was coming home! Griffen kept the glee he felt off his face in case the other players misunderstood it. He would be so glad to see her. Then he was going to give her a piece of his mind for running away and not letting him know where she was for months. He put his cue away and headed toward the lobby.

Fox Lisa waved to Griffen from a table near the front of the room. Feeling light on his feet in spite of his lack of sleep, Griffen loped over to tell her. He swept her up, cue and all, and gave her a big kiss.

"Well, thank y'all," Fox Lisa said, her eyes shining as he put her down. "What's that all about?"

"Val's on the way in."

"Wonderful!" Fox Lisa said. "She okay?" Griffen nodded. She gestured toward the two men and a woman who were playing on her table. "Do you need me to bow out here?"

"How are you doing?" Griffen asked, peering at the scoreboard.

"Winning."

"Then don't stop," Griffen said. "If I need your help, I'll yell. I promise."

"Well, see that you do." Fox Lisa leaned close to him and put her lips to his ear. "Maybe you can do something about the man who's been staring at us. I'm okay with it, but it's been bothering Natalie something awful. I'd speak to him, but you're an official of this event."

"No problem," Griffen said. He checked the time on his cell phone. "I have a minute. Which man?"

Fox Lisa turned Griffen's shoulders so he was facing the rows of seats near the left corner of the hall. A knot of onlookers sat there in twos or threes, talking among themselves, eating popcorn, drinking or smoking. Griffen couldn't figure out who Fox Lisa meant, until the form of Rose coalesced into view behind a man in sunglasses leaning on a cane and a neatly dressed tawny-skinned woman in the front row. As he recognized them, Griffen felt an inner jolt that shook him to his feet. The hot spark in his belly started dancing up and down.

"I know who that is. I'll take care of it."

Fifty-one

Griffen marched over to Duvallier and glared down at him. The shrunken cheeks molded themselves into a pleasant smile as Duvallier removed his cigar from his mouth.

"What are you doing here?" Griffen demanded.

"Well, hey there, Griffen. Good afternoon to you, too. You remember Miss Callaway?"

Griffen felt shamed into politeness.

"Hello, Miss Callaway. Nice to see you. What are you doing here, Mr. Duvallier?"

"I paid my money. I want to see what happens."

"What are you talking about?"

Duvallier peered up at him over the tops of his dark lenses. The red eyes glinted.

"I sponsored a few players. I intend to win a majority of your prizes."

"You what?"

"I have a few friends from the old days. They don't need the money, but they like a chance to match sticks against the young people. I love a good competition. Why, you been playin' with my old pal Elmer. A real pro. Wipes up the floor with the competition. My other old boys is the same."

Griffen was horrified but fascinated.

"You brought in a ringer. A *dead* ringer."

Duvallier grinned, showing square teeth in the shrunken gums.

"Might put it that way. Nothin' in your rules says that the players got to be among the living."

Griffen began to have a creeping feeling that few of the people in the room, except for the reporters, and maybe not all of them, were human. Shape-shifters, dragons, dead people . . . But he refused to be distracted.

"You can't stay here."

Duvallier took a drag on his cigar and blew a stream of gray smoke at Griffen. Griffen coughed.

"Can't make me go. It's a public event, for a wannabe elected official."

"Yes, I can," Griffen said. About ten yards away, he spotted Harrison making his rounds at the perimeter of the room. He strode over and grabbed the burly police detective by the arm.

"What's your problem, McCandles?"

Griffen hauled Harrison over to the seats and pointed down at Duvallier.

"Arrest this man!"

Harrison looked from the elderly gentleman in dark glasses to Griffen and back again.

"On what charge?"

"Attempted murder!"

"Whose murder?"

"Penny Dunbar."

Harrison gave him a glance that asked if Griffen was in his right mind or not.

"That Penny Dunbar? The one who's doing a victory lap around her table?"

"She looks pretty alive and kickin' to me," Duvallier agreed. "You barkin' up the wrong tree, son." He eyed the detective up and down. "Say, ain't you Oscar Harrison's boy?"

"Yes, sir," Harrison said, then went very still. "Do I know you, sir?" Duvallier took off his glasses. The red eyes blazed into light. The cop didn't back away. Griffen admired him for standing his ground. "Yeah, I thought that might be you, Mr. Duvallier. McCandles, you don't want to kick over this anthill."

"I have to," Griffen insisted. "Rose told me that Penny's life is in danger!"

The eagerness on Harrison's face made Griffen's heart turn over.

"Is Rose here? Where is she?"

"Back there," Griffen said. He pointed to the second tier of seats, but the voodoo queen had disappeared. Harrison's face fell. Griffen was sorry to disappoint him, but his mission was urgent. "Duvallier told me that he was going to have Penny killed!"

Harrison sighed and took a notebook out of his pocket.

"Did you say something like that, sir?"

Duvallier tried to look outraged, but his eyes twinkled with sparks.

"I certainly did not. You don't get to put words in my mouth, Griffen. I ain't no danger to that girl's life!"

Griffen goggled at him.

"But you said . . . what about you trying to kill her?"

Duvallier tipped a length of ash onto the carpet. Miss Callaway tsk'ed at him. Duvallier patted her hand. "Haven't you felt like strangling her now and again over the last few months? She could drive a man to drink. I told you *a man* asked me to kill her. Don't have to do that. He'd really be happy enough if I drove her out of the race. That's gonna happen real soon now. I work in mysterious ways. Would I kill my own great-granddaughter?"

Griffen put a finger in his ear and wiggled it, but he knew he had heard correctly.

"Your . . . what?"

Duvallier grinned around his cigar. He exhaled a huge puff of smoke.

"Sure enough, son. That girl's a chip off the old block, a real deal-doer and bargain-maker. I just don't want her in this race. She can't win it, and she's beating her head against a wall for nothin'. She won't listen to me. I even told her I'd back her in a decade or so, but she wants everythin' right now. I'm just playin' both sides. And getting' paid for it, I might add." He gestured toward a pale-faced man with light brown hair who stood among the onlookers near Penny's table. "He's gonna get what he wants for his candidate, but I ain't doin' nothing to Penny. She's done plenty herself."

"So you have no real power," Griffen said, looking down his nose at the old man. "You know a bunch of zombies and ghosts who play dirty tricks for you."

Duvallier was unmoved by the insults.

"You don't know a damned thing, and that's a fact, Griffen. I thought you was more mature than Penny."

Griffen felt his temper flare. Smoke jetted from his nostrils. He moved toward Duvallier, who beckoned him with an upturned hand.

"Come ahead, boy. Try. You'll be sorry, but come right ahead."

A heavy blow fell on his shoulders, and Griffen found himself being hauled backward. Harrison kept hold of him.

"Leave it, McCandles. He said he's not going to do anything to her. Leave it!"

Griffen blew one more gust of smoke. He raised a threatening finger toward Duvallier's nose.

"All right, but one move on Penny, I will consider it to be your responsibility. I'll take you to pieces."

Duvallier laughed and tapped more ash on the rug.

"You can try, son. You can try."

Griffen retreated. Harrison kept an arm on his shoulders until they had moved away from the spectators.

"Count to ten, or whatever you have to do," Harrison said. "Duvallier's a power in this town, has been for decades. He's a pain in the butt, but he doesn't lie. He doesn't have to."

"Well, if he's not the threat to Penny, who is?"

"I haven't heard anything. McCandles . . . ?"

Harrison hesitated, his face in a blank mask. He'd already shown enough emotion for the day.

"I'll tell you if I see her again," Griffen promised. Harrison nodded and moved off to continue his patrol.

"You're hiding her! You can't keep her from me! She has

my grandchild!" a female voice shrilled. Malcolm's voice replied, loudly but calm.

"I have not seen her, but if I had, I would not inform you."

"You're lying!"

"Please," Malcolm said, his expression pained. "Why would I lie? Please leave. You are not welcome here."

"No! I will not let you put me off. We'll have it out right here and now!"

Griffen looked up. Malcolm was in the doorway, arguing with someone too short for Griffen to see over the crowd. But he didn't need to see her to know it was Melinda. Griffen strode to his uncle's side. Melinda wasn't alone. Her two pet goons loomed at her back. Two other men stood nearby, a tall, good-looking man with blue eyes and wavy black Superman hair, and a smaller, slender man with blond hair. Griffen's dragon sense went off on the tall man. The other was a puzzle. He had no time to figure it out. The reporters, looking for new material to perk up the rather tame feature pieces they were taping, saw an altercation brewing. They nudged their photographers and cameramen and started to move away from the players, toward the scene of the action. Griffen opened his stride to get there ahead of them.

"There he is, the uncle-to-be!" the small, stout female said, holding out her hands toward Griffen. She bore down on him and attached herself to his arm like a clamp. "Where is my grandchild's mother?"

"Come with me," Griffen said, holding on to her hand firmly with both of his. He tried to steer her out of the room. She didn't move an inch. He felt as if she had taken root in the hotel floor.

"Oh, no," Melinda said. She looked around her as if for the first time. "I'm not going where you can ignore me. What is all this? A party?"

Inwardly, Griffen wanted to grab a pool cue from the closest table and smack her with it, but he produced a friendly, easygoing smile. He lowered his voice.

"Melinda, this is a bad time. We're running a fund-raiser

here. Uncle Malcolm and I are supporting a candidate for governor."

Melinda waved a hand.

"Yes, I know! That's how we found you. We went to your apartment first. Imagine how impressed I was when I saw all those flyers for this event! And all for nothing! But it did tell me that you would be here now. It's all working out for the best."

At that moment, the candidate herself, detecting the depletion of her audience, had come to see what the fuss was all about. By the spark in her eyes, Griffen saw she knew Melinda. She put on all her charm and extended a hand.

"Hello there. I'm Penny Dunbar. I'm running for governor of Louisiana."

Melinda ignored it. She eyed Penny up and down, dismissed her, and turned back to Malcolm.

"Oh, yes, your little puppet girl. The novelty candidate."

"My record is as good or better than anyone else's in this race," Penny said.

"Good enough is hardly good enough," Melinda said.

Horsie broke through the crowd and interposed herself between the two dragons.

"Well, it seems you must be from out of state, ma'am," she said. She brandished a handful of flyers and tucked them into Melinda's hand. "Representative Dunbar has a sterling record of backing law enforcement and education."

"Putting lipstick on a pig doesn't change the fact that it's a pig," Melinda said, ostentatiously dropping the pamphlets onto the floor.

The reporters grinned avidly over their recorders and notebooks.

"Is that what you say to yourself in the mirror every morning?" Penny asked, sweetly. She glanced over her shoulder at her security escort. "Winston, would you remove this *person*."

Winston moved forward with the inevitability of an avalanche. Griffen pushed Melinda into his grasp.

"Yes, Representative. Ma'am, will you and your party please come with me?"

Melinda backed away, trying to break his grip.

"Physical intimidation! Is this how you treat potential donors? Help me!" She turned to the reporters. "They're attacking an old woman because they don't want the truth about their penny-ante candidate to come out!"

Horsie's mouth dropped open. She appealed to Griffen.

"Can't you get this woman out of here?" she begged. "This is ruining her!"

A puff of cigar smoke enveloped them all. Griffen coughed. Without looking, he knew that Duvallier was there at his elbow. The big man with the light brown hair stood beside him, looking uncomfortable.

"She's already ruined," Duvallier said, gleefully. "We're just witnessin' the burial of the corpse."

"Please stay out of this," Griffen said.

"Naw, gonna enjoy the show! Did I introduce you to my friend, Mr. Sandusky? Albert, say hi to Griffen."

"Uh, hi," said Albert.

Melinda put a dramatic hand to her forehead.

"Police brutality! I'm going to faint! I can't take this torture!"

Horsie grabbed Griffen's arm to get his attention. "Stop her!"

"How?" Griffen asked.

"Ma'am, no one is hurting you," Winston said calmly. He held on firmly. Melinda writhed, managing to look feeble and frightened in the cameras' harsh light. Malcolm was furious. He tried to push the press back, away from Melinda.

"Nothing to see here, folks," he said. "The tournament is still in progress."

"Griffen!"

Griffen spun toward the sound of his name. He looked over the heads of the crowd of reporters.

Through the doorway of the ballroom staggered Gris-gris and Mai. Between them was Val. His sister looked exhausted.

Her face was red, and wisps of her long blond hair had escaped from the long plait over her shoulder. She wore a rumpled light blue sweat suit that had stains on the jacket. He was amazed at how large her belly had become since he had last seen her. Griffen pushed in between the onlookers, most of whom turned to see what was going on.

The tall, black-haired man was right behind him, his face taut with concern. He hurried toward Val with his arms out.

"Val! Are you all right?"

Gris-gris let go of Val's arm and breasted up to the man. He reached into his jacket and came out with a shining curved knife. The man backed away a pace.

"Who the hell are you?" Gris-gris demanded. The man offered him a pleasant smile.

"I'm Mike. You must be Gris-gris. I've heard a lot about you."

The dealer was in no mood for appeasement.

"Well, I don't know nothin' about you! Get away from my lady!"

"Hey!" Mai shouted. "She's heavy!"

Griffen swooped in and got a shoulder under his sister's arm just as she started to slump. He helped her to a chair. She clutched her side as if it hurt her. Mai sat down beside her and held her hand. Val was breathing heavily. Griffen didn't like the pinched look of her face.

"Are you all right?" Griffen asked.

Val grinned wearily up at him. "Just can't run like I used to. I'm all off-balance. Had to park blocks from here and run. They'll probably tow our car."

Griffen laughed with relief.

"You're safe now. I'll take care of it when this is over."

Mai wrinkled her nose up at him.

"Do I not even rate a hello?"

So many questions urged themselves forward in his mind that Griffen hardly knew where to start.

"Valerie!" came a triumphant shout behind them.

As if magically recharged, Melinda flipped Winston

backward like a cardboard cutout and shoved reporters aside. The blond man trotted behind her, exuding a proprietary air.

"There you are, darling! Now, you didn't have to leave in such a hurry. Why didn't you tell me you wanted to visit New Orleans?"

In spite of her exhaustion, Val regained her feet. She held her arm tightly against her side. Griffen headed off Melinda and glared down at her.

"How dare you kidnap my sister!"

Melinda was unapologetic. "She came with me of her own accord."

"I didn't intend to stay forever," Val insisted.

"You should have given me notice."

"Why?"

"Because you're working for me, sweetheart," Melinda said.

Val's face turned even redder.

"That job was fake. Everything was a sham!"

"Not my affection for you, Valerie. It's clear you need medical attention." Melinda sniffed. "And a shower. We need to get you back. Henry, help me take her out to the car."

The blond man reached for Val's hand.

"Come with me, dear," he said. "We'll get you a penthouse suite while we're waiting for the plane home."

"Oh, no!" Val said. She sidled a little unsteadily to the left. "Don't let him touch me!"

"Don't be silly," Henry said, with an imperturbable expression. "We only have your best interests at heart."

He reached for her again. Val dodged him. Henry followed her as if he could read her mind. Griffen moved to intercept Henry. He didn't know why Val was so frightened of him, but it didn't matter. If she feared him, he was Griffen's enemy.

Griffen had a good head in height on the other man, but Henry moved with surprising speed. Gris-gris and Mike broke off their argument to block Henry from following Val.

"He ain't gonna touch her as long as I'm alive," Gris-gris said. He tossed the knife from one hand to the other. It flashed in the air. Henry held out his hands, touching both men on the arms.

"Now, there's no need for violence," he said. Mike's expression softened, but Gris-gris looked more fierce than before. He glared at Henry.

"You can't charm me, demon. I wearin' my witch-bag."

Henry tried to move past him. Gris-gris held the knife up to his face.

Val squeezed backward between a pair of chairs into the second row and made for the open door. She clutched her side as if it hurt. Mai put an arm around her to help her run. Henry dodged his pursuers and ambled swiftly after her.

"Come back, dear. Everyone is looking at you!"

"Leave me alone!"

Mike raced past Griffen and leaped into the air. He tackled Henry and brought him down to the carpet. Camera flashes went off all around them. Mike hauled Henry to his feet, hauled back his fist, and punched him in the jaw. Henry's head snapped back. He went limp and sank to the floor at their feet.

"Now, why did you do that?" Melinda asked. She signed to her minions to pick up the blond man and lay him on a row of chairs.

"Because Val said he's a threat," Griffen said. "It's over, Val. You can come back."

Val and Mai halted just past the registration tables. Jerome escorted them over. Griffen gave Val a hug.

"We are going to have a long talk later."

Val raised her chin defiantly. "Yes, we are."

Gris-gris tapped her on the arm.

"Hey, lady," he said.

"Hey, Gris-gris," Val replied, smiling though tears were standing in her eyes. Gris-gris took her face between his hands and kissed her solidly on the lips. Val wrapped her arms around him and hugged him so tightly he squeaked. Mike watched them, somewhat dismayed.

Mai stood by, seeming small and forlorn. Griffen gathered her in his arms. It felt good to hold her after so long. The questions he needed to ask her didn't seem as important at that moment.

"Thank you," he whispered. "I owe you."

"You most certainly do," she said.

Fifty-two

Malcolm stalked over to confront Melinda, his usually passive face furious.

"I hold you responsible for this catastrophe," he said. "You had no right to interrupt this event."

"Me?" Melinda said with an air of injured innocence. "They're the ones who assaulted my secretary. Look at him!" She swept a hand toward the unconscious Henry.

"Don't you worry," Penny said, descending on them with the press and the police at her back. "I will be pressing charges. Detective Harrison!"

"Yes, ma'am?" Harrison said. Penny pointed an imperious finger.

"Take these . . . *people* into custody. For disturbing the peace and endangering the public!"

"Yes, ma'am." Harrison nodded to his brothers-in-uniform, who came forward with handcuffs and plastic restraints.

As they arrested Melinda and her bodyguards, from the rear of the ballroom came four men in white coats and flat painter's caps. Griffen only had a moment to register their curious presence before a pale, naked man dashed into the chamber.

"Hey," Jerome said. "Who's the streaker weirdo?"

The man paused for a moment on the threshold, panting and drooling like the Tasmanian Devil, then tore straight toward Val. It took a running dive and latched onto her ankles. She screamed and punched at it.

Griffen gawked, but he was surprised into inaction only for a moment. Gris-gris reacted first. He leaped on the male's back and dragged its head up. It had no hair and heavy-lidded eyes like a lizard.

The bald white monster! It looked just as Holly had described it.

Gris-gris held his knife to its throat.

"You let her go this second!" he hissed.

Like a snake, it writhed and flipped over onto its back. Gris-gris flew off into the chairs, scattering them like toys. The spectators had retreated, screaming. The creature made another leap at Val. Malcolm and Mike grabbed its legs. They dragged it several feet. It twisted and fought loose. It raked a handful of claws down Mike's chest, tearing half his shirt off.

"Don't hurt him!" Val screamed.

Mike pulled back. His skin, dragon-tough, was unmarked. Val let out a sob of relief. Gris-gris crouched in a fighter's stance, knife in hand, moving for an opening. Griffen and Jerome joined in the fray, trying to restrain the crazed demon. It seemed determined to get at Val no matter what was in its way.

A fifth man in a white coat appeared at the doorway. He pointed at the naked male.

"There he is, men! Grab him! We need to get him back to the asylum!"

George! At last!

The five demon hunters converged on the group to help subdue the creature. It bit and clawed like a wolverine. Even ten of them weren't enough to hold it down.

Griffen glared at Melinda, as the bucking, kicking demon bit his ear.

"This is your creature!" he said. "Call it off!"

"I can't," she said, peevishly. "Henry is the only one who can control it! And you ruffians knocked him out!"

"I can control it," Penny said. Confidently, she pushed her way into the midst of the group. "Hey, fellah," she called.

Her musical voice caught the creature's attention. Slowly, Penny started to move, the dance seeming to come into her from her feet upward. She writhed and twisted, closing her eyes to listen to music only she could hear. The room fell oddly silent.

The cameras focused on her. Penny moved her hips and shoulders. Her hands fluttered upward and down again, describing without words a paradise of sensation that Griffen yearned to know. He could tell that every male in the place experienced the same feeling. Instead of a blue T-shirt and khakis, he pictured her in translucent veils, sparkling with jewels.

That included the demon. It stopped struggling. Its beady eyes fixed on the strawberry blond woman, following her every move like a hungry dog seeing its dinner approaching. Penny sidled closer, her eyelids lowering suggestively. The demon watched her with fascination, its muscles sagging, falling limp. Penny danced a step nearer and whirled, her hair streaming behind her.

The demon's nostrils twitched. It threw up its head suddenly. Before the posse of dragons and demon hunters could tighten their grip on it, it kicked loose. It had caught Penny's scent.

Dragon!

It leaped for her, hands clawing for her neck. She fell to her knees. It throttled her, screaming wildly to the ceiling. Griffen scrambled after it, catching one cold, naked foot in his arms. The demon hunters swarmed it, trying to separate predator from prey. There seemed to be no way to control it. It raked its clawed feet down legs and bellies, drawing blood from the shape-changers.

Suddenly, Duvallier was in their midst. He shoved past George and his men and put a finger to the demon's forehead.

He whipped off his dark glasses. The red eyes almost crackled as the flames behind them brightened. The demon cringed.

"You got no right to be here," Duvallier said. He put his hands on the creature's shoulders and pressed downward. It slumped to its knees. Griffen watched, astonished. It *whimpered*. It had taken a dozen men to subdue it, and Duvallier had taken it down with a touch.

The others rushed in to help Penny up. She had trouble swallowing. Her long, slender neck had purple bruises on it. Fox Lisa and Horsie put their arms around her, straightening her hair and clothes. Unfortunately, the cameras were right there to record her in her disheveled state.

Horsie moaned. "Guys, please! She's been assaulted! She needs to go to the hospital."

Duvallier let go of the creature. It sat on the floor, its head nodding limply. Black handprints marked its shoulders.

"It won't be no trouble now," he said.

The demon hunters swarmed in to wrap it up in restraints. Four of them hauled the now-quiescent creature out of the room. George stood on the threshold.

"Sorry, folks. Escaped lunatic. Got to get him back for his therapy." He followed the others out.

"Well, son?" Duvallier said to Griffen.

Griffen was impressed and respectful. "Is that something you can teach me to do?"

Duvallier laughed. "If you live long enough to grow some wisdom, I'd be proud to teach you some things. Fire's been my friend a long time. It ought to be yours, seeing as how you have the heredity."

"Take 'em down," Harrison said, pointing at Melinda and her escort. The other two police officers moved in with hand-cuffs. Val waved an arm in protest.

"Don't arrest Mike!"

"Ms. McCandles?" Harrison asked.

"He didn't have anything to do with that thing, I'm sure!"

"How do you know?" Gris-gris asked. "He came in with 'em!"

"I came here to defend Val," Mike insisted.

"She's my lady!"

"Well, she's been my girlfriend for the past several months."

"You got to her while she was hypnotized. It don't mean nothin'."

"I'm not going to argue with you. She made a choice, and the choice was me."

Val turned to confront them. Both of them had had their clothes torn to rags by the bald demon, but they were already fighting over her. Part of her liked it, but the rest of her was fed up with conflict.

"Enough. Enough already!" she barked. "I belong to me, not either of you! If I choose to sleep with one or both of you, or a whole platoon, it's *none of your business*!"

"Hear, hear," Mai said.

"Whatever you say, lady," Gris-gris said, contritely. "I just missed you like a piece of my soul."

"I have come to love you, too," Mike said. "These months with you have been magic."

"Oooh," Val said.

At the soft noise, Mike looked hopeful. Val was annoyed. It wasn't meant for him. She clutched her side. A pain hit her in the ribs. No, it was lower than that. Agony rippled through her belly. She sagged to the floor. Everyone suddenly came to loom over her. Her lower body felt as if it didn't belong to her. The baby kicked fiercely at her from the inside, as if demanding to be free.

"What's wrong?" Griffen shouted. He knelt beside her and held her hand. Val tried to answer him through the haze. Mike's and Gris-gris's faces swum over her head.

"Wrong?" Melinda said, breaking away from Harrison. "Nothing's wrong. Everything's right. She's having this baby, that's what's going on!"

"*Now?*" Griffen asked.

"Looks like it!"

"But it's months early, isn't it?"

Melinda looked concerned. "It's the second baby that takes

eleven months, you know. The first one can come at any time." Her answer was flippant, but she did look worried.

"We'd better get her to the hospital," Griffen said.

Ms. Opal bustled up and took Val's other hand.

"I called the paramedics and told them two stretchers instead of one. My, my, but this was an event!" She looked sternly at Griffen. "Y'all gonna pay for the damages, gentlemen."

"Yes, Ms. Opal," Griffen and Gris-gris chorused.

The ambulance screamed away along Baronne Street. Gris-gris and Mike had both insisted on riding with Penny, Val, and the paramedics. The police cars had departed with their cargo. Griffen wished he could be a fly on the wall to listen to Melinda trying to reason with Harrison. The irresistible force was about to meet the immovable object. He watched until the red lights were out of sight, then went back inside to deal with the chaos of the interrupted fund-raiser.

A man in a red T-shirt lettered with ST. GEORGE'S HOSPITAL fell into step with him. Griffen glanced at it and kept walking.

"You were late. What happened?"

"Mai took my car. I need to find out from her where they left it. Goddamned Prius had no power in the mountains. It just crawled up the slopes. I was lucky to get here the same day as that demon. Lucky Debbie called in all local hunters. The extra manpower and my expenses are going on your bill. Your sister led me on a real wild-goose chase.

"But did you really bring her back?" Griffen asked.

"She would not have gotten away from Melinda without my help. That thing is a watchdog on her estate. No, I did not escort her to your presence. Yes, I was instrumental in getting her out."

"Okay," Griffen said. "I'll pay the bill. Thanks. Are you all right?"

George grimaced.

"I've got a score to settle on my own account, but nothing that can't wait. But I want to talk to your zombie friend. I want to know how he did that."

"You and me both," Griffen agreed. "Come in and have a drink. The bar's open for another half hour."

"Thanks." George opened his phone and hit a key. "Debbie? Mission accomplished. I'll send you the sitrep, but you're not gonna believe it. It's a doozy."

Malcolm sat on a chair beside the registration tables. His mien was glum. Griffen stood beside him and surveyed the remaining players. One wall had several dents in the plaster where chairs, and bodies, had flown into it. A pool table had been knocked halfway off its trestle. Griffen fervently hoped the slate bed hadn't been cracked. A quality table like that cost about twelve thousand dollars.

The camera crews had gone. The majority of the spectators had fled, screaming, and were probably giving their side of the story to the press. Griffen dreaded watching the evening news. It wouldn't be good for their side.

Malcolm cleared his throat.

"I am afraid that the majority of the donations will need to go to pay damages," he said. "After the prize money is deducted, I fear there will be little left to pay campaign debts. It would seem that Representative Dunbar's run for governor is over."

"I know," Griffen said.

Malcolm looked up at him.

"Though we were unsuccessful in our enterprise, allow me to say that I appreciate all of your efforts in this matter, Griffen. I am glad to see how well you are growing up. I cannot say I fully understand this city or your relationship to it, but you have done well. You are, as your friend Jerome might say, the big dragon here."

"Thanks, I think," Griffen said.

Fox Lisa and Mai came over, arm in arm. They gathered Griffen in a three-way hug.

"How are you doing?" Fox Lisa asked.

"I need a drink," Griffen said. "And about eighteen hours sleep."

He felt a tap on his shoulder.

"Wait a minute, you can't go yet," Elmer said. "We still got a match to finish. Mr. Duvallier wants to see it."

"Not really," Griffen said.

"Yeah, really. You promised him."

Griffen gawked.

"No, I didn't."

"Sure did," Elmer said. "You told him that in exchange for letting Penny alone you'd face his champion. That's me."

"You?"

The other man grinned. He took off his sunglasses. Griffen could see that his eyes were unnaturally sunken—or perhaps not so unnaturally, if you considered that Elmer was a walking corpse.

"I was national champion three years running in my day. I want to see if you can beat me. Twelve frames so far. Come on, son!"

Griffen followed him back to the table in the middle of the room. Maestro was waiting for them. He racked up the balls and stood back. At the side of the room, Duvallier and Miss Callaway sat placidly watching. Duvallier waved to Griffen.

Griffen took a deep breath and chalked the tip of his pool cue. He didn't have to help out with Penny's campaign any longer. He could go back to his business. His uncle said he was proud of him. His sister was going to have a baby. Life had turned from bad to good in the course of an afternoon.

He leaned over the table. The worried hubbub had given way once again to gentle banter and the peaceful clacking sounds of people playing pool.

Griffen drew back his cue and broke. The one ball shot

away from the pack and rolled toward the far-left pocket. Without waiting for it to land, he moved a quarter of the way around the table, sighted down his stick over the cue ball at the two. He tapped it and watched it scoot into the nearest pocket.

The tension of the last months drained away. He fell into a rhythm of angle and shot that was like a dance. He let himself move with it. He sank the nine ball. One frame down. Elmer racked the balls. Griffen broke them. Two frames. Three frames. He was going to run the tables until they pried the cue out of his hand. He wasn't the greatest pool player in the world, but there and then, he could not lose. He felt it. He would defeat Duvallier's champion and bring the whole mess to an end.

Fox Lisa brought him a glass of Irish whisky. Smiling, Griffen took a sip and leaned over to take his next shot. He could take the eight and nine together. It was a tricky play, but he knew in his mind exactly how the balls would fall.

Outside of the cloud of contentment in which he was wrapped, he heard a chuckle.

"You know the joke about savoir faire?" Elmer asked.

"Yeah," Griffen said.

The dead man smiled.

"You have savoir faire, man."

ROBERT (LYNN) ASPRIN, born in 1946, is best known for the Myth Adventures and Phule series. He also edited the groundbreaking Thieves' World anthologies with Lynn Abbey. He died at his home in New Orleans in May 2008.

JODY LYNN NYE lists her main career activity as "spoiling cats." She has published forty-two books, including *Advanced Mythology*, fourth in her Mythology fantasy series (no relation); six science fiction novels; and four novels in collaboration with Anne McCaffrey, including *The Ship Who Won*. She has also edited a humorous anthology about mothers, *Don't Forget Your Spacesuit, Dear*, and published more than a hundred and ten short stories. Her latest books are *Robert Asprin's Dragons Run*, fourth in the series begun by Robert Asprin, and *View from the Imperium*, first in the Thomas Kinago series. She lives northwest of Chicago with her husband, author and packager Bill Fawcett, and their cat, Jeremy. Visit her on the Web at sff.net/people/jodynye.